Rite of Summer

Tess Bowery

This is a work of fiction. Similarities to real people, places, or events are entirely coincidental.

RITE OF SUMMER

First Edition, 2018.

ISBN: 978-0-9866184-9-9

Written by Tess Bowery.

http://tessbowery.com

Dedication

To the love of my life, for making everything feel possible, and to my London Ladies, for beginning it all.

Contents

Chapter One

There were few things in the world as perfect as Evander's prick.

It was neither misshapen nor too small, nor curved oddly to the side. When it rose with his arousal, jutting hard and red-tipped from the cloud of golden curls at the base, it was as magnificent a creation as the Tower of Pisa all the way over in far-distant Italy.

If Stephen were to write odes and sonnets—on pricks in general or Evander's in particular—they would not focus on the look of it, but the feel. On the heavy weight that filled Stephen up and broke him open, in arse or mouth alike; on the heat of his skin, so soft when so much else about him was rough; on the salt-slick slide as he thrust in over Stephen's tongue and held there, gasping.

Evander's prick was the epitome of all things that were erotic and beautiful in the world.

Loving the man would be easier if Evander didn't think so as well.

The thought veered too close to blasphemy. Better to focus on the task at hand.

The noise of the busy London street carried on outside the shuttered windows of their lodgings. Inside, all was quiet but for their panting breaths and the wet slide of spit and skin.

The uneven floorboards pressed ridges into his knees, his lips stretched around the prick in his mouth. The taste of Evander's arousal mixed with the remnants of the wine they'd shared, passing the same bottle back and forth until there was nothing left but dregs.

There was little hope of a breeze on the best of days, and this sultry summer afternoon was not one of those. Evander had persisted in wandering around in only his linen shirt and drawers, the light garments clinging to his lithe frame and his blond hair sticking, damp, to the back of his neck. Accompanied by the utterly obscene way he lifted the bottle to his lips, it had made their current position inevitable.

Stephen's fingers clenched on Evander's thighs, dug into the solid dips and curves of his muscles, stroked across the smattering of fair hair. His own prick ached, hard and damp, his trousers too tight and harsh where they rubbed. He dropped a hand to palm himself. The pressure was the barest edge of relief, muted by the wool and linen of his clothing. He groaned aloud, the sound muffled around the thick cock in his mouth.

Evander thrust in reaction to the vibrations, his fingers clenching in the bedclothes. Gasps spilled from his lips as he arched, threw his head back and came.

"Come up here," Evander ordered, the command softened by the drowsy satiation in his voice.

Stephen swallowed around Evander's prick one last time before he pulled away. It fell from his lips with a wet and obscene pop, to lie, gleaming, against Evander's muscled thigh. Stephen let Evander draw him up onto the bed and he crawled to his usual place, nipping lightly at Evander's flank as he moved. Salt tingled on his lips, both of their bodies damp with the sweat of exertion in the midsummer heat.

Evander seized Stephen's face in his hands and kissed him, tongue delving into Stephen's mouth. He licked in and Stephen opened for him, passed back the taste of Evander's own release from tongue to tongue. His prick throbbed in further urgency at the heat of it, the taste and feel of him. Evander consumed him, fire and molten steel.

Evander's fingers slipped down inside Stephen's fall front, wrapped around his aching prick, and words were no longer possible. They vanished from his mind as soon as he tried to focus on any particular one. He wasn't good with them at the best of times, preferring always to let music speak for him, in the rhythm of the notes and the scrape of the bow across the strings.

Evander hummed a discontented note. His mouth closed over Stephen's again, tasting like him, salt-sour and familiar. His oiled hand gripped and glided along the length of Stephen's prick.

"What are you smiling about?" Evander asked, pressing firm, cool kisses along his throat.

Stephen tipped his head back and Evander ran his tongue down the length of Stephen's throat. "I was thinking of you," he reassured him. Life was always easier when Evander was pleased. "How much like Michelangelo's

David you are, stretched out for me in the sunlight."
Stephen paused, then, and grinned. "Except for certain
things, of course, in which you far surpass the original."

Evander soaked up the compliments, as he had
embraced the sunshine before, lounging across the narrow
bed. "The Greeks had a strange position on male beauty."
Evander laughed, his pride repaired.

Stephen couldn't form coherent thoughts against the
pressure of Evander's hand on his prick, on the strength of
the fingers wrapped around him. Evander pressed his thumb
firmly beneath the head, dug in just a little with his nail so
that the shock of pain and pleasure mingled and combined
inexorably.

"Come for me, my muse," Evander murmured in his
ear. He wrapped his hand up and over the crown of
Stephen's prick, then scraped his teeth across Stephen's
swollen earlobe and bit down. The momentary pain shot
down through his body like lightning, met the coiled and
heavy arousal in his gut. He released, hot and sticky, into
Evander's palm, the ache in his body fading in time with the
pulse of pleasure wrung from him.

Evander rolled away and rose to his feet the moment
Stephen's body stopped trembling. He crossed the room and
took up a kerchief to clean himself with water from the jug
on the nightstand.

Stephen stretched, reaching his fingers above his head
until his shoulders popped in agreement. The mugginess of
the midsummer air made his skin clammy as the sweat dried
in prickling pools behind his knees and in the crooks of his
elbows. It would be so much nicer to have Evander back
beside him, to curl against his body and lie there, languid

and warm. But such things did not please Evander's sense of aesthetics, and so Stephen sprawled inelegantly and alone across the bed, linens damp beneath him from sweat, oil and come. The bedclothes would stick to his skin once everything began to dry. He would have to peel himself from them, the creases red across his back and lingering longer than the memories of the pleasure itself.

The pillow had ended up on the floor; reaching for it was too much effort. He would stay here, drowsy in the summer afternoon, listen to the clatter of the carts over the cobblestones and the laughter of the children running in the street below.

If they only knew what grotesque acts took place just above their heads; Stephen felt a rush of amusement mixed with trepidation at the thought. Fat Annie must certainly suspect. Their landlady was too much a woman of the world to entirely mistake the sounds that the two young men occasionally ripped from one another, or to wonder at their lack of interest in the Covent Garden girls who whistled low at men passing by along the road.

There was more muscle to Evander now than there had been when they first took these rooms. Stephen played in the inns for pennies and Evander wrote his music by the window, the better to preserve their few precious guttering candle ends. The rent, small as it was, had been too much sometimes, but Evander had always been there, his blue eyes and easy charm buying them one reprieve after another.

Those days of penury and hunger were long gone now, had ended when the Earl of Coventry had seen Stephen play.

Or, to hear both the earl and Evander say it, when the Right Honorable Earl had heard Evander Cade's compositions as faithfully rendered by Stephen Ashbrook's violin. He had offered Evander a patronage, instructions on the sorts of music he liked best, a stipend enough to feed and keep two in reasonable accommodations, and a hope of better things to come.

Stephen, it must always be remembered, had been included on sufferance. The patronage, the lodgings in Holburn and the income to pay for it all were Evander's.

Stephen sighed at the thought, staring up at the wooden beams of the angled roof above him. Someday, that would change. He would find a new patron or work of his own that did not require him to flatter Coventry, as Evander did, in thanks for his generosity and connections.

He was not a fool to think himself so talented that he could get by in life without the assistance of a patron at all, mind you. But, somehow, when he had his bow in his hand and Rosamund's living wood tucked securely beneath his chin, her neck humming with his heartbeat and his breath, their song ascending into heaven—

Somehow all the connections and society in the world ceased to matter.

And *that* was probably why Evander was poised upon the brink of true professional success, and Stephen was still something of an afterthought.

His postcoital discomfort proved too much to ignore, finally, and he peeled himself from the sheets with a groan of protest. Evander was putting a kettle to boil in the sitting room, from the sounds of it, and going through the mail that had been delivered while they were out. They had stumbled over the folded envelopes under the door earlier, too intent upon each other's bodies to stop and deal with mundane matters.

Stephen washed, the water splashing cool over his face and sweaty throat. By the time he had found trousers and a fresh shirt, and had thrown his fouled garments aside for the laundress, Evander was sprawled full-length and half-dressed along the settee, reading his letter. A satisfied smile settled on his face, turning his golden beauty momentarily smug and dark.

The expression vanished as he sat up, the shadows changing as he moved, the twist to his features nothing more than a trick of the light. He swung his legs down and beckoned Stephen over, draping his legs across Stephen's knees once Stephen took his usual place at the end of the faded green cushions.

Evander was humming a bawdy tavern song, and Stephen stroked his calf lightly. It was the sign of a good mood, as though their lechery before had not been enough to prove it, and the last remaining knots in Stephen's shoulders untangled themselves.

"Something pleases you," he ventured, arching an eyebrow at the letter. The paper was fine quality, and what he could see of the wax seal and the writing was familiar. Coventry, then, and with good news.

"You please me," Evander countered, and he reached a hand out to toy possessively with one of the dark-brown curls that lay on Stephen's shoulder. He kept his hair unfashionably long, true, but it was simpler to tie it back with a ribbon when he played than to worry about having it cut on a regular basis. And Evander liked it.

"My life is but to serve you," Stephen replied dryly.

It was, as always, a joke. As always, Evander laughed.

"We—that is, *I*, and he knows that you and I are inseparable—have received an invitation." And there Evander paused with a flourish of the letter, waiting for a reaction before he carried on. He had more of the born performer in him than most actors of Stephen's acquaintance.

An invitation—and it had to be a request to perform. That was something worthy of a little pretension! The previous year had been a lean one, the earl's mourning for his late wife putting a temporary halt on his usual festivities. The Countess of Coventry had been considerate to the last, mind you; her early spring death ensured that her youngest daughter's first Season would only be delayed by a year, rather than cancelled for two. *"Polite of her,"* Evander had commented when the news came. Stephen, for once, had kept his thoughts rather firmly to himself.

This summer had been much better so far. More performances meant more exposure to the wealthy families of the bon ton. And the more in demand they became, the greater the likelihood of future commissions.

The possibilities were exciting, especially given the smile on Evander's face. It had to be something enviable. Vauxhall again, perhaps, or a grand concert at Coventry's London home. The manor had a ballroom so large that he could host forty couples and still have room for a sideboard. The acoustics in there were a marvel, the resonance such that it would make a howling cat sound like a boys' choir singing "Te Deum".

"Go on," Stephen urged, not entirely because Evander was still waiting for his reply. He ran his hand along Evander's bare calf, his trouser leg pushed up to his knee. Unruly blond hairs stuck up in all directions. Evander hated unruly, and Stephen smoothed them down again.

"To a house party," Evander announced smugly.

A *what?* Images of Coventry's grand ballroom crumbled to dust.

Evander did not look up from the letter, which gave Stephen a chance to rearrange his face into something that did not show his dismay. "Very exclusive, as special guests of Coventry himself. There shall be a command performance of 'Nocturne', and we shall be wined and dined as kings. There!"

He set aside the letter, brimming to overflow with self-satisfaction. "I told you he would like the piece, and now look. We are to be guests in the house of an earl! You would never have believed such a thing was possible when we first met, love—now look at what we have accomplished."

A house party in the country? How could he possibly feign excitement about that? Far from the pleasures of playing for a full room or dreams of a grander stage yet, a house party meant confinement to an audience of ten or fifteen at the most. There would be interminable days filled with guns, dogs and riding about in circles, and even more excruciating nights sitting about in parlors, miming charades and losing at cards to frowsy dowagers in muslins three sizes too small.

Evander was watching him in expectation, his eyes bright.

If it were for a week, perhaps it would be tolerable. A week to press palms with the earl's nearest and dearest and make some new connections. Then escape back to London, where the air was thicker and heavier at the end of summer, but at least the people and the streets were his own.

He bit back the sigh that threatened. "For how long?" he asked, keeping his voice as mild as he could manage.

Evander scanned the cramped black handwriting one more time. "Six weeks," he replied, exultant. "Depending, of course, on the weather and how the company enjoys itself. We are to leave on Wednesday next; he will send a coach to fetch us."

A full month and a half? "No," Stephen declared, shaking his head. "That will not do." To Evander's startled look, he said only, "I have a prior commitment. Phillips arranged for he and I to play Lady Ailsford's soirée a fortnight from now."

The Ailsfords were known for their "little parties" which invariably involved half of high society. To appear on his own merits, to have the opportunity to play a program of his own design, rather than worry about whether his choices would be found wanting—

"Cancel it," Evander ordered blithely, and he refolded the letter along the original crease lines. Stephen stopped stroking over the arches and balls of Evander's feet. "Or have Wren take your place. The earl has commanded a performance, and I cannot find anyone else in time who knows my music half as well as you."

"But..." Stephen began to object, though everything Evander had said was true, "...we will be isolated, away from all our friends, with only Coventry and his set for company."

"Come now," Evander wheedled. "The Season is all but over; Lady Ailsford will have an empty house this time of the summer. An opportunity like this comes along but once in a lifetime, and we must make the most of it. Who knows who else he will have in attendance—earls, marquesses, perhaps dukes! We will find ourselves in greater company than ever before."

"I would prefer not."

Evander's pale-blue eyes flashed dangerously and an edge crept into his voice. His legs were heavy in Stephen's lap, his muscles tensed as if for battle. "I would do it for you. Do you not care about me?"

And there was the challenge. Accept the invitation and maintain all as it was, keeping Evander's affections as well as Coventry's, or refuse. He'd find himself on the outs with both that way, and with a cold bed until Evander's temper could be placated. For an offense this grave, it could take months.

"Fine," Stephen conceded, and he forced away the sigh of discontent that rose up inside. Trusting Evander had gotten him this far; it was only stubbornness and his vague dislike for Coventry that were giving him qualms about it now. "I will write and beg a postponement. If it means so much to you, we shall both go."

Evander's face brightened again, the sun restored to the world. "You will not regret this," he promised, all tension gone from his jaw. He set the letter aside, and with a gleam of mischief in his eyes, tucked one foot down in

Stephen's lap. He dragged his toes slowly along the soft bulge of Stephen's prick.

What was he— *Oh.*

Evander grinned. "It is a massive house, you know," Evander began, as though delivering a confidence. "With galleries and gardens that extend for miles. Coventry described it to me once. We will have *hours* of uninterrupted leisure."

He dug his foot down farther and pressed it, firm and strong, against the front of Stephen's trousers. "We'll kiss and we'll swive," Evander sang, putting lyrics to the tune he had been humming before, his eyes alight and his smile infectiously lascivious. He was utterly ridiculous and delightful, and Stephen could not help but laugh as his body began to respond to Evander's excitement. "Behind we will drive, and we will contrive, new ways for lechery..." Evander finished his bawdy chorus by tangling one hand in Stephen's hair and using it to pull his head back.

Stephen's breath caught with the spike of desire, his throat exposed to the press of Evander's lips. "All right!" Stephen laughed breathlessly. "I've agreed already, I need no bribe to convince me further."

"Oh, but you do," Evander said, letting go of his hair and slinking his hand down to replace the press of his foot. "We shall make a game of it, defiling his house in as many ways and places as please us. Think of the thrill!"

Stephen's prick was thinking of little else, rising under Evander's touch, as it always did. The man was insane, the suggestion as distractingly tempting as almost all of his ideas were. If one servant saw them, though, in the wrong place, at the wrong time—Evander's social climbing would end rather abruptly. As would their necks.

"Think of the risk," he pointed out, one last-ditch effort to talk some sense into the man before he too was carried away by the contagion of his delight.

"There is no risk," Evander shook his head before detangling himself and crawling across Stephen's body to straddle his lap. "We are Coventry's favorites; no one can touch us now."

His kiss was one of triumph—full, wet and dirty.

Stephen kissed him back, ran his hands up the firm muscles of his thighs and buttocks, cupped the round swells of Evander's arse tightly in his hands.

"A month or more in the country, surrounded by the rich and the powerful." Evander spoke between kisses, his hands braced on either side of Stephen's head. "This will be a grand adventure, Stephen. It could change our lives."

Perhaps. Stephen allowed himself to be swept up in Evander's enthusiasm, in the heat of his mouth and the solid surety of their bodies entwined. But could life truly get much better than this?

"And what do you think?" Mr. Meredeth, owner and proprietor of Meredeth's Music, as his father had been before him, leaned over the counter between them to watch as Stephen flipped the pages on the new sonata.

"Mad," Stephen declared, "and brilliant. It shall take me a month at least to learn this properly." He passed over far too many of the coins he had been carefully saving for just this moment.

The coins fell into Meredeth's hand with gentle clinks. He counted them calmly, stowing the fee away with a smile. He could only have ten years or so on Stephen, fifteen at the most, and yet there were already threads of gray in his short brown hair. It was thinner on the top as well, but he was a man of the sort who never seemed to run to fat, no matter what other indignities age tried to inflict.

"Is the missus not feeding you well enough?" Stephen joked while Meredeth wrapped his packet for him. "I could span your wrist with my finger and thumb, man."

"The missus is as good a cook as you'll find anywhere." Meredeth puffed up proudly. "But running after customers all day and children all night, ah! There's no way to eat enough to keep up." He patted his stomach, hollow as it was, with a wink and a grin. "You'll find out, when you've got little ones of your own."

And that was easily the most unlikely prediction for Stephen's future that he'd ever heard, but he laughed nevertheless. "I'd have to be able to afford a wife first," he answered as though delivering a confidence, a pat reply that would lead to no further questions.

Meredeth set his own elbow on the counter and leaned in just as conspiratorially. When he spoke, though, he pitched his voice loud enough to be heard through the open door to the small shop's back room. "I'll tell you a secret— work them hard enough and they pay back their overhead quickly." And he winked.

"John Meredeth, you stop with your foolishness!"

"And here she comes." Meredeth straightened and turned to face his wife, whose lack of height and equally slim figure did nothing to reduce the impression of her ferocity.

"Morning, Mrs. M."

She ignored Stephen at first, swiping at Meredeth with a sodden dish towel.

"And to you, Mr. Ashbrook." She curtsied prettily, then smacked Meredeth's hand as he tried to slip it about her waist. "You see what I put up with?" she asked him rhetorically.

"Should've married me, then," Stephen teased. "I'd treat you like the queen among women that you are."

"Well now!" Meredeth pretended to object to the banter. "And in front of me, yet."

Mrs. Meredeth laughed at her husband and exchanged a look with him of such infinite fondness that it seemed even more of an intrusion to watch than had Stephen come upon them kissing. She leaned across the counter and patted Stephen on the cheek. "You're far too young and far too pretty, my dear boy. We'd never have gotten on. You'd be better use to some calm and lovely creature with a taste for tunes." She slung her dish towel over her shoulder again and headed back through the door to the living space behind. "Ask him about the lessons!"

"I am to ask you about lessons," Meredeth said dutifully. His solemn nod was enough to make Stephen grin again. "Our Susannah's old enough now—we were wondering if we could engage you for it. Despite all this…" he waved at the shelves of sheet music, the instruments that lined the walls, the once bare panel by the door now pasted thick with bills advertising concerts and entertainments from around the county, "…I never did learn pianoforte, and Mrs. M. simply doesn't have the time to sit with her."

The middle child of the Meredeth brood was a quiet and serious little girl, her mother's big brown eyes peeking out from her father's slim face. Even if she turned out not to have the knack for music, she wouldn't be difficult to manage for half an hour at a time.

"Gladly," he replied, and would have said more but for the thunder of hooves outside and the rattling of a coach pulling up outside the door of the shop. Those would be Coventry's horses and his driver, but how could he have found Stephen *there*, unless—

"Come on, then!" Evander leaned out of the coach door and waved to catch Stephen's attention. "We'll be late starting!"

"And that would be me, off," Stephen apologized, tucking his parcel under his arm. "We'll be gone about six weeks. Shall I call on you to make arrangements for lessons once I return?"

"Do so. Six weeks in the country, such a hardship!" Meredeth laughed at him and his disgruntled expression, and waved him off merrily. "Come home with a sweet farm-fed bride!" he called out, the end of his words muffling as the door swung shut behind Stephen.

He swung himself up and into the coach, tucking the precious package out of the way, beside the seat. The driver had them moving within moments, Evander already sprawled easily across the seat opposite.

"I don't know why you still go in there," he said, a frown on his face. "The selection's much better at Bland's, or even Clementi's." He toyed idly with his pocketknife, carving slivers out of an apple and eating them off the blade. "The other customers are better situated as well." It was hard not to watch his tongue and lips as he ate, and Evander caught Stephen's eye with a knowing smirk.

How to describe the feeling that kept pulling him back to Meredeth's? The warm smiles of those who knew him, the cozy, familiar sense of a well-loved space, the knowledge that, even though all money had been firmly settled between them, there were some debts that could never be fully repaid. Evander would not understand.

"They're able to order what I need," Stephen said, shrugging. "And they were so kind to us when we first came to London. Extending credit on account to a pair of starving boys is hardly what you'd call a smart business move."

Evander did *not* understand. "And they continue to reap the rewards of it from your patronage, so it was hardly an ill-conceived one," he pointed out, gesturing with a piece of apple stuck to the end of his knife. He must have seen something cross Stephen's face, for he softened his smile a moment later. "You're a sentimentalist, dear Stephen," he said fondly. "That will be your undoing one day."

"Perhaps I am," Stephen replied, stealing the apple slice and popping it into his mouth. The juice splashed tart and cool across his tongue. "Better that than unfeeling."

Evander's cheerful disdain aside, it did not seem like such a terrible thing to be. It had a much lower likelihood of getting them in trouble than, say, Evander's hedonism. And now, to be moving among powerful strangers for a month and a half, their relationship of the sort that could never be discovered—it could prove a problem.

Two artists from humble origins, sharing lodgings, was common enough, mind you, that even the most respectable of society matrons would not blink. Stephen could think of a handful of men of equal stature who lived exactly as they did, but for whom pursuit of cunt, not prick, was their favorite pastime. So there was little to give them away in *that*.

The raids, at least, would not be a problem for them while they were away. There were a handful of common houses in the back streets of London where, at least until recently, men of a certain inclination could go to drink and flirt and remain unmolested by either women or the law. For years they had slipped by, disregarded, but lately the magistrates had found them a useful target.

It had only been seven months since sweet Dr. Taylor had swung for buggery, his body hanging for the ravens at Portsmouth. He had possessed surgeon's hands, a tribute to his profession, and Evander had exclaimed in delight over his lush and eager mouth. Less than a year ago, the three of them had spent the better part of a night at play in an upstairs room at the Kit and Barrel. Now those precise and clever fingers fed the worms.

Life would be easier if he could summon up some passion for a girl, enough to marry her and take her to bed with frequency enough to keep her content. It was hardly an uncommon thing, though mightily unfair to the bride. But he had yet to meet a girl, however pretty, who could compete with the curve of Evander's arse or the strong cut of his jaw.

They would need to be far more careful.

Chapter Two

12 June 1810

Dear Sir,

I am writing to you

I have been reliably informed

Please forgive any impertinence that you may sense in my initiative. I take up pen to write because I have been informed that you have interest in the services of a painter.

The letter sat in front of Joshua on the sloped writing desk, his handwriting slanting across the page in stark-black contrast to the fine laid paper. He would have to recopy the whole thing once he had the wording down—one did not send a letter to a viscount filled with crossed-out half starts. Even if he *was* of French extraction. That he had escaped the oncoming hordes of Napoleon's army and removed himself to Belgium was a mark in his favor, but that didn't change a man's innate nature.

Dubious ally or not, though, Sophie would browbeat him until he had it written, and her tongue could be sharp. He may as well get it done.

It was a good beginning, at least, the right notes of supplication and hints at informed connection. He dipped his pen in his inkwell again, tapped it idly on the rim and drew a clean sheet toward him to begin anew.

Sunlight filtered through the tall windows that lined one wall of his studio, the rays landing warm on his back. Motes of dust flickered in the sunbeams, a hint of a breeze setting them to dancing. A handful of stretched canvases sat along the wall, their untouched surfaces waiting to be transformed. The rest of the Earl of Horlock's household puttered along in their routines beyond the double doors, but inside his sanctuary, all was calm.

He was placing the final stroke of his name on the bottom of the page when the back door opened, and a head crowned with a rich braid of dark mahogany peered around the jamb. Sophie Armand, the countess's abigail, scanned the room and when she deemed it safe, entered. Sophie was a French refugee, supposedly; charming, also supposedly; and counted uncommonly beautiful by men who were far better equipped than he to appreciate such things.

"Are you writing it?" She crossed the room lightly, her simple calico dress swirling around her, and perched nymphlike on the edge of his table. "Have you finally made up your mind?"

"I've written," he said, fighting the urge to curl his arm around the top of the page to prevent her from reading. "So you may leave off as soon as you please. But I'm undecided on whether to send it." He leaned back in the finely carved wooden chair to show just how unconcerned he was about the entire business. "I don't see why you're so keen on expanding my clientele. I'm very well situated exactly where I am." A vague gesture across the expanse of the studio illustrated his point.

"You're boring where you are," Sophie replied, and she slid the letter out from under his hand. She had lost the gentle lilt of the fashionable accent she affected when around anyone but him, her earthy, prosaic—and rather more English—roots betraying themselves. "And it's making your pictures boring."

"I paint portraits, Sophie," he chided her. "I can hardly spice them up beyond reality. Would you have me add an attack by bears to Gosling's commission? I daresay his three little sons would be very pleased by the change to their nursery."

"Not a bear, but perhaps a wildcat? It would match their mother's temper." She gave as good as she got, and he chuckled softly in response. "I *mean*, you're bored with people. There's no life in their eyes when you paint them. Not anymore. You need to take a risk occasionally, find that spark again."

"I take plenty of risks," he objected, the treads of the familiar conversation reassuring. It was still disconcerting to have become the focus of Sophie's latest improvement project, though it was easier on the nerves to consider it a pleasant affirmation of her friendship. Thanks be to God that she had decided to focus on expanding his professional aspirations instead of trying her hand at matchmaking.

"Then why are you still here with the old bat?" Sophie snorted and he stole the letter back from her to scan it for errors one last time. "If it's only for the creature comforts, I shall be cross with you."

"Careful," he warned, his focus on the page. "That's your employer you're speaking of."

"And your cousin's great-aunt or whatnot. I know. That hardly changes the fact that she's beastly," Sophie proclaimed bitterly.

"Behave," Joshua said mildly. She never did, of course, and their friendship had been partly forged on laughing at the foibles of others. But there was a token attempt that had to be made, and a smile played over his mouth regardless.

It was a generous mouth, he knew that from standing and staring at himself in the glass as he'd painted his self-portrait. Self-portraits were the fashion these days, after all, and one *must* remain fashionable. (That was the countess's voice in the back of his mind, and he sighed to himself.)

So, a wide mouth, perhaps too wide. His hair was still thick, but it was that unfortunate shade of strawberry blond that looked so well on a pretty girl and foolish on a man approaching twenty-five. He kept it short, for convenience more than anything else. Not for him the foppish stylings of the bon ton.

He could only pretend to be so many things that he was not. No matter how much Sophie attempted to "improve" him.

"I shall not." Sophie laughed in response to his admonishment, and hopped lightly off his writing desk. "And you shall come to see the wisdom in it. You will go to the Continent and become the darling of the proper set, fêted at the courts of Europe." She seized his hand, her small one all but vanishing in his palm. He abandoned his papers and let her do it.

"Those not currently embroiled in war," he reminded her as she hauled him to his feet, stronger than she looked.

"Fie on you and your predictions of doom! Come— you shall have to know how to waltz if you are to make a proper impression." She placed his hand on her hip and seized the other, humming as she led him backwards in lurching steps.

There was no choice but to play along, and soon enough she had him laughing as well, even as he stepped on her feet and tripped over his own.

"No, that will never do!" she said delightedly. "Three steps, like so. Da-*da-da*, da-*da-da*!"

He watched her feet, hands resting obediently where she had placed them, and attempted to lead as she demanded. "Watch your toes if you dance with me or your 'one-two-threes' will leave you crippled."

"Turn me under your arm, and all will be forgiven." Sophie moved with easy grace, and not for the first time he wondered at it. He turned her and she spun out, laughing.

"Now where did young Miss Armand learn to waltz, hmm?" He was not about to admit it, but the steps started to come a bit more easily as he watched her feet.

"'Miss Armand' learned at some fancy boarding school, no doubt." Sophie tossed her head imperiously. "But *I* picked it up from a pretty Viennese girl in London. Her dancing was very much in demand, you know," she replied archly, a much longer story behind those words. "You shall have to know it too if you are to make your grand impression!"

"You shock me more and more every day." Joshua twirled her around his studio gallantly. "Now tell me, minx," he said after they had stopped to catch their breath, Sophie tucked neatly under his arm. "Why should I leave all this?"

"Because we grow or we die, dear heart. And you are slowly dying." Sophie stepped away from his brotherly embrace.

Joshua stayed where he was, folding his arms before him as he turned her words over and around in his mind. "What of you?" he asked, to have something else to consider.

Sophie shrugged, trailing her finger across the top of his writing desk. "I will forge on, as I have always done. William is fond of me and has good prospects for a serving man. If not there, then Mr. Glover in town has a ready hand with the compliments, and a staymaker's wife would always be in fashion. We shall see what comes of things. Now…" she picked up the letter and put it into his hands, "…you must send it."

She poked him in the ribs with one finger. It did not hurt, but he tilted away from her jab out of habit. "I have a letter to send to Evangeline as well, but you must pay postage for both together."

"Now I see your scheme, minx." He folded the letter into a neat packet, regardless.

"Fiddlesticks," Sophie said, but she took the letter from his fingers and tucked it away in the bodice of her gown with a smile.

Joshua patted down his pockets without commentary, passing her a half sovereign. "Put that under the seal when you close it up. That should cover costs, if not a little more for the postman."

"You're a good man, Joshua Beaufort," she teased gently. "And you should be painting kings on the Continent, not doddling about, sketching her ladyship's terriers."

A sharp voice carried in from the hall, and Sophie stopped to listen. "And speak of the devil. There's *Madame* now, and my cue, m'sieur, to take my leave." The accent came back in as easily as she had let it go in the first place. She slipped out the back door of his studio with a wink and a finger pressed to her lips. The door clicked closed behind her as the Countess of Horlock made her entrance through the front.

She was not a tall woman, nor broad, though she took up an astounding amount of the air in a room with the force of her presence alone. The countess had accepted middle age with as much grace as anyone could hope, and the years had acted on her not as a sop, but as a whetstone. Her children were married off and about their own business, which left her a great many free hours for social activities and general meddling in the affairs of others.

At the moment she seemed in a pleasant-enough humor, a letter unfolded in her hand.

Joshua rose and bowed. "Lady Horlock," he opened easily, swinging his hands to clasp them behind his back. "What brings you to me on this fine afternoon?"

Lady Horlock looked him over as though doing a survey of his component parts, taking in his ruffled and slightly breathless state. She all but shook herself, a slender gray goose settling her feathers. "We've been invited to a party—Horlock, myself and you. The Earl of Coventry invites us to stay at Belmont House for six weeks. He is having the men in to hunt and some women for civilization, no doubt."

Invitations here were hardly unusual; Joshua's inclusion in one, slightly more so. He raised an eyebrow at the description. "Then why me, Your Ladyship? Surely I am neither invited for the hunt, nor to improve his civility."

Her lips pressed together but curled at the corners, despite her attempt not to smile, and she indicated his studio with a sweep of her hand that encompassed all. "He is a devotee of your art, my dear young cousin. Perhaps he is interested in a companion piece to that dreadfully indulgent self-portrait of yours that he bought last year. Apparently those have become all the rage.

"I cannot say that I understand everything about the 'art world'..." and she pronounced it so that he could all but hear the marks about the words, setting them off, "...but he appreciates your talent, and that reflects well on this house."

And on her patronage choices, naturally. "Do you know who else is expected to attend, madam?"

The countess tapped her gloves against her hand in consideration, a movement which drew his eye. "The Chalcrofts, I presume—their daughter is hardly to be separated from Lady Charlotte these days. The Talbots as well. They always have reached higher than their station. Lord Downe and his sons." She levelled him with a steely eye, her glace flickering to the back door and then away. "I expect you to behave properly around the debutantes. I am not so blind as you think, cousin, and as long as nothing disrupts the fair running of my house, I will say nothing. But if you intend to go courting, especially among the ton, I will know about it first."

Joshua seducing Sophie was about as likely as growing wings and flying himself to the moon. On the other hand, the more that she suspected him of one sort of misbehavior, the less she would be inclined to go sniffing for others.

"Oh what tangled webs", and so forth and so on.

"Of course, Your Ladyship," he replied, his lips twitching, and doing his utter best to look innocent.

She arched a fair eyebrow at him and patted his cheek indulgently, as though he were a boy caught stealing biscuits from the kitchen. "Other than that…" the countess continued, drifting about the edges of the room and flickering her eyes over some of the unfinished canvases and sketches, marking, noting and filing away for later examination, "…Coventry's own family. As he is positing this as some sort of 'artists' retreat'—for the cachet, one supposes—his pair of catamites are certain to attend."

The insult slipped from her mouth so casually and with so little venom that it would have been easy enough to mistake it for something of no importance. All his cheer dissolved away, bubbling down into a grim and familiar reminder for himself to keep the faint and noncommittal smile on his face.

"…honestly, it would be wiser not to be so closely associated with such a libertine, but Horlock will have his grouse, come hell or high water, and so there is nothing for it."

He knew who she meant, of course, who did not? He had no particular proof that they were as she described—he had not frequented the taverns or the stroll in years. There would be a great many men moving in those circles now whom he did not know.

But he knew of Ashbrook and Cade.

Even if they were not lovers, they were a match designed for art. One dark and one fair, both slim, middlingly tall and with the vaguely transparent look that came from too much time indoors and not enough outside of the city.

Most of society had worked itself into a dither about the composer—slightly taller of the two, more classically handsome in that popular Grecian sort of way—who strutted about the halls and streets of London as though he himself had brought Euterpe down from Olympus to be his personal muse. But it was not Evander Cade whom Joshua could not forget.

It was generally known that Stephen Ashbrook played only for Mr. Cade—or could it be that Cade wrote for Ashbrook? When they appeared together, when Cade's music came to life under the rosin and horsehair in Ashbrook's hand, angels themselves wept for the sheer beauty of the sound.

He had seen them once at a concert in the Vauxhall Pleasure Gardens. The trees had arched in dark, forbidding shapes above the walkways and paths, lit from below with gleaming golden lanterns. Four men stood arrayed with instruments and bows, the composer standing before them with his arms high. All were dressed and polished, handsome and skilled, but only one had drawn and held Joshua's eye.

Ashbrook was dark seduction to Cade's polished gold, his lips perfectly shaped, his shoulders broad. He played with his eyes closed, an expression of such ethereal joy on his face, as though he had been carried away in the ecstasy of sound.

Joshua's hands had itched for paper, to limn him out in swift, bold strokes and commit the embodiment of *music* to the page.

His hands had been empty, and the moment passed uncaptured. He had tried, later on, in pencil and in charcoal, on pages that lay unfinished and tucked away inside a sketchbook on his shelf. Either his memory or his hands had failed him, because nothing he had drawn had come close.

That had been a year ago. Despite the distance of time, he still felt something indefinable twisting low in his gut at the thought of meeting the man face-to-face.

Perhaps it was indigestion.

Lady Horlock finished her circuit, apparently satisfied. "William will see to your clothes, and you must gather what supplies will be useful to you. Bring things for portrait taking, and silhouettes." She tapped her gloves against her free hand again, lips pursed in thought. Little wrinkles were forming at the corners, catching the daylight in less flattering ways. "Coventry has Charlotte yet to marry off, and a pretty picture of her would likely not go amiss."

"Bringing stretched canvases might seem a little presumptuous," he felt obliged to point out.

"Nonsense," she replied crisply, and he revised his mental tally from one canvas upward to four. "If Coventry wants artists, then a lawn full of artists he shall have. And," she continued, her expression softening again into something that looked like nostalgia, "the grounds are beautiful. You shall have a chance to indulge in landscapes. Coventry may be louche and a libertine, but he has a lovely house. Be ready for the carriage after breakfast tomorrow."

The door clicked shut behind her and Joshua was left in the company of his thoughts, his sketches and the dust motes sparkling in the sun. Summer in the country was not a terrible thing, despite his nerves.

No. He would not say "nerves"—that suggested that he expected something to happen. This was one party among many, and there was nothing to be nervous about.

At the barest minimum, despite his vague and probably baseless suspicions regarding Cade and Ashbrook, the trip would be entertaining. And that would have to do.

Chapter Three

The wide main road opened up to a long and winding drive as Coventry's carriage began the turn. The trip had been as easy as these things ever were. That meant Evander and Stephen crammed cheek by jowl into the small carriage for two days, bumping along rough and muddy roads until Stephen had turned altogether green. It had taken over an hour for his stomach to resettle once they stopped for the night, despite the cold cloth that Evander had brought for his head and the cup of sweetened tea he'd pressed into Stephen's hands.

At least this second day had been better, the air fresher and his innards no longer attempting to turn themselves into a knotted cravat along the way.

The sky stayed clear, a vibrant summer blue, only spotted by a handful of white clouds. A vast lawn extended up to the house, so carefully trimmed that it must take an army of gardeners to maintain its image of perfection. Small rocks kicked up around the carriage wheels as they approached the immense stone front of the house, wide white stairs angling down to meet the ground. Flowerbeds extending along the front displayed carefully planned bursts of brilliant color, all of it regulated, pruned and controlled to within an inch of its existence.

Stephen swung down from the coach and paused to breathe in the air. It was, he was forced to admit, far fresher than the smoke and grime of London would ever permit. For a moment his head actually seemed to swim, as though he were waking up from half sleep.

In the shelter of the coach, hidden from view of the house, Evander let his hand drop briefly to drift against Stephen's arm. "Are you well?" Concern was written on his face, doing battle with anticipation and excitement.

Stephen nodded. He could hardly do otherwise, and the longer he stood in the drive, solid ground beneath him, the better he felt. "I am," he said, and Evander brightened. "Go ahead; I'll follow directly."

Evander's long, easy stride took him easily across the verge to where a trio of young women sat, their pastel gowns and bonnets arranged strikingly against the green of the grass. They had sketch pads and boxes of watercolors scattered around them, though only one seemed to be at all employed in their supposed pastime. Their chaperones, two older women, sat some distance away with sewing in hand, a veritable wall of dark-silk disapproval.

"Mr. Cade and Mr. Ashbrook, at last!" Lady Charlotte, Coventry's daughter—and the only one of the girls whom Stephen could put name to—rose to greet Evander as he approached. She was honey-haired and gleaming in the sunlight, curls escaping from the bottom of the bonnet that framed an elfin, heart-shaped face. She curtsied low and he bowed, flashing all three of them that wide and generous smile.

Stephen followed in Evander's trail, bowed as Lady Charlotte performed the introductions. It was to be Miss Talbot in the green shawl, her dress plainer than the others, and Lady Amelia Chalcroft with the darker hair and the purple ribbons. How on earth he was going to be able to tell them apart after they had changed for dinner, though—ah well. Take each challenge as it came.

"What a pretty picture you all make," Evander said. "I wish I were a painter rather than a composer, that I might have a way to capture this moment for myself forever."

Stephen would not roll his eyes. He would *not*.

Evander's flattery had a different effect on the ladies, though, and Lady Charlotte tipped her chin up in an imperious lift that was so very like her father. "You shall have to compose a new dance for us then, Mr. Cade," she declared, "and Mr. Ashbrook shall play."

Stephen nodded in his turn. "It would be my honor. My regret shall be that it keeps me from joining you in the dance, but your pleasure itself shall be my reward." Evander beamed at him, hands clasped behind his back and the sun gleaming off his hair, and all their ridiculous squabbles of weeks past were forgiven and forgotten.

Lady Charlotte clapped her hands together. "Oh, very prettily said!" she exclaimed with a girlish laugh. "You will give our dear Mr. Cade some competition this summer!"

"More than just Mr. Cade, I think. Did you know we have a painter here as well?" Miss Talbot interrupted, eager as a new puppy.

Lady Amelia cast her eyes up to the heavens, behind Miss Talbot's head.

"Mr. Beaufort," Miss Talbot continued on, oblivious, "who does such beautiful portraits. He came in with Her Ladyship, the Countess of Horlock yesterday. We were trying to convince him that it would only be proper if he were to give lessons! See? We have our paints and books." She raised a hand to her lips in a gesture born more from practice than honesty, and her eyes lit up. "You must help us convince him!" She was addressing Stephen, for the most part, though her gaze kept wandering to Evander. "Won't it be a lark?"

God help the poor man. It was only Stephen's luck that none of them were angling for music lessons yet.

Evander was in his element, at least, his eyes alight. "I shall, but on one condition," he promised.

Miss Talbot positively beamed. "Name it."

"You'll spend as much time at dancing practice as you do at painting, or I shall have been implicit in my own undoing."

Oh, for heaven's sake.

"If you'll excuse us, ladies all," Stephen interrupted before the chaperones could rise like storm clouds from their perches. Their weighty stares were enough—there was no need to court further danger. "I must drag Mr. Cade away to pay our respects to our host. We shall have the pleasure of your company at dinner tonight, I presume?"

"Indeed you shall," Lady Amelia replied coolly, the only one of the three who didn't seem entirely swayed by the meaningless social patter and Evander's amiable charm. In a perverse sort of way, he liked her a little better for it.

Evander fell into step beside him as they crossed the lawn back towards the house. His ebullient mood was as infectious as ever, but, even so, Stephen could not resist a small poke. "Laying it on a bit thick, weren't you?"

"I don't know about that," Evander replied, never breaking his easy saunter. "Lady Charlotte's likely to oppose her father on the color of the sky, simply for the sake of opposing him. It's better to stay on her good side than be caught between their swords."

"Your mind is a labyrinth, my *dear* Mr. Cade." He wasn't wrong, though. There was every reason to suspect that Coventry would be happier than Charlotte herself, when some poor sap finally carried her off to another region of the country. At the very least, his house would be a great deal quieter.

"And yours entirely too guileless, my *dear* Mr. Ashbrook." Evander smiled knowingly, casting a sidelong look at Stephen as they mounted the stairs. "I think the winsome Miss Talbot has her eye on you."

He was teasing, the dreadful creature, but there was no time to respond. The door opened and the footman stepped aside to allow them entrance to the grand front hall of Coventry's country house.

The hall was a marble-clad masterpiece of modern architecture, a winding staircase soaring up to a mezzanine on either side of the space and carved balustrades fencing off the gallery above. Tasteful statuary lined the pedestals in the hall, cherubs and seraphs in white draperies carved so fine as to appear as translucent as silk.

Age had not treated Coventry with all the kindness a devoted patron of the arts might have deserved. He was as broad of girth as of shoulder, though he had once been a sportsman to be envied. His suit was of the finest cut, and his light-brown hair had gone to white at the temples, his sideburns all to gray. He extended his arms to the two men as they approached, and they bowed, Stephen a half beat behind.

"Gentlemen, welcome." Coventry clapped Evander on the shoulder as he straightened his head, and nodded affably to Stephen. "I trust your trip was uneventful?"

"Most comfortable, sir, thank you," Evander lied without a flinch or flutter, sparing Stephen from having to comment. The state of the roads was hardly the earl's fault, but discussing the first day of travel spent trying not to embarrass himself all over the coach was hardly scintillating conversation. "And thank you again for your kind invitation. We met the ladies outside—are there more guests yet to arrive?"

"There are indeed! This promises to be quite the party," Coventry promised with a gleam in his eyes. "Viscount Downe and his sons will be arriving later. They're Irish, you know, but Downe's a pleasant fellow otherwise and we shan't hold that against him. We shall have some excellent weather this week for hunting." He rubbed his hands together in barely repressed excitement.

The thought of riding was an entertaining one, though Stephen would be happier to go without the hunting. Too many years of city living were going to be his downfall, especially if the aim was not to embarrass their host.

"We're honored to be included among such august company, sir," Stephen said, and Coventry preened.

"Not at all! The honor is all mine, I assure you. Now, you must be road weary, and I'm afraid you've entirely missed the sideboard. But Gregory will show you to your rooms and arrange for a tray to be sent up if you're hungry."

The livery-clad butler, as tall and stately as Coventry was gregarious and round, bowed, hands clasped behind his back. He looked askance at them over a great eagle's beak of a nose, and whatever thoughts that passed behind his narrowed eyes, he betrayed nothing. "Sir."

He escorted them up the long and winding staircase and past a gallery hung with portraits. They hardly had time to mark any of them as they were led along the hall. Another flight of stairs led to their suite of rooms, which turned out to be a pair of bedrooms and a sitting room with high, arched bay windows that caught the afternoon sun. The room was done in the pale yellows and greens that had been so fashionable a few years before. Their trunks had been brought up, one just beyond the open door to each bedchamber.

Stephen made his way to the window and twitched aside the curtain. Their view was of the back gardens, brilliantly colored flowerbeds leading the eye down a gravel path toward a copse of trees, and off to the left, a hedge maze of some complexity. It was brilliantly green, well tended and dreadfully pastoral. The countryside's beauty paled in comparison to the vibrancy, the *urgency* of a single day in London.

His boyhood had been surrounded by a different sort of nature, the fenced-in swaths of crops and pasture on either side of the long dirt road that wound down to the schoolhouse. He'd seen them in the dark, half the time, trailing along behind his father with books wrapped in a leather belt to keep them from falling. He could still feel water seeping in through poorly patched holes in the bottoms of his boots, feel Margaret's little hand clenched in his, hear the lowing of the cattle and Farmer Benton's enormous mean, old bull that liked to charge the fence until it shook. The schoolhouse was always cold when they arrived, the room only beginning to warm hours after Father started the fire.

Stephen shivered. Oh, for the cozy closeness of their lodgings. It might not have brocade upholstery, but they had only a flight of stairs dividing them from tavern tables full of jolly companions and the pulsing heartbeat of the city.

"Dinner will be served at five," Gregory said, not entering much farther than the door. "Clare shall be up to draw you baths in the meantime, that you may recover from the arduousness of your journey." His message delivered, he retreated, closing the door behind him with a stately click.

Evander turned once to take it all in and flopped down on the ivory settee, still in his boots. He held out his hand and Stephen crossed the room to claim it, glancing back at the door over his shoulder. It remained closed, secure against intruding eyes.

He squeezed Evander's ink-stained fingers in his own, and Evander beamed at him with satisfaction and wonder.

"We've managed it, Stephen—look at us. A vicar's son and a schoolmaster's boy, received by a peer of the realm and hosted in luxury. We are *here*."

Later, the road dust washed away, Stephen stood in front of the glass and tugged his cravat into place. The suit was not a fancy, bespoke thing like Coventry's, but it fit him well enough. The black-wool dress coat closed neatly across his chest, his frame trim but not overmuscled. The green waistcoat had been Evander's suggestion. Something about bringing out the green flecks in his eyes, which he himself had always considered to be more of a muddy brown. Still, it all sat well enough that he could go down to dinner feeling rather dashing, rather than the awkward country boy he still was inside.

Evander wandered out of his bedroom then, looking as much the fashion plate as ever. His golden curls hung perfectly in place—all but one, which drooped ever so slightly across his forehead, as though daring someone to loop a finger in it and tug. He looked Stephen over, and all he said was "hm".

Stephen frowned back, trepidation rising in his chest and squeezing gently at his throat. "What's wrong with it?"

Evander stepped in closer and refolded his lapels, brushing away an invisible speck of dust from Stephen's shoulder. "Nothing!" he replied, though he worried again at his lower lip. "Certainly nothing. Only— No, never you mind. It will be fine, I'm sure."

And what good did that do, to hint that something was wrong but refuse to follow through? He bit back the urge to pursue the issue, tugging his coat into place with a sharp gesture instead. "We've a little time before dinner. I thought I might take a look around. Will you come?"

Evander shook his head and Stephen felt an odd twinge of relief. "I've a few things to take care of first, but I'll be down shortly. Go on without me."

Stephen let himself out, the hallway continuing on ahead for what seemed like half a mile. It was ludicrous to have a home so large that the only way that it could possibly be filled was by importing other families. A wealthy man with four children, say, or even five, could get along quite well in a house half the size, with six bedrooms, a suite for guests and six or seven staff to tend to it.

It was exactly the sort of property Evander yearned for and spoke of with longing that bordered on avarice. It was also the kind of place where, as Evander always managed to suggest through word, look and gesture, Stephen would never manage to fit in.

He shoved his hands in his pockets, then guiltily pulled them out again. How many times had Evander lectured him on the importance of cutting a proper figure?

Damn him, anyway. He was as much a child of poverty as Stephen, if not more so. He was the youngest of a full litter of children, while Stephen's parents had only been burdened with two to clothe and feed. Where did he get off putting on such grand airs?

It was hardly Evander's fault that he had such a keen and critical eye, mind you. He hadn't grown up in a large house, but in a cottage on the edge of an estate much like this one. He had learned, watching little quirks and habits of the wealthy, and been generous enough to pass those tricks on to Stephen in turn. They were able to pass among the proper folk now, be lauded and loved for their talents and not judged on their poor family names.

Stephen had taken advantage of all of it with little qualm before. Why did it stick in his throat now?

He should find Coventry's conservatory and see what sort of arrangements he could make for practicing. He had not been able to do anything of the sort in the coach, naturally, and had been too drained and ill at the halfway mark to do anything more strenuous than drink some broth and fall into uneasy sleep. His fingers ached from lack of use; his knuckles cracked when he curled them.

But his violin was back in the suite, and returning meant making conversation again.

It could wait.

Noises sounded from the first floor, murmurs of conversation and the swish of silk skirts, and Stephen turned into the open archway on his left rather than go downstairs just yet. The portrait gallery stretched out before him, long rows of paintings hung along the facing walls. Shadows clung to the walls, the sconces not yet lit.

The images were mostly of the standard sort: prettily posed ladies with various small dogs, simpering children, doughty-looking gentlemen with swords on their hips. Some of them were rather more dubious, a weedy-looking, young man with a highly unfortunate chin, chief among them. One good stiff wind would knock him flat on his arse, and that chin would act as a sail.

A handful of portraits in a newer fashion looked like more recent additions. The paintings themselves fit the mold of the others—delicate brushwork, the sitter looking off to the side or down in modesty or up to glory, depending on nature, sex and inclination. All but one. The palette was still muted, but the straightforward pose and the natural life in the expression of the sitter stopped Stephen in his tracks.

The man in the portrait was not classically handsome. His mouth was too full and his hair too red for that, his jawline perhaps a little too soft. But his eyes crinkled at the corners with secret mirth, as though sharing a very private and personal joke with the viewer, and those lush and generous lips curled up at one corner. He sat in a smock and his shirtsleeves, a palette on the table behind him. His head tilted very slightly to the side, like he was listening to some secret, lively song. His eyes caught and held Stephen, gray as storm clouds over the cliffs, a hint of blue that was the clear sky breaking through, and a knowing look that struck some chord deep within that Stephen could not immediately name.

He wanted—

Well, he wanted a great many things. But never before had a *portrait* been responsible for a curl of longing or desire twisting its way up from the center of his being, some vague and wistful sense of thwarted desire focused on that arresting stare.

I wonder if he would look at me that way in life.

I wonder who he is.

A faint scuff of feet behind him was all that gave Stephen warning before someone spoke, and he managed neither to whip around in surprise, nor jump like a child caught where he shouldn't be.

"He's not a particularly good-looking fellow to deserve such lengthy scrutiny."

The voice was an unfamiliar one, a warm, rich tenor that verged on a deeper range, a faint Northern accent coloring the tone.

"I suppose not," Stephen replied, pausing to allow his heart to slow before he introduced himself, "if you value men solely based on looks. But there is more life in his expression than in all the other portraits put together. Either the sitter was a man of uncommon vivacity or the painter was exceptionally fond of him."

He turned and looked at the man standing behind him.

His hair was shorter now, and he was dressed for dinner, his cravat impeccably tied and tucked into a cream waistcoat. The man from the portrait stepped into the gallery, framed by a shaft of light that fell across the floor from the hall. His eyes had not been exaggerated. They had been perhaps underplayed, and that gray-blue gaze regarded Stephen with a peculiar intensity. He was a little taller than Stephen, his frame of very pleasing proportions, and had a controlled energy to his walk that suggested strength lying beneath the layers of wool and linen.

"Or he was his own painter," the newcomer said, his lip quirking up in that selfsame knowing smile, "and both irredeemably prone to vanity and in desperate need of an honest friend to check him in his fancy."

"I should say otherwise," Stephen replied, the compliment easy to make. "It appears to be the very copy of life." *Careful!* It was all well and good to flatter and tease when flirting with the ladies, but this man was still a stranger. "Stephen Ashbrook, at your service."

The other man hesitated, but only for a moment, and bowed in return. "Joshua Beaufort. A pleasure, sir."

Something about the light in the room suggested an edge of color rising to Beaufort's cheeks, a faint flush that vanished a moment later. "Though, I should confess, your name was already known to me. I saw you play last summer, at a chamber concert at Vauxhall."

That thrill of recognition would never become tiresome! Still, modesty demanded a different sort of reply. "Then I should have given you another name so that you would not have made the connection," he joked, beating back the urge to let his tongue tie itself in knots. "I promise that I have made some effort to improve since then."

Beaufort. His eyes kept playing over Stephen's face, his shoulders, his hands—the scrutiny made it difficult to focus on the conversation. He smiled, and his eyes were warm. "If your playing has improved, sir, then I hesitate to ask if you have brought your instrument. I don't think my nerves could take a performance better than that."

"You flatter me."

There was a hint of something in Beaufort's expression, beyond that careful smile. The way he held himself, carefully poised and controlled, his gaze lingering perhaps a breath too long on Stephen's mouth when he spoke, a gleam on his lower lip when he moistened it.

Perhaps—

Was Beaufort playing with flirtation, or was he merely being kind to a fellow artist? In the years Stephen had been living in London, he had not once seen Beaufort at the taverns, or on the stroll in Moorfields where less careful men went to find their fun. That meant little, mind you. He could be circumspect, or live nowhere near London, or have a lover at home to whom he kept faith.

He was not beautiful, but he was exactly the sort of sensual that made Stephen wish Evander were there to charm him and flatter him and convince him to come to their bed.

"Not at all. I was particularly moved by the third variation. I am sorry, I don't know enough about music to describe it, but perhaps you know the one I mean. There was such passion in your playing of it that it utterly transported me."

Stephen's ears flushed hot at the tips and he ducked his head like a child at the praise. It was ridiculous! He'd had compliments plenty of times before, ovations and applause aplenty. But none of it had been delivered with that delicious intensity and a gaze that held him as though he were actually someone important.

He should mention that Evander was also a guest, redirect Beaufort's compliments to the appropriate place, but something held his tongue. "I do indeed, and you're very kind to say so. It is one of my own favorites, which I suppose can have an effect."

Beaufort's nearness was having a very real effect on *him*. That mouth was all too much. He would likely make soft, breathy sounds when Stephen nipped at it with his teeth. He would press his tongue against it, draw Beaufort's lower lip between his and taste the heat beyond it—

Noises of conversation and laughter filtered up from below, as well as the sound of feet on the stairs. Stephen blinked and realized with a start that he and Beaufort were standing quite close together in the half dark. There was something dangerously intimate about it, and he stepped quickly back to a safer distance. "It sounds as though the hordes are gathering. Time to make an entrance, I believe."

Beaufort glanced at the door, and by the time he turned back he was remote again, dispassionate and cool. He nodded, whatever moment of connection they'd been sharing seemingly dismissed from his mind. "It would appear so." He gestured to the door. "After you, Mr. Ashbrook."

It was unseemly and a little bit ridiculous, but Stephen could not help the flicker of disappointment that flared as he walked out into the well-lit hall. Beaufort did follow him as he clattered easily down the stairs, Lady Charlotte and the other guests already amassing in the parlor.

There was the world-weary Earl of Horlock with his pinch-faced countess, whom Stephen knew of from a carefully maintained distance. She paused in her conversation with Lady Chalcroft to stare at him over her pince-nez, like a caricature of a gargoyle, and he bowed with carefully precise courtesy. The chaperoning crows—Mrs. Talbot and Lady Chalcroft—paid little attention. The girls giggled together on the couch behind them, now in fancy evening gowns and ribbons woven in their hair. It was too bad they didn't seem to be wearing the same colors as their day dresses because it took him some effort to match their names to their faces.

"Gentlemen and Ladies!" Coventry entered not far behind them, saving Stephen the effort of requesting proper introductions. Evander was close on Coventry's heels, perfectly pressed and put together. "The table is laden—shall we process in? Let us not stand too heavily on ceremony, for we are all friends here. Or at least we shall all be soon enough!" Coventry winked to his daughter's companions with the broad and exaggerated gesture of an older man who knew he would not be taken seriously.

The countess had been in her grave over a year, Stephen reminded himself, as the ladies rose and teased him in return. It would not be unheard of for Coventry's eyes to wander once more. From the calculating look in Lady Amelia's eye as she hung off of Charlotte's arm, Stephen was not the only one to make that observation. Miss Talbot trailed the other two girls, not seeming to mind being relegated to the back of their cluster.

Mr. Beaufort looked back and held his gaze just a moment too long before processing in to dinner.

Well, well. And a good evening to you too, sir.

Chapter Four

Joshua lowered himself into the armchair in his room and untied his cravat with a peevish snap.

"That bad, was it?" Sophie asked from the chair opposite, her legs curled under her. She closed the book in her hands, tucking it into her lap. It said something that he wasn't the least bit surprised by her presence, though by all rights he should have been appropriately scandalized. He could always tell her to leave, as though that would do any good. The girl was like a cat—she went where she pleased and did what she liked, and woe betide anyone but her employer who tried to force her otherwise.

"I had no idea," Joshua said, checking first to be sure the door was most securely closed, "that her ladyship had such strong opinions about the idea of gas lighting."

"Ooh, yes, did she get on about that again? 'Those gas lines will be a blight on the city'," Sophie imitated bitingly. "'They're an invitation to treachery and a first stage toward a new Gunpowder Plot', to hear her go on. And did you know that they're sinful as well? Apparently our Lord and Savior would prefer candlelight."

"Lord save us from the march of progress." Joshua sighed and rubbed his forehead. Exhaustion nipped around the edges of his eyes, his shoulders aching. "You were quite right, by the way." He glanced up at Sophie, not too tired to add to her amusement. "Lady Chalcroft's got her eye set on Coventry for her eldest. The two of them would set on her rivals like a pair of wild dogs if they thought it would get her a handspan closer to a coronet."

"I said as much." Sophie nodded in agreement, running her fingers over the embossing on the leather cover of her book. "She's got mean eyes, that one, and the daughter's not much better. Mrs. Talbot, on the other hand…she comes a daft creature, but she's smarter than you'd think. I was speaking with her girl, Poppy, while we were airing out the gowns? She said the family's come on hard times since their boy caught sick. They need a good match for the miss, and fast."

"You would make a remarkable spy," Joshua observed, only mildly caustically. "Have you never thought about entering the diplomatic corps?" He itched to remove his jacket, but Sophie showed no signs of leaving.

"If I thought they'd take a girl…" Sophie smiled sweetly, "…in an instant. Now…" she pointed at the center of his chest and arched an exquisitely crafted eyebrow, "…what of those musicians? The girls downstairs were all atwitter, and I'll not leave until I've heard your impressions."

Joshua schooled his face into something which he prayed resembled indifference and shrugged expansively.

Sophie's eyes narrowed.

"There is not much to tell," he said in an attempt to put her off the scent. Not that it was at all likely to work, but he had to try. "Mr. Cade and Mr. Ashbrook attended dinner, they were seated down at the other end of the table from me, and we did not speak beyond pleasantries after our introductions."

There. None of those things was in and of itself a lie. The musician and composer had been seated by Lady Charlotte and the Countess Horlock, while Joshua had ended up entertaining the Chalcrofts and fending off Mrs. Talbot's increasingly unsubtle hints about painting lessons.

And, though it was a technicality, all of his conversation with Mr. Ashbrook had taken place before they had been formally introduced. That conversation was something he would keep most firmly to himself, Sophie's curiosity be damned.

Sophie's eyebrow had climbed higher on her forehead while he had been lost in thought, and he made a dismissive noise at her. "Out with you now, I'm for bed."

"D'you need a powder for your head?" Sophie rose languidly, book in hand. "I can fetch one, or some brandy if you prefer."

"No, thank you." Joshua rose with her from force of habit. "Only some sleep."

"G'night, then." Sophie slipped out, with one last, pointed look, and closed the door behind her.

He followed behind to bolt it fast, then tossed his cravat over the back of his chair. He stripped efficiently, doused the light and collapsed onto his bed in nothing but his shirt.

He should have known better than to approach the man in the gallery. It had been temptation too strong, Stephen Ashbrook standing right there before him. He had intended to take the chance to reassert their respective places, meet him as a person and banish forever the fantasy that had lingered since Vauxhall. Reality should never come close to the things fevered imagination could dream up.

Ashbrook had indeed been different than expected, but in ways that did nothing to stop the lurch in Joshua's gut at the sight or thought of him. He had left his hair to grow long over the year, and it curled about his neck and face in rich, dark waves. His eyes, which had simply looked brown from a distance, were flecked with green, his lashes impossibly long against the high curve of his cheek. He was not girlishly pretty, despite that. Ashbrook was every bit a man, from the breadth of his shoulders to the slim taper of his hips.

And it had been a long time since Joshua had taken anyone to his bed.

Those warm, walnut eyes had lingered a moment too long on Joshua's lips. He had come very close to succumbing to the unasked question.

Ashbrook and Cade, he reminded himself, and tried to bring up images of the two speaking together after dinner, heads bent in quiet conversation. Ashbrook had a lover. He had no need for Joshua's fumbling attentions.

And yet. Ashbrook had flirted—it *had* been flirting. He was not yet so far gone in his solitude that he could no longer recognize the flash of interest and the subtle mark of a kindred spirit in another man's eyes.

For a moment, however brief, Joshua had been desired.

It rushed hot through his body, flared deep in the back of his mind and burned down his spine, settled in the deep pools of his understanding. If those few moments of connection were all he could have, it would have to be enough.

Sleep, normally a welcome lover, forsook him for warmer beds. Joshua tossed and turned in his sweaty sheets, in that half space between dream and waking. Every time he dozed off it came back, that feeling that he was reaching for something, only to have it turn to mist and slip from his fingers the moment they closed about it.

He rose and dressed again by the faint glow of moonlight. A small stub of candle was enough to light his way, and he went wandering. The almost-full moon shone in through the bay windows in the upstairs hall, turning everything it touched to shades of silver, taupe and gray.

Silence reigned, not the quiet of the grave, but something more wholesome and peaceful. It was late enough that all the servants would be abed, and not yet time for the parlor maids to be slipping through the rooms to set the next morning's fires. Darkness closed about him when he turned the corner and left the moonlight behind, his tiny flickering flame the only thing holding it at bay. He was a ghost, passing melancholically and unseen past closed and barred doors. Once he was gone, there would be none left to mourn him.

Joshua turned another corner and then stopped, the flicker of light below a door banishing all of his morbid thoughts. The double doors led to the music room—he remembered that much from the tour he had received upon their arrival. The countess had been disinterested, he had marked it more from curiosity than anything else, and they had moved on.

Now someone else was there.

Ashbrook? His treacherous pulse beat faster before he could calm it, but who else would it be? The master of the house was no music lover, to be hanging about his pianoforte in the dead of night. Unless one of the ladies was indulging in a secret assignation with her music master—hardly likely. The man was fifty if he was a day, and with a potbelly to match.

No music echoed down the hall, but even through the door he could hear the soft susurration of voices, both male, and the creaking of furniture. He needed to know, though he could probably guess. His feet moved one in front of the other despite his nagging impulse to turn around and return to his room. The candlelight flickered again, below the doors and between them. The latch had not been properly set.

Someone gasped, a sound followed by a low and guttural moan that quickly cut off. Or had that been a sob? Despite himself, he pinched out his candle and put his hand to the door. What if someone inside was injured or ill? Just because it sounded like something other than that—

It swung silently at his touch, the hinges well oiled and the door heavy. He stopped it before it could open farther than an inch or so, but that was more than enough for the image to sear itself into his memory.

The hushed and muffled noises that emerged from the room were musical indeed, but not the sort that could be

59

played upon a harp. Two bodies writhed and rocked into one another in the center of the room, a portrait of lusty abandon. Candlelight gleamed golden and warm on Cade's long, lean thighs, his trousers pushed down about his knees. Ashbrook knelt on the upholstered armchair in front of him, his fingers clutching tightly to the headrest, clad only in his shirt. A pair of trousers lay in a heap on the floor.

Cade's fingers sank into the flesh of Ashbrook's hip, digging hard enough to leave dents. That fair skin would be marred tomorrow with pink and purple marks, the constant low ache a persistent reminder of their fucking. Ashbrook's shirt clung to him, the sweat-damp fabric clinging to the dips and shadows of his muscled back and shoulders. Cade bent low, pressing kisses to the bumps of Ashbrook's spine with every snap of his hips. Cade's buttocks clenched in time with the slap of skin against skin.

God above, Joshua would pay any price imaginable to be the one leaving marks like that, to feel Ashbrook's body clench around his cock, to drive into him and wring gasps of pleasure from his throat. Ashbrook arched deliciously, his neck and back a perfect taut bow. He groaned and bit his lip as Cade laced fingers in his dark curls.

Cade pulled back, tugging Ashbrook's head up and baring his throat. The curve of it in the flickering shadows was devastating, the angles of their bodies and the punishing thrusts of their movements a punch to the gut that sent Joshua reeling back a step.

His breath heaved faster, loud even to his own ears. They must be able to hear it, had to realize that he stood there, hardening inside his trousers, at war with himself. He should respect their privacy, turn and walk away.

And yet. They had a suite entirely to themselves—why plan an assignation in a public room if not for the thrill of the possibility of discovery? Better that it be him than one of the maids or, heaven forbid, one of the chaperones or Coventry himself. Perhaps it would be better if he stayed where he was, if only to raise the alert if someone else should happen to come by, someone who would be less…understanding about their particular proclivities.

Yes, he would be doing them a service. He turned his back, pressed his forehead against the cool, solid wall.

In the meantime…Joshua pressed the heel of his hand against his cock, fought the urge to thrust against it, to roll his hips into the friction. He tried to will it down, to force his pulse to slow to normal. Mathematics—that could work. Times tables, if he could remember them all, or the order of precedence of the current peerage…

Another creak and gasp from behind him made him turn, and the sight drove all thoughts of leaving out of his mind.

Cade had knocked Ashbrook's legs wider where he knelt on the chair and slotted himself more snugly between them. He slid again into Ashbrook's body and his own head tipped back in exultation, his face contorted with pleasure and lust.

Joshua ached. He ached and he *throbbed*, and pushed against his palm despite it all. What if he were there, beneath Ashbrook as Cade was above him? He could not see Ashbrook's cock from this vantage point, blocked by the hem of his shirt. He would be big, though, full, red and long, hanging thick and heavy between his thighs, the crown gleaming with the wet evidence of his desire. Yes, and he would thrust into Joshua's mouth as Cade thrust into him—

Ashbrook panted and reached back, sank his nails into the meat of Cade's thigh and urged him deeper, faster.

Heat suffused Joshua's body, his cock hot and hard inside his trousers. They were too tight, the buttons pressing into sensitive flesh, and it would be so easy to undo those buttons, slip a hand inside and stroke himself. He could practically taste Ashbrook's skin, could imagine what it would feel like to slide his tongue up, from the shadow of his clavicle to the Adam's apple that bobbed with every swallowed moan.

Joshua stepped to the side, craned his head to get a better view. Good judgment? What was that compared to this?

There—he could see Ashbrook's prick now, as large and well-formed as any man could ever desire, hard and slick with precome that made the silk-soft skin gleam. It bobbed up against the flat plane of his stomach with each thrust and roll of his hips.

Ashbrook let go of Cade and wrapped one hand around his own prick. He stroked himself, the tip thickening and lengthening more than before. He panted, gasped for breath, his lips red. They gleamed wet in the light, parted just so.

What would it be like to slide his own prick between them, to feel the hot slick of Ashbrook's mouth enveloping him? He would be so beautiful like that, his lips stretched full around the root of Joshua's erection, his own skin shining slick with spit as he thrust—gently, so as not to hurt—and Ashbrook's tongue circled and pressed and rubbed, like that—

The strangled cry ripped from Joshua's throat, too quickly to smother.

Ashbrook's head snapped toward the door, Cade's eyes stayed closed and his face tipped up toward the ceiling.

He was unmade, undone, discovered in his voyeurism!

The only saving grace would be that they could not expose him, but Ashbrook would surely despise him. Joshua staggered backward, remembering too late that his hand was pressed rough against his prick through the fabric of his trousers. No dim lighting could disguise the bulge of his erection or what, precisely, he had been doing there.

Ashbrook's eyes met his and went wide, but he said nothing. He stared, and Joshua stared back, caught, paralyzed. Ashbrook's hand moved faster on his own prick, tight and rough. He fucked back onto Cade's cock in violent motion, and his gaze on Joshua was *hungry*. He came with a shudder and a strangled, quiet cry and sob. He shot his emissions over the fingers of one hand, gripping white-knuckled to the chair with the other. And all the time, his eyes stayed fixed on Joshua.

Joshua turned, all bravado gone. He walked, five steps later broke into a run and did not look back to see if anyone followed.

Half an hour later, in bed once more with the door securely locked and barred behind him, he was further from sleep than he had ever been. The images kept running through his mind, unbidden and…

No. He could not lie to himself. His fantasies had been made flesh, and the memories were welcome. Ashbrook and Cade were beautiful, both alone and together, light and dark, gold and onyx, sun and shadow. They moved with sure knowledge of each other's bodies and with the confidence of old lovers, and Joshua ached in envy and thwarted desire.

His body stirred as he lay there. Alone, with no one to condemn him for his lusts, Joshua took himself in hand to answer. Ashbrook's fingers were slender, strong and precise in their movements. He would know exactly where and how to touch, when to tighten his grip and when to tease with short, quick strokes.

Blood and heat rushed to Joshua's prick as he closed his fingers around his shaft. It hardened in his hand, the smooth skin heating, stretching, throbbing as his prick expanded into the circle of his palm. He stroked himself with a few slow and languid tugs at first. His foreskin slid easily over the crown, sending little shivers of pleasure and heat rippling through him. It caught for a moment on the small gold ring that pierced his cockhead, the burn immediate. He flicked the ring with his nail, a jolt of pressure and pleasure reverberating down to the root of his prick and into his spine.

His last lover's hands had been clever, his mouth hot and wet, capable of so many distracting things. That mouth had slid down over Joshua's prick, so slick and slow. He had tongued at the base of it, worked his way back up to circle the head with such deliberate and drawn-out caresses that Joshua had been a shaking, trembling mess by the time Charlie had allowed him to come.

Yes, think of Charlie. It was safer that way.

The gold rings that had winked in Charlie's nipples had been a revelation, souvenirs from a voyage to far-distant lands. Joshua had vaguely expected tattoos, maybe scars. A sailor's life was fraught with danger, and Charlie had been an able seaman, not an officer able to shut himself away in a cabin with charts and books. And then, alone in an inn room that smelled of wood smoke and wine, Joshua had peeled the shirt from Charlie's body, with trembling and eager hands, and been unmade.

When Joshua had taken those rings between his lips, toyed with them in his fingers, Charlie had spent himself untouched—an amazing sight. Joshua had suckled at the metal, fascinated, rolled the ring between teeth and lips, pulled back at it and laved the sting with his tongue. Charlie had convulsed, cried out for God and for mercy before his prick jerked and he splashed wet, white and hot between their bodies.

Joshua had not known such a thing was possible until he saw it for himself. And then he *wanted.*

"Where else can it be done?" He had asked, lying in Charlie's arms, his body replete. He'd smoothed his thumb over the red marks of his teeth left on Charlie's shoulder and arm, tugged gently on the leftmost ring and watched his nipple harden to a pebble. Then, *"That. I want that."* It was the closest thing to impetuous madness he had ever allowed himself, his pulse beating loudly in his ears, the drumbeat of the ocean.

Dashing, fair-haired Charlie had done his best to talk Joshua out of his mad plan. He capitulated—finally, after weeks of henpecking—procured the necessary items with a warning and a fierce scowl.

That delicious night, alone in the bed piled high with pillows, Joshua gripped the headboard with both hands, his nervousness taking over. Charlie opened the brandy and drank, but didn't swallow; he kissed Joshua with it, fed him the liqueur from mouth to mouth until Joshua's limbs were loose and his body languid.

"You can still back out, you know."

"No—I want this."

He had come close to refusing when Charlie turned the needle in the candle flame, the metal glowing red-hot in the fire. Still, he steeled himself, gripped the headboard more tightly and imagined himself elsewhere. The pain had been brutal yet brief, the euphoria that drowned it moments later far more intense than any discomfort.

Joshua had had cause to regret over the course of the next few weeks, naturally, until the first time his cock hardened without stabs of pain. He had taken himself in hand that first time, so tentatively, so carefully, as though it were the *very* first time and he still imagined he might break. Until his thumbnail scraped across the ring and it shifted against the hard and glistening head of his prick, and he *understood*. He had released harder and more violently than ever before in his life, into his own hand, with Charlie watching and applauding his display.

It was like that even now, that brilliant rush of pleasure-ache and fullness, the wound long since healed and Charlie's bones, crew and ship all resting at the bottom of the indifferent sea.

Two years since the storm took his ship down. Two years since Joshua had removed himself back to Horlock's estate, there to paint portraits of large ladies with small dogs and retire at night to a cold and empty bed.

Now, though, he could close his eyes and see Ashbrook's face, his lips, his hands. Two years was longer than any widow ever mourned a husband—he could have this without guilt. He could allow himself, just once, to indulge.

Joshua stroked himself again, ran his hand along the silk-soft skin of his prick, aching with the doubled need of unspent lust. A gentle tug at the ring sent coils of heat down through his groin, building and pooling at the base of his spine.

Yes, this he could have—the image of Ashbrook's mouth, red, red lips that parted, plush and inviting, when he drew breath to speak. He would paint those lips with his fluids, rub his prick across them and press just the tip inside. Ashbrook's tongue would curl around the ring, tug on it, suck at the place where the gold joined his body. His hands would clench around Joshua's buttocks, urging him closer, pulling him in so that he could thrust deeper, slide heavily across Ashbrook's waiting tongue.

His fingers would—

Joshua slipped two fingers into his mouth, his other hand still circling his cock. He sucked on them, laved them with his tongue, imagined for a moment that it was Ashbrook's prick there, stretching his mouth open and leaving trails of salt-sweet across his lips and tongue.

His fingers wet, he let them slip from his mouth and trailed them down his body. They left streaks of damp on his skin, raising gooseflesh as he went.

He crooked his knee up, gripped tightly at the head of his cock and twisted his hand up to run his palm across the head. His other hand slipped between his legs, and he pressed the pad of one finger against his arse, traced circles of cold fire along the sensitive skin.

Fuck me.

It would have been easier with oil, but for one finger alone his body opened, slick with spit to ease the way.

Joshua shuddered and gasped aloud into the silent room, waited for a moment for the stretch and burn to fade into need. He rocked down into it, crooked his finger to find that ephemeral *something more*. It was not his own hand that fucked into him, opening him up and filling him, but those long and slender fingers that danced across a violin's strings with such deceptive ease.

There—that made his prick jump against his stomach, a trail of precome leaving wet marks against the linen of his shirt. An impatient shove sent it up to expose the pale expanse of his stomach and the fine red-blond hair that trailed down to the nest of curls at the base. He fucked up into his own grip, rocked down onto his fingers and imagined Ashbrook's fierce mouth. He could almost feel the nibbles at his hip, the way Ashbrook would suck Joshua's balls into his mouth one at a time. He would take Joshua's prick deep, so deep, into that perfect throat and swallow around him, his fingers twisting up firmly into Joshua's body until he was nothing but a shaking mess of need.

Desire pooled deep inside him, and his balls drew up tight, tight against his body. Lightning flared behind his eyes, a white-sharp jolt that flashed out through his arms and legs, leaving his fingers tingling and his toes curled so tightly that they cramped. He bowed up off the bed, his emissions spurting wet and sticky across his stomach and his chest, coating his fingers with the evidence of his lust.

Later, his skin cool where he had washed and his clean shirt stiff against his skin, Joshua sank into bed for the third time that night. He should have been exhausted, his body sated, but his mind whirled at much the same pace as before.

He was hell bound. That much had been assured since his first hesitant, adolescent explorations in the hayloft, the lines of Thomas's slim, brown body as new and exciting as discovering his own. How much more could covetousness possibly add to his tally of sins? At least there was one thing in his favor—it was nothing more than infatuation. And that, given time and distance, would inevitably fade.

After this torturous summer he would move on, forget Stephen Ashbrook, and they would all be the better for it.

Sleep circled, dubious, outside his reach. When he closed his eyes, all Joshua could see was a pair of green-flecked eyes and slim fingers playing a waltz upon another man's skin.

Chapter Five

Guests were not expected for breakfast at any particular hour, thank goodness. Stephen rose late, the soft bed pulling him back down into hazy dreams every time he began to wake. He lay there for a while, even with his eyes open, feeling the warmth surrounding him, the way the pillow sank down beneath his head, the delicious ache in his body from the previous night.

He should get up, take some time to practice before eating. He needed some pretense at a respectable schedule if he was not to drift entirely into indolence and excess.

The lushly appointed conservatory looked different in the bright light of morning, the dark, sultry night replaced with clear sunshine and a gentle breeze. He amused himself by sitting in the armchair they had defiled the night before, to run his scales. It gave him a clear view of the open door as well, which triggered its own memories.

Beaufort. How long had he been watching, and how much had he seen? Enough, obviously. If Stephen had noticed him earlier, could he have been convinced to join them? He and Evander coupling would make a gorgeous picture. (Because of course it had been Evander who drew his gaze. Evander would settle for nothing less.)

The fingertips on his left hand ached with the delicious soreness of use after two days of nothing, and the heady smell of rosin lingered in his nose. His stomach churned and growled, demanding attention. Breakfast first. The rest would have to wait.

The earl was already in the hall when Stephen came down the stairs. He was dressed for riding and pulling on a pair of leather gloves. "Good morning!" Coventry greeted him effusively. "I trust you found your accommodations to your liking?"

That, he could answer in absolute truth, given his silk and feathered nest. Imagine what it would be like to have that as one's normal state of being! It was no wonder the rich preferred to stay at home and have guests come to them.

"I've never known better," Stephen replied, and Coventry's smile grew wider. "Your house does you great credit."

"And my cook does me more so!" Coventry patted his girth with a self-deprecating laugh. "I'm riding out now— my physician is after me to improve my exercise, and the weather is fine. We shall have a little hunting to begin the day. Horlock and Cade are already at the stables. Feed yourself and join us."

There was his first dilemma of the morning. Should he accept and spend the morning riding in the sunshine— which would also include listening to Coventry wax on to his friend about his properties and cottages, taking the occasional potshot at some poor defenseless grouse, and watching Evander at his most sycophantic in front of *two* earls—or demur and risk spending the morning with no one around but a gaggle of giggling girls and their mother hens?

There was always the conservatory.

"With your permission, sir, perhaps tomorrow?" Coventry's ebullient smile began to fall toward a frown, and Stephen hastened to explain. "Two days on the road did not lend itself to practice time. I should put some hours of work in before I get any rustier." Waggling his fingers in demonstration put off Coventry's visible disappointment.

"Of course." Coventry nodded his permission. "Very understandable. It will be a better group tomorrow as well, once Downe and his sons are here. We shall make a proper party of it and bag some beauties for the table." He clapped Stephen jovially on the shoulder. "Enjoy your practice. I hope we shall have the honor of enjoying the fruits of it."

"If my strumming and plucking amuse you, then it would be my pleasure," Stephen replied in an equally jovial tone. He clasped his hands behind his back in an attempt at the casual ease that this sort of conversation demanded.

Coventry gave him a look that suggested he'd said something wrong, but he simply nodded again. "Something to be arranged then," he said, a little cooler toward Stephen than before, and headed for the front doors. "Have a good morning, Mr. Ashbrook."

Why couldn't every conversation be as amiable as those with his friends back in the city? Every word spoken here had to be selected like fruit at market, turned over and measured in the hand to check for bruises and for poison.

Bread, jam and coffee procured, Stephen ate quickly before anyone else wandered in to trap him in a conversation. Without Evander to use as a distraction, he would inevitably misstep in some other hideously unfortunate way.

The sun was streaming in through the tall windows in the conservatory by the time he returned to it, and the dark wood of the beautiful pianoforte gleamed like burnished bronze. On a whim, Stephen opened the lid and ran his fingers along the keys. It sang to him, not as perfect a sound as Rosamund's, but with its own sweet charm. He let his fingers glide across the keys of their own volition and struck up a sweet, simple dancing tune that seemed to send the curtains to pirouettes. Here he had no audience, no critical composer standing guard, only music, a faint summer's breeze and the midmorning sun to warm him through. The tight knot between his shoulders eased and released, tension ebbing further from him with every passing moment.

But he was flirting with a mistress when his one true love lay untouched in her felt-lined bed.

A flip of the latch on the violin case and he lifted the lid, exposing Rosamund's sleek brown lines to the light of day. Her maple body and spruce neck had been made in the Stradivarius style, her skin polished to a gleam by years of careful waxing. She settled against his collarbone as though made to fit. Or perhaps, over the years, he had grown to accommodate her shape.

Stephen needed no sheet music for this. The exercises poured forth as purest muscle memory—first scales, then fingering. Once his hands were loose again he set to playing Evander's "Adagio", slow and sweet, the first piece he had ever written for Stephen. The notes were lazy winter evenings entwined in each other's arms, new wine and old cheese eaten from willing and supple fingertips. It was hope and promise and a thousand other things that, like those long, dark nights, had begun to fade in the light of summer and years of slow disillusion. The music, at least, was his to keep.

The sun was at its zenith in the sky by the time Stephen set down his bow. His fingertips tingled and blood rushed back to them as he placed Rosamund back in her case. The world outside called to him, the breeze at the window toying with his hair. A walk, then, and a chance to explore on his own. There was as of yet no sign of the hunting party's return.

Stephen left the house by way of the kitchen doors, a hunk of fresh bread in one hand and a piece of good cheese in the other. Coventry had not been wrong about his cook. Gravel crunched beneath his feet once he was out of the kitchen yard. The light danced merrily through the leaves of the trees that shaded the path, casting dappled shadows over the ground. The breeze rustled through them, and birds sang somewhere, and it was all exceedingly quiet and dull.

Where to now? He could explore the garden or wander down the drive and take a walk toward the small village they had passed on the way in—

No. Lady Charlotte and her adherents were coming around the corner of the house and making their way in that very direction. Charlotte had a basket over her arm, covered with some fancy embroidered cloth, and Miss Talbot wound daisies between her fingers as she idly knotted them into a chain. Lady Amelia followed them closely, a couple of ladies' maids making up the last of the party as chaperones. Miss Talbot stopped suddenly, reaching behind to jerk the train of her dress, somehow caught in Lady Amelia's shoe.

The squabbling began and Stephen pressed himself back into the shadows. Whatever they had planned for the day, he wanted little part of it. Conversation there would be the same as at dinner, no doubt, all discussions of people he only knew as faces in an audience or names on a newssheet. He turned and faded away, heading off along the path toward the garden that had been his first temptation.

The jeering voices of boys were more of a city sound than anything he'd expected on an estate, and Stephen turned off the path and moved through the trees to follow the noise.

A girl stepped lightly across the lawn, her dress simple and plain, her dark hair bound up around her head and a large basket tucked beneath one arm. She steadied the basket with the other, resolutely not looking behind her at the stableboys, baby-faced but tall enough to be almost considered men, who catcalled to get her attention. She stooped—perhaps she had fallen?

And Stephen broke into a run. "Oy!" Stephen shouted, and the boys stopped.

The girl straightened, her basket on the ground, and whipped her arm. Something small and round struck a stableboy and he turned to run, his friend hot on his heels. The girl threw again and again, pelting them with a hail that struck heads and backs and fleeing legs. By the time Stephen got close, he could see the hard, green crabapples in her hand.

"And stay gone!" she shouted after them. "And you, sir…" she laughed, her accent French, with faint shades of something else in the undertones, "…are you a knight in shining armor, come to save me? As you can see, I do not require it."

"No 'sir'—good Lord!" Stephen replied, his hands coming up to forestall her. "I'm only a common man, trying, on occasion, to be a good one. Mr. Ashbrook, at your service." He bowed.

The name seemed to spark some kind of recognition in her. "Sophie Armand, at yours." She curtsied prettily, despite the last few apples still in her hand. She dropped them and scrubbed her hands off on a kerchief tucked into the waistband of her apron. "Now, if you'll excuse me, I must get this back up to the house. My mistress will be expecting me."

She bent to pick up her basket but he got there first, hoisting it with ease. It was heavier than it looked, filled with damp muslin, and he upwardly revised his first impressions of Sophie's strength.

"Permit me," he said easily when she began to protest. "It's a bit of a walk yet."

Sophie's fists went to her hips. "I could never! You're a guest of his lordship's…"

"Ah, so you do know me!"

"…and it would not be proper." Something in the imperious tilt of her head reminded him of Margaret, and he forced the half-tempered pang of regret back into the recesses of his mind. His sister was at least a hundred miles from here, his memories of her years old, and this girl was a stranger.

"Then stop me," he teased, and she pouted.

She tried to grab for the handles and he began walking, his long stride putting her at a disadvantage. "You were right and I was wrong," Sophie said after he slowed and she caught up. Her brow furrowed at him dangerously. "You are no gentleman."

"But I am your chivalric knight…" he slowed to match her pace, "…and I will see you safely delivered. Are you here with one of the other guests or for Lady Charlotte?"

"I serve the Countess of Horlock," Sophie replied.

The name rang a bell—the sharpened old axe at dinner who had a strong preference for candlelight. More importantly, though why it should be so he couldn't quite say. Lady Horlock was Mr. Beaufort's patroness, which meant that *this* girl could know *him* and the secrets in his sea-storm eyes. For no reason in particular, Stephen's pulse beat a little faster.

"I'm her abigail and no one of importance."

"Do they teach bowling at French girls' schools?" he asked, and her head jerked up. Why should that question make her wary? "You'd make quite the addition to a cricket team."

"If more girls were taught to throw, m'sieur, some might be permitted to stay girls longer, instead of being made women before their time."

"Point well taken." He hitched the basket up a little higher on his hip, giving himself a moment to think. "Mr. Beaufort makes an interesting addition to the summer's party," he said after a moment, as casually as he could. There was no reason *not* to ask after one of the other guests, and it was safer for him to enquire about a fellow gentleman than, say, the countess. "We do not see him at all in London. At least, not that I can recall. Does he not like town?"

"He prefers the country these days," Armand replied, and the look she gave him was sharp and penetrating. He resisted the urge to squirm under it, returning it instead with wide and unblinking eyes.

"Does he have a wife or sweetheart secreted about in some small cottage there?" he asked. If he kept his tone as light and casual as possible, then she would not suspect the faster thrum of his pulse, nor the lump in his chest that formed at the idea. "I find it hard to imagine willingly trading in the energy of the city for a pastoral life, not for a man who could easily sell enough canvases to make a good living on his own."

"There's no Mrs. Beaufort, not as far as I know." She raised an eyebrow. "I shall let him know about your interest."

While there was nothing to it at all, Stephen's blood ran briefly cold.

"Though, if you have a sister in mind for him, I don't think she'll find him to her satisfaction."

There were a dozen things she might have meant by that, but that hardly mattered; if she exposed his clumsy curiosity to Beaufort, then at least *he* would be able to put two and two together. Unless Beaufort had told *her*, in which case…

In which case Stephen was doomed before he had begun, so he may as well carry on as he had been. Trying to unravel probabilities and plots made his head ache.

"No, no, sister," he replied with all haste. "And there's no need to pass on any message. I was only making conversation."

"Hmm," she said, and did not explain herself.

They had reached the kitchen yard and Stephen set the basket down upon the low stone stoop with cheer more forced than natural. "And here you are delivered, fair maiden. Will this suit?"

"It will. Though why I should thank you for something I never asked for is beyond me."

His expression must have betrayed his startled amusement. Perhaps she thought he was flirting and was responding in kind? That thought sank like a stone, and he winced.

"I am doubly chastened, then," he replied, more subdued than before. She shook her head at him with a moue of irritation, lifted her basket and headed inside with a deliberate and disdainful flick of her skirt.

He was alone in nature once more, the clattering and banging coming from the kitchen windows the only signs of human life around. He wandered down the path again, this time choosing a different route. The garden lay ahead, and the hedge maze beyond it. He had little else to do now but be left alone with his thoughts. Perhaps there would be something worth finding in between those carefully pruned and tamed rows of domesticated shrubbery.

Chapter Six

Curls, sinuous and sensual, unspooled under Joshua's pencil. He stopped for a moment, used the pad of his little finger to smudge the lines, blur them into one another to soften the edges. The chin, then, following the lines that he had sketched in from memory—strong and sure, clean-shaven, with a divot barely visible below the rounded lobe of his subject's ear.

He sat back on the bank of the creek and examined his shading with a critical eye. The sketch of Ashbrook stared up at him from the page. There was an expression on his face that Joshua had not intended to place there. He looked introspective, thoughtful, possibly affectionate; it was close to the expression on his face when staring at Joshua's self-portrait. At the same time, though, some of Joshua's own fantasies had obviously intruded. The man in the sketch regarded his creator with openness, not jest, nor flirtation, nor teasing, and that was wholly unlike the man Joshua had seen at dinner.

That man was closed off, a shell and a pretense, his expression a polite mask.

It had been different, somewhat, in the gallery.

Very different again in the conservatory, his head thrown back with pleasure, his mouth open.

It was foolish. Joshua closed his eyes, a familiar throbbing beginning in his groin. This was not the time or place to dwell on *those* memories! He had to save that for later consideration, when he could properly indulge in the memory of Ashbrook's arms trembling as he held himself up, or the way the flush of lust extended down the sleek, firm curves and shadows of his throat and clavicle.

Idiot.

He opened his eyes and brought his pencil back to the page. Shading in around the eyes helped, turned them harder, cooler, more distant. He was not a child, to be dwelling on an infatuation. The man was very pretty, yes, with a cock that begged for sucking and arms that curved with sinuous lines of muscle, but that was *all*.

There were many other pretty men in the world, and some of them were even musicians.

The creek burbled along at the base of the hill, adding a gentle chorus to the other sounds of the outdoors. Perhaps he could be excused for his distraction because he neither saw nor heard the man coming up behind him until the other spoke.

"What do we have here?" said the voice.

Joshua's heart stopped beating for a moment. He may or may not have yelped quietly, and he slammed his sketchbook shut. *Too late? How much did he see?*

"A wandering minstrel and a riverside artist, a pleasant combination." Ashbrook spoke easily, though his eyes tracked the closed cover of the sketchbook as Joshua laid it aside. "May I join you?"

And here it came—exposure, censure, disgrace? Ashbrook could not make the incident public, of course, but he could certainly convey his disappointment and disdain in private conversation. On the credit side of the ledger, perhaps that would be enough to cure Joshua of his ridiculous infatuation.

Joshua did not ask the first question that came to his mind—*whatever for?*—instead, he merely nodded. What would his voice do if he spoke now? Would it stay steady or break like a growing boy's?

Ashbrook paused, staring at the creek for a moment, and at the reeds along the edges that blew in the intermittent breeze. He hitched his trousers and sat. The dark-gray wool pulled snug around his upper thighs and hips, outlining the rounded swell of his arse.

Joshua's mouth went dry.

The slap of flesh on flesh, the way he had pushed back to spear himself more fully on Cade's cock, dark curls stuck to the back of his neck and damp with sweat—

Ashbrook stared out at the river for a while, his arms resting deceptively casually on his knees, his fingers, long and slim, always in motion. He tapped out a hypnotic rhythm on his calf, seemingly unaware that he was doing it. A cloud wandered across the sun and cast his face in shadow, the dark pools of his eyes fading. For a moment, just one, he looked sad, unsure and a little bit lost.

The cloud passed, the sun shone down on them both, and Ashbrook's curls gleamed in the light. They sat in silence so long that the birds began to sing again in the bushes behind them. Ashbrook tracked a sparrow as it flew overhead, leaning on his elbows and tipping his head back to keep the delicate creature in view as long as possible.

"Do you prefer to sketch outdoors?"

The sound of his voice after minutes in quiet startled Joshua, and he had to think about his reply before he made it.

"There is only so often one can paint armchairs and be satisfied," he said finally. Ashbrook snorted a rough and startled laugh, and Joshua felt his lips tug up in a small smile. "The light is better," he explained, this time more gently.

So they were not about to discuss the events of the previous night. While the thought soothed some of the tension in his gut, he found himself oddly disappointed at the same time.

Ashbrook nodded sagely, as though Joshua had said something deep or important, and dropped to lie in the grass. He sprawled there, loose-limbed and boyish. "I met your Armand this morning," he said unexpectedly.

"Sophie?" Joshua's fingers curled around the cover of his sketchbook.

Ashbrook followed the movement, his brow furrowed.

Joshua ducked his head, flipped his book open to a blank page and took his pencil in hand again. "She's hardly *my* anything," Joshua replied, though why should he feel the need to explain? Simple shapes began to rough out under his fingers—vertical strokes for the bulrushes, a handful of curving arcs to mark the sinuous lines of the riverbank. "She works for the countess as well. Though we are, of course, acquainted."

"Of course." Ashbrook pushed himself up on his elbows, still heedless of the damage the damp grass could do to his coat and trousers. "She's quite the hoyden, once you look beneath her elegant coiffure. I came upon her teaching some ruffian boys quite the unforgettable lesson in manners."

That scene was one he could picture with ease, and Joshua's smile flickered again. "She does that."

Ashbrook seemed to have little to say in return, and the quiet fell upon them once more. He lay too close, his knee a scant inch from Joshua's, near enough to bump against it quite innocuously should one of them choose to move.

He wanted to; it would be so simple. Just press his knee a little farther to the right and soak in the heat of Ashbrook's body for himself.

Ashbrook's attention momentarily stolen by flocking birds on the other bank, Joshua could hardly be blamed for taking the opportunity. His eyes drifted, made careful study of the particular arc of Ashbrook's cheekbone, the curve of his mouth, the distant expression in his eyes. The dimple below his lower lip where it pushed out in something that, on Joshua, would look petulant at best. On Ashbrook, it was an invitation to debauchery of the worst sort.

Apart from Cade, away from the sparkle of champagne and chandeliers, Ashbrook appeared almost…small. Utterly normal. Human.

For a moment, only he thought he understood, could see in the depths of his imagination—Ashbrook spread out before him, his face as open and vulnerable as it appeared just then, something more than scorn or distant amusement welling up in those depths. *Please, Joshua, I need you—*

Joshua forced his eyes down to his paper again, added a handful of lines that would eventually become a duck.

"Why do you?" Ashbrook blurted out, a startled look flashing across his face, as though he had not anticipated his own question. "Work for the countess, I mean." He recovered, bracing himself backwards on his outstretched arms, and the casual air he affected was too obviously that. "Lady Charlotte mentioned at dinner that you're related," he explained himself, eyes flickering to Joshua and then away again. "Doesn't that make you an aristocrat as well?"

"Like any man whose skills do not tend towards useful things," he began dryly, the self-deprecation within aimed entirely at himself.

Ashbrook barked with laughter again, which was more gratifying than it should have been.

"I found myself in need of a wage and a roof. The countess—my great-aunt once removed, I believe the situation to be—was kind enough to provide both in return for some flattering pictures and the assurance of her name appearing regularly in the best papers. I presume your patronage with his lordship was founded along similar lines."

That was, most likely, the longest speech Joshua had given in Ashbrook's presence. It was a distinct pleasure to note that his voice had neither broken nor stammered once during the entire thing. Perhaps he was getting better at ignoring the way Ashbrook's pulse thrummed at the side of his throat or the soft divot beneath his ear that would be warm against someone's lips.

A shadow fleeted through Ashbrook's eyes and was gone.

They would have to play cards someday, Joshua reflected with some level of amusement. Preferably for money. Ashbrook's inability to hold a closed face was appalling.

"Something like that," Ashbrook agreed, and appeared happy to let the conversation lie there for the time being.

"It is good that you still find the time to draw for your own pleasure," he ventured after a moment, following the distracted movements of Joshua's hand as he fleshed out the sketch. "Unless Coventry has already been after you for commissions."

There was something amiss in the way he spoke, dancing around something obviously weighing on his mind. And yet his queries were, on the surface, innocuous and even pleasantly light conversation.

"No commissions yet," Joshua replied, roughing in the shapes of distant trees before laying his pencil down along the sketchbook's spine. The wood was smooth from his fingers, the paper rough. "Though I have been reliably warned to stay away from the south lawn while the young ladies are about with their watercolors."

He was rewarded with a laugh from Ashbrook that seemed more natural than anything else so far. "Indeed, you would be wise to take that advice," he joked in return. "There is such a marked lack of young and titled men here so far that anyone even remotely appealing to the eye is like to become targeted as a plaything."

"Remotely appealing?" Joshua fired back. "Hardly a rousing recommendation in my favor."

Ashbrook did not rise to the obvious bait, laughing and pushing himself to sit fully upright again with his arms balanced easily on his knees. "As working men both, I rather think we fall under that lesser category, regardless of the prettiness of our eyes or mouths. Unless, of course, you have a coronet stashed at the bottom of your paint box."

As a suggestion and an invitation, Joshua had received and given many both more and less blatant than having his mouth called "pretty", but this one he deliberately ignored. "I am a bit amazed that you did not ride out on the hunt this morning," Joshua said instead, not looking up to see whether Ashbrook's marvelously expressive face registered any reaction. "You could avoid female companionship for the entire day with little additional effort."

He expected another joke, perhaps another invitation, but Ashbrook once again surprised him. This was becoming something of an unwelcome habit. "It's not to my taste," was all he said, the flirtatious laughter gone from his voice.

Joshua did look up, settling himself to face Ashbrook instead of the riverbank. "How so?"

Ashbrook's gaze stayed fixed on the steady flow of water down the lazy slope of the hill. "I'm no stranger to death, but to take a life myself seems anathema."

Such sentimentality! Another surprise, and Joshua would do best to stop trying to keep track, for Ashbrook was soon going to surpass every record.

A small sound must have escaped him because Ashbrook glared at him sharply. "You're laughing," he said, his eyes snapping. "You think me foolish."

Haste, haste, or he would lose this moment forever, and he had not yet memorized the curve of Ashbrook's lashes against his cheekbones when his eyes were soft and honest.

"Not at all," Joshua corrected, keeping his voice as easy as he could. "Life is a rare and precious thing. Who is man to make the decision to end one, when he cannot restore the dead back to breathing in return?"

"Now I *know* you're making fun," Ashbrook replied, allowing himself to be gentled back into ease. The tension ebbed from the set of his shoulders and the tightness faded from the set of his jaw.

"Perhaps I am." He tempered the comment with a careful smile. "Or perhaps I am entirely serious."

A distant horn sounded and Ashbrook startled, looked out toward the woods and then back to the house. "That sounds like the party returning." He changed the subject. "I suppose I should go and greet them and see what bounty they return with." He rose easily, limbs uncurling and his muscles moving sleek as a cat's beneath the fine wool of his suit. "If you will excuse me, sir."

"Of course," Joshua answered, for what else could he say? *No—stay here and pose for me and I shall draw you from life instead of flawed memory?* And so Ashbrook brushed loose blades of grass from the seat of his trousers and headed off toward the main house without a backwards glance.

Avoiding the south lawn was easier than avoiding the mistress of the house turned out to be. Joshua had barely stepped foot inside the hallway, finally abandoning his fruitless attempts to sketch, before he was set upon. His afternoon was lost to educating the debutantes on still-life painting, while their chaperones sipped tea and stitched idly at handkerchiefs and cushion covers.

The talk revolved entirely around Viscount Downe and his two eligible sons, who were due to arrive before dinner. He'd met Downe a handful of times; the man socialized with Horlock. He was utterly remarkable, purely for his unremarkableness. He was neither thin nor fat, neither tall nor short, and had the singular distinction of having no distinguishing features whatsoever. He could always be counted upon to lose just about as much at cards as he had won in the previous hand, and when he passed from this life, the existence of his sons would be just about the only mark he would leave on the world to prove that he had ever been.

The thought was chilling, far out of proportion to the man who had inspired it.

His sons took after their mother, apparently. And with the three men, along with their retinues, the house would be full and the party would truly begin.

Finally able to make his escape once the ladies retired to dress for dinner, Joshua closed and locked his bedroom door behind him. A few minutes' peace was all he needed— no Sophie barging in to learn his gossip or William hovering about to fuss over his clothes. He kicked off his shoes and flung himself backwards onto the bed, sinking into the bedclothes. There was no one to see; he could be allowed his moment of dramatic excess.

His life was not an exciting one. Things were simpler that way, and he was reasonably content with his lot. The absolute last thing he needed was a flirtation with a handsome rake like Stephen Ashbrook, and all the complications he carried with him.

He would *not* fuss over his clothing for dinner. It hardly mattered what he wore, as long as he was presentable enough for her ladyship's honor. He was not here to woo, and there was no one whom he was trying to impress. He could easily lie there another quarter of an hour and still rise in plenty of time to dress neatly and serviceably, in whatever William had laid out for him.

Half an hour, four attempts at tying his cravat, and two hissed and insulting conversations with his mirror later, Joshua tugged his best waistcoat down to straighten an imagined wrinkle at the lapel, and left.

He found himself back in the gallery a few minutes later, the candles from the hallway casting their faint light only so far into the long chamber. Some of the paintings there were old friends, others altogether new and deserving of a little attention, even if they were examples of the stilted styles of previous generations.

"I can't *find* it!" Lady Amelia complained to her mother as they passed down the hall. "I know I left them on my dressing table."

"Really, child, you mustn't be so careless. Those earrings were your grandmother's!"

"Perhaps one of the maids…"

The silence that fell after they passed didn't last nearly as long as it might. It was no conversation that caught his attention this time, but a discreet cough and a shadow that blocked out some of the already faint light. Joshua turned, and his heart most certainly did *not* contract at the sight of the young man in the doorway.

Ashbrook stood casually, his hair caught back in a velvet ribbon, his cravat high and hiding the marble column of his throat. He smiled, distant and playful.

Damn that formal cravat, anyway.

"This is becoming habit," Ashbrook said, and Joshua drew himself up tall in response.

He nodded politely, because that was the safest thing to do.

What was *not* safe was flirting again, not after what he had seen. There was too much heartache there, too much lonely desire, all of it blended together in the teasing invitations of a man who would not be his.

"A thing needs to happen more than twice for it to be called a habit," Joshua replied, a little more sharply than perhaps he meant to.

Ashbrook did not blink at the rebuke, only grinned and, *damn* him, because all Joshua could see now was the way his eyes had widened at the end of his lovemaking, the little astonished gasp that had escaped him as he spent himself.

"Shall we reconvene here tomorrow and see what becomes of it?" Ashbrook asked, and Joshua forced those memories back to where they belonged.

He had been allowed to watch, once, for whatever private reason of Ashbrook's, but it could go no further. "You presume a great deal."

"How so?"

He wished to play games—fine. Joshua would play games as well. "I may have other plans for tomorrow. A meeting could be utterly impossible."

Ashbrook stood with his back to the light and it was all but impossible to read the expression in his eyes. His mouth, though, quirked up at the corners and Joshua hated the spark within him that responded.

"Would you not find the time for me?"

They treaded dangerous waters. As much as Joshua longed to take his face in his hands, to kiss and press him, all of this chatter could still be explained away if regrets took hold. None of it yet *meant* anything.

"Please, do not toy with me like this. Return to your partner and leave me to my own devices." So much for his promises of self-control, of keeping back, holding his desires private. He clamped his lips and tightened his teeth on his tongue to prevent himself from saying anything else unfortunate. *Double damn!*

Ashbrook tensed, his eyes still on Joshua. "I've offended you, but I cannot guess how."

In for a penny…

Impulse drove him, even as the gong sounded downstairs to call them all to table. "Can you not?"

That won him a frown and a squint, as though Ashbrook was trying to divine some deeper meaning behind his words. They had been born purely of the moment, though, no greater thought behind them than thwarted selfishness.

Joshua left the gallery by the other door and descended the staircase toward the light and sounds of the party assembling for dinner.

Chapter Seven

Beaufort was an utterly impossible man to read. Stephen spent too much time through dinner puzzling over the man's implacable expression, so much so that he had to be nudged under the table twice before remembering to offer some of the capon to Miss Talbot. He ran between extremes, flirtatious and inviting one moment, and then cold as hoarfrost the next. Stephen had thought, surely, after last night, he would have been induced to say *something*. The way he had looked at them from the doorway, the naked lust in his eyes—and there could be no doubt *now* about the nature and form of Stephen and Evander's desires.

So why did he resolutely refuse to meet Stephen's eyes? The jellied meats were certainly not that interesting. Embarrassment at being caught out? There were some who did not enjoy watching or being watched. For an artist, though, that seemed a bit preposterous.

"Don't you agree, Mr. Ashbrook?" Miss Talbot asked from his elbow, all wide eyes and firm breasts cresting over the low neckline of her dinner gown. Pearls gleamed cream and white around her throat and in her ears.

"Oh yes, certainly," he tossed off diffidently, and she flashed a smile of triumph at Coventry. Now, what had the question been? His mind had been running in circles and he had missed the conversation.

"Now how do you expect any man to say otherwise when asked by so charming a young person?" Coventry chortled from his seat at the head of the table, and Miss Talbot colored prettily while Lady Charlotte looked affronted.

The conversation moved on—the advantages of returning to town post-hunting season had apparently been the topic of choice—and it became apparent that Stephen's lapse had gone mostly unnoticed. By all, that was, except Evander, who arched an eyebrow at him over the rim of his crystal goblet and drank his wine in silence.

Stephen cringed inwardly, putting on a charming smile to hide the curl of dread in the pit of his stomach. He would be in for a lecture later; there was no getting around it. Stephen gripped his own glass around the stem and tossed back the last mouthful inelegantly. He grimaced as it went down, the warmth of the alcohol spiraling out in tendrils to stroke the edges of his prickling nerves. Candlelight danced on the silver and crystal laid out on the table, white faces gleaming hollow and expressionless in the reflections in the dining room windows.

Lady Amelia laughed at something, Lady Charlotte leaned over to murmur a comment in Evander's ear that made him turn and smile, and the matrons clucked at each other like gossiping geese in a farmyard.

Suddenly and acutely, he missed the tavern back home, the rough wooden tables and the faintly sticky feeling of the wooden floor, the honest laughter of his friends, the smells of ale and pipe smoke thick in the air.

Down at the far end of the table, Beaufort didn't look his way. Not once.

Evander, miraculously enough, said nothing as dinner was cleared and the women decamped to the parlor. He was in fine form by the time the port had been passed around and they had rejoined the ladies, though, every comment and passing observation a little barb or another aimed directly at Stephen.

Which, he supposed, he deserved. He had come close to embarrassing Evander tonight with his inattention at dinner. Of course he would be cross. "And the noise when he first picked up the music—he set cats in the alley to crying back at him in better harmony."

"Not all of us can be geniuses on our first attempts," Stephen replied, as mildly as possible. He felt brittle behind the smile; how many of the others could see it? He laughed with them. "We cannot all be you, Cade."

Evander chuckled and Coventry tipped his glass in recognition of Stephen's willingness to take the joke. Beaufort looked away, his jaw clenched.

"Do play for us," Lady Chalcroft requested from her comfortable seat on the sofa, her book left aside on the small table.

Her daughter had joined the whist game across the room, and she had been casting her eyes about the room looking for some other diversion since.

"And you needn't even go looking for your violin. There is a lovely pianoforte here. Amelia played so pleasantly on it when we visited in the spring. Don't you agree?" Lady Chalcroft smiled winningly at Coventry.

Miss Talbot dropped her cards.

Stephen schooled himself not to look at anyone else, for fear he would laugh aloud. Subtle, the mothers were not. But, then, they had only a few years to get their poor girls turned out of the house and into someone else's before they were stuck with them forever, so subtlety must take backseat to expedience.

"The pianoforte is not *your* forte, is it, Ashbrook?" Evander asked, all innocence and half in his cups. "Perhaps we would be better to allow the ladies to demonstrate how it should be done."

"On the contrary," Beaufort spoke up from his seat in the corner, where his head had been bent over his sketchbook. Lady Charlotte looked at him in surprise. He kept his voice mild and even, and Stephen stared.

"I've had the honor of hearing Mr. Ashbrook play and he is quite the equal, if not better, to any I've heard before or since."

Defense from a most unexpected quarter. As Evander shrugged and demurred, Stephen felt a small burst of hope and gratitude for it. "I cannot argue against a man's personal taste, especially when it turns in my favor," he replied with a smile that was impossible to hide behind any affectation. "Though perhaps the glamour of the concert hall and the beauty of the compositions affected your opinion too much in my direction," he did add, more as a sop to Evander's mood than to anything else.

Beaufort gave him a measuring gaze that was not the easy cheer he had hoped for, but was infinitely better than being ignored.

With that encouragement, Stephen sat himself at the pianoforte and flipped up the lid. The instrument was heavily decorated, meant more for showing off to guests than to hold a tune. The sound was not as rounded and clear as that of the piano in the conservatory, but it would do nicely enough. Lady Charlotte stationed herself at his shoulder and presented music for him to choose, but there was only one option in this case. And he did not need reminders.

Stephen pressed his fingers to the ivory keys, and Evander's "Nocturne" flowed from them, as perfect and as haunting as the first time he had heard it played. Conversation slowed and stopped, eyes turned to him and lifted him up, gave him the rush that surged through his veins, that magic that drove him to be *better*.

He glanced up, once, to take the measure of the room. Evander watched them intently, Lady Charlotte still standing behind his shoulder. And beyond Evander, in the corner of the room, Beaufort sat terribly still, like a statue of a man, his face rapt and his eyes fixed continually on Stephen.

The last few notes tailed off into silence, followed by applause. Stephen stood and redirected it. "The composer, Ladies and Gentlemen." He gestured at Evander who clasped his hands behind his back and bowed, taking it all as his due.

Beaufort frowned, a little crease appearing between his eyes, and he sat his hands back in his lap.

Lady Charlotte took the stage after that and Stephen was pressed into service himself as a page-turner, then the other young ladies naturally had to prove their own worth, especially now that the party had filled out. Lord Downe's sons were a pair of youngbloods of the swaggering sort, all bluster, finely trimmed coats and the unconscious arrogance carried by handsome, young men of means everywhere.

By the time music had been changed over for cards, Stephen was thoroughly done with the crosscurrents and careful stepping of society conversations. The smiling was beginning to leave him with a permanent case of dry teeth, and the need to measure every one of his words six or seven times, and then consider the likelihood of Evander's disapproval on top of it, made his head ache right above his left eye.

Wide doors led out onto a terrace of sorts; Beaufort had stepped out not long ago to take some air. Stephen made his apologies to the older Mr. Downe, tugged his coat into place and followed.

Beaufort stood alone at the far end of the terrace, his hands clasped behind his back and his chin tipped up to gaze out at the vast field of stars above. He stiffened as Stephen approached, his shoulders drew up and his spine went straight, as though preparing himself for something unpleasant.

Stephen leaned on the railing in, for the moment, something that could pass for companionable silence.

Beaufort shifted beside him.

What to say that could take them back to the afternoon, or even the previous evening? It had been so much easier to talk to him then.

"Thank you," he said after a moment. "For what you said, earlier. Cade has a sharp tongue at times, but means no harm."

"I only spoke the truth," Beaufort said simply, and his voice was warm again, like when they had been sitting together on the bank of the river. "It is unfair for him to call attention to what he thinks of as your shortcomings and leave you unable to defend yourself."

"Oh," Stephen said wryly, "but I have a great many shortcomings, and Cade works diligently at correcting them all. We come as a matched set and I must represent him well."

"Now that I *had* noticed," Beaufort said, his voice as dry as the desert sands of Arabia, and Stephen barked a laugh of surprise.

Were they to talk about this *now*? Here, in the dark, with the stars wheeling by overhead? The rapid beating of his heart was surely enough to alert everyone inside that Stephen's mood had made a decided turn for the better.

He leaned on the balustrade and cocked his head to regard Beaufort more fully. His red-blond hair was shorter than Stephen generally preferred, but it would be soft to the touch, especially if he stroked it where it lay on the back of his neck.

"You have excellent eyesight, to see such things in the dark of night," Stephen tried. Wordplay had worked with him before…

"Nighttime is often more revealing of character, I've found." Beaufort didn't fall into his opening, but neither was he walking away. Perhaps his transgression, whatever it had been, would be forgiven after all. "Of secrets, and the things people are willing to do when they think no one's watching."

"Or when they wish someone were," Stephen countered, turning to stand with his back against the hip-high railing and fold his arms.

Beaufort's suit cut across his chest in a perfect arc, leaving the hint of waistcoat and shirt visible below. What would he taste like if Stephen pulled his shirt free from his trousers and ran his tongue across that flat plane? Would he be ticklish and squirm away, or arch and beg for more?

"I prefer to think of night as freeing. Under cover of darkness we can act as we were made to do and absolve ourselves of the sins of lying and false witness."

Beaufort was quiet, then, his breath catching as though he wished to say something. He did not. Finally, he glanced up at Stephen, his body perfectly still and under rigid control. God, he would be beautiful when taken apart, lying down on a bed and stroked until he begged—

"And what of the sin of covetousness?" he asked, and Stephen blinked. "Thou shalt not covet thy neighbor's property."

OH. Pieces of a puzzle he hadn't known he was constructing snapped more fully into place.

"That only applies to things that are owned." There was no sense in obfuscating his intent much longer—he spoke as plainly as he knew how. "And as Parliament only recently confirmed, one cannot own men. God's own Church has seen fit to ensure that we cannot make marriage vows to each other, so there are none to be broken."

Come to my bed. Let us all feel whole together, at least for a little while.

"Are you suggesting—" But Stephen would not learn what Beaufort thought, because at that moment the doors swung open and a giggle of girls swished onto the terrace.

"You are avoiding us!" Lady Charlotte put her hands on her hips and tilted her chin imperiously, her eyes sparkling. "We need at least one more gentleman for the men's team for charades, so you simply must come inside."

Beaufort had gone quiet again, leaving it to Stephen to make the expected noises. "You say you need only one, but there are two gentlemen here," he objected with an easy smile. "Which of us is to have the singular honor?"

Lady Amelia made a gesture with her head that suggested her exasperation. "Whichever does not run fast enough, of course," she said, and was thoroughly shushed by Miss Talbot in response.

"We shall return presently," Beaufort interrupted.

Stephen was pulled along with the group, despite that, and he cast a last glance back over his shoulder as he stepped once more into the light and the noise.

"Now, we shall have to pry Father away from his cards."

"Will you speak to Mr. Downe, dear Amelia? He will listen to you, surely."

Beaufort stood in shadow, a frown creasing his forehead, the light of the moon playing silver on his shoulders and his face. He was ethereal, pale and beautiful in his concern.

The door swung closed behind Stephen, and the image was gone.

The next day brought a mess of rain and thick black clouds blocking out the sun. All were trapped indoors, restless and ill at ease, and Stephen escaped to the conservatory at the earliest possible opportunity. The quiet was enough to soothe his spirits, despite the peals of thunder that made the glass panes in the conservatory rattle in their frames.

By the time he emerged to dress for dinner, Lady Charlotte was holding court on the parlor couches. Lady Chalcroft had a death grip on Lady Amelia's arm as the redoubtable elder lady chattered away relentlessly to poor Coventry. The earl looked about ready to chew off his own arm in order to escape, nodding away with faint despair in his eyes. But where—

There. Beaufort was chatting with the Horlocks and Mrs. Talbot, his hand resting lightly on the back of the countess's chair. He nodded and smiled briefly at Stephen. Relief then, followed by vague disappointment as Beaufort turned back to his conversation.

His disappointment only magnified over dinner, with no decent conversation to be had. Then to cap off the evening, Beaufort excused himself at the end of dinner on account of a bad head, escaping the drawing room and the evening's activities with enviable ease.

A hand settled heavily on Stephen's shoulder as he watched the door swing shut, and he jumped at the touch. It was only Evander, though, and he too was watching the door. His bottom lip stuck out a little, the beginnings of a childlike pout, and he pulled it in before Stephen could poke fun.

Evander sat on the footstool by Stephen's side and rested his elbows on his knees, his glass of port dangling loosely from his fingertips. It was his second one of the night, following a number of glasses of excellent wine at dinner, and it had all left him in an expansive mood.

"You like him," Evander murmured quietly, keeping their conversation easily out of earshot of the men discussing their hunting dogs over by the fire. One of his hands moved, just so, and he brushed the edge of Stephen's knee with the side of his little finger. His touch laid sparks along Stephen's skin, made him feel daring and wild.

"He has a good eye for art," Stephen replied, something inside him demanding that he hold back. Some things, surely, could be his alone? "And I can hardly fault his taste in music," he teased.

"Certainly not." Evander grinned wolflike. "And his fine form does no harm to his presentation either." He paused to drink, brought the crystal glass up to his lips and laid it there, the dark-red port swirling inside.

Stephen swallowed compulsively. Damn the man. Evander knew all his dreams, all his desires; he had helped him to discover them in the first place.

What was he up to this time?

"Four fine pups in the last whelping," Coventry proclaimed from the fireplace. "I've arranged to breed her to Corkerton's mastiff next."

Downe scoffed. "Careful with that one—he talks a bigger game than his dogs can prove. That mastiff's part hound, or I'm a shopkeeper."

"He's very pretty," Evander continued, softly, so softly. The others in the room would have no idea what sins he was proposing right beneath their very noses. Evander's eyes gleamed with excitement. "And artists have wonderful hands. Do you want him?"

Stephen pondered it for a moment, and a moment only. Beaufort was a fantasy, a lovely, lush-mouthed man with a still and quiet soul. He had all but suggested, the night before, that he wanted at least one of them. (Evander, most likely—everyone wanted Evander. He was gold and sunlight, slim hipped and lithe.) If Evander invited him, Beaufort might come.

He had stayed to watch them fuck.

The conservatory had been Evander's wild idea, the first room on his list. He had pulled Stephen through the hallways, biting back giddy laughter so as not to wake the house. Stephen had thrown the latch, but it must not have caught. He'd been distracted, after all, when Evander pulled out the oil and kissed him so fiercely. He had dropped to his knees then and there, hanging on to the overstuffed red wing chair for balance. He'd taken Evander's prick in his mouth and sucked it to hardness, listening for the desperate and hungry noises Evander made that told him he was ready.

Evander had pulled him to his feet and spun him, bent him over the chair and slid two fingers home, thick and so, so slick. First his oiled fingers, then his tongue, hot against the sensitive skin of his arse and below his balls. And then— oh then—his prick had pressed home, Evander's hand coiled in the thick locks of Stephen's hair, holding him tightly in place. Evander had fucked into him, his cock thick enough to break a man in two.

Then the gasp, a shuffle of feet—looking up in a panic, sure that they had been discovered—

It had been Beaufort standing there, his perfect mouth open in shock and surprise, his hand on the door and the other pressed firmly against his own prick.

He had *stayed*. More than that, he had watched them fuck, stroked himself as he did so. How could anyone resist?

Stephen had looked up, held Joshua's eye as he watched Stephen's gorgeous degradation. His release had been harder and more satisfying than anything had in months, perhaps longer. Perhaps ever.

Knowing that Beaufort had wanted them, had taken pleasure in the sight of them, had probably gone back to his bedchamber and fucked his own hand to thoughts of them—

Stephen crossed his legs and settled his arm to hide his mild distress.

Evander bit the inside of his cheek, his eyes bright and merry. "I see that you do," he said softly, a promise in every movement of his lips. "Shall I get him for us? Bring him to our bed to please you?"

"I…" Stephen began, then remembered quickly whom he was speaking to, "…I don't need anyone but you to please me," he replied, equally quietly. Evander preened, and Stephen chuckled. "But you are too good to me, and he might well be amenable. Perhaps if we approach him together? I believe I've exchanged more words with him than you, and he seems to have a tendency towards shyness."

"Shyness is an excellent quality in a girl and foolish in a man." Evander dismissed his warning with a wave. "But as you wish. You know I live to make you happy."

"This would," Stephen agreed, his heart still beating too rapidly, even as the rest of his body subsided. Flirting was one thing, and something Stephen could sometimes manage without putting his foot in his mouth, but with Evander's charm working for them, there was little to no chance that Beaufort would refuse. No man of their inclination ever did.

When he came to bed, though—it would be because he wanted Evander, and not Stephen. A horrible thought. But if he preferred to touch and be touched by Evander, at least Stephen would have the pleasure of watching two beautiful men tangle together. He could put aside the quick rush of jealousy to at least see that.

"This would indeed."

Chapter Eight

Cynical as he was becoming, Joshua had anticipated some kind of confrontation with Cade. The man had Ashbrook under his thumb; Cade would soon know everything that had passed between them.

The sharp and dangerous looks thrown his way at dinner did little to dispel his foreboding. Cade hovered over Ashbrook all evening—his hand at the man's waist or resting on his elbow—or loomed behind him as if to remind Joshua that Ashbrook was his. The easiest escape was to beg off early after dinner and retire to his room. He had no taste for dramatics, not anymore, and florid declarations and threats of vengeance were all too gothic to be borne by rational men.

So when Cade and Ashbrook approached him as he sat in the sun on the east lawn the following day, it took him a moment to recover from his surprise. Cade was smiling, for one. It was hardly an uncommon thing—the man turned his charm on and off like a profit-minded Bankside girl. But this time, it seemed almost sincere.

The sun gleamed in Cade's golden hair, the breeze tugging at his coat to make it fall just so, as though even nature herself were dedicated to making him as attractive as any human being could ever claim the right to be. His trousers, a very fashionable cut, cupped the curves and sinews of his legs to great advantage, and it did not take much imagination to pair the look with the memory of Cade driving into Ashbrook, his face flushed with exertion.

Ashbrook, two steps behind him, appeared somewhat more nervous. He'd caught his hair back from his face with a ribbon, and his fingers toyed with the flaps of his waistcoat pockets as though he had little to no idea what to do with them. He looked down and swiftly clasped his hands behind his back.

No one else lingered in the area. The ladies had taken themselves off to pick berries, baskets and parasols in hand, and the report of guns from elsewhere announced Coventry, Horlock and the Downes' current diversion.

Joshua set aside his sketchbook; it would do no good for either man to see some of the things he had put down on the pages.

"Gentlemen," he greeted them with a polite smile, his cheeks rebelling at it, "I didn't hear your approach."

"I hope we're not intruding." Cade ignored any answer he might have made, sitting down beside him, completely certain of his welcome.

Ashbrook sat on Joshua's other side, settling one booted foot beneath him. A dark curl fell across Ashbrook's jaw, blown there by the breeze, and Joshua stepped firmly on the sudden urge to reach out and brush it back into place.

"It is a beautiful day," Cade said, "and there is fine company. And yet you prefer to sit alone? You puzzle me, Mr. Beaufort."

Cade hadn't come to berate him; he could begin to relax. "I think I am a reasonably simple man at heart, as most of us are. I apologize for any disruption to your world view," he added with a wry grin that Ashbrook seemed to find amusing.

"I happen to like puzzles," Cade replied instead, and turned to let his leg fall lightly to the side. He knew and loved the light, that much was obvious, and the daylight loved him. The midmorning sun turned him into an angel. (Cast from heaven, perhaps. He could be painted in such hues, nude, of course, and with broken wings to suggest his fall.) Cade only smiled at his scrutiny, warm and inviting. "And I think, perhaps, you might as well."

"You think I am like you?" Joshua asked, cutting swiftly to the meat of the matter. He stared at Ashbrook, at the deep-brown eyes that looked deeper and darker yet under the sun's shadow, at the skin below his jaw that begged to be bitten and marked.

"I think you are much more like us than any of the others," Ashbrook replied with soft intensity. "You like…art…as well."

His meaning was now quite, quite clear. *Goodness.* "I am very fond of art." He did take the opportunity to indulge in a little bit of sarcasm. "Considering that it is how I earn my keep."

Ashbrook tilted an eyebrow in a look that was probably meant to be irritated but came off closer to amused. "But, yes," Joshua relented, with a crook of a smile that he could not quite hide, "I take your meaning. I find the male form to be a subject of which I am particularly fond."

"So Ashbrook tells me," Cade murmured, and he locked eyes with Ashbrook over Joshua's head. "He has also suggested that you might be amenable to joining us in a…" he paused, then laughed softly, "…let us say an art-appreciation session, then, if we are to continue this game."

"Let us drop the pretense." Joshua suggested, even as his pulse began to race. "As we are alone here. What, precisely, is on offer? For I presume this is an offer you are making." Or was it a game, one meant to break him, for Cade's amusement?

"A night," Ashbrook replied softly, hopefully. *He* was the angel, dark and potent. "That is all. One night, the three of us, free from the eyes of others and able to play out our fantasies and pleasures. You're not opposed to such things?" Ashbrook was watching him, perhaps to gauge his reaction. His warm eyes pleaded with Joshua, his lower lip gleaming with a hint of moisture from where he had been chewing at it.

He shook his head, and Cade nodded appreciatively. "I've rather enjoyed them, on occasion," Joshua admitted, because to show anything else would be to tip his hand too easily.

Was this to be his devil's bargain? Go to bed with Cade as chaperone, in order to know the texture of Ashbrook's skin, the weight of his cock on Joshua's tongue, what it felt like to be the one to bring him to the heights of passion? He was doubly damned, if so, because he was going to accept. It had been too long since he had lost himself in someone else's pleasure.

"I would be pleased to join you," he answered as calmly as though they were arranging a time to take tea. "I assume you have a time and place in mind?"

Ashbrook's eyes dropped to Joshua's mouth. He could swear that the man's throat bobbed compulsively when Joshua ran the tip of his tongue across his bottom lip.

He coughed, and Cade replied, "Our suite, midnight, after the house is abed? There will be less notice of corridor creeping taken at that hour."

Joshua inclined his head as Cade rose and gestured.

Ashbrook scrambled, albeit slowly, to his feet.

"Midnight," Joshua repeated. "I look forward to it, sirs."

"As do we," Ashbrook said, all dark molasses of a voice. He seemed as though he was about to say more, but Cade beckoned and the two left, heads bent together in conversation.

Joshua waited until they were out of sight entirely before flopping back to spread his arms wide against the grass.

What had just happened? Had he honestly just now been invited to bed with both Cade and Ashbrook? Had he just *accepted*?

Good God Almighty. He would not survive the anticipation.

His body stirred restlessly at the images his mind had begun to form, and he sat up instead. Fourteen hours, a dinner and an evening to get through yet—he would be better off finding some more productive way to distract himself.

And the day had started off so normally.

The afternoon alternately dragged and raced, half the time moving too slowly, and the other, half hours vanishing each time Joshua looked at a clock. He changed his mind a dozen times. He would not go. He could not *not* go. After the evening's socials he paced the length of his room twice, three times, back again, wearing a path along the rug that surely the maid would notice.

Until that morning, he would have said that Ashbrook intrigued and Cade disdained him. And now? Now he was upside down and backwards.

On the surface, there was little enough to shock. Many men took liberties, the sorts of which women could not dream. Joshua had heard braggarts speak of all manners of arrangements before, in a dozen combinations of number, sex and preference. Previous lovers had delighted him with lascivious tales of other affairs, of beautiful men of all complexions and sizes, of ready cocks, deft hands, hot mouths and arses. How many of those stories had been true and how many told purely to be exciting, he had never been sure. Nor, at the time, had he cared.

He was no blushing innocent, that was the main point. No, his torment stemmed purely from the men themselves. If he suspected for a moment that Cade would ever take the subservient role, he would take a great deal of pleasure in holding him down and fucking him, in shaking that damned arrogance down to a begging, mewling mess of sweat and lust.

But then there was Ashbrook, whose fingers ran over the pianoforte's keys with such agility that it was impossible to watch without imagining himself beneath those clever hands.

And even that was not the entire truth. It was not only about Ashbrook's hands, or his mouth, or even his taut muscle. Joshua had apparently developed a humiliating interest in that crooked little smile from the riverbank, the flash of uncertainty in his eyes before he asked a question, the purr low in his voice when he said something intended to be suggestive.

The light that shone from his face when he was lost in his music, that begged—no, *demanded*—to be captured in paint and on canvas.

A better man would send a note announcing a change of heart, abandon all notions of making love to Ashbrook and leave them to their own devices.

Joshua was not a good man.

Still, in the moment of truth, he hesitated one last time. The door to Ashbrook and Cade's rooms stood silent and ominous before him, a portal through which, once he entered, his world would be forever changed.

Only he could be so dramatic over a casual assignation. *Honestly, Joshua. So much for your distaste for dramatics. You should have been a playwright, not a painter.*

There was still a chance to change his mind. He could turn and leave, go back to his room and spend his night in respectable and solitary sleep. Or take a risk, attempt something daring, violate Sophie's expectations of his "boring" life and prove—what? That he was still a young man, with a body that lusted and a heart that yearned for things it could not have?

Joshua let his hand fall heavily against the door, then instantly regretted it. The door opened almost immediately, as though Ashbrook had been waiting there. A frisson of excitement and a hint of dread coiled deep within his gut. He collected himself, forced his eyes and mouth into a calm and personable smile that showed little of his shaking nerves.

Ashbrook's bottom lip was red and full, as though he had been biting at it, and something else entirely tangled up inside Joshua. He'd taken off his coat and only his shirtsleeves covered his arms, in fine linen that was not nearly transparent enough for Joshua's liking.

"Come in," Ashbrook said quietly, and he stepped aside. Ashbrook kept his eyes fixed on Joshua—as though, what? Afraid that he might vanish? At least until Joshua was within the lushly appointed room and Ashbrook closed and bolted the door behind him. "So that we're not interrupted."

Joshua took a minute to absorb the atmosphere of the rooms: the pale upholstery on the furnishings, the two doors, one on either side, which would lead to bedrooms. A fire smoldered low in the hearth, coals glowing darkly red and murmuring softly to themselves, the room lit further by an oil lamp in the corner.

Cade lounged on the settee. He too was dressed only in his shirt and trousers, legs sprawled wide and arms stretched out to either side. His hair curled about his face, his parted lips wanton and already debauched, and a surge of unexpected desire pulsed through Joshua's veins. Cade met his eyes, then let his gaze wander, slow and uninterrupted, down along the length of Joshua's body, with no attempt to disguise his hunger.

That thrummed along Joshua's veins—the rush of *being desired*—and he flinched when fingers ran along the back of his neck and broke the spell.

"Let me take your coat," Ashbrook suggested, so close beside him that Joshua could smell the oil in his hair.

Joshua shivered at the faint brush of warm air against his cheek when Ashbrook spoke, but managed a clipped and careful nod. "Thank you," he murmured, and for some reason, surprise flashed for a moment in Ashbrook's green-flecked eyes.

He slid Joshua's coat from his shoulders with careful hands.

"Do you do this sort of thing often?" Joshua asked Cade coolly because someone had to break the hush and make this odd situation normal. He crossed the room and poured himself a drink from the decanter, the brandy tumbling into the glass in a spill of rich amber.

Cade reached out to pull Ashbrook into his lap as the other man walked by too close. "Indulge in carnal excesses, you mean?" He was teasing, his voice warm with laughter.

Joshua drank, the glass cool against his lips and the fine liquor burning a trail down his throat.

"As often as possible."

Ashbrook looped an arm around Cade's shoulders, but kept his eyes on Joshua, even as Cade reached up with a finger to tip his chin. Cade fixed his mouth on Ashbrook's, their lips sliding together in familiar and easy passion.

Ashbrook's eyes closed, his long lashes sweeping the curve of his cheek, and his hand tangled in Cade's hair.

Joshua gripped his glass tightly, a rush of blood making his head swim. They were achingly beautiful together, a creation of some god or another and designed to fuel myths. He was a fool to think that he could ever share a place in their bond.

His lust, though—it saw only Cade's hand sliding down between two firm, young bodies to unbutton Ashbrook's waistcoat. Joshua's prick twitched, a slow and steady ache of want throbbing low in the base of his spine. He could ignore it for the moment, aside from the bulge that surely they would notice any moment now.

Ashbrook broke the kiss, swiped at Cade's lips with the tip of his tongue, then extended a hand to Joshua. "We did not ask you here merely to watch again," he said, his voice husky and low, and Joshua's breath caught.

He downed the last of his brandy and felt a flash of pleasure at the way Ashbrook's eyes followed the movement of his throat. Glass set down, he stepped forward, caught Ashbrook's waistcoat as Cade pulled it free from his arms. Joshua wound his hand in Ashbrook's fall of dark curls.

The locks were as soft as he'd imagined, curling around his fingers as sinuously as any girl's, though the face below was the opposite of girlish.

Cade kissed down Ashbrook's throat, pulling a soft gasp from him. Ashbrook's eyes locked, pleading, on Joshua's. Joshua tugged at Ashbrook's hair, gently, gently; Ashbrook gasped again and his hips rocked into Cade's as though by reflex.

Is that how it is? The rush of it burned through him, the possibility and the need, and Joshua tugged again, slow and firm. He drew Ashbrook's head back, careful not to pull him to a point of any real discomfort, and held him there.

Cade bent his head to suckle at one of Ashbrook's nipples, now exposed and hardening in the air.

Ashbrook's mouth fell open, his breathing heavy, his bottom lip plump and apple red.

Joshua bent his head and pressed a kiss to those lips, closemouthed and chaste, gently exploring. Ashbrook opened beneath him, slick-wet and hot inside, and Joshua traced the contours of his mouth with the tip of his tongue. Ashbrook moaned beneath him and Joshua tugged gently at his hair again. Ashbrook trembled, and when they parted, took in a long, shuddering breath.

Cade's hands were between their bodies and Ashbrook's hips rode up into him in a slow and easy rhythm.

Joshua was fully hard now and aching, his trousers and his skin both too tight. "I am a painter," he began, reaching out for Ashbrook's hand to pull him from Cade's lap. "I make love first with my eyes. Let me see you...both," he added, almost as an afterthought.

Ashbrook's hand closed around his, and once he was on his feet, he pulled his shirt off over his head with barely a moment's hesitation.

He was as Joshua had imagined him, long arcs of muscle, firm without being overburdened, the breadth of his shoulders tapering down to a slim waist, that vee of muscle accentuating the Aristotelian perfection of his hips. His trousers tented obscenely over his cock, and Joshua's mouth watered.

Cade's eyes flashed wide at the command, but he shrugged as though it meant nothing to him. "Let me never be accused of impeding art," he drawled, rising smoothly and easily to his feet. His clothes joined Ashbrook's shirt on the floor within moments, his cock half-hard and bobbing as he moved. "Do we pass inspection?"

He laughed, sublimely confident in his answer, and with good reason. His cock was thick, of excellent proportion, and it swelled into desire, even as Joshua watched. Despite everything, Joshua reached out and took it in his hand, fascinated.

Cade shuddered at the contact, his prick heavy and smooth in Joshua's hand. He stroked it once, again, the silk-smooth skin rolling easily under the callouses that marked Joshua's palm. Cade was a statue of masculine perfection, and his cheeks flushed obscenely red when Joshua slid an arm around his waist to hold him in place. He stroked again, circling his palm over the crown, wetness beginning to pearl there.

A low and pained groan behind him was quickly followed by arms encircling him and hands at his waist. He stroked Cade swiftly once more, because it had been a very long time since he had had another man's prick in his hand. Cade responded with a thrust up into the circle of his fingers, then dropped his hands to pull at Joshua's waistcoat.

Ashbrook pressed against his back, the hard line of his cock rubbing firmly against Joshua's arse. "Come on," he urged, and took Joshua's hand. "The bedroom."

"Naked first," Joshua ordered.

Ashbrook grinned at him, a wild and unfettered look of delight. He turned and made a show of it, shook his rump at the pair of them as he divested himself of trousers and smalls, raising his arms over his head and turning around once more to display his wares.

"And how do you like my handsome toy?" Cade murmured, but even his interruption could not break the spell.

Ashbrook was no marble statue but a living, breathing man, dark hair scattered across his chest to accentuate the curves of his muscles. A trail of similar hair ran down from his navel to the root of his cock, which jutted red and hard from a nest of tight, dark curls. His foreskin pulled back, and the crown of his cock gleamed in the lamplight.

"Handsome indeed," Joshua agreed, and he dropped to his knees.

Ashbrook gasped.

He seized Ashbrook's hips in his hands, to hold him steady, and drew his tongue up along the length of his shaft in one long, fluid motion.

Ashbrook cried out once, then jammed his knuckle into his mouth to muffle the sound. His other hand wavered around Joshua's head, finally settling on his shoulder.

Joshua brought his mouth down again. He licked around the ridge of Ashbrook's cockhead, collected the salt-sour evidence of his desire on his tongue. Ashbrook gasped again, his hips flinching in Joshua's steady grip, but he was strong enough to prevent Ashbrook from choking him.

He sank down, eyes closed in bliss, his own prick throbbing and untouched, still trapped behind the fall front of his trousers. He took the head of Ashbrook's cock in his mouth and suckled at the tip. He flickered his tongue out and around the edges in delicate tracery that left Ashbrook a groaning mess above him, his hand finally clutching in Joshua's short-cropped hair.

"Please, *please*," Ashbrook begged, his voice cracking.

Joshua would have given him anything at that moment, his hands clenched around the gorgeous firm swells of Ashbrook's arse, his cock heavy on Joshua's tongue, his nose filled with the glorious musky scent of man and sex.

This, *this* was what he had been missing, the feel of another body against his, a scent not his own, the thick slide of a cock between his lips, feeling shudders run through Ashbrook's thighs as Joshua swallowed around his hard, hot prick. He could stay like this forever, just this, teasing and suckling, feeling Ashbrook come apart beneath his hands and mouth, the surge of power that came from taking him to pieces inch by velvet inch.

Until Cade pulled them apart, his mouth closing over Ashbrook's and claiming him, kissing the gasps away from his lips.

Ashbrook's prick slid out of Joshua's mouth and he was empty again. He rose to his feet and Ashbrook pulled him in, Cade sandwiched between them.

Cade tipped his head back for a kiss but made a face at the taste of Ashbrook's precome in Joshua's mouth. The more fool he.

They stumbled and tugged toward the bedroom door, Joshua's clothing finally joining the rest on the floor. The bedroom was lit only with candles that cast thick shadows across the room, but for a moment Joshua's keen eyes caught what had been hidden from him before. White scars—thin, old, regular but well healed—crossed Cade's back in a grid pattern. An old whipping, or more than one. But when had Cade ever been a sailor?

It stayed a mystery for another time, though, as Ashbrook joined Cade on the bed. They kissed and stroked each other with the ease of long familiarity, and Joshua palmed his own cock as he watched.

"Come on," Ashbrook commanded him, imitating Joshua's own intonation from before. His eyes dropped to Joshua's groin as he approached the bed, and Ashbrook's eyes widened. "What is this, now?" he asked, reaching out and running his thumb across the gold ring that pierced through the bottom half of Joshua's cockhead. The sharp pleasure made Joshua gasp, his hips buck forward despite himself, and Ashbrook laughed with delight. "Evander, have you ever seen such a thing?"

"Does it please you?" Joshua asked.

"Oh yes," Ashbrook breathed out, stroking him gently, too gently, his fingers playing up and over and around Joshua's prick until he was close to screaming for the lack of pressure or friction. "I like it a great deal. Does it hurt?"

He looked up, his face all concern, but his finger hooked on the edge of the ring and he tugged deliberately.

Sparks of need and want and *take* burned along Joshua's spine. He rolled into Ashbrook's palm, taking the friction where he could find it, needing more, so much more.

"No," he got out after a moment, when the flare of desire had subsided.

Ashbrook palmed him maddeningly slowly, Cade's prick in his other hand.

"It did when new," he amended, "but now it is for pleasure."

"Can you fuck with it?" Cade asked, his hand trailing down over Ashbrook's chest. He reached out and traced the pad of his thumb across Joshua's lip.

Joshua opened his mouth and sucked him in, rolling his tongue around Cade's thumb as though it were Ashbrook's cock pressing down on him again.

"I want to find out," Ashbrook purred, his voice a challenge. He tightened his grip and twisted his palm up and around the head, tugging Joshua's foreskin over the ring and back down again. He dropped his hand to slide between Joshua's legs to toy with his balls, rolling them softly in his hand.

Oh God, yes. To sink into Ashbrook's body, tight but yielding to him. He would be so slick and sweet once Joshua had opened him up, spread oil over his prick and pressed inside—

Cade shook his head. "Not this time," he ordered briskly, and Joshua's heart sank. "I want to see your mouth on him…" Cade continued, taking charge as though it was his rightful place, "…while *I* fuck you." He flicked Ashbrook's nipple with his thumbnail and Ashbrook arched up into both their hands, obviously happy with the idea.

Joshua chased down the burn of disappointment with two things—*mouth*, to which his body answered a resounding *yes*, and *next time*.

"If you're content with that," Joshua asked Ashbrook specifically, letting go his prick and sliding both hands into his hair to cup his face.

Ashbrook murmured his assent and Joshua kissed him, moving his lips softly over Ashbrook's mouth until he responded in kind.

A hand wrapped around Joshua's prick again while another stroked his back, yet another sliding down the cleft of his buttocks. He spread his knees wider and allowed the intrusion, sliding his tongue into Ashbrook's willing mouth. He no longer knew which hands were whose, stroking him and petting him, touching the tight, hot skin of his hole and circling it with just the right edge of pressure. He thrust up against Ashbrook's stomach in response, wild and dirty, whispering promises and endearments into his mouth.

Cade bent Ashbrook over, moving them on the bed until there was room enough for all three.

Ashbrook kissed his way down Joshua's body as Joshua settled back on his elbows. He nipped and sucked at Joshua's nipples until they stood in tight peaks on his chest. Joshua chased the heat of his mouth when Ashbrook withdrew.

Joshua pushed himself up to take a better look.

Cade knelt behind Ashbrook, two fingers sliding into Ashbrook's arse. Ashbrook rocked back, fucking himself on Cade's hand, his cheeks burning red. His cock and balls hung thick and heavy between his legs, swaying as he moved.

"Please, please, Evander," he begged. "I'm ready." His eyes met Joshua's, pupils so wide that his dark-brown eyes were all but black.

Joshua surged up and kissed him, kissed him and felt the surges of his body as Cade filled him up and withdrew, again and again and never enough.

"Suck him," Cade ordered, and Joshua nodded.

"Please?" he asked, and slid up to allow Ashbrook some room.

Ashbrook ducked his head and traced his mouth down along Joshua's hip. His breath puffed hot against Joshua's skin, teasing and not close enough.

Joshua fisted his hands in the sheets to prevent himself from grabbing Ashbrook by the ears and forcing him into place. His tongue flickered out, teasing as Joshua had done to him, and Joshua groaned with the agony of it. He forced his eyes open and stared down the length of his body. The sight of Ashbrook's mouth stretched around him was too much, combined with the wet brush of Ashbrook's tongue over the head of his cock.

Ashbrook looked up at him, his mouth red and bruised. He held Joshua's gaze firmly and opened his mouth and throat, sliding down to take Joshua all the way in. Heat encompassed him, surrounded his prick, and Ashbrook's tongue pressed up along the bottom as he pulled off with a pop. The ring caught on Ashbrook's bottom lip and tugged, sending fire to burn along the base of Joshua's spine and ignite between his legs, over and over again.

Joshua would die from this, there was no alternative.

Then Ashbrook gasped and shuddered, his nose pressed tight to the root of Joshua's cock and his mouth hanging open.

Cade pushed into him, hard and vengeful, his fingers tight enough on Ashbrook's hips to leave dents in the firm flesh.

Ashbrook sucked Joshua in again and grabbed for his hand. He laced his fingers through Joshua's and squeezed tightly as he sucked and bobbed, the friction of his mouth and his throat driving Joshua upward until speech was utterly impossible.

They matched their rhythms, sweat prickling behind Joshua's knees. He wound the sheet around one hand and hung on, the other clasping Ashbrook's fingers with desperate connection. He wanted to thrust, to plunder and own, only Ashbrook's other hand splayed out across his hip and his own waning sense of care preventing him.

"Close," he gasped out as his vision began to white around the edges.

Ashbrook's response was to suck harder, to let go of Joshua's hip and wrap his fist around the base of Joshua's cock, hard and tight. He closed that beautiful mouth around the tip and worked the base with his tongue, tracing under the ridge, laving that spot at the base of his slit where touch was so, so sweet. He tugged at the ring with his lips, ran over the loop of metal with his tongue, then sank down to take Joshua in again entirely.

Joshua arched, his body taut as a bowstring, and he released into Ashbrook's mouth. Ashbrook rose up, then took him down one more time, drove Joshua's prick deep and swallowed around him, the muscles of his throat fluttering around the very tip. His eyes were brown with flecks of green that glittered in the candlelight, his lips vermilion-red.

The world went white.

Grunts and gasps greeted Joshua when he returned from his haze of semiconsciousness, Ashbrook pressed up on his arms above him. Cade fucked into him, bent low and biting marks into Ashbrook's shoulders and spine. Sweat beaded on Ashbrook's forehead and in his hair, gleaming along the line of his throat.

Joshua licked a stripe of wetness up the center of his own palm. He wrapped his hand around Ashbrook's prick and pressed his thumb up and over the head.

Ashbrook groaned and cursed, arching his neck so that Joshua could kiss and bite at it, Ashbrook's prick sliding slick and sweet through the mess of Joshua's saliva and his own hot precome.

Cade finished with a muffled grunt and a full-body shudder, pulling himself free moments later.

Ashbrook moaned and sighed, rolling down into Joshua's grip. Joshua twisted his hand, rolled his palm and tightened his fist, stroking his thumb across the slit, pressing down on the spot beneath. Ashbrook jammed his knuckle into his own mouth to muffle his cries and came silently, spilling white and hot across Joshua's fingers.

Joshua stroked him through his tremors, pulling gently at his cock as it spurted once, twice more, then slowly began to soften.

Cade waited until his shaking stopped, then rolled off the bed with no words of explanation.

Ashbrook's arms trembled from the strain of holding himself up.

Joshua wiped the mess off on the sheet without a thought, then stroked his hands up and over Ashbrook's shoulders. "Settle," he murmured softly, and Ashbrook collapsed gently on top of him.

His hair clung to his face in sweaty ringlets, and Joshua brushed them back, tangled his fingers in Ashbrook's hair as he pillowed his head on Joshua's chest. His arms came about Joshua in what felt like exhaustion and reflex rather than affection, but it was an intimacy that Joshua had not enjoyed in far too long. How could he deny himself this? He passed his hands over Ashbrook's skin instead, tangled in the curls at the base of his neck, traced the bow of his lips.

"You were so good," he murmured quietly, an endearment for Ashbrook alone, and squeezed the hand that still laced tightly with his. "So good to me."

Ashbrook buried his face in Joshua's side and said nothing, but his heartbeat slowed a little against Joshua's chest and the tension ebbed from his shoulders.

Joshua dared to lean in to steal a kiss, and tasted his own sour musk on Ashbrook's lips. "You are beautiful," Joshua dared to whisper and that got a response, Ashbrook lifting his head to stare at Joshua with wide eyes.

"You're blind," he murmured back, a smile playing on his lips. "Or mad."

Cade returned then, with wet cloths and towels in hand, that they might clean themselves and restore the modicum of dignity allowed three naked men in one bed.

Ashbrook let go of Joshua's hand and sat, tidied himself in quiet. When Joshua rose to find his clothes—for the invitation had most certainly not extended to being discovered there in the morning—Ashbrook had his nightshirt on and a jovial smile back upon his face.

Joshua liked the just-fucked look much better on him, for the openness in his eyes that drove away the brittleness lurking just beneath.

"I thank you, gentlemen both," he said finally, though his smile was for Ashbrook alone. "It has been a most entertaining evening. I hope…" and here his veneer cracked a bit, though if he was lucky, Ashbrook would be the only one to notice, "…that we might reconvene at a later date to further our discussions."

"I think that can be arranged," Cade replied, smoothing a wet towel across his perfect face. "There are subjects yet untapped, after all," he added with an indelicate waggle of his eyebrows, and Ashbrook laughed, seeming to get his feet back beneath him.

"Indeed there are," he said and nodded to Joshua. "A pleasure, sir."

Joshua nodded back—was he unwilling or utterly unable to meet Ashbrook's eyes now, lest he see the vulnerability lurking there? "Until next time, then." He drew his coat about him like a shield or suit of armor and let himself out.

Chapter Nine

Warmth. Everything around Stephen was warm and soft, an arm looped around his waist, Evander's chin tucked into Stephen's shoulder. It was endearing and unusual, in a heavy kind of way. Stephen lay there for a few minutes, feeling the even rise and fall of Evander's breathing, before rolling out from underneath him. Evander muttered something under his breath and jammed his head beneath the pillow, while Stephen padded softly into the main room of their suite. They would need to tidy up and unlock the doors to let the servants in shortly, and it would have to at least appear as though someone had spent the night in Evander's bed.

Stripping the covers down and moving the pillows around was simple enough, but absurd. How had Stephen come to the point, within a short week, where he was concerned about placating servants and hiding the evidence of his unnatural congresses? One more point in favor of returning to their cramped lodgings as quickly as possible, where they could lounge naked in each other's arms all day if they so chose.

Regret cut through him sharply. They'd leave the country house at the end of the party to return, just the two of them, to London's hectic streets. Their friends would be awaiting them with open arms, and the raw effervescence of the city would bring him back to himself again. But now, unexpectedly, there were some things he would miss.

Evander had never called him beautiful.

(Lovely, yes; inspiring, certainly; but never *beautiful*, or with such whispered reverence.)

Beaufort had worked his body over with his mouth and hands, then kissed him with tenderness. He'd held him close, whispering the sorts of endearments that sounded shabby and lukewarm in the daylight, but meant everything in the dark.

Unsettling, that was what it was. Glorious, and brilliant, and unsettling in a way that shifted the ground beneath his feet. What to do?

Evander had enjoyed himself, certainly. He adored having the attention of two, of someone watching while he fucked Stephen, of watching Stephen with someone else. He would be easily amenable to a repeat. So would Beaufort, if his reactions had been anything to go by.

It was hardly infidelity when your lover was the one who had proposed it in the first place. The knowledge that Beaufort found him amiable enough to return meant nothing more than that. It would be foolishness to read anything into it other than three like-minded men enjoying their youth and freedom.

There—it was decided. Stephen washed his face and hands a second time, and returned to his room to begin the process of cajoling Evander out of it.

With the ice now thoroughly broken between them, Beaufort proved excellent company. And, oddly, Beaufort seemed to prefer *his* company to Evander's. That was disconcerting—Evander had always been the pivot upon which their triangles wheeled.

Stephen couldn't find it within himself to complain.

Though Beaufort had not called him beautiful again. Not since that first night.

"So tell me," Stephen asked aloud as they trailed along at the rear of the riding party, one of Coventry's more docile mares flicking her tail angrily beneath him, "if you could have any life you wanted…" he ducked a branch that Beaufort easily avoided, Evander oblivious from his place nearer the front of the group, "…any path at all. What would it be?"

Beaufort chewed his lip in that gesture Stephen had come to recognize as honest consideration. His hat shaded his eyes so that Stephen couldn't see them properly, even when he turned his head to answer.

"I like my profession as it is," Beaufort began. He sat his horse easily, the bastard, and seemed no more discomfited by its size and strength than as if it were a small foal.

"You would change nothing?" Stephen raised an eyebrow at the suggestion. Surely he could not be entirely satisfied. There were times when Stephen caught him looking out at the sky, his mind a thousand miles away.

"I didn't say that." Beaufort's horse shifted and he clucked quietly at it, bringing the creature back in line. "If I could have any life I liked, I should like to be successful enough to choose whom—or what—I paint. To either have the annuity or the clientele to know that, even if I chose to indulge only my own fancy, I could still sell enough canvas or draw on enough income to support myself. Lady Horlock has been more than generous," he added quickly, glancing over his shoulder, but there was no one behind them to overhear, "but painting portraits to order is not the best way to keep one's skills honed."

"I imagine not," Stephen replied. "But surely there are enough variations in sitters and in landscapes to keep it interesting. It is not at all the same as practicing the same piece twenty or thirty times in a row."

"Apparently," Beaufort's reply came, dry and acerbic, "there are only five or six styles of drawing room considered fashionable these days, and three stylish cuts of gown. Why it should be so and not the reverse I cannot begin to decipher, but perhaps it is one of those things not meant for the male mind to comprehend. Once you have seen one matron in her day dress or fellow in his Sunday suit, you may as well paint the rest from rote and consider it a job well done."

Stephen laughed, and the sound echoed off the trees ahead.

Evander slowed to wait for them, but his attention was immediately redirected by Lady Charlotte on her dapple-gray.

They were left to themselves, and Stephen let out his held breath. "I think perhaps you would be happier, my dear Mr. Beaufort, to live without the oppressive presence of other people around you at all. Would you be content with your paint box, a cottage and an endless parade of different sunsets?"

Beaufort tipped his head back and forth as though considering it seriously, and one corner of his mouth curled up in a genuine smile. "Perfect solitude, I think, would become as endlessly dull as an eternity in society." When he looked at Stephen next, his eyes were as warm and soft as his mouth. "But give me the company of one beloved friend," he said quietly, Stephen's pulse racing at the wistful look in his eyes, "and a village with a good tavern not too far away, and I would say you had described paradise."

It was a lovely image, if far too provincial for Stephen's usual tastes. Someday, though, Beaufort would find a friend for whom that too seemed to be perfection, and he would seal himself away in the country forever. A cloud passed across the sun above.

Some of the party ahead of them on the trail broke into a lively canter, the trees opening up into a lovely green field spotted with brilliant patches of wild flowers. Miss Talbot's mare pranced prettily, her rider's hands light on the reins, and Coventry applauded.

"Your turn, then," Beaufort said, and Stephen snapped back to attention. "What would you change?" Beaufort kept his eyes facing forward, looking at the path and the field, and a small tic flickered at the edge of his jaw. He glanced at Stephen, his expression softening. "If anything," he added.

"I have what I want," Stephen said, the easy answer. "Though a more secure income would surely never go amiss." It wasn't true, of course—he could think of a great many things he would change if he had the power.

Evander's occasional cruelties, for one—replace them with the immense kindnesses of which he was also so perfectly capable. "I have my music."

"That is all that you need?"

"Music and an audience to perform for," Stephen amended. "Is that not enough?" He cocked his head to take in Beaufort's response, but his horse decided to slow down her pace and crop mouthfuls of the grass from the side of the trail. He tried pulling her head up, but she did not obey.

Beaufort sidled up and took his reins for a moment, applying a gentle correction that had her moving again within a moment.

"Thank you. She is as stubborn as Cade."

"And with hair almost as pretty," Beaufort said quietly, his eyes sparkling with amusement, and Stephen chuckled. Beaufort handed back his reins, and their fingers brushed together, a tentative touch of skin on skin. Beaufort's hand was rough where the scars and callouses of his work marked his long fingers. Neither said a word, but the warmth curling low in Stephen's belly was comment enough.

"When I play," he continued, "people *listen*. I can bring them to heights and depths of pure emotion, change their moods for the better or for the worse. I can make my audience feel what I wish them to feel."

Beaufort's smile slipped. "What Cade wishes them to feel, you mean. You play his feelings, recite his lines and not your own."

"Why does that bother you?" Stephen asked in real confusion. "Many musicians also compose, but few particularly well. I am hardly the only player to make the music of others."

"Because I have heard you play," Beaufort answered, which was not an answer at all, "and listened to you at practice these past few weeks."

That, Stephen had not known.

"Sound travels from that room, sometimes," Beaufort added hastily, and the curve of his ear turned pink. "You have talent and skill. You understand music in ways not many do. You could be so much more than just his mouthpiece."

His words struck so close to some of the things Stephen had secretly considered that for a moment it seemed as though Beaufort had developed the power to read men's minds. To write his own music, choose his own programs, develop a patronage and a following as himself, not as "Cade's player"—

But mind reading was as impossible as the dream itself. Evander would be hurt, so desperately hurt. And to even begin, Stephen would either need to deceive him—quite impossible—or strike out alone, with neither funds nor support.

"It is not so easy to begin again." Who knew that better than he who had done it once already?

Beaufort flickered an eyebrow up, the only indication he had heard anything.

"In any case," Stephen said, "you don't know that I could be anything more than what I am today. Society's tastes are so capricious that what is popular and praiseworthy now will be out of fashion and unplayable tomorrow. For all we know, the winds of change will bring trumpets as the fashionable instrument next, and sculpture rather than paints, and both you and I shall be out of a trade."

Beaufort's look of irritation was well worth the price of his silence.

And Stephen had some things that bore thinking about.

Lady Amelia caught Beaufort at his drawings the next evening as Evander accompanied Stephen's violin on the ornate pianoforte in the parlor. Beaufort's perfectly shaded sketch of the two of them at their instruments made it all the way around the room, much commented on, before the poor man could finally get his hands back on the page.

Evander demurred, but Stephen, at least, ended up promising to sit for a proper sketch the next day.

It turned out to be far more entertaining to attempt his own watercolors than to sit still for Beaufort's pencils. It was more amusing still to dab color on the brush and aim for Beaufort's nose rather than the paper. If they ended up with paint on their shirtsleeves and wrinkles in their cravats, they were easily cleaned up before anyone could discover them behaving like fools.

"What in the world would you have done with yourself…" Stephen laughed, wielding his damp cloth to dab green paint from the hollow of Beaufort's throat, "…if you could not have become a painter? Surely you're fit for little else." The room was empty but for them, the curtains drawn, and he risked it, pressing a kiss to the spot he had just cleaned. Beaufort lifted his chin to allow it, his laughter rumbling against Stephen's lips and his pulse fluttering faster than butterfly wings.

"Schoolmaster, I suppose." Beaufort returned to wiping his hands clean with the rag from his pocket. Stephen shivered, but Beaufort seemed not to notice. "A tutor. There are always families looking for art lessons for their daughters, and I can set figures if I need to."

"That's a hard life." Stephen shook off the moment of memory, the bone-deep chill of fingers and toes that never quite warmed through. "Though, of either of us, I think you have the better temperament for it."

"Perhaps," Beaufort said easily, and stole a kiss from Stephen's lips. His mouth was warm like sunshine, seeping into Stephen's pores and warming him from the inside out. "What of you?" he asked, turning away to close his paint box, a smile lingering on his lips and in his eyes. "If you did not have your music?"

"If I did not have Cade, you mean," Stephen answered honestly and without thinking it through.

Beaufort tensed, his shoulders tight and head bowed.

"My parents wanted me to go into the army. My father was a schoolmaster and not at all wealthy, and the army would have been something secure." And he had done the opposite of their desires, had run away and abandoned his king and country, become a layabout and a coward.

"You?" Beaufort laughed incredulously, but it was not the condemnation for which Stephen braced himself, the damp and paint-spattered cloth clenched tightly in his hand. "You, so kindhearted that you cannot even bring yourself to hunt for the table? What did they expect you to do?" He was all kindness and good humor, reaching out to cup Stephen's jaw and trace his lips with the pad of his thumb. *"Flatter* the enemy to death?"

Stephen snorted, could not help himself, and tipped his head forward so that their foreheads touched for a moment, trading soft breaths between them. "Hardly," he said after pulling back and tucking the rag into Beaufort's waistcoat pocket. "But as you can see, I did not go through with it."

"No, apparently not." Beaufort cocked his head and stared, then gestured impatiently for him to continue.

The best way through was to make light of it, however painful the sting of old thorns. "I ran away with the vicar's son from the next town over. A schoolmate of mine, you see, who happened to have something of an ear for musical composition."

"And so genius was born," Beaufort murmured, a crooked smile on his face and a thoughtful expression in his eye. "You two have made quite the name for yourselves since."

The writing desk looked sturdy enough and Stephen hopped up on it, bracing his hands on the edge. The wall was cool against his back, even through his waistcoat, a welcome change from the heat of the day. "We made a bargain, back then. Evander would write the best music in the world, I would play his compositions and we would be each other's bulwarks against a cold and uncertain life."

Beaufort raised an eyebrow, but said nothing unkind. "It appears to have worked out rather well for both of you."

His paints stored away and his brushes cleaned, he rested his arms on the edge of the table, between Stephen's knees. He smiled up at Stephen from that unfamiliar angle.

"Better now," Stephen said. The flash of guilt that had come with the kiss was foolish; Evander had long ago given him permission to dally, as long as Evander knew beforehand and had first say in with whom. And he had approved of Beaufort from the beginning.

Stephen kissed Beaufort again, and his doubts vanished entirely.

Beaufort yearned up into him, his indecently dexterous hands splayed out over Stephen's thighs.

"Much better now."

Beaufort picked up music lessons better than Stephen did painting, given that he could already read the notation with a little bit of skill. He had not sat at a pianoforte in at least a decade, however, and his fingers showed it. The first two missed notes in his scales got no more than a glance from Lady Charlotte, curled up in a chair by the window with a book she only pretended to read. The third earned them a muffled giggle and a rustle as she turned a page ostentatiously. Beaufort took it in his stride, but his jaw worked and a vein throbbed in his temple when his thumb hit the wrong key and a sour note rang out.

"My music master would strike my knuckles with a willow switch if I were so persistently awful," Lady Charlotte advised archly. Thankfully, she rose to take herself and her maid away before Stephen said something impulsive and ill-advised.

"What a pity it had not been her bottom," Beaufort murmured *sotto voce* after they were alone again. "She might have developed a personality less 'persistently awful' in the process."

"And you wanted to be a teacher," Stephen teased. He pushed Beaufort over a few inches on the padded bench so that he could sit beside him. Beaufort slid over easily, his presence a warm and solid thing on Stephen's left when he sat. "Where is your vaunted patience now?"

"Tried," Beaufort said dryly, his sea-gray eyes twinkling with repressed humor. "I would feel sorry for Coventry, except that Lady Charlotte has a considerable dowry and so, I imagine, will not be his problem for too much longer." He set his fingers to the keys again, carefully copying the positions of Stephen's hands.

"Here, like this—" It was easier and much nicer to slide his hands over Beaufort's, laying each finger on top of one of his student's to adjust the curve and placement of his fingertips. The heat of him was a lure, the faint scent of oil from his hair an intoxication. The way he arched his eyebrow in skeptical disbelief and amusement, a chastisement Stephen would gladly take.

"Fine, then," Stephen said. "Do it yourself." He let go and ran a rapid scale up the high end of the keys, just to be perverse.

He did watch while Beaufort copied the movements, his own rendition of the scale hesitant but correct. A few runs later and he had improved, so much so that he was embarking on sheet music by the time the doors downstairs opened and the hunting party returned.

"So what would your music master think of you now?" Stephen asked, turning the page for Beaufort as he doggedly plonked his way through a simple air.

"He would be cringing behind his horrid old pipe and disavowing all responsibility for the way I turned out," Beaufort replied, with an ease that suggested he really had studied from a music master as a boy and not the kind of scraped-together lessons given by the postmaster's wife after school.

He missed the next bar, though, and had to backtrack, which made Stephen feel a little better about Mrs. Collier and her careful instruction. "I had no idea you came from such privilege," he did tease, though. "Perhaps I should be looking for your name in the gossip pages next Season. Shall you be setting your cap for Lady Charlotte and her magnificent portion?"

"Hardly," Beaufort replied, thumping a sour note. He began again from the top of the page, at Stephen's gentle tap, a wry smile tugging at his lips. "I am the third born of the second son of nobody particularly important in the first place. My one claim on society is a distant relation to Lady Horlock, and that plus a shilling will rent me a room for a night."

It was the most he had told Stephen about himself—in words, anyway. He was loath to let the conversation trail off into nothingness, even as Beaufort frowned at the page and walked his fingers carefully through the run of eighth notes that had stymied him the first time.

"And is that how you came to study music and painting?" Stephen asked once the difficult section was over. "Learning the genteel arts to please distant aristocratic relatives?"

Beaufort let his hands rest on the keys. "My parents had the kindness and the ability to encourage my interest in art, on the understanding that I either had to become good enough to find myself a patron or clientele, or industrious enough to find myself some other living. Luckily, the former won out. I doubt I would have made a good clergyman." He had the audacity to wink at Stephen. His lips quirked up at one corner in a grin that promised mischief, and Stephen was done for.

"Come to bed tonight," he murmured low, even as voices rose up the stairs and the clattering of feet could be heard in the hallway. He shivered as he spoke, his lips barely brushing the round swell of Beaufort's earlobe, close enough to bite. "Cade and I shall make confessions of all our worldly sins."

"All of them?" The reply came, hushed and breathless.

"All. And then, with your blessing, Father Beaufort, we shall commit a dozen more."

It was Cade who induced them both to join him on the lawn on sunny days. With the three of them and young Mr. John Downe at play, the shuttlecock proved too valiant a foe for the ladies. The ladies dropped about on the grass, pastel flowers in the sunshine, to egg the men on with cheers and applause for pleasingly dramatic efforts.

Downe smashed the shuttlecock and Stephen dove for it, landing hard on his shoulder in the grass. He swung up at the last moment and his battledore connected, sending the small cock flying back up into the air.

"Rise, rise up, fallen warrior!" Lady Amelia urged him gleefully, but Stephen flopped onto his back and waved a hand in the air in surrender instead, his forehead damp with sweat.

"Go on without me, I am done for. Avenge me, Cade!"

Evander stepped into his place against Downe, and Beaufort passed a cup of lemonade Stephen's way.

"You abandon your post," Beaufort teased, handing over a damp handkerchief.

Stephen mopped his brow before handing the linen square back.

Evander and Downe drove the shuttlecock back and forth through the air, their arms swinging strong and their faces golden in the sun.

"I concede to the greater sportsmen." The glass was sticky in his fingers, the lemonade cool and sharp against his tongue.

"Is there salt in this?" Lady Amelia asked suddenly.

Lady Charlotte frowned. "Not in mine."

"Nor mine. Perhaps it is your imagination?" Miss Talbot replied, wearing one of Lady Charlotte's bonnets.

Hardly earth-shattering stuff. The girls' attention taken elsewhere, Stephen murmured for Beaufort's ear alone. "Besides, this way, I can appreciate the view. Now I see why you took up art as a profession."

Beaufort's laughter, when it was genuine, sounded the way a fire in winter felt—warm and homelike, through and through.

Five young men, three silly debs, two chaperones, two earls, a countess, a viscount and a veritable brace of footmen were hardly, Stephen reflected to himself alone, what he would call a picnic. "Add a partridge in a pear tree and we have ourselves a carol."

"That could probably be arranged." Beaufort came up beside him on the front lawn, the rest of the group assembling slowly. He had some sort of straw monstrosity on his head that cast his entire face in shadow, spotted through by pinpricks of light that shone through gaps in the weave.

"Good Lord," Stephen greeted him cheerfully, "what is that thing eating your head? I think a bird's nest has landed on your hat."

Beaufort shook his head and sighed as though aggrieved. "Thus speaks a man who has never been concerned about freckles."

"They can be pleasing on the right person."

Beaufort's cheeks pinked up in a highly gratifying way. Evander came out of the house then, followed by Lady Charlotte and her maid, and then they were all off in a herd like the strangest collection of cattle—or gaggle of geese— to ever wander the dirt roads.

The footmen carried the bulk of the food and the accouterments, as was the way of things when one was wealthy, though Stephen carried a blanket over his shoulder. Evander had taken two picturesque little baskets from the ladies and was playing at being the gallant.

"Mr. Cade!" Lady Charlotte waved back to them, blonde curls bouncing about her shoulders and her bonnet ribbons flying.

Until he was summoned to better things, that is. Evander thrust the baskets into Stephen's hands with a distracted "Take these, won't you? There's a chap" before hurrying off to answer the call. Charlotte tucked her arm securely through Evander's and led him away.

Beaufort arched that eyebrow of his and took one of the baskets off his hands until they arrived at the bank of the pond.

White-linen cloths had been spread over the deep-green grass, chairs and parasols set up around the perimeter for the ladies who preferred them. Ribbons fluttered gaily from the stakes used to keep the cloths down at the corners. The breeze ruffled the edges of the cloths and sent the multihued silk streamers to dancing. The water stretched out before them, clear and rippling on the surface, kept full by the river at which Stephen had found Beaufort sketching three weeks and half a lifetime ago.

The party went much the same as most days at the house. That is to say, Stephen made casual and polite conversation with the company, Evander flirted with the girls, the young bucks boasted of their affairs in London, and Coventry watched benignly over them all, his hands clasped across his belly like a jovial patron saint, occasionally tipping his head to say something to one or another of his guests.

Stephen wandered away after a while, the quiet of the water's edge drawing him closer. Frogs stopped their measured song as he came close, only to start again farther down around the shore, and he nodded in sympathy.

"Can't say I blame you," he said aloud, smiling at himself. "Sometimes everyone needs to get some distance from people."

Footsteps crunched on the stones behind him. Beaufort approached. "I hope I don't count as people," he said hesitantly. "Because if it's solitude you seek, I'll take my leave and think you none the worse for it."

His heart had not sped up at Beaufort's approach, because that would be ridiculous. He liked the man, of course he did! They had become, Stephen liked to think, rather good friends over the last few days.

"Not total," Stephen promised, and hopefully the faint rush of heat to his cheeks would be accounted for by the warmth of the midday sun. "Only escaping the conversation about topiary, for I fear I have little to contribute."

Beaufort nodded approvingly, and that funny, warm sensation swelled inside his chest again. Sunshine and peace, desire and kindness, it all blended together into something lovely and too far beyond his clumsy words. "A wise commander knows when to hold fast, and when to make a strategic retreat."

"I am glad that I have never been in position to be a leader of men, in that case." Stephen stooped to pick up a flat stone from the water's edge. It sat well against his finger, round and smoothed by the waves. "I've never been good at knowing when something is a lost cause." He flicked his arm and the stone spun from his hand, skipping lightly—once, twice, thrice—across the still surface before sinking beneath.

"I should probably be grateful for that persistence," Beaufort replied with a secret smile meant only for Stephen. He followed Stephen's lead, finding his own stone and letting it fly. It skipped beautifully, making five graceful arcs before it too vanished below the water's surface and sank from sight. "You told me not long ago," Beaufort said casually, though the glance he threw Stephen's way suggested that he had something more serious on his mind, "that one man could not own another. Why, then, do you allow Cade to treat you as he does?"

That stopped him short, bent over with his hand among the rocks. Stephen crouched down on his heels, turning a pebble over in his hand. It gleamed dark silver in the sunlight where the water had marked it, dun and drab on the side that remained dry.

"He is my oldest friend," Stephen began because while Evander could be mercurial, he did not *own* him. He did not mistreat him, and what he did, he generally had good reason for. "The only one who has ever believed in me. He wants me to be a better man than I am."

There. That was the truth, and surely answer enough. Stephen stood and whipped the rock into the water. It sank without bouncing.

Beaufort crouched, then stood and skipped his rock across the rippling waves. "He wants you dependent on him, and on him alone. Does he permit you to have friends whom he has not himself approved, or pursuits not related to his own needs?"

He reached out a hand to touch Stephen's shoulder, his eyes shuttered and wary. Stephen pulled away. "You don't know him the way I do. I've seen his vulnerability, the way he needs me."

Beaufort didn't take the bait as Evander would have; he neither snapped nor railed nor drew upon his vocabulary to heap imprecations on Stephen's head. Instead, he simply took his hand back and searched for another rock. "Need and desire are not the same thing as respect. Or love."

Stephen snorted and shoved his hands into his pockets in defiance of good manners. "Can men such as we even know what love is?" he asked, striving to keep his tone as elevated and impersonal as he could. "We are not made for it."

"That sounds like Cade talking," Beaufort corrected him, his voice sad and gentle. "Men such as we need it more than anyone else. As you once so correctly pointed out, God does not permit us to make holy vows. Love itself is all we have." He skipped another stone, ferocious and hard, his coat flying about behind him with the force of his movement. It bounced six times, then one more, then disappeared. "It is not good for man to be alone," he quoted, and Stephen recoiled.

"You quote the Bible at me? Fine, then." These verses he knew, as Evander knew them. As Evander mumbled them in his nightmares, those that ended with tears, cries for mercy and Evander calling out his father's name. "Man shall not lie with man as with a woman, it is an abomination."

Beaufort flinched and Stephen felt a perverse rush of satisfaction at the crack in his cool exterior. Then he felt nothing but guilt.

Beaufort shook his head, his eyes as gray and stormy as the sea. "Our bodies may be sinful things, but we are also human. Our hearts were built to love and be loved in return." He spoke quietly and reverently, as though he really believed it. It was a good belief, a thought that lifted instead of terrified, made something small and cold in the middle of his chest unfurl, just a little, and begin to sing. "Falling from grace cannot change that."

Stephen moistened his lips, made as though to reply, but words would not come. He nodded once, then again with more finality. When he found the air, he only said, "You *would* have made an excellent clergyman, Father Beaufort. Will you come to bed tonight?"

"Of course."

A shriek and a splash came from back over the embankment, around the other side of the pond, ending the conversation. Beaufort jogged up the slope to see what happened, Stephen following behind.

Miss Talbot had already been fished out of the pond by the time they caught up to the rest of the party, her dress splattered with mud and sodden curls of hair hanging limply about her shoulders. She sputtered and sulked until a blanket was found for her shoulders, and she was settled in the sun in the best of all seats to dry, her mother fluttering around her like the broodiest of all hens and Lady Amelia conspicuously distant.

Never a dull moment.

Again and again, Beaufort came to their bed. Not every night, for there were evenings when the parlor games ran long and the wine flowed freely and sleep was all any man craved. But some nights, when the wind blew outside or the house retired early, and no force alive seemed able to induce others from their beds, Stephen would murmur an invitation and a soft knock would come at their door.

This too fell into a pattern, of sorts, though between them they could come up with an infinite number of variations. More often than not it happened like so— Evander would draw them together, touching and stroking his fill, his hands roaming and sating himself with hot, hard flesh.

Stephen would find himself on his knees, taking one or the other or both into his mouth and hands, sucking and stroking until his entire world was nothing but this excess of skin and sweat and burning want. Pricks slipped against his cheeks, between the cleft of his arse, come splattering hot against his chest, his lips, across the small of his back. Marking him, claiming him, both of them together.

Evander would fuck him then, with Beaufort watching or touching. Sometimes Stephen would get to suck Beaufort while Evander fucked him, the ring first cool, then hot, on his tongue. Or Evander would finish in Stephen's mouth and watch the rest, stroking himself leisurely as the other two amused themselves.

That was best, for he had both of them then, the taste of Evander lingering on his tongue while Beaufort opened him up, first with his fingers and then with his cock. The gold ring stroked deeply through him, pressing rough against a cluster of coals inside.

It had intimidated him the first time, not knowing how it would work. The ring seemed so much larger and more dangerous to Stephen's tenderest flesh as Beaufort slicked his red and eager cock with oil.

"It should not hurt you," Beaufort said, laying Stephen down on his stomach. "But if I do, you must tell me, and we shall stop."

He pressed against Stephen's back, his cock sliding thick and easy between the cleft of Stephen's buttocks, and Stephen's hips jerked up. More—he needed more than just that slide and gentle pressure, the slick pass of hard flesh over his hole. He was empty and needed to be filled up, hungry and desperate to be fed.

Beaufort ran his hands down along Stephen's outstretched arms, warm and still slippery with oil, and laced his fingers through Stephen's without another word. They lay there just like that for a moment, Beaufort's hips undulating and his cock rubbing hard and hot against Stephen's lower back, their panting breaths echoing in his ears.

He needed, he wanted. He was so empty, with Beaufort's fingers gone from inside him, and the promise of his cock right *there*.

"Do it," Stephen groaned. He rocked his hips up to make absolutely no mistake about his request. A gasp that sounded like Evander's came from the chair beside the bed, accompanied by the slick sound of skin on skin. Stephen's cock ached—heavy, full and untouched—and he thrust against the bedclothes with a whimper. "Do it now. Someone needs to fuck me now, else I die."

"We can't have that," Beaufort laughed softly.

He pressed his mouth against the back of Stephen's neck, then scraped his teeth across that same spot, stinging and salving the skin in one. He moved, the heat and pressure were gone from Stephen's back, and Stephen whimpered.

It was only a second before Beaufort's hands were on him again, pulling his hips up to slide a pillow beneath them. Beaufort's hand brushed Stephen's cock and the little bit of foreign pressure sent a flare of pleasure spinning through him. He pushed down to chase the friction, but Beaufort pulled away too quickly.

"Bastard!" Stephen gasped, and rutted down into the pillow in desperation before Evander's hands stilled his hips.

"Now, now," Evander chided him. Stephen could see his cock from this angle, already most of the way back to hard. He nudged at it with his nose, all that he could reach, and Evander's hips jerked. "Behave, or I'll take care of him myself."

Not that, never that! Stephen bit his lip as Beaufort's fingers trailed down his inner thigh, a cool line of oil and sweat drying on his skin where they passed.

Evander ran his hands down Stephen's back, held his buttocks open and ready, his fingers curling along the edges of Stephen's hole.

He fucked back onto Beaufort's fingers when he slid them inside again, curling and probing and driving him to the brink of madness. Four hands on him, three fingers inside, his nose and mouth full of the heady smell and taste of sex, full but nowhere near full enough—

Then, thank God and all the saints cursing him from heaven, Evander let go so Stephen's hips could move freely. He pinned Stephen's arms above his head instead, hands pressed flat against the mattress.

Beaufort's weight settled between Stephen's thighs, though with his face down he could see nothing. Then pressure, a hint of cold and a slow, agonizingly slow, slide inside.

Stephen was going to split in two. He ached and yearned, the sting of stretching fading, to be replaced by pressure as he was filled up entirely. Beaufort was too large; there was no way Stephen could take him all, and the ring— *Oh. That* was what it was for!—as it bumped against the nut-sized spot on the inside that turned Stephen's arms and knees to jelly.

Beaufort's cock filled him up, pressed him open until there was no sensation in the world other than that, the pain of the stretch and the pressure against his insides, the slow drag of skin on skin and the way Beaufort's hands smoothed, comfortingly, over his lower back.

Stephen sobbed once, and Beaufort stilled, his balls pressed up against the skin of Stephen's buttocks. "I can stop," he said quietly, his voice thick with strain.

Evander's hands shifted on Stephen's wrists, relaxed and released.

"If this is too much, I'll stop."

"No!" The sound burst out of Stephen, and Evander laughed. "If you stop now I will hunt you down, you and your children's children," Stephen threatened.

Beaufort rocked his hips, just once, as punishment. He stroked across that spot again and Stephen's toes curled. He let out a low and trembling groan before he could stop himself. Beaufort lay down half atop him, rested his hips against Stephen's buttocks, his arms on either side of Stephen's head and laced his fingers through Stephen's.

Evander settled into his chair again, still close enough to reach them should he choose to, his thick and angry cock in his own hand.

Beaufort kissed Stephen's neck again, wet and sloppy this time, rocking his hips in and then out as they started to find their rhythm. Each stroke seemed to go deeper, set more sparks blazing in the base of Stephen's spine.

He craned his neck to catch Beaufort's mouth in a kiss, and they mashed their lips together, hot, slick and filthy wet. There was nothing elegant about it; Stephen pushed his hips up as their mouths collided, fucking himself back onto Beaufort's cock.

Evander stroked himself in time with them, thrusting up into the circle of his fist. Stephen watched it, his eyes fixed on the red-purple head appearing and then vanishing down between Evander's fingers.

Beaufort reached a hand beneath him, his fingers hot against the skin of Stephen's hip, and he wrapped those long, elegant artist's fingers around Stephen's cock.

He stroked, and Stephen cried out, the sound ripping from his throat. The need to *push* and *thrust* and *take* burned through him and he shoved his hips forward, pressed into the tight grip of Beaufort's fist.

Evander fucked his own fist, dipped the pad of his thumb into the slit and smeared a trail of precome across the skin. He held himself so Stephen could see every motion, see but not touch.

Beaufort changed his rhythm to match, fucking into Stephen with fast and shallow thrusts. The pool of fire in his spine coiled tighter and burned hotter with every tug, every slick slide of fingers over the head of his prick and push of thick cock into the core of his body.

His balls drew up tight, so tight, and in the distance he heard someone chanting "please, please, please more…" before realizing that it was him. He chased something, three steps behind, his skin on fire and his insides aching, throbbing, burning for it.

Beaufort picked up speed, hand and body alike.

There, there, oh *there*! Stephen exploded, shooting hot and sticky over Beaufort's hand. He forced himself back onto Beaufort's thick, beautiful cock to push the last of his release out of his shaking and exhausted body.

Again.

Again.

He collapsed to the bed, and Beaufort let go, pulled *out*. The emptiness that followed was soul crushing, his body alone and abandoned.

Until hands flipped him over as he lay there panting.

Beaufort straddled him, pinning his hips down again as easily as he had before. He held his own cock in his hand, jutting, curved, toward the sky in blood-filled fury, and the grimace on his face betrayed his desperation. His hair stuck to his forehead and his cheeks, all askew and utterly unmade, his fair cheeks flushed red, his pupils blown so wide that the color of his eyes was impossible to see.

Stephen slid his hand between Beaufort's legs to roll his balls in his palm, stroke and tug at them.

They drew up tight to Beaufort's body and Beaufort bit his lip, hard. He stroked himself with a deft flick and twist of his wrist, once, twice, then he was gone, his head thrown back and body arching. His come splashed hot over Stephen's stomach, pearled in the sparse dark hair on his chest.

"Dear God," Beaufort said, his chest heaving with exertion and from orgasm, his hands clenching and unclenching in the bedclothes, his feet tucked beneath him and his weight resting on his knees on either side of Stephen's hips. "Dear God."

"God, I think," Evander said lazily, sprawled with one leg over the arm of his chair, his cock softening slowly against his thigh and his stomach splattered white with his own come, "has very little to do with this."

"Dear Gentlemen, then," Beaufort replied, and the rise and fall of his chest began to return to a more normal pace, the bright-red flush of lust starting to fade from his cheeks. He stared down at Stephen, his eyes as fair and gray as the sky over the Channel.

"I am," he said simply, catching his breath with a small, soft, bitter laugh, "utterly undone."

Chapter Ten

The face that stared back at Joshua from the mirror was not his own. At least, it didn't resemble the same old Joshua Beaufort. The bags were gone from beneath his eyes, his smile came easier, and somehow he looked…happy. Not simply content, but *happy*. And it was entirely Stephen Ashbrook's fault.

He should have stopped it weeks ago. He would have been better off refusing the invitation to the house party in the first place. Then Ashbrook would have stayed an unattainable, distant fantasy, instead of a very real, very *human* man. Because a human man was easy to love.

Love—the word was trouble. Better by far to keep thinking of these feelings as nothing more than infatuation, inspired by fornication and midsummer madness.

He could not stop thinking about it. About watching Ashbrook sink to his knees, or pressing tender kisses into the yielding firmness of his thighs; of course it was about that. But neither could he make himself forget the smile that creased the corners of Ashbrook's eyes when he laughed, the way he hummed softly under his breath in quiet moments, the callouses on the fingertips of his left hand, the constant sense of motion that surrounded him. Each of those had, in such a short time, become something precious.

That itself was a perfect demonstration. Joshua sighed as he allowed William to help him into his coat, of why he was better off alone. He formed attachments too quickly, with too little provocation, and almost certainly with all the wrong people.

This could not end well.

And speaking of the wrong people—William slipped out to attend to his other duties, and Sophie caught the door before it closed. She stepped inside after a couple of quick and hushed words with the young valet.

Joshua stared at himself in the mirror rather than turn to face her, tugging at the edges of his cravat for something to do with his hands.

"Hullo, stranger," Sophie teased him gently, batting away his hands and stepping into his line of view. "This will never do," she tut-tutted, untying the length of linen and snapping it out with a flourish before wrapping it carefully around his neck again. Her hair smelled faintly of hay and sunshine, and coiled darkly around her head under the pale-white linen of her cap.

"Did you come in simply to correct my dress?" Joshua found his voice, smiling down at her.

She tilted her nose up pertly and wrinkled it at him, tugging his cravat into a perfect knot. "Someone has to do it." She stepped back, seemingly satisfied, but her eye on him was critical.

"I don't see much of you at all, these days," Sophie said, trailing her finger across the top of his dressing table.

She rubbed her fingers together to rid herself of a faint trace of dust, her brow furrowed. "It's only to be expected, I suppose."

What was she hinting at? "How so?" Joshua asked, honestly confused. "It is much the same as it was at home—you have your duties and I have mine. I can hardly be blamed for the distance between the servants' and guests' quarters in this house."

"And when you are about…" she looked up at him with a sharp eye and a knowing smile, "…you are so engrossed in Mr. Ashbrook that I think I could dance naked on top of your trunk and never once be noticed."

Had Joshua been in the midst of drinking or eating something at that moment, he surely would have choked. As it was, he winced, the only outward sign of his loss of composure, and shook his head. "Please…" he laughed, "…let us not resort to that."

"I shall not," she replied with a toss of her head. "But I shall persist in this: you have become close with Cade and Ashbrook." And there was no question in her tone, only statement of fact.

He would not demean her by lying. "I have," he replied, leaning around her to pick up his pocket watch and fob. "They are entertaining friends and closer to my station than Lord Downe's sons. Does that disturb you, my having other acquaintances?" he asked kindly, making a game of it. "I cannot spend all my time downstairs among the maids."

"And here I thought you cared little for them." She was fishing, her eyes bright and mouth slightly parted. The early morning light fell across her fine features, highlighting their delicacy and giving her a kittenish air. "You were not so impressed back home."

Joshua attached his watch, checked it and slid it into his waistcoat pocket. "Cade grows on me," he admitted.

"And Ashbrook?"

He most emphatically did *not* blush, but looking her in the eye was impossible. "I like him well." He pulled out his watch again and wound it instead.

Sophie stepped up behind him then, her hand on his arm and her eyes too old and too knowing to fit the rest of her face. "How well? As well as any man did like a maid?"

Joshua closed his eyes and swallowed hard against the anxious twist that sat in his throat. That Sophie suspected his preferences was nothing new. They had never spoken of it, but it rested there, an undercurrent of understanding between them.

There had been one night years ago, the true beginning of their unlikely friendship, when she had come to him—a new lady's maid, and never as shy as she should have been—with a bottle of good wine in hand. They drank, talked, lay down chastely side by each, and she left in the early hours of the morning as good a maid as she had come to him. Something in that had proven him to her, and they had been as fast as siblings since.

Even so, there were some things one did not say aloud, not in company not similarly engaged.

"Those are dangerous suggestions, dear heart," he said, his voice a hard whisper. "I suggest you keep them to yourself."

She shrugged nonchalantly. "You don't shock me, you know." She looked at him with eyes so genuinely affectionate that the gut-churning burst of *fear-panic-run* began to fade. "I saw more than enough growing up in the stews. Unless you somehow involve dogs or cattle, there is little I can think of that would offend."

"That, I can promise you, is well out of my sphere of interest," Joshua grumbled darkly. He should have known. Sarah Harlow, once a penniless whore's bastard, was a great deal more worldly than Sophie Armand, the delicate alter ego of a lady's maid she had invented years ago. "If you must have me say it, then so be it. I am a buggerer and buggered alike. What do you want from me?"

"If you think I did not know years ago, you are a fool." She leaned in and pressed a soft kiss to his cheek. He felt, rather than saw, her shake her head. "But attend to your danger," she said, and he blinked. What now? She closed her fingers around his upper arm, her voice pitched soft and low. "The old bat has begun asking questions about the amount of time you have been spending with Ashbrook, and with Cade. You would be better served putting some distance between you."

Damnation! He would almost rather lose a limb than sever his understanding with Ashbrook now! Three more weeks would be nowhere near enough time to explore all his desires, but it would have been a magnificent beginning.

"Thank you," he said coolly, tugging his waistcoat and jacket into place. He nodded to the door and she made for it, her disappointment showing plainly on her face. She meant well, and he was treating her poorly.

Damn.

He forced his face into a look less severe, and Sophie let out a held breath. "Thank you," he said again, far more kindly than before. "I shall take that under advisement."

"See that you do." Sophie ducked her head and slipped out of the room again. Lavender perfume lingering in the air and the disquiet settling deep into Joshua's soul were the only signs that anyone had been there at all.

The house still lay in relative quiet as Joshua came down for breakfast. The ladies were outside; flashes of skirts and bright bonnets went by the window as he crossed the hall, the others slowly making their way to find themselves coffee, tea and toast.

So Lady Horlock suspected something. Was it possible that they had been discovered? He rather thought not.

Only once in his midnight wanderings had he come across another living creature in the halls. Silly Miss Talbot, she of the heaving bosom and fluttering eyelashes, trying to find her way back to her own room in the early hours of the morning. Lost, she'd said, after searching for a servant to bring her a drink of water. Escorting her back had only taken a moment. He had almost forgotten the exchange, lost in his own preoccupations.

She could hardly have mentioned his being out of bed without revealing how she knew, and getting into far more serious trouble herself.

There were always the servants, of course, and servants invariably gossiped. But if that were the case, then certainly Sophie would have intercepted and said something long before now.

No, Joshua decided, entering the dining room and bowing to the lords and ladies already there assembled, he had nothing at all to worry about.

"Sodomites," declared Lord Horlock, as Joshua took his seat, "deserve their fates for their offenses to the Almighty."

He froze, half in and half out of his chair, utterly speechless. Had they—was that directed—? Good God, they were discovered, after all, and would have to flee. He kept his face absolutely still and lowered himself into his chair. "Good morning to you too, sir," Joshua said politely, and Lord Downe guffawed.

"You've startled your good painter." Lady Chalcroft tittered behind her cup of tea. "We discuss the news, Mr. Beaufort, nothing more. And such a miserable topic for over such a fine breakfast, wouldn't you say, Lord Coventry?"

"Yes, indeed." Coventry shook his head.

Cade and Ashbrook entered behind him, freshly washed and dressed, Ashbrook's eyes lighting up when he set them on Joshua.

Joshua managed a confused smile in return.

"A grim topic indeed. For who among us…" Coventry gestured expansively with his fork, "…has not sinned somehow in mind and body, hmm? As long as they hurt no one, then I see no reason for all this business with arrests and executions."

Joshua had always found the phrase "his blood ran cold" to be a dramatic exaggeration, a cliché favored by gothic writers who had little creativity of their own. In that moment, he discovered the truth of the sensation and was hard-pressed to find better words to suit.

"I fear," he began, moistening a mouth gone very dry—Cade was taking his seat on the far side of Lady Chalcroft, Ashbrook across from him beyond Downe—but his eyes were fixed on them all, "that I have not seen a paper for some days. What news are we discussing?"

"Trials and tribulations," Lady Horlock pronounced, the words rolling off her tongue with great satisfaction. "It turns out that this was an excellent time to remove from the city, for the entire thing has gone to Sodom and Gomorrah whilst we have been away. The magistrates have arrested more than thirty men for all sorts of sinful dealings, the likes of which I cannot *begin* to fathom or describe. They are all to stand trial for it." She gestured, her cup tilting dangerously in her hand.

"I had heard it was only twenty-seven," Lord Downe said, his mouth full of jam.

Cade and Ashbrook had gone very, very still. "Whereabouts was this?" Ashbrook asked, his tone a mastery of forced casual inquiry.

Lady Horlock looked at him with sharp eyes over the rims of her pince-nez, then at Joshua for a half beat too long.

"The White Swan, the paper said, up on Vere Street," Downe answered again, and Joshua knew the place he meant.

There had been clubs and molly houses in that district for decades, long before he had first made his way down to the seamier districts of London. They would presumably remain there long after he was dead and buried. The streets around Lincoln's Inn Fields boasted a number of establishments where a man could go in safety, could flirt and be flirted with, could drink and bed with friends or strangers and could forget for a few hours at a time that he was hated for it everywhere else.

And now this. *Thirty men arrested.* There would be trials next, their names and their families dragged through the quagmire, all honor stripped from them and secrets laid bare. Then would come executions, by hanging, or hours in the pillory to be beaten and cursed by finer, morally upstanding citizens.

"They harm their own immortal souls and drag the rest of us into perdition with their unnatural practices," Lady Chalcroft said airily, "bawds and procurers alike. I say it is about time. There are too many dark corners about town that could use with a good cleansing. Let the magistrates tackle Covent Garden next, and those girls who drag poor men down into a life of blasphemy and lust."

Lords Downe, Horlock and Coventry alike focused quite intently on their tea and cups of chocolate, Downe himself turning red about the ears. The conversation thankfully veered away entirely after that. By the time the girls joined them, Cade had almost found his tongue again, Ashbrook was still very quiet and Joshua's appetite had entirely fled.

How many of them did he know?

He had been so far gone from such activities for long enough; his name would never come up in interrogations. Cade and Ashbrook, on the other hand, were frequenters of such establishments—the Swan among them. While the raids meant slightly more caution on Joshua's part until the news blew over, for them it must have hit very close to home. The abstract distance he tried to keep was sickening him enough.

The few bites of bread he had managed to choke down curdled in his stomach, and Joshua excused himself as soon as he was able. Flagging down a footman was not difficult, and he pressed a coin into the young man's hand. "A paper, if you please, the most recent one from London to be found in the area." Off he went, leaving Joshua alone in the hallway with nothing but his worry to keep him company.

The paper came to Joshua quickly. He tucked it beneath his arm and hastened out-of-doors to read it in some privacy. His room had a lock but felt too confining now, too much like a prison cell. He needed the security of the breeze in his hair, the sun's heat beating down upon his shoulders and—if he was lucky—the two men who would understand his agitation.

He found them in the stables. Ashbrook stood, shadowed and still, brushing one of the horses in long, hard strokes while Cade paced and fretted, saying nothing.

"I have the paper," Joshua said by way of greeting, closing the wide door fast behind him. "Is there anyone else in here?"

Cade shook his head. "We are alone." He gulped from the glass of wine he held like a ship's lifeline clenched tightly in his fist. "Read on. What has London to say for itself?"

Ashbrook buried his hands in the horse's mane and hung on, his knuckles white. Joshua could run over, gather him up in his arms, hold him and promise to keep him safe, force Ashbrook to make the same vow to him—but he did not.

"The rumors are true," Joshua said, his heart heavy and solid as a stone inside. He flipped to the correct page and began to read from the small print there. "About eleven o'clock last Sunday evening, three separate parties of the patrol, attended by constables, were detached from Bow Street upon this service."

He skimmed ahead, the self-congratulatory notes in the text churning his stomach. He could envision the scene all too easily. Men, tired from their long day's labors at tanneries and butchers' blocks, bricklaying and store minding, gathered together for drinks and storytelling.

Once, he had been a fixture at just such events, one lover or another sprawled easily in his lap.

They would have felt free to give affection, to kiss their lovers' lips, to be greeted with amused catcalls rather than fists for daring such an unruly display. Couples would have been going up and down the back stairs to the rooms above, to lie together, rut together, explore the pleasures and secret places of each other's bodies.

Until the heavy fall of hobnail boots outside, the banging of fists on wooden doors, the screams and crashing glass, fallen lanterns, muskets and fire. And everything, everything in ashes.

"This paper says twenty-four arrested, which is better still than thirty," Joshua carried on, swallowing against the prickle of hay in his nose and the dryness in his mouth. "They are to have a hearing in two months' time, to be tried for crimes against nature and man."

"If the magistrates have no evidence," Ashbrook suggested, resting both palms flat against the horse's steady flank, "perhaps they shall all be released."

"Perhaps," Joshua replied, though it seemed unlikely. Such things had happened before. Three years ago, a hanging; four years ago, another raid; three years before that, arrests that saw three men executed. "But there is more here. Two days ago, a young man named Dickenson was convicted of sodomy with a drum boy in the guards."

"I know him," Cade interrupted. "He is younger than we are, not yet two and twenty. The same as his pretty Ganymede. They fancy themselves in love. What of them?"

"Dickenson was pilloried for it, his drummer boy hanged." The words were ashes and bile in his mouth.

Ashbrook's shoulders sagged miserably, and for a moment it looked as though he might drop to the ground under the weight of it all. He remained standing, however, and after a moment he resumed brushing. "Read on," he commanded, pale as the grave.

"They placed him in the pillory at Charing Cross," he began, paused, then carried on when neither Cade nor Ashbrook interrupted him, "where he received the most pitiless pelting from the indignant multitude, with mud, eggs, turnips and other missiles… In the course of the first ten minutes he was so completely enveloped with mud and filth that it was scarcely possible to distinguish his back from his front, and it was with the utmost difficulty that the peace officers could prevent him from being torn to pieces by the mob."

"No more," Cade snapped, his voice as quick and sharp a lash as any whip. "I'll hear no more. They were incautious.

They should have known—anyone could see that Cook and Yardly were not our friends. They were landlords who cared for nothing but coin, and the fastest way to get it." His voice cracked, broke, and he drew in a breath, put on an elegant face of uncaring, like drawing curtains across the final act of a tragedy. "And now we see the folly of trusting anyone who does not have as much as we to lose." He drained his glass and flung it, shattering the crystal against the back wall of the stables. The pieces hung in the air, a thousand broken rainbows, before falling to vanish into the dirt and scattered hay.

He turned on his heel and stormed away, slamming the doors open to the day, then closed behind him.

Ashbrook started to follow, his face dark, then stopped. He walked across the floor to join Joshua instead, sinking down to sit beside him on the hay bale.

Their sides pressed together, comforting and solid, as nothing else had been this morning, and Joshua could not stop himself from leaning over farther. There was this, at least, in a world gone entirely mad. Normal people would look at them and see nothing but evil; he could only feel desperate, clinging on to distant hope.

Ashbrook laid his arm across Joshua's back and his head upon his shoulder, his solid presence a comfort.

"Did you know them?" Joshua asked quietly after hours seemed to have drifted by.

Ashbrook nodded, and there was exhaustion laced through his voice when he replied, "Yes, though Cade knew them better. I don't understand all this hatred," he continued, not moving from Joshua's half embrace. "Unless this is our punishment for sin. Why can we not be left alone to live our lives as we choose?"

The question cut to the core of things, and Joshua closed his eyes. Pain sliced through his heart, knowing the things that were impossible. And a glimmer of hope, for the things that weren't. "In some places, we could be. England is not the sum total of the world." A different sort of image of his own future began to build itself behind Joshua's eyes, wheels already set in motion.

Ashbrook turned his face in to press his lips against Joshua's throat. "Perhaps," he sighed, his eyes closed. Joshua buried his face in Ashbrook's curls and hung on. "But it is the only one I know."

The door dragged against the dirt. His head jerked up and he looked around, only to see Sophie flying in at top speed. She had been running, her hair in disarray, and she gestured at the two of them with wild hands.

"There you are!" she proclaimed, and gave them both disgusted looks. "I've been looking for you everywhere," she addressed Joshua alone. "I told you to be careful, but do you listen? The old bat has her wind up, now that you three vanished together, and one of the scullery girls said she saw you coming down this way."

Cade was already gone, but the two of them alone together, the paper in his hand— No, it would not do at all to be found here.

"We need to run," Ashbrook said, coming to the same conclusion.

"There's no time!" Joshua could see movement and people out the window, coming down the path. "If we leave by the door they'll see us."

Ashbrook looked around, then lit up. "Then we'll have to find another way." He bolted up the ladder into the hayloft like he were a circus performer or a sailor's monkey, too rapidly for Joshua to copy.

"Here." He handed the paper to Sophie, about to try his best regardless, but the door at the far end creaked as someone pushed it open.

Sophie jammed her hands through his hair to rough it up, grabbed pieces of straw and shoved them down her bodice.

"Sophie!" he hissed, and she stomped on his foot.

Shuffling and rustling came from the hayloft, and a flash of boot gleamed in the light as Ashbrook squirreled himself away.

Sophie pressed the paper to her suddenly heaving bosom and set her eyes wide, as Downe and Lady Horlock entered the stables together. "Of course I'll…" she began breathlessly, pressing close to his body and—

What in God's name was she playing at?

"Mr. Beaufort!" Downe called out.

Sophie squeaked and jumped away from him as though she had not just been pressing herself up against his thigh like a cat in heat, "…take this message up right away, sir," she said in the breathiest, worst attempt at faking a conversation he had ever heard, glancing sidelong at Downe and Lady Horlock, and managing to blush crimson across the tops of her cheeks.

He needed to revise whatever he might have thought about her acting abilities. The girl should be on the stage full time, instead of mending Lady Horlock's linens. "Yes, thank you." He was red himself now, though not from the falseness of the scene they were apparently now committed to playing out.

"Ah, Lady Horlock, Lord Downe..." he turned his attention toward the others and Sophie, managing to look both demure and debauched simultaneously, scurried out the door under Lady Horlock's heavy glare, "...what a surprise to see you. Here."

A noise came from the hayloft that sounded suspiciously like a strangled cough.

"Apparently so." Lady Horlock turned the full force of her steely-eyed anger on him now. "Were we interrupting something, cousin?"

"I was just...er..." he was a terrible liar when put on the spot, that was what he was, "...looking at the horses. I had a thought to paint some of them, perhaps in the field, and wanted to get a look up close."

"I am confused as to how my abigail became involved. You don't need her for that."

"No," Downe said, and he was smiling with more sympathy than Joshua had ever seen on him before, "no, but she certainly brightened up the place."

"Armand happened to be passing and I asked her to take a...message for me. Up to the house."

"Honestly—" Lady Horlock drew herself up to full height, but was then interrupted herself.

"Yes, well." Downe shook his head and tut-tutted. "We shall let you get back to your…er…horses," he added, more amused than Joshua felt, certainly. "I don't suppose you've seen either Ashbrook or Cade around, have you?"

The hay rustled. Joshua froze. "Not since breakfast, my apologies." Inspiration then— "I believe Mr. Cade was heading for the gardens. But he would certainly be better able to tell you than I."

Lady Horlock drew breath to say more, but Downe caught her by the elbow and guided her toward the door. "There, you see?" he said as they left. "Nothing more exciting than what you already knew…"

The door swung closed behind them. He counted to ten, then collapsed onto the hay bale, his breath coming fast and shallow.

Up in the hayloft, Ashbrook let out a string of sneezes.

"I am starting to hate that woman," Joshua said with feeling.

Ashbrook slid back down the ladder, straw in his hair and a smile on his face that wasn't there ten minutes ago. "You're terrible at that," he informed Joshua, and what was there to do but laugh?

Joshua shook his head ruefully.

"I had no idea what she was going to do," he confessed. "I suppose we should be grateful that it worked. This time." Because they would not be able to pull off that kind of trick again.

"I am," Ashbrook said firmly, and he sank his fingers into Joshua's hair and pressed his lips in a tender, closemouthed kiss. "Now, check me over," he requested, brushing straw from his trousers and shaking his head to settle his hair. "I cannot have straw about me if I'm supposed to have been walking the gardens with Cade."

"We'll have to be more circumspect." Dreadful, terrible, awful thought. But necessary. "At least for the next little while."

Ashbrook seemed more hopeful, watching the door with careful eyes as Joshua straightened his clothing a little more diligently than was perhaps called for. "This will settle," he said, more wistful than sure. "It always does. And then we can go back to being as we were."

"Perhaps." Joshua finished, and tended to his own repairs. "I shall leave first; they know I was here. You follow in ten minutes, as long as the coast is clear." He hesitated, Ashbrook's face still pale and his eyes rimmed with a hint of red.

Joshua cupped his cheek, rubbed his thumb over Ashbrook's lips in an unspoken promise, then turned and left. Before he did or said something that he was going to regret.

"You're ridiculous," he told Sophie later as they passed in the hallway.

"And you're still alive," she retorted, her jaw set. "It's worth a little ridiculous."

She had a point.

A few days passed with no more bad news, only watchful eyes following their movements. Slowly, with every report of another man released for lack of evidence, Joshua's temper and his nerves began to ease. He kept his careful distance from the other men during meals and after dinners, balancing that out with his desire not to have any new distance remarked upon.

If Cade found himself making a fourth for cards more often than not, however, while Ashbrook instructed one of the girls at the pianoforte or was prevailed upon to play for dancing, and Joshua spent his time at spillikins or silhouettes…that was the beauty of good company and a house party. There were always so many clever diversions to choose from.

Night followed night, and there were no more murmured invitations.

On the seventh day, Joshua stood on the terrace and stared out at the setting sun, the soothing wash of oranges and reds not as much a balm to the nerves as they should have been.

"Would you be content with your paint box, a cottage and an endless parade of different sunsets?"

"But give me the company of one beloved friend, and a village with a good tavern not too far away, and I would say you had described paradise."

Now, though, he should add "freedom from the magistrates" to that list.

His heart ached.

A scuff, a cough, and Joshua turned, his heart palpitating wildly in his chest at the sight. Ashbrook stood there, ill at ease, silhouetted, in the doorway, by the firelight behind.

"I am sorry," he said quietly. "I didn't realize there was anyone out here."

"No matter." Joshua shook his head. There was a great deal that still needed to be said, but this was not the time. They needed to be prudent, at least for a little while longer. "I was about to return indoors; you may take your ease in as much solitude as you desire."

Ashbrook made a soft noise and strode two long steps onto the terrace, to where he would be hidden from viewers inside by the pillars. "Please," he said quickly and quietly, "I know there is good reason for it, but promise me this separation will not be forever."

The words seared themselves into Joshua's mind, burned themselves there, where he could stop and examine them and turn them over like precious pearls whenever he so delighted.

"I miss you. I wager Cade does as well." From the laughter rolling out of the room behind them, that seemed less likely.

"And I you," he murmured, his best reward the way Ashbrook lit up when he said it. Utterly impulsively, his heart riding roughshod over his better judgment, he said, "Not tonight—the party is too wild, will go too late, and sleep will be too light for most. Tomorrow?" *Please, one more time before this all falls to pieces.*

"Tomorrow," Ashbrook agreed. He headed for the railing, but as he passed, he reached out with one finger to stroke the passing palm of Joshua's hand.

The line seared him, burned him and left him weak, attached an invisible cord to him that would tether them together for eternity.

That, or Joshua was a hopeless romantic who fully deserved any mockery he received, now or at a later date.

"Good night," he said as he headed back inside. *Good night.*

It did not begin as well as one would hope.

Cade was in a fierce mood from the moment Ashbrook opened the door to Joshua's knock. He lounged again upon the settee, his trousers on and nothing else, a glass of brandy in his hand. No greeting came from his direction, though his eyes ranged down the length of Joshua's body and then away, as though finding him wanting.

Ashbrook's enthusiasm was not feigned, at least, his hands on Joshua as soon as the door was closed and locked fast behind him. His banyan and shirt ended up thrown across the back of one of the chairs, Ashbrook's hands sliding hot across his naked chest.

His mouth was slick and sweet, and Joshua chased the hot flare of brandy across his lips. "You've begun without me."

Ashbrook only rubbed his rough cheek against Joshua's freshly shaven one. "Then you shall have to hurry and catch up."

That was no hardship. Joshua cupped Ashbrook's face in both his hands, drew his thumbs slowly along the pushed-out pout of his lower lip, then settled them along the strong line of his jaw. Ashbrook's evening stubble pricked roughly against his fingers, the flat plane of his chest pressed up against Joshua's, and everything about him was firm, hard and beautiful. Joshua kissed him, pressed his mouth against Ashbrook's and traded a breath back and forth between them.

Ashbrook's eyes were always dark, but now they were even darker, gone black with desire. He kissed Joshua back, hands tangling strong in Joshua's hair.

Until another pair of hands snaked between them, fumbling first with Ashbrook's fall front and then with Joshua's, Joshua had forgotten that Cade was even there.

They stumbled to Ashbrook's bedroom, leaving trousers and stockings in untidy piles on the floor. Cade pressed Ashbrook back, then, more surprisingly, pulled Joshua in to meet him. The lamp burned low in the room, turning the white bedclothes a dusky gold, and Cade maneuvered all three of them back toward the bed with strong and determined hands.

Joshua went, his cock hard and caught between his and Cade's stomachs. The back of his knees hit the edge of the mattress and he sat, the mattress sinking behind him as Ashbrook joined Cade and him from the other side.

Cade held his face in both hands and kissed him, slid his tongue between Joshua's lips. Joshua opened to him, kissed him back with equal force. Ashbrook knelt behind him, the heat of his body warming Joshua's back better than any fire, molten lava in the push of his prick against Joshua's spine. His hands moved across Joshua's chest, circling and pinching his nipples, tugging at them one at a time with the pads of his fingers.

Sensation curled through him, the heady taste of brandy on Cade's lips, the insistent thrusting of his tongue that mimicked everything Joshua wanted elsewhere. His cock hardened fully, rose up, begging to be touched, mouthed, stroked with firm and unrelenting pressure.

He ignored it, his hips twitching where he sat with the insistent urge to seek out friction. Joshua turned, instead, reached out a hand to grasp Ashbrook's prick. He gasped as Joshua stroked two fingers between his spread thighs, around his balls and up the length of his shaft. Joshua seized it and pumped it quickly, Ashbrook's foreskin sliding easily over the head, slick with the first drops of precome.

And then for the second—but Cade was not yet hard. His prick hung warm and thick with some sign of arousal, but dangled between his legs as though they were not all naked, all beautiful, all desperately reaching for some signs of affection in a world gone absolutely mad.

"Come here," Ashbrook said, his voice thick with lust, and he let go of Joshua to reach for Cade. He took Cade's prick in hand even as Joshua stroked *him*. Ashbrook bent to set his mouth to Cade's tip. His tongue licked out and around the head as Joshua watched, those wicked brown eyes flashing up at Joshua as though to say, *See? I perform for you.*

Joshua watched, untouched, breathless and aching, his hand stilled for a moment on Ashbrook's prick. Ashbrook sucked just the half-covered head of Cade's cock between his lips. Ashbrook swirled his tongue around the thickness of it, pink and wanton, flicked the tip of his tongue across the crown.

Joshua's hand tightened on Ashbrook's cock and Ashbrook bucked into his hand. Cade seized Ashbrook's hair in his fist and Cade hissed air out between his teeth, his hips rocking up to thrust deeper into Ashbrook's mouth.

Ashbrook pulled away a minute later, Cade's now-hard prick slipping from between his lips with a wet popping noise. Ashbrook turned, his eyes alight, and he tackled Joshua down to the bed, straddling his hips. His prick stood proud between them, thick and with a vein that pulsed along the bottom. He was so perfectly proportioned as to be unreal, his muscled thighs holding him poised above Joshua as though he was about to sit on his cock with no other preparation, a notion both terrible and divine all at once.

The mattress dipped again as Cade rejoined them, his hands rough and less eager than they were angry. He pulled at Ashbrook until he was sitting back on his heels, his lips parted and his weight resting on his arms, then slid a hand between his legs to press two oiled fingers between the cleft of his buttocks. Ashbrook jerked up, stiffened, his erection softening slightly as Cade fingered him. Cade himself was flagging again, his prick back down to half-mast.

"Does something ail you, Cade?" Joshua asked, and he took Cade's cock in hand. It was a goodly size, of excellent vigor, and he had never before lost his nerve when they were in bed together.

Joshua stroked him experimentally, felt blood rush in to heat and stiffen Cade's prick once more.

But then the same dark storm cloud settled low over Cade's fine features. He pulled away and sat back. "I am well enough, thank you," he snapped.

"I think not," Ashbrook replied, all concern, and reached out for Cade's hand.

"Enough," Cade barked, and Ashbrook flinched. Cade stood, taking himself to the edge of the bed and then descending to the floor in a step that looked too easy. "I am done here. Continue on without me."

Ashbrook rose to his knees, all confusion, and Joshua sagged back against the pillows in defeat.

"Evander!" Ashbrook pleaded, which was demeaning in and of itself, not even considering the person to whom it was addressed—and the one doing the addressing. "Please."

Trousers and one stocking retrieved, and his cock flaccid, Cade scowled at them both. "Glut yourselves on carnal urges; I have better things to do." The door to the sitting room slammed shut behind him; then another muffled thud announced the slamming of his bedroom door.

Ridiculous, petulant child! How much would it have cost him to allow them this? And now Ashbrook would follow, and that was that—one final chance and now it was over.

Ashbrook groaned, brushed his sweat-damp hair out of his eyes and rose to his feet to go after Cade.

Joshua grabbed for his arm instead, pulled Ashbrook down to lie on top of him, chest to chest and hip to hip.

Ashbrook resisted, looked at the door, but one more gentle tug at his hand ended his show of reluctance. He sagged his weight down against Joshua's body and allowed Joshua to wrap his arms close around him.

His head rested under Joshua's chin, his cheek cushioned on Joshua's chest, and his legs between Joshua's thighs, where Joshua'd let his knees fall open. Ashbrook's weight was a comfort, thick and solid, pressing him safely down into the sheets.

His tongue darted out to taste Joshua's nipple and trace a gentle wet circle on the surrounding skin. He mouthed at it once, twice, their hips rolling together in an easy and instinctive motion.

"He's ridiculous," Ashbrook said, his words partly muffled against Joshua's chest. His cock caught on the edge of Joshua's hip, then slid up and over the skin, and back down.

All that Joshua had ever wanted was here, in this slow glide of bodies, Ashbrook's stomach a glorious source of pressure.

"He is," Joshua conceded, gasping softly. Ashbrook rolled his hips in that same precise way again, grinding his hipbone against Joshua's gold ring. "Do not give in to his tantrums or we shall never hear the end of it."

Ashbrook groaned, pushing himself up to kiss Joshua, slowly and desperately thoroughly. "What would you have me do instead?"

Joshua flattened his hands and ran them down over Ashbrook's back, cupping and kneading his gloriously round buttocks. "I intend to follow his instructions and sate myself with fucking. Say you'll join me?"

Ashbrook laughed, rolled his hips in a circle so that he almost impaled himself upon Joshua's fingers and nodded his assent. "How would you have me, then?" he asked, and the weight in that question—in the opportunities in their solitude—suddenly struck home.

Ashbrook forever played the boy in their games, on his stomach or his knees, taking Cade and Joshua's cocks in his arse or mouth, with groans of pleasure and desire. But now, here, there was only the two of them—no rules, no old habits and no overseer.

"Any way that pleases you, and as often as pleases you," Joshua promised in the abstract, and he locked his mouth to Ashbrook's.

Ashbrook wriggled inelegantly, his cock bouncing against Joshua's, which startled a laugh out of Joshua. "You please me," he said with a grin.

Joshua put his hands to Ashbrook's chest and pushed him up to sitting, slid his own legs out from underneath. His prick protested at the loss of the pressure and the heat, the delicious friction that had him pearling liquid at the tip and yearning.

"Here," Joshua suggested, and he straddled Ashbrook's crossed legs. He slid down until he was sitting on Ashbrook's muscled thighs, their cocks in line, side by each, and pressed snugly between their stomachs. His hands went around to cup the back of Ashbrook's head, his feet tucked securely beneath Ashbrook's knees.

His mouth yielded when Joshua leaned in to claim it, opening for him like a flower. He tasted sweeter than the finest wine, of brandy and the heady flavor of musk, hints of Cade's own particular taste lingering from when Ashbrook had licked and sucked him.

The remembered image ripped a groan from Joshua's throat—Ashbrook on his knees, Cade's prick thrusting between his lips, gleaming and red.

Bucking up against Ashbrook's cock and belly relieved some of the desperately mounting urge for pressure, but it was nowhere near enough. He sagged back, his breath coming heavily and quickly, and Ashbrook met his eyes.

He too was laughing breathlessly, his hands clenching tightly around Joshua's hips and buttocks. Ashbrook slipped his fingers farther around, skimming across the hot skin of Joshua's arse, circling his hole, ever closer and closer.

He pressed the pad of his thumb down across the entrance, not sliding inside.

Joshua writhed and jerked, pushing backward to get more of that pressure and sensation.

"You like that." Ashbrook laughed and caught Joshua's lower lip with his teeth. He bit down, just hard enough to make it sting, then released him and kissed him so deeply that Joshua lost his breath.

"I do," Joshua gasped out, and, attempting to still the rocking of his hips, was utterly fruitless.

More—he needed more than just this teasing game. He needed Ashbrook beneath him, or above him, mouth, hands, arse, cock inside him, anything!

Ashbrook rocked with him, sliding his prick along the slick already beginning to gather on their stomachs. One hand continued to play around his arse, the other between his legs, stroking him and cupping his balls. "And I like this as well."

There was precious little space between their bodies, but there was enough to work his hand between them. Ashbrook paused long enough to give Joshua a quizzical look, one which vanished when Joshua wrapped his hand around both of their pricks together. He stroked up, catching his thumb just under the ridge of Ashbrook's cockhead.

Ashbrook moaned in response, pressing his mouth against Joshua's throat. There was the sting of teeth; then he sucked at the spot, passing over it with the flat of his tongue. Ashbrook thrust up furiously into Joshua's hand, their pricks sliding against each other and through the circle of Joshua's calloused fingers.

"I am surprised you are not a musician, sir..." Ashbrook gasped and laughed at the same time, gripping Joshua's hips and holding him steady, "...for you play me like your instrument."

Joshua groaned and shook his head, for there was a light in Ashbrook's eyes not entirely attributable to the way his cock slid, faster now and faster, between Joshua's fingers. He rocked up, himself, squeezing his legs tight round Ashbrook's thighs to give himself purchase.

"That is a terrible line," he advised, uninterested in hiding his smile. "I am surprised you have any prospects at all, never mind two, if that is your best approach."

"I have worse," Ashbrook teased back. "And no need for better, because from all appearances, I have won." One hand remained on Joshua's hip, still holding him firm, and the other Ashbrook brought between them. He fit his fingers between Joshua's around their pricks, holding them both in a grip so tight that Joshua's entire body trembled with the pleasure of it.

They stroked together, fingers laced through each other's, pumping their cocks with fierce determination. Joshua kissed him, thrust his tongue into Ashbrook's mouth with the rhythm of their bodies, sucked and bit at his lip, desperate and wanton.

"Please," Ashbrook begged, and Joshua ran his thumb over the head of Ashbrook's cock, dipped down into the slit and then around the ridge.

His reaction was electric, a pink-red flush running down his cheeks and throat to color his chest as well.

Joshua looked down between their bodies and the sight of it—oh, torture and bliss! Their swollen and wet pricks vanished into their fists, the purple-red heads reappearing over and again. Ashbrook's cock pressed hard against his. The slick, solid length of it slid against the base of Joshua's, the head bumping hard and hot against the ring looped through the crown of his.

It was too much, too much!

Ashbrook squeezed their hands tighter on the upstroke and Joshua was gone, his balls drawing up and fire exploding outward from the very base of his spine.

His release spurted, white and thick, over their hands. Ashbrook flung back his head and laughed with delight as he dragged their hands and his prick through the mess.

Joshua ran his tongue along the prickly line of his throat, bit down at the soft place where it joined Ashbrook's shoulder. Ashbrook's entire body jolted and froze. He made a noise like a sobbing moan, one Joshua had never heard before, and then he too was coming, his emissions joining Joshua's in hot ropes over their hands, stomachs and thighs.

They stayed like that for a moment, Joshua seated in Ashbrook's lap, one hand cupping the back of his head and the other laced around their slowly softening pricks.

Ashbrook held on tightly, his one hand entwined with Joshua's, his other dug fast into Joshua's hip. Their chests rose and fell together as they fought for breath, Ashbrook's forehead gleaming with a sheen of sweat.

Joshua tipped his head forward and rested his forehead against Ashbrook's, skin pressed against skin.

Ashbrook kissed him and slowly untangled his hand from around their cocks. Joshua's muscles sagged, exhaustion taking hold, and they tumbled sideways to land on the bed in a heap of sweaty and sticky limbs.

A bowl and jug rested on the side table, a cloth beside them, and Joshua stretched out, brushing the edge of it with his fingertips. Another inch—there, he had it, damp and cool against his fingers. He cleaned them both, and Ashbrook blithely dropped the cloth off the side of the bed, to be dealt with at some other time.

He settled between Joshua's thighs, his head resting on Joshua's chest, and there he stayed, pressing tender kisses along Joshua's ribs.

"Thank you," Joshua murmured, and Ashbrook's lips echoed the words against Joshua's skin.

Joshua slid his hand into Ashbrook's hair and stroked his head gently. He traced the edge of Ashbrook's ear, the tendon along the side of his throat, the rises and valleys of his spine.

Ashbrook found his free hand and took it, closing his fingers between Joshua's and holding tight.

Joshua bent his knee and set his foot among the bedclothes. He caged Ashbrook between them, his own precious thing.

Ashbrook buried his face in Joshua's chest and wrapped his arms tightly about him.

This would not, could not, last. The world outside still hated them, and Cade's tantrum would no doubt have its own repercussions.

Worst of all, before the sun rose, he would have to be gone—back to his own room, the four posts standing as silent sentinels over a cold and empty bed.

No. He would not allow himself to consider that now. There might be trouble coming, but for this single moment, all was contentment, satiation and peace.

Surely they deserved that much.

Chapter Eleven

Beaufort was gone by the time Stephen struggled into solitary wakefulness. Only the rumpled and dirty sheets suggested that anything but quiet slumber had taken place; those, the cloth on the floor and the lingering scent of him impressed into Stephen's skin. He rose to wash and dress, sorting the chamber into something resembling respectability. If the servants chose to believe he'd brought a girl in the previous night, so be it. Sweat, after all, was sweat.

The day dawned bright and cheerful, but an anchor wrapped chains around Stephen's heart. The distraction of carnal bodies could only last so long.

Every name in the newssheet had a face he remembered. Each one had been a friend or a former lover to a friend—laughing, joyful boys and men who would be forever tarnished now by rumor, gossip and hate.

He had lain with some of them in the past, with Whittington and with Tanner, their bodies thickly muscled and tinted golden by the sun. He'd cheered Evander on as he'd taken Ellis's member into his mouth and tried— ultimately in vain—to encompass the monster in its entirety, sung lewd ballads over pots of ale with Colchester while Yardly filled their plates with stew and good brown bread.

Yardly and Cook had turned traitor. It was impossible to believe of their two jovial innkeepers, but the records surely didn't lie. They had turned their backs on the men who had put faith in them, pled guilty to maintaining a bawdy house, and now a body that Stephen had admired in all its youthful perfection swung on the gallows, to be picked at by crows.

Stephen's gut overturned and he lunged for the chamber pot, his stomach thankfully empty but for bile. He rinsed his mouth when the retching finally ceased, his eyes watering and his stomach cramped tightly in sailors' knots.

Evander. If ever he needed comfort and loving arms about him it was now. Evander would chide him, call him ridiculous, make him understand just how little his fears actually meant in the grand scheme of things. And then perhaps he would put his arms about Stephen and hold him as Beaufort had the night before. Just long enough to make the shaking stop.

His knock on Evander's door received no answer. He called out, knocked again, his arms wrapping back around his unhappy gut to hold himself upright. This time Evander answered with a low and angry grumble. "I'm asleep."

"Obviously not, or you would not be answering." Stephen waited a few minutes more; perhaps once he was more fully awake…

It was not to be. While Stephen was reasonably certain the door was unlocked, barging in to demand attention was not the sort of action that would end well. Resting his forehead against the cool solidity of the wall helped, some.

He stumbled back to his own room instead of waiting any longer. He was weak, weak and foolish to feel things so deeply. How could he help it, though? How could Evander sleep peacefully, knowing what would be waiting for them when they returned home?

He fumbled with his waistcoat and frock instead, tied a cravat about his neck and pinched his cheeks to rid himself of the pallor of the grave. Company would do him better than brooding alone, thinking about a hundred things he could not change.

If Evander could not be a comfort, at least he had Beaufort.

Or not.

Beaufort was at breakfast, true, but his formal bearing and rigid back did little to encourage Stephen to approach. He nodded, made a small smile, so utterly at odds with his affectionate demeanor from the night before that Stephen had to remind himself forcefully of the kind of peril they all faced. He, like Evander, was no doubt doing as he felt best to protect them all.

The topics at breakfast seemed to have moved on entirely from perversion and arrests to hunting and riding, subjects about which Stephen was only marginally prepared to add anything of value. He spent most of the casual meal observing.

Coventry's high spirits and Miss Talbot's easy laughter made for bubbling contrast to Lady Chalcroft and Lady Horlock's murmured conversations. Evander surrounded himself with the remaining young ladies and bucks, holding court of his own down at the far end of the table, and all around Stephen the world hung in a state of enforced and brittle gaiety.

Stephen rode out with the men that day. Beaufort, as was his habit, did not. The heat had abated a little, replaced with a clean, fresh breeze, and Coventry had found him a docile enough horse that did not seem prone to throwing either shoes or riders. He carried a gun but found excuse not to shoot it; Evander's hands were less valuable than his own in case of a misfire, after all.

Evander did not speak a single word to him on the ride back, despite the three birds tied to his saddle horn. Stephen probably deserved it.

His bed was empty that night; his dreams were dark and ringed in fire.

Stephen was being punished, though Evander refused to tell him his current sin. Given the mood he was in, it could have been anything.

It was easier to assume that Evander was more disturbed by the news than he had let on, Stephen decided four days later, with both his lovers still distant.

Evander spoke little with Stephen and never to Beaufort. He rode out with Coventry and his friends instead, or whiled away the evening hours paying court to the debutantes.

Did Stephen honestly have the right to feel upset? Evander was a tender soul, after all, and such things struck him very deeply. He teased Stephen for his sensitivity and moods, traits that he always seemed to regard as an intensely personal failing, but he was no less easily bruised. Stephen rather liked it.

Men could be just as passionate about life as women, if not more so, and to allow people to touch the depths of your soul was a precious thing. So Stephen liked to think, anyway. Evander would snap out of it, given time. In the end, everything would once again be as it was, despite the vast expanses of cold sheets on either side of Stephen in his large and empty bed.

The door to the suite closed. Stephen sat up in that bed and frowned, but no other sounds followed. His banyan hung on the bedpost and he drew it close around himself, padding quietly out into the sitting room. Dare he hope that Beaufort had come? Even now he could be waiting, his arms open—

He had not and was not, and when Stephen knocked softly at Evander's door, there was no response. He had to open it, sure again that Evander would be sleeping, his blond hair tousled across the pillow in golden disarray.

The bed was empty.

Stephen headed back to his own room, more troubled than when he rose. He dragged the armchair closer to the banked fire and settled himself in it, wrapping his counterpane around himself. He would sit up, wait for Evander to return, in case there had been some trouble. Had something happened elsewhere in the house? Perhaps

Evander would need his assistance, and it would be better if he was already awake and ready to be of help.

Shackles clapped around his ankles, he shuffled forward through the mud. More mud splattered on the side of his face, the cold, wet slime dribbling down into his shirt collar.

The crowd jeered and yelled.

"Sodomite!"

"Catamite!"

"Arse boy and whore! How many do you bend over for?"

Stephen woke with a gasp, the sunlight that streamed across his room through the gap in his curtains cutting across his closed eyes. Faint images of a dream flickered around in the back of his mind and then were gone, only a faint sense of troubled sleep lingering behind to plague him. Where was he and what happened?

Memory filtered back slowly as he struggled into consciousness, his eyes sandy and his mind in a fog. He sat in the armchair by the fire in his room, his bedclothes in disarray and his banyan puddled on the floor before him. One corner stuck through the grate and he yanked it back away from the coals. No singes or scorch marks there to betray his clumsiness, thank God!

Evander's bed had been empty last night. He had sat up to wait—

And fallen asleep.

It was a very good thing that he had never been hired on as a night watchman because he had done a piss-poor job of the whole thing. He struggled free of the counterpane wrapped around his legs and the chair.

No one was in the sitting room, and he had a flash of memory of making this same trip in the darkness. He rapped on Evander's door, once, twice, and this time was greeted with a groan.

"Are you up?" Stephen called. "May I enter?"

Both were answered in the affirmative. Evander sprawled across his bed in nothing but his shirt; golden hair tumbled down around his face. His eyes were bleary from interrupted sleep, and he flinched when Stephen reached out to caress his stubble-rough cheek.

Stephen leaned in to press a kiss to Evander's lips. It stayed chaste and gentle, and Evander pulled away without further encouragement.

"I trust you slept well?" Evander asked, showing no interest in the answer.

"Well enough," Stephen answered, and there was something in Evander's eyes that he did not like, a set to his jaw that suggested—what, he was unsure—but there had to be a reason for it. "I am troubled with bad dreams," he admitted. If he were open, perhaps Evander would be inspired to do the same.

"They will pass," Evander promised, his eyes flickering to the door. He squeezed Stephen's hand and brought it down from his face, all the while with a smile that did not reach his eyes.

"Have yours?" Stephen asked, no longer interested in dancing about the issue. "I heard you leave the room last night—did you need wine to help you sleep?" There were better solutions that he could suggest, certainly that he had applied many times before and could help bridge the chasm forming between them.

"Leave?" Evander's brow furrowed and he blinked twice in succession, his brows all up and innocent. "Not I."

"I heard the door, and then your bed was empty." Stephen began to explain himself, then stopped.

Evander was toying with him, perhaps, and now he would admit that he had, in fact, been caught.

"I was in the suite all night," Evander said instead, and with such powerful confidence in what he said that Stephen was hard-pressed to disbelieve it. Except that he had seen with his own eyes— "You must have been dreaming."

And that… No, he had not been. He remembered it too clearly, the feel of the floor under his bare feet, the doorknob in his hand, the drag of the armchair across the floor to place himself before the fire when he returned.

"You said yourself that you are being disturbed by nightmares, dear heart." Evander interrupted his train of thought as it began to whirl, pressing one of Stephen's hands between his own. "Let them not trouble you in the daylight. I know I have seemed uncaring of late—it is only because everyone's suspicions have been aroused." He seemed to be reading Stephen's mind, the lines of his palm, and seeing the truths written there. "I am concerned for all of our safety."

It could have been a dream, couldn't it? Stephen had imagined himself lying awake when he heard the door shut, but, then, might that not *also* have been a dream? He remembered flashes of dark images before and after, those ones indistinct and not at all like the memory of crossing their rooms. But dreams took different forms and changed one moment to the next. How could he be sure?

His own mind was a tangled mess, thick from lack of sleep—or, perhaps, disturbing dreams and sleepwalking—and the only thing certain was Evander's hand in his.

"A dream, yes," he agreed, only half believing it. "Of course. And I understand. I do not have to like it, but I understand. And once we are home again, and safe," he added for good measure, "we shall have to make up for all the time we are now losing."

"Of course," Evander agreed too easily. He dropped Stephen's hand and stood, dipping his own hands into the bowl of water on the nightstand.

"I will leave you to dress." Stephen rose, his heart lighter than it had been, but his mind far more troubled. If he was mistaking dreams for something real—or so unsure of his own mind that he was allowing himself to be convinced that reality was no such thing—what then could he do to save himself? "And see you at breakfast."

Another beautiful day dwindled into late afternoon, the sun making her lazy way down the clear-blue arc of the sky. The conservatory could only hold Stephen so long, and he found himself wandering the corridors of the house once more. His footsteps fell quietly in the upstairs rooms, most of the guests at play elsewhere and the staff carrying out their duties with reverent silence.

It was too much, too quiet, too heavy and stately and still. He needed the tavern with its laughter, the chaos of the city streets, the market and music shop and all the things that sang to him of life and joy. He clattered down the main stairs, but turned away from the front door.

The kitchen door was directly to his right and he took it instead, no footman here to watch everyone's comings and goings. A block of cheese and a hunk of bread came easily enough to hand again, with a giggle from a scullery maid, and soon he was out the servant's exit and into the orange and gold light of late afternoon in the kitchen yard.

Beaufort was here.

Stephen refused to allow his pulse to do anything so trite as skip. His gut clenched, instead, in an entirely unwelcome and unforeseen way. What was wrong with him? Until now, until this, his mood had never been so dependent on the presence or absence of another, and now Beaufort had become the arbiter of his joys, just as Evander—

That was a dangerous line of thinking, and he would not travel down it.

Beaufort was not alone, either, that lady's maid bowing her head close to his in intimate conversation. They did not touch, not until she laid a hand upon his arm and nodded toward where Stephen stood, his hands full of bread and cheese. Beaufort said something else and Armand nodded, then slowly departed, casting a long and knowing look at Stephen as she did so.

"Mr. Ashbrook," she said coolly as she passed. Her stare unsettled him, reaching right through his eyes and taking note of every flaw she found.

By the time he had even begun to consider a reply, she was gone, the kitchen door closing behind her.

Beaufort stood and watched him, hands clasped behind his back, his spine straight and formal as any parading soldier.

"Good day to you," Stephen said loudly enough for any passing observer.

"And to you." Beaufort nodded, and as Stephen got closer, he could see Beaufort's eyes without shadows to block them. They were dark, a sea during a thunderstorm, with bags underneath as though he had not slept. Was he also afflicted by nightmares and dreams of faces he might never see again? "On your way somewhere?" he asked politely, his eyes flickering to Stephen's hat, his coat and the provisions in his hands.

Drawing within arm's reach, Stephen glanced at the house. No curtain twitched to suggest a hidden observer. "I am off to wander the woods in search of peace of mind," he admitted candidly. "Will you take a turn with me?"

Beaufort hesitated, his lower lip curling to sit between his teeth. "I cannot," he said after a minute, his rejection sounding reluctant. That was a foolish thing to pin his hopes on—a sound in a voice—but it was something. "I am to meet Lady Chalcroft soon to discuss plans for a portrait of her daughter. Work, you understand."

"Of course." *No,* he wanted to say. *No, I need you, your company, your advice. I need to know that the world will make sense once we leave this place. We are all bleeding and pretending that we are whole.* "I understand completely." He mouthed the polite words instead, and something inside him curdled, curled small and died. "I'll not take more of your time."

He walked away quickly, before Beaufort could call out to him, if he even cared to, and refused with all his strength to take even the smallest look back. Birds sang high in the treetops and the grass was green underfoot, a verdant lawn that gave way to twigs and a compressed dirt path as the thicket grew thicker and the forest enveloped him.

Honestly! He was being a child. They had another fortnight in the house, by Coventry's original invitation, and anything at all could be survived for two measly weeks. Then they would be out from under the watchful eye of society matrons and lords, and Evander would relax. Perhaps they could even keep correspondence with Beaufort and arrange to see him again at some later date, when they would not be so closely observed.

Yes, that was the way to think about it—a temporary inconvenience. He and Evander had faced obstacles greater than this in their lives together so far. This would go down in their shared memories as a summer of tragedy and almost-tragedy.

Because—and this was where his breath caught and his heart ached desperately—if they had not come to the country house, then the chances were very good that they would have been there, at the Swan, with the others. Their friends who had *died*, or who now languished in cells, while he and Evander sat in luxury, their only concern not being discovered by the chambermaids.

A wave of nausea swept up and over him again. Stephen dropped down to sit on a fallen log and put his head between his knees, breathing deeply. He kept his bread and cheese in his stomach, this time, but it was a near thing. *Foolish, weak boy! You are safe. What have* you *got to be upset about?*

Feet crunching through leaves made him sit upright again and run his hands through his hair to try and remove any evidence of his failure of nerves. His sour face and the dark circles beneath his eyes he could do little about. Who was it? Coventry or Downe? One of the servants? Armand, perhaps, come to threaten him again for endangering Beaufort's reputation and forcing her to put her own on the line.

It was none of those.

Beaufort himself appeared from behind a tree, trudging up the path and casting about in both directions as though looking for something. Or someone. Not discovered yet, Stephen stood, and Beaufort's hesitant smile when he caught sight of him was enough to dispel some of the anger and pain.

"You found time for a walk after all," Stephen called out, hands in his pockets, and he waited for Beaufort to come abreast with him along the narrow trail.

"I did." Beaufort spread his arms, a sketchbook tucked beneath one and a roll of pencils in his back pocket. "As you see, it occurred to me that the weather might turn in the next few days, and I should make sure to get all my outdoors sketching done before any rains begin."

"Clever."

"I thought so." Beaufort spread out his coattails and perched himself on Stephen's fallen log, his sketch pad on his knee. "And if I happen to come upon an amiable companion and engage him in conversation while I do so, well..." he hesitated, as though convincing himself more than anyone else, "...so be it."

Stephen sat again, keeping a foot of distance or so between them. Beaufort's hands played over the page when he opened his book, charcoal-smudged fingers tracing the grain of the paper. Beaufort looked down, his hair too short to do anything but curl forward slightly around the shells of his ears, and it would be so simple to reach out, reach out and run his own finger—or the tip of his tongue—along that same pink edge, brush his hair back, taste the heady musk of his throat and mouth.

Beaufort drew out his pencils and began to sharpen one, casting a sidelong glance at Stephen. His lips parted, full, fair and fine, but he said nothing. He dropped his head and looked back down at his carving.

"Armand is an interesting girl," Stephen said, because if he stared at Beaufort's clever hands much longer without other distraction, he was going to end up on his knees, drawing Beaufort's fingers into his mouth and suckling as though they were his cock. Not so helpful in present circumstances.

"That she is," Beaufort replied neutrally, but his eyes dropped to Stephen's mouth and lingered there, his gaze burning, for three seconds longer than Stephen could bear.

"*Are* you and she...?" he asked the question, more to distract himself than anything else, with visions of Beaufort bedding another. *Perhaps that would be enough to slice you out of my mind.*

Beaufort, much to his regret and joy, shook his head. "No." He followed Stephen's gaze, then shrugged lightly. "There are many who take pleasure in both the male and female of the species. I am not one of them, except on purely aesthetic grounds. Women's curves do very well for gathering light and shadow in interesting ways."

He sketched as he spoke, the trees resolving themselves into columns that twisted and marched across the page. A few quick marks outlined the squirrel, now sitting on a high branch and telling them off with faint chitters and squeaks. "Have you ever?"

"Bedded a girl?" In any other company Stephen would have had to laugh, make some sly and knowing remark that would paint him as more experienced than he was. "There's nothing wrong with girls; I've known one or two. The risks are different, of course, and I've no interest in being a father. Though I suppose," he laughed, "better that than imprisonment."

"Jail may only last a fortnight," Beaufort said, and his wide mouth quirked up at the corners. "Fatherhood is a life sentence."

"Indeed. One that some men are better suited for than others." What next? Tell Beaufort how, these days, his thoughts only turned to him? That his heart leapt at the sight of him coming through the trees? Where had his sense of self-preservation gone? It had flown free the moment Beaufort had appeared again, seeking him out above all others. *Him.* "Though while I've shared pleasure with their bodies, I've never felt for any girl the way my heart beats for—"

"For Cade," Beaufort interrupted.

Yes, Stephen would have said if Beaufort had asked that only four weeks ago. Now he paused, tasted around the edges of the thought. The shadows played over Beaufort's face, the hints of red the light brought out in his strawberry-blond hair, the spot at the back of his neck that made him harder than iron when Stephen bit and licked at it.

He finished his sentence a different way. "For the solemn beauty of men."

When Beaufort looked at him, when his mouth and eyes smiled together and his eyes were the soft gray of a cloudy, early morning sky, it only added more proof to something that he already knew.

When Stephen checked to be sure they were alone, then leaned in and kissed him, he was sure. The words bounced around in his fevered brain as Beaufort's lips— soft, dry, an addiction sweeter than strong drink or laudanum—played under his.

I need you.

And oh God, *thank* God that Evander liked him too.

It would be a good thing for all of them, Stephen decided, staring at his own face in his mirror as he attempted to tie his cravat, if they went to bed together again. It had been more than a week since the news had broken about the raid at the White Swan, since Evander had stormed out of bed unsatisfied. Let them have one more night, to sate themselves on each other. A chance to release a little tension would do everyone a world of good.

Assuming, of course, that Evander would speak to him for long enough to hear him out. He had developed the habit of having something else pressing to do at any given moment, and, frankly, it was getting ridiculous. One would think they really were only colleagues, and newly acquainted ones at that, rather than men who had first sucked and fucked each other when they were barely out of school.

The house hovered in that odd state between silence and chaos, in the gloaming after the day's activities and before the bell rang to call them all to table. The women would be off primping and preparing, pinching their cheeks and setting their curls. Coventry would be closed in his study with his letters, as he always was this time of day. Servants bustled around through the back stairs and in and out of empty rooms, giving the place the impression of a beehive, but one in which the bees had only left the room moments before you entered.

Evander had not been in his chamber, nor was he in the conservatory.

The gallery remained empty, with no Beaufort to fill it, and he paused only briefly to pay his respects to Beaufort's portrait. Those knowing gray eyes stared at him solemnly now, some trick of the light taking away the amused twinkle in his painted expression. He could trace the brushstrokes with his eyes, map out the places where his hands and lips had been, imagine the taste of Beaufort's skin, his mouth, the salt of his sweat.

Enough—the hunt was on if he wanted to catch Evander before dinner. If all went according to plan, he would have both of his men in his bed again in less than six hours, and fantasy would be unnecessary.

A low murmur of voices sounded from the door that led into the library, the door propped open to allow some semblance of a breeze through the south-facing rooms. One sounded like Evander's—what luck! The other was female, alas. So much for hoping that he might find Evander and Beaufort together and deliver his messages all at once.

Stephen opened the door.

Evander stood by the fireplace, and he was most definitely not speaking to Beaufort. He bent his head over another blonde one, two pairs of lips moving too lushly and too intimately to be anything but the conversation of lovers. Evander had one finger coiled in a curl of Lady Charlotte's hair, his thumb pressed against the bare skin below her collarbone. She stared up at him, her chest and cheeks rose flushed, her lips parted and pink swollen from kissing.

"…are my muse," Evander was saying, "my love, all in all to me…"

"All in all to me. The reason I hear music at night and wake with songs on my lips."

Stephen knew that speech very well. His pulse thrummed in his ears, his breath catching in his throat.

There would be an explanation. Evander always had a reason.

The door slipped from Stephen's fingers. It slammed shut with a sudden bang that echoed in the long chamber.

Evander and Charlotte jumped, turned to see him standing there.

She relaxed, oddly enough, and Evander lifted his chin, unabashed, to stare Stephen down. "Ashbrook? What do you want?"

His cravat was partially untied—Stephen noticed that. His hair was mussed, and he wore a jewel on his watch fob that Stephen had never seen before. It glinted gold in the sunlight, gold like Evander's hair. And Lady Charlotte's.

Why, he wanted to yell. And, *what are you doing?* Evander had never shown interest in women! He flirted, obviously; it was all innocence. All part of his grand games. He occasionally encouraged Stephen to pursue his own entertainments, but Stephen had taken no lover that Evander had not known about beforehand, had not helped him choose, come to bed with, petted and stroked and claimed for his own as well.

Was that not our agreement? Never said in so many words, but implied in every jealous glance and murmured assent, in every evening at the Swan or Boar that saw Stephen glued to Evander's side while he stalked their game for the evening's *mutual* pleasures.

And now this—professions of love, sweet words that Evander had whispered in Stephen's ear so many times before.

That was supposed to be his reward for the arguments and the silent nights. The one promise that he had been able to rely on through every indignity, each subtle insult and deliberate misunderstanding.

Evander beds other men, but he loves only me.

He could say none of this here. He was no jilted lover in front of Lady Charlotte, had to struggle to swallow against the bile that rose up, stinging and thick, to burn his throat.

"My apologies," he managed to get out, every syllable dropping into silence that rippled like the surface of the pond. "I did not mean to disturb you."

"Think nothing of it," Lady Charlotte said, her voice a silken serpent.

Evander said nothing.

The door—he had to leave. A million words slammed against the inside of his skull, none of them wise, all of them important. The handle slipped in his fingers, twisted like some living thing that he could not get a grip on. He grabbed for it one last time before flinging himself out of the window began to seem like a viable escape route, and this time it turned. He ran.

The murmuring began again inside. Conversations bubbled up from the main hall below, servants moved through the rooms, setting tables and bringing food. He could not stay. He needed time. Time alone to think and prepare what he would say, what questions he would ask that would make Evander give him the right answers. Memory played tricks on him, serving up images of the past weeks that now made sickening sense.

Their heads bent together as Evander guided her through a piece on the pianoforte, blond on blonde.

The two of them cantering ahead when the group had gone riding, returning with mud-splashed hems and secret smiles.

Tossing and turning on the cool sheets, listening out of habit for the sound of breathing that wasn't there.

He had never once imagined this.

How many nights has he gone to her bed instead of mine?

How many times has he laughed at my ignorance?

How stupid have I been, and how long has this been his plan?

Stephen stumbled back toward his room, catching a passing maid by the arm. "Give my respects to the earl," he said clumsily, letting go of her arm when she pulled back in surprise, "but I am unwell. I will not be down to dinner."

Let Evander make love to the earl's daughter across the dinner table, under it, over every chair and by every fireplace in the house if he wanted to. Tonight, at least, Stephen would not be there to watch.

Chapter Twelve

Ashbrook did not come down to dinner. His seat sat empty, a maid curtsying prettily before Coventry to make his excuses.

Cade was a slow-simmering fire of banked rage in the chair opposite. He played his part well, certainly, chatting with the ladies on either side and keeping the conversation both light and utterly insubstantial, but the darkened blue of his eyes and the set of his jaw suggested another story. Joshua watched him from the corner of his own eye, only half-attentive to Lady Chalcroft's conversation on his left.

Lady Charlotte spoke less than usual, her hands clasped before her and satisfaction radiating off of her. She cast kittenish eyes at Cade, which was nothing new. More surprising were the intent stares she kept giving her father, as though waiting for something to be said. He, on the other hand, was so busy talking up his hunting dogs to Miss Talbot and her mother that he missed the entire spectacle.

No one brought up London news, for which Joshua could only be grateful. Even Horlock and Lady Horlock kept conversation to the weather (fine), the weather in general at this time of year (not always so fine) and the possibility of a picnic the next day (only if it stayed fine). It was all he could do to sit there, not to glance over at the empty chair between Lady Amelia and Lady Horlock, to imagine the comments that Ashbrook would be making under his breath or the sly grin he would shoot across the table, meant for Joshua's eyes alone.

The end of the meal came as a surprise and a moment of almost unbearable relief, Charlotte rising to lead the ladies out. He could stay long enough to take brandy with the men, then make his own excuses and slip away. Away from under Lady Horlock's watchful eye, it would not rouse suspicion. And then?

He faltered. He would look ridiculous if he ran off to check that Ashbrook was well. The man was grown and didn't need a nursemaid petting him over every headache and ill turn of the stomach. No, he would stay for the hands of whist and the talk of literature, however long into the night it lasted.

Joshua was well done making an idiot of himself over men.

Chapter Thirteen

He found no rest in his room.

Stephen paced, his coat off and his cravat loose around his neck. He flung himself backward onto the bed in a gesture so dramatic that even the actors in the Haymarket would laugh at his overacting. And none of the restless motion helped the itching displeasure under his skin, the anger and the shame commingled, the *humiliation* of it all.

And why should he be feeling any of those things? Men were liars and ruled by their pricks. One only had to look at the number of ladies thronging Covent Garden by night to understand that. Marriage vows meant nothing, even to those who *could* make them.

Sooner or later, there would have had to come a woman who held some sort of fascination for Evander. Perhaps that was it. Stephen stared up at the white ceiling and counted the shadows made by the flickering candle in the window. Lady Charlotte was the angel come to lift Evander from his life of sodomitic lusts, and Stephen would be left behind to feed the fires of hell.

If it were so expected, so natural, why did he feel so hollow? Why did his chest ache and his stomach feel tangled, the image of Evander and Charlotte embracing impressing itself upon the blackness every time he closed his eyes? Man and woman were designed for each other; the Bible said so. Man and man—pleasure in temporary release and companionship, with a side order of sin. And nothing more.

Until an hour ago, more or less, he had known intimately what shape his future would take. Now there was nothing there but the uncertain void.

What time was it, and how long had he been up in the room, feeling the shift of the earth upon its axis? If dinner was over he could find Beaufort, perhaps steal some time alone to take counsel, feel the comfort of Beaufort's arms around him. He had no qualms now about following through on the promises in that gentle forest kiss, even without Evander's by-your-leave.

And then—

And then he had no idea.

Still, it was the beginning of a plan. Stephen rolled to his feet and headed for the door, not bothering with coat and cravat. He pulled the door open and froze, foot still raised. Evander stood on the other side, one hand raised as though to knock, his face dark as thunder.

Stephen stepped back reflexively. Evander pushed his way inside. The door closed behind him, and Evander turned the key to lock it. His whole body tensed, his movements tight and perfectly controlled, the vein throbbing at his temple.

"Do you do this on purpose to humiliate me?" Evander hissed, his hands balling into fists. He loomed, as much as a man only an inch taller or so could loom, and Stephen fell back another pace.

His heart thrummed, his mouth went dry and his palms wet. Now what, when Stephen was the one with the right to be angry and distraught?

"You're an embarrassment. They were asking after you and all I could say was 'I don't know'."

Stephen backed up a step farther, his instinct first, as always, to put distance between them, even as he remembered how much Evander hated that. His anger from the afternoon still simmered, a low-banked fire, flaring now in the face of Evander's fury.

"I?" He sounded incredulous, which would only enrage Evander further, but there was no hope for it now. "I am not the one jeopardizing everything. What would you have me do when I saw you with that snippet of a girl?" The edges of the world started to go red, and Stephen struggled to keep himself from shouting. "What lies are you playing at now? 'You are my muse'…hah! Have you also told her that she is the first who could ever stir your heart?"

Evander shook his head and sneered at Stephen, his perfect upper lip curling in a hard and unforgiving parody of itself. "You are being ridiculous. Are you trying to play the cuckold now? We've never been married, you and I. The sins we commit have been ratified by no sacraments."

"And that gives you license to break our agreement whenever it suits you?" He wanted to throw things, to punch him, to make a scene of the sort that had never, ever been permitted, to loose the bubbling rage that was only now surfacing from some dark place inside him.

"I have done nothing wrong," Evander proclaimed, drawing himself up with the full and straight spine of the righteous man. "I know full well what you and *Beaufort* have done without me. And now you accuse *me* of being the one to defile our bed? You're the worst sort of hypocrite, Ashbrook, and if either of us is to be making apologies, it should be *you*."

And that was utterly wrong...wasn't it? Because it had been Evander himself who had said "do what you will" and left the bed, it had been Evander who pointed Joshua out and Evander who had made the first invitation. Surely feeling some measure of affection for the man who had had his cock up Stephen's arse was an acceptable thing. The two situations were in no way comparable.

Were they?

"You gave us your blessing!" Stephen protested, far less sure of himself than he had been ten minutes ago. "I may well have liked him first, but we agreed together that he should come to our bed. I have in no way deceived you! Unlike what you're doing, which I still cannot fathom!"

"That much is obvious," Evander said coldly. His hands unclenched and a cool, appraising smile replaced the hot anger on his face. "Don't you understand?"

He stepped forward and took Stephen's face between his hands. It took everything Stephen had not to recoil, his jaw clenching. Evander took a deep breath, his shoulders settling, and when he opened his eyes again there was a glimmer of the man whom Stephen knew.

"I'm doing this for us," Evander said kindly, steel behind his words. His touch was too much, crawling and uncomfortable. A log popped in the hearth and the fire jumped, casting Evander's face in shadow.

"For us? How does that make any sense?" Space, air— he needed both.

Evander dropped his hands away but kept talking in the sort of voice used to gentle a wild horse or a dog. "Use your head, Stephen. If I marry Charlotte, we will never have to strive again. I will have money, money to compose and travel, and never have to scratch and scrape and bow to those who hate me."

"Us?"

Evander blinked. "Eh?"

"You said you were doing this for 'us', but all you say now is 'I'."

Evander shook his head in annoyance, blond hair falling into one eye. He pushed it back, Stephen's golden idol, and frowned petulantly. "You know I meant 'us'— don't try and get out of this with distractions and semantics. You have been cruel to me, Stephen, when all I want is to make our lives easier."

"And now you say 'our'," Stephen said, emboldened enough to take a step forward and point a finger at Evander, risk his wrath and ruin, "when I know you mean 'your'. Anger is like wine, Evander—it brings out the truth in the words we try to hide behind. You are a small and petty man, interested only in your own advancement."

He regretted the words as soon as they were out, not for what he had said—which was true, frankly—but for what it would lead to. The surge of power, though, that sudden notion of indestructibility, of feeling ten feet tall and broader than the mountains—that, he could cling to for protection.

Evander's tune changed, and the hands that had been balled into fists now reached out to Stephen in palms-up supplication. "Stephen," he wheedled, "you're angry, I know. Don't you know the truth? *You* are my muse. Everything I write, I write for you."

"I forgive you," Evander declared magnanimously, "even though you're being unreasonable. Get some rest, and in the morning all will be well again. You'll see that I'm right. I need you, you know that. I cannot write my masterworks without my muse beside me."

"So write for Charlotte," Stephen said, his "unreasonable" anger still the one thing fueling him. "I am sure she will appreciate it better than I at the moment."

The firelight played ugly tricks on the lines of Evander's face, his sneer cutting deep into his brow and cheeks. "She's a silly girl who wants her father's attention. If I can use that to make our lives easier, who could blame me for trying? All three of us will have what we want. Money, security, connections—"

"You are insane." Charlotte's only purpose in life was to make a good match and advance her family. For that, she needed someone titled and wealthy, not a rogue of a composer with all the lusts of a grim Greek god. "Even if you ruin her—a girl whose only crime is being silly and rebellious and a little bit in love with you—even if you make her shame so paramount that she has no *choice* but to marry, the gentry always have options. Coventry will marry her to the King of *Spain* before he gives her to you!"

Evander went completely still, then his head moved forward, his eyes intense and dark, blazing like the sun. When he spoke his voice was a hiss, all the more dangerous for his tight control. "You are ungrateful and have always been ungrateful. Nothing I do ever suits your moods. So be it!" he exclaimed, and despite himself, a bubble of cold dread formed in the pit of Stephen's stomach. "If I am so terrible to you, then I no longer want *you*. Run to your precious *Beaufort...*" he spat the name out as a curse, "...and let your new lover attempt to make you happy. Because apparently I cannot ever do so."

That— No. That was the opposite of what he wanted, was it not? The evening was supposed to end in reconciliation, in Evander's reassurance that he still had a place at his side.

So then why was the word "finally" echoing in the back of his mind? Ungrateful wretch indeed!

The memories came next, Evander's voice, his father's, all of it blending into a cacophony of reminders.

"We are partners, you and I—I will write the music and you shall play my tunes, and the world shall love us both."

"You're hapless, boy, and the army's the best place for you. You'll spend your whole life searching for a leader to take charge of you because you haven't the stones to rule yourself."

"They come to hear my *music, you know. It is* my *voice that sings to them from your strings."*

"Evander!" Stephen could get out no more, the weight of what he had just done crashing down upon him.

Evander shook his head, his lip curling, and he unlocked Stephen's bedroom door. "I will hear no more. As of now, and thanks to you, our partnership is at an end."

Chapter Fourteen

Joshua should have known better. He had been a fool to follow Ashbrook into the woods, had known the loss of control it would lead to. And yet. The afternoon had been a scene of perfection, down to the last detail. The breeze had tossed Ashbrook's curls around his face, dark on cream, and his lips had tasted of summer rain.

"Come to bed tonight," he had asked—begged! *"I will speak to Evander."* And Joshua had believed him.

Why should he not? The universe had seen fit to give Joshua a gift in the shape of a ridiculous musician who hated to kill animals and rescued serving girls from farm boys. (Who had a mouth made of heated silk and fine brandy— smooth, soft and burning like fire.)

Joshua had believed him.

And now the clocks had long since struck the hour of two, the world outside dark and still.

Cade had not looked his way the rest of the evening, not even to glower, and no message had been waiting beneath Joshua's door when he retired.

He had been far better off, Joshua mused, staring into the glowing red embers of the fire, when he had restricted his activities to tension release and nothing more. Caring this way for someone brought only dashed expectations and disappointment.

And if he wasn't careful, he was going to end up a character in an opera, all brooding and no spine.

He had been invited to Ashbrook's room. He would at the very least go and find out more.

The suite was empty. No one answered his quiet knock and so, on impulse, he tried the door. It opened for him, unlocked, the sitting room tidy and the fire banked low in the hearth.

Ashbrook's room was in disarray, his jacket from the afternoon and his muddy-bottomed boots tossed over a wooden chair, and his bedclothes rumpled as though he had flung himself upon them and lain for a while. They were cool when Joshua smoothed his hand over them, so he had been gone for some time.

Joshua left as softly as he had arrived, closing the doors carefully behind him.

Where is the first place I go when I am upset? The studio and my charcoals. Why should he do anything different?

The doors to the conservatory were closed, the faint strains of music from the other side low and melancholy. The doors swung open at his touch, neither locked nor barred. For a moment he regretted intruding. He froze; even breathing too loudly might break the enchantment.

Ashbrook had indeed turned to his music. The dirge poured from his violin, cradled gently beneath his chin. His eyes were closed, his head bowed, his dark hair pulled back into a ribbon with a few tendrils escaping to frame his face. He stood at the side of the room, as far away as possible from the chairs upon which Joshua had once watched him fucking. The memory was no longer one which could set him to blushing—it had been the beginning of something both dear and dire and, even so, he would not change it.

No embers glowed in the fireplace, only a handful of candle ends burning in a stand set on top of the sideboard. The shadows in the room leapt and jumped with the movement of the air, the flames guttering as Joshua softly closed the door. The golden light caught every movement and sweep of Ashbrook's arms as he played, the discordant minor key not something Joshua had ever heard before. He played out his heart and soul in something wholly original, and Joshua would bet money that he would never be able to repeat it.

He seemed not to have heard the opening of the door. Joshua could only stand and watch, Ashbrook's movements so desperately intimate. He could never capture it in paint, the agony on Ashbrook's face, the introspection, the bow and sweep of his body as the music flowed through and out of him. *A series of sketches, then, pencil studies of movement and line, overlapping in sequence.* Then perhaps he could hold on to some miniscule portion of this visceral beauty.

His chest clenched and he swallowed hard against the lump that seemed to suddenly appear in the center of it.

Breathing became difficult, the air in the room thin and insufficient.

Ashbrook drew his bow down along the strings in one last long, solemn cry of pain, the fingers on his left hand trembling more than the vibrato called for as they pressed against the strings.

That pain echoed in his eyes when he opened them, lifted his head up from the base of the violin and let it slide down from its perch on his shoulder. He saw Joshua then, put the instrument and bow in the case at his feet.

There was red in the picture that didn't belong there, a discordant note in the harmony of the palette, spotted crimson on the cuff of Ashbrook's white sleeve. That broke Joshua's paralysis and he crossed the room in three long strides.

Ashbrook seemed half in a daze himself, his cheeks rough with stubble growing in, and darkening circles beneath his eyes. Ashbrook closed and opened his fingers reflexively, looked down as Joshua took his hand and smoothed out the tense and strained tendons. He had played through his callouses, the skin cracked and broken on already worn fingertips. Red blood seeped between the splits in his skin, pooling under his close-trimmed nails.

"What are you doing here?" Ashbrook asked, distant and dazed, as Joshua patted down his pockets in search of his handkerchief.

"Looking for you," Joshua replied, too sharp with concern. Ashbrook flinched as Joshua began to clean his fingertips, and he pressed more lightly against the broken skin. "You were not at dinner," he began again. There was not as much bleeding as it had first seemed, but he could not be left unattended to, either way. "Nor in your room. I was concerned."

"You went to my room?"

The dispassion in Ashbrook's tone made Joshua look up, and his face was as closed off as the rest of him. *Waiting for a blow to fall,* Joshua imagined, apropos of nothing.

"I did. Neither you nor Cade was abed, and the hour is late. I wondered, perhaps, if something had happened between you." It was a leading question; the answer was obvious. But now was his chance to find out the truth.

The story he got, though, was told quietly and with little emotion, as Ashbrook's eyes focused on Joshua's hands moving and the wreck he had made of his own fingers—that, he had not expected.

"What does he imagine?" Joshua ground out between gritted teeth, letting go Ashbrook's hand and folding his handkerchief to keep the smears of blood concealed. "That he will simply go on as he has been, find someone new to kowtow and grovel before his *greatness*? He has used you shamefully," he stated firmly. "You are not to blame here."

Ashbrook rubbed the tips of his injured fingers with his thumb, wincing. He shook his head, still not meeting Joshua's eyes. He sat on the floor, his back against the pianoforte. He tipped back his head and rested his wrists on his bent knees, a statue of a man in contemplation.

Joshua joined him without invitation, settled on the floor beside him and tucked his banyan around his own legs to better ward off the nighttime chill.

"I said things I should not have." Ashbrook broke the silence and scruffed the fingers of his good hand through the stubble on his chin. "Accused him without thinking things through. In one short argument, I destroyed everything I have been working for, everything I walked away from my family for. I wanted to be a musician, more than anything, to make my living and my fortune through my song. And now—"

"And now you still have that chance, only without that albatross of a man weighing you down."

Ashbrook barked out a short, discordant laugh. "You don't understand. Without him I am nothing."

How could a man capable of so much artistic vision be so unrelentingly blind? "Without him," Joshua said, resting his hand on Ashbrook's knee, "you have a chance to be a man of your own making. Cade has shown you his true colors. Believe him. And," he added vehemently, "he is not the only composer in England, nor is Coventry the only patron."

"Who, then, do you recommend?" Ashbrook said sharply. "With Evander a favorite of the earl, they will do damage if I walk away. I must beg for forgiveness and a return to grace." He scrubbed his hands up his face and pressed the heels of his palms into his eyes. He sagged, and it would be so easy to lean over and draw Ashbrook into Joshua's arms, but he gave off an aura of *"touch me not"* that even a blind man could see.

"They know too many of my secrets," he said, defeated. "If they expose me, I am a dead man."

Joshua bit his tongue. *Good Lord, the man was defeatist.* He seemed unwilling even to *try.* "Cade cannot expose you without exposing himself—what would he do?

Accuse you of buggery with someone *else*? That he just happened to hear about?"

"I'll have to apologize," Ashbrook said, "and pray he forgives me. There are better musicians who would give anything to play for him. If I am not his lover, he will have no reason to keep me. Then I am a dead man."

"Listen to what you're saying," Joshua protested. "Think about the compromise you're considering. If he would have you beg and grovel for his favor when he is so clearly in the wrong, that is not affection, or love. That is mutually assured destruction."

Ashbrook looked up at him with eyes glazed over in anger and in self-loathing. Joshua needed to control his tongue or he would lose whatever tenuous connection was making Ashbrook listen to him now.

"If he did not have power over you," Joshua continued, softer now, reaching out to take Ashbrook's hand, "tell me. Would you return to him or not? As lover or as player?"

The silence dragged out as Ashbrook considered the question. When he finally spoke, his answer was cryptic and his voice hushed, "Do you have to ask that question, after today?"

Which part of "today" did he mean? Tender and loving kisses in the woods, or the revelations and the fight which followed?

"But that is not how things are," Ashbrook said, and took back his hand. "I have to live in the world, not in a fantasy, and reality tells me that I am done for. It is *Evander's* name that draws crowds, not mine. And a performer must have an audience. Without him I have no home, no living, no life."

Enough. The self-pity sat as badly on him as a flowered bonnet on a pig, making a mockery of everything he could be. Joshua surged to his knees, rising up a few inches above Ashbrook's head to give his indignation a better platform.

"So you are content to live not only as a pretty jewel in a box, but a slave or painted whore as well?" The words were harsh, but all the better to snap the man out of his bout of sulking. Somewhere in the back of his head he could imagine Sophie laughing herself absolutely sick at the hypocrisy in it, in *Joshua* of all people telling off someone *else* about lying and staying dependent on another!

"Even if you can bring yourself to work with him again, you do not have to give him yourself as well as your music," he urged.

It made little impact. Ashbrook pushed himself up from the floor, grabbed for the coat he had left draped over the pianoforte. "My music *is* my self," he said fiercely, denying everything else that Joshua had begun to know. His compassion, his humor, the way he lost himself sometimes in dreams, the loyalty that made him the kind of man so deserving of pure and absolute love—and the least likely to receive it. "Beyond that, without that, what else am I?"

"A man. A heart. Someone who deserves better." Joshua stood and faced him down.

All Ashbrook did was shake his head. "Maybe I deserve this," he said, which made no sense.

Joshua reached for him, but Ashbrook stepped away, leaving Joshua adrift, unmoored, with no notion what to do or say next.

"Press me no further," Ashbrook said firmly, and Joshua's heart thumped painfully in his chest. "I am not angry with you, but I can cope with no more tonight."

If he argued, he would be as cruel and controlling as Cade, and yet if he let Ashbrook walk away now, was there any guarantee that they would find themselves alone again? The summer was not so long that they had endless days to while away. Soon enough they would all leave this house and its velvet rooms, the sunny parlors and days that only reluctantly faded into evening.

The cold of the winter sea would take them all one day. He felt something similar to that leaching frost even now.

Let it take him. He was used to swimming alone.

Good God in heaven, the man's melodrama is rubbing off on me.

Joshua nodded, once.

With his head low and his mouth pressed into a tight line, Ashbrook left the conservatory and let the door close softly behind him. The sound of the latch echoed in the room.

Where would he go now? Back to Cade? To brood alone somewhere in the garden? Whatever it was that Ashbrook needed, Joshua was apparently not it.

Joshua fell into sleep eventually, but his night was filled with dark and sinister dreams. He lost count of the number of times his eyes flew open, of the thick sensation of some nightmare creature sliding away just out of view, the world tilting dangerously and his white-knuckled grip on the sheets barely enough to keep himself from falling. The dreams vanished as easily as they had come, leaving him with nothing in the morning but a mind fogged by exhaustion.

A clock somewhere chimed the hour—seven—too early by far to go in search of coffee and sausage, but too late to return to bed. Joshua rose, washed, dressed, all in a haze, his thoughts whirling by and yet too insubstantial to pin down.

The light in his sitting room was all wrong for any kind of work so early in the morning; it would not be useful until at least midafternoon. Joshua paused in the middle of his room, his sketchbook and charcoals in his hands and momentarily at a loss. The parlor was no good. He would look everywhere and see Ashbrook's smile, his ear daubed with blue paint, a streak of green across his cheek. *The merry sound of his laugh, the crinkles in his smile—*

Outdoors, then, to take advantage of the sun. There would be chance for solitude there, and a bench to keep the dew from his seat.

Yes, he decided a few minutes later, sitting on the carved granite bench. This would do nicely. The rolling green side lawn extended away in front of him, the high and silent façade of the house a looming presence behind and the sun glimmering down from partway up the sky. *This is perfect. Silence, light and no people to confound me and make life difficult. If only it could always be this way.*

"And good morning to you, stranger."

Naturally.

Sophie sat beside him, settling down onto the bench as though she meant to stay awhile. Her hair was bound up beneath her cap, an apron tied around her waist. The sewing basket under her arm suggested her errand. "You're hiding again." She had dropped her accent, the false French lilt pointless when he knew full well that she was as English born as he.

"I am not in the mood," he cautioned her. Normally her teasing could jolly him back to smiles from just about anything, but today was different.

"I see that," Sophie began, deceptively mildly. "Are you and your lover on the outs again? He is causing you more pain than pleasure, on the whole." She opened the basket and rummaged within, taking out a handful of tangled skeins of brightly hued silk thread.

"Sarah!" Joshua hissed, the girl's real name slipping out in his panic. He turned, scanned the lawn, but there was no one to be seen. "Still yourself, woman, or you will have me turned into a new flag over the house."

"Still *yourself*," Sophie-Sarah said. She picked through the tangle until she found the loose end of a pink thread and began to unwind it from its fellows. "We are quite alone. Why do you think I chose now to speak?"

"Regardless," Joshua insisted, his cheeks growing hot, "it is no good for you to worry about my well-being and announce my crimes in the same breath."

"What I worry about is your attachment to a man who leaves you looking like a widow in first mourning, instead of someone enjoying the flush of youth and love," she said pointedly.

Joshua braced his elbows on his knees and ran his hands over his face, scruffing his fingers through the hair on the nape of his neck. "I am not attached," he muttered.

"Hmm." Sophie made a noise that he ignored. The pink silk caught and she worked the knot free with her nails, drawing out the skein to pile the free end in her lap. "And that is why you are a broody hen out here and he is sulking in the drawing room, naturally."

"Ashbrook is sulking?" He spoke before he thought. That reaction was to be expected after Cade's actions the previous night, he supposed. Foolish enough to think that he might be upset over *Joshua* or anything that he had said. Joshua was the interloper, the variable that had upset their careful balance. He had no right to feel proprietary.

"Oh indeed." Sophie nodded solemnly, and he had fallen right into her trap. "He plunks one note upon the pianoforte, like so…" she tapped the air with a single, dramatic finger, "…and then he sits his chin upon his hand and sighs 'aye me'…" Sophie pressed her palm to her cheek, "…like so. And then he faints for grief." She flattened the back of her hand against her forehead and pretended a swoon, her head tipping back and her eyes closed.

"Wench." Joshua snorted, a smile twitching at the corners of his lips.

Sophie beamed at him in triumph.

"I do not think to speak for him…" Joshua sighed after a minute.

He could not lie to her. There was little point. A certain lightness settled in his chest. To be able to speak of it, freely and without euphemism—it was a freedom he hadn't imagined he needed. Or could ever have.

"I…like him well. He infuriates me," he added quickly, and Sophie chuckled. "But I find myself at odds when he is out of sorts with me."

"And that sounds like every marriage I have ever heard of," she replied. "Except, of course, for the presence of his other lover."

"That may well be over," Joshua confessed. And he had been overlooking the obvious answer—Sophie had the ear of the rest of the house. She might know more than he did about the circumstances surrounding…everything, really. "Cade has been bedding Lady Charlotte, and Ashbrook caught him at it yesterday."

That got her attention away from the tangled silks, her eyes going wide. He hadn't expected the wide grin that followed. "That explains a great many things," she said, almost to herself. "And I take it whatever agreement exists between you three does not extend to noblemen's daughters."

"Apparently it did not." Joshua shrugged, the world seeming to fall into more tangible order the more he talked it out. "Ashbrook confronted Cade, Cade was vehemently unapologetic, Ashbrook and I had words, and now here we all are, at arm's length to each."

And put like that it was so simple, was it not? Except that he could find no easy remedy. No power on earth would compel him to play go-between now.

He opened his sketchbook, the pages falling apart to a well-creased spot in the binding. Ashbrook's face looked back at him from a dozen different poses, each one a futile attempt to capture the radiance of his animated beauty.

"Indeed," Sophie murmured, winding the loose pink silk around her fingers in careful layers, "I see how it is." That skein wound, she tucked in the end and sat it carefully back into her basket. Green next, the slippery threads clinging around a rainbow of other colors so tightly that unpicking them seemed impossible. "Tell me, do you love Mr. Ashbrook for himself, or because he so desperately needs to feel lovable?"

That stopped him dead. Her question was a riddle and a paradox, for wasn't the beauty of the human being in the yearning? In the *something* in people's eyes that burned to be more than what they were? It was utterly missing in some, replaced by flat satisfaction and stagnation…

He was an idiot.

But he had never said "love".

"Does it matter?" he asked finally.

"For you? Yes."

She was not about to let him off the hook upon which he dangled. Fine, then. If he had to articulate it, he would.

Joshua's fingers curled around the charcoal and he flipped to a blank page, the black smudges already creeping across his skin. He outlined a curve that became a cheek, a cheek that fed down into a strong jaw, a dark curl that brushed against a naked shoulder, the collarbone winging out in an arc that would seduce da Vinci himself in his quest for human perfection.

There had been bruises there the last time, stained by Joshua's mouth. The marks had stood out, red and lush against Ashbrook's skin, begging to be sucked at, bitten and made darker again. All in service of the fantasy that was the word "mine".

"When I first looked at him, I saw a demigod," Joshua began, biceps and triceps emerging on his paper as he'd seen them last, arcing under his lips and straining to the touch of his hands. "Beauty unparalleled and entirely out of my reach." And then a mark, a love bite on the column of his throat, the crook of one finger and the callouses there from his playing, the cracks that bled onto his palms and stained his skin with red. "Now he's human, frail and vulnerable in ways I could not have imagined."

Sophie made a soft noise.

"And stronger in so many others."

Ashbrook's torso, the angles of his hips, dark shadows concealing the hollows of his thighs and the tangle of curls at his groin. Joshua smudged the charcoal across the divots and curves there, shielding Ashbrook's prick from the viewer's eye.

I share this with Cade, I will not share this part of you with the world as well.

Another soft sound came, not unlike a snicker, but when Joshua looked up, Sophie was diligently bent over her work, green silk thread coiling now around her deft fingers.

"I don't know that I love him," Joshua finally confessed, each word a painful admission. "Not as such." He drew Ashbrook's eyes, his eyelids closed, the shadow of his lashes skimming across his cheekbones. But that wasn't the entire truth. Softer, then, the hole inside his chest hollow and empty. "But I do know that I very easily could."

Sophie's smile, when he met her eyes, was gentle, tender and utterly out of place. She reached out and closed the sketchbook on his fingers, hiding his ridiculous scribble from view. "Be careful, dear heart," Sophie said, as warm as the summer sun that had risen higher in the clear-blue sky. "That is all I ask."

"All?" he asked, his eyebrow arching with his grin.

"Well…" she tossed her head and laughed, "…if you're offering, here." She handed him her handkerchief. "Clean that mess off your hands and help me wind these skeins."

It was too easy, too familiar, and Joshua took the kerchief with a soft chuckle. "As my lady commands," he said, wiping the black smudges from his fingertips. She kicked him. That too was easy and familiar, and the chill inside him began, slowly, to thaw.

"Uneventful" used to be the highest praise Joshua could give his days, one blending into the next in an easy, unbroken rhythm. Until Ashbrook and the passion in his eyes, until Cade and his plays for power, and until the fractures beginning in the careful walls he had built to keep out the world. That this current day was uneventful sounded more like a curse than a blessing.

After leaving Sophie in the garden, he'd given himself over to wandering, traipsing across the fields and woods in a search of a decent background for Lady Amelia's portrait. He found nature aplenty, but none of it sang to him.

Not until he returned to the clearing and the fallen log, thick with the memories of Ashbrook's lips, the tenderness of his hands on the sides of Joshua's face, the way the light had played in his hair, bringing out highlights from the summer sun.

The words they'd spoken ran together in his mind, a blurred collage of thwarted dreams.

Come to bed tonight. / I miss you, I crave your touch / I will, I will.

He went back to the house.

The hallways were no better, the ringing of girlish laughter and the movements of the dozen family members and guests eliminating any chance for real peace and quiet. He'd read his book twice through and nothing else in the library could hold his attention. It was despite himself that he ended up back in the gallery, among his old and silent friends in their gilt and walnut frames.

Uncomfortable and unpadded as it was, the old bench set back against the wall was better than sitting on the floor. He folded himself down onto it and slouched there, elbows on his knees and his chin resting on his hands, the stillness broken only by the distant echoes of voices from downstairs.

Soon, he would go back to the quiet of the estate, the sprawling generosity of his studio, the tree-scattered hills that spread out toward the horizon. The days would continue to roll by in banality, unchanged except for visits to clients, visits from subjects for their sittings, dinners with his cousins-cum-patrons, where he simpered and smiled and lied about his life.

His own eyes stared back at him from his mockery of a self-portrait. The expression there was nothing at all like the face that stared back at him in the mirror every morning.

Charlie, bold, wild and free, would have hated everything about the complacent hypocrite he had become.

But not entirely, for even now a letter sailed across the Channel, pushed by fair winds to an unknown future.

So he might still be rescued from himself. If Sophie's cousin's employer had any need, of course, for a painter. It was a spark of hope, at least, that he was not as bad as all that. He still had the chance to change.

And what if my life could change still further?

He'd avoided thinking about it before, distracted himself with a thousand other things when his mind veered in that direction.

Ashbrook will never leave Cade. Too much of him was already in Cade's hands, under the most insidious sort of lock and key. Joshua had made himself as content as possible with the three-way friendship, though it was no secret that his affection for Ashbrook was far more particular.

It almost felt safe, now, to picture it. A cottage, a studio, the stars, all the things Ashbrook teased him about. And more.

The warm press of arms around him in the night, a firm, broad chest on which to lay his head. Ashbrook's face cast in shadow, tilted up toward the sky as the sun splashed golds and vermilions across the clouds. Coming into the kitchen in the morning to the smell of coffee and bread, Ashbrook working at the kitchen table, his shirtsleeves rolled up, his fingers stained with ink and his hair still tousled from sleep. Spending the day in front of a canvas, color pouring out across the white field to take the shape of his dreams, working to the sounds of symphonies being rehearsed in the other room.

The world was not that generous.

The scuff of a foot in the doorway, deliberate and loud in the otherwise quiet hall, caught his ear. Joshua looked up, his heart picking up a faster pace, his hands suddenly clammy with sweat because he knew, *he knew*, who it was going to be.

Ashbrook looked well the worse for wear, his head bowed and his hands stuffed in his pockets like any vulgar workman. His eyes were shadowed—had he been crying? Whether he had or not, his hangdog expression and the woebegone slump of his shoulders said enough.

Joshua's breath caught in his throat and he rose to his feet before he could overthink it. He did stop before he took a step, however.

I am done making a fool of myself over men.
Hah.

He should say something poignant, something meaningful and rich, words that would thrum in Ashbrook's ears the way Joshua's pulse beat in his, words so carefully chosen that they would shame writers in their craft. He needed to find the phrasing to explain himself, to make Ashbrook see how his self-destruction was unwarranted and unnecessary, make him fall into Joshua's arms and repent of Cade and Cade's cruelty entirely.

"I didn't see you at breakfast this morning," Joshua said.

Idiot.

"I didn't come down." Ashbrook came fully into the room, glancing behind him once before crossing the floor in a couple of long and hasty strides. "Last night…" he began, nervously at first. He gathered strength as he spoke, though, and the shadows under his eyes were not as dark as they first appeared. "I owe you an apology. I said things to you I did not mean."

It would be so easy to forgive, pretend that nothing at all had changed with the shattering of the third leg of their triangle. "We all say things when upset that we are ashamed about in the light of day," Joshua offered as his concession. "You've been under great strain."

"Nevertheless," Ashbrook insisted, "you were offering counsel and I closed my ears."

He glanced behind them again, and then cautiously to each side, before stepping in closer. Not touching, but enough so that Joshua could see the fleck of green in his brown eyes, the faint stubble coming in along his jaw that he would have to shave off before dinner, the wrinkles in his cravat where it had been hastily and carelessly tied. He moistened his lips with a quick flicker of his tongue.

"Allow me to apologize," Ashbrook murmured, his voice like molten honey. And like honey could be, it was too sweet, too cloying to be believed.

Joshua's body, on the other hand, seemed to think otherwise, reverberating to the timbre with desperate yearning. He was a moth and Ashbrook the flame, the compass needle drawn inexorably to the magnet.

Damn him, anyway. Joshua shook his head. Things could not go back to the way they were.

"I'll come to your rooms no more," he said, and there was a small part of him that took immense satisfaction in the way that Ashbrook faltered and his face fell.

And then, naturally, the wave of guilt and need that overrode his common sense.

"I have no wish to duel with Cade over your honor," he added gently. The flash of surprise that blanked out Ashbrook's expression was his reward, then the sour and vaguely exasperated frown that followed.

"Come to mine." He extended the offer impulsively, regretting his weakness as soon as he'd made the decision. "But only if you come alone. I'll have no truck with Cade after the hurt he's done you."

I would have had it like this in the first place, though there was beauty in seeing you throw your head back in pleasure as you fucked. I only wish it had been my prick buried so deeply inside you, my hands on your cock, watching us in a mirror that reflected our unique and private passions...

He was a mess, a disaster of a man, and bringing Ashbrook back to his room would only compound it.

"I'll have as little as possible to do with him myself," Ashbrook promised, his eyes bright and his color high in his cheeks. "You were right yesterday, and that is what I came to tell you. Surely he and I can be adults about this business, continue to play music as partners, without sharing a bed. We can each do as we please. And what pleases me is you."

One more look around and then he turned those eyes on Joshua again, the heat simmering deep in those dark depths. "Please," he said, "let my body speak where words fail me."

Joshua was helpless, hopeless, sunk. "Midnight," he replied, his mouth gone dry. "I will wait for you then."

Chapter Fifteen

When was the last time Stephen had been the one to sneak to another man's room under cover of darkness? He couldn't remember.

Leaving had been easy, Evander locked in his own bedroom since they'd returned from dinner. The small bottle of oil, mostly empty, hung heavily in his pocket. His hair, still damp from bathing, clung to the back of his neck.

There was a thrill to it, a rush of freedom, lightness in his feet; he did not need Evander for this. Beaufort wanted him, him *alone*, and that knowledge went a long way toward easing the tender bruising around the edges of his soul.

He knocked, waited only for a moment until he heard a murmur of assent. He opened the door.

Beaufort stood by the low-banked fire, his jacket off, his cravat hanging loosely around his neck and his shirtsleeves rolled up to his elbows. He had a book in his hands, and his expression when Stephen entered—joy, surprise, trepidation mixed—softened the strong lines of his face.

He didn't expect me to come.

And that thought was enough to send the guilt spiraling up through him. *My fault, for making him doubt.* He knew how to fix this, how to make Beaufort understand just how beautiful, how *necessary* he was.

He closed and locked the door behind him as Beaufort set his book aside. The warmth of the room suffused him, thick over his skin, or was that from the heat sparking in Beaufort's eyes? His strawberry-blond hair sat tousled, spiking and tumbling as though he'd been running his hands through it, and even now his fingers drummed nervously on the mantelpiece.

"I promised I would be here," Stephen said, and Beaufort's shoulders relaxed.

"So you did." A smile tugged at the corners of his mouth. "And here you are." The firelight traced shadows on his skin, played in flickers over the curve of muscle in his arms. The hollow of his elbow beckoned, the skin there soft, easy to mark and turn red-purple from kissing and biting, yet easy to hide under a coat in the light of day. There, or the divot at the base of his throat below his Adam's apple, a pool of shade nestled in the parted placket of his shirt.

Stephen swallowed against the dryness in his mouth, the anticipation beginning to curl below his stomach. He crossed the room in easy strides, and before Beaufort could speak, Stephen cupped his face in his hands.

Their lips met in a crush, fierce and thorough, and he swallowed any words of protest Beaufort might have let out.

Beaufort's hands came around Stephen regardless, gripped his waist, his fingers splaying out over Stephen's hips and clutching tightly enough to leave marks. He kissed back, the tip of his tongue tracing the edge of Stephen's lips until Stephen opened for him.

Beaufort tasted of cognac and smoke, the thick, dusky flavor of a pipe, the bright and fresh cut of soap and underneath it all the scent of leather and oil, paints and thinner. Stephen could live inside that potent masculine scent, wrap it around himself, drink it in—drink *him* in. He would contain and embody him, kiss him just like this forever, until their lips were bruised and bleeding and nothing lay between them but skin.

The hard nudge against his hip suggested that Beaufort had no objections. Stephen sank his fingers into Beaufort's close-cropped hair, held him in place while he kissed his lips again and again, thirsty as a man dying in a desert. Beaufort gripped his arse and pulled his hips in closer, locked his body tight against Stephen's and ground them together.

Stephen bit along the line of his jaw, his ear, his throat, nibbling and suckling at the tender skin his cravat and collar would normally hide.

"You seem to be feeling better," Beaufort said breathlessly, pulling back for a moment, his hips still tight against Stephen's and his prick a heated weight against Stephen's thigh.

"I panicked last night—I didn't know what to think or how to feel," he confessed. *Useless, hopeless, a wayward child in a man's body*…except now he had Beaufort to give him hope.

"And now?"

He was hardly about to admit the deprecations that had been pulsing through his mind. "I'm feeling you."

Beaufort snorted out that laugh that meant *"I'm putting up with you because you're beautiful"*. He squeezed Stephen's arse through the fabric of his trousers, his fingers roving down to press into the cleft of his buttocks, massage the space between. The sensation was muted through the layers of wool, but Stephen rolled into it anyways, and everything burned.

He would lose his tenuous sense of control over the situation if he allowed that to continue, and tonight was supposed to be *his* apology.

"Let me," he asked and ordered together, stepping back half a step and pulling Beaufort's hands up to his hips again. "Let me show you how much I care for you."

Beaufort's eyes flashed with uncertainty again, and Stephen kissed the look away.

Believe me.

He stroked his hands down Beaufort's sides, the linen warm from body heat, and tugged until his shirttails came free. Beaufort hummed approval against his lips, gasped when Stephen grazed his teeth across the plump lobe of his ear. It only took a second to drag Beaufort's shirt up and over his head, and tangle it around his wrists.

"What are you doing?" Beaufort tensed, but didn't pull away.

"Trust me?"

Oh, he looked beautiful like this, the creamy linen tangled around the gorgeous muscles of his forearms, his stomach taut and nipples tight. Stephen bent his head to

247

suck one of those rigid pink nipples into his mouth and flick at the tip with his tongue. Beaufort's hips canted toward Stephen, and he could just drop to his knees right now, undo his trousers with a flick of a button and suck that gorgeous prick into his mouth—

"Fine," Beaufort relented, a smile in his voice. He pulled against the linen binding his wrists, and Stephen caught it to hold him steady. "But no biting anything off," he cautioned with a short and nervous laugh. "I am overly fond of all my parts."

"I solemnly swear. I'm also very fond of your parts." Stephen nodded, keeping his face as serious as he could in front of the laugh that pressed against his lips.

Stephen stroked Beaufort's chest, ran his fingertips lightly across the smattering of red-blond hair that gave brilliant texture to the warmth of his skin.

Beaufort's shoulders shook, his lips pressed together, but the laugh escaped him anyway. He arched his neck for Stephen's touch, his skin warm and inviting. He rolled his shoulders forward to drop his bound hands between their bodies.

Stephen set his hands against those shoulders, pushed him experimentally.

Beaufort rocked back a step, then caught himself. "What are you doing?"

A few more steps like that, Stephen following, and they made it to the bed. One last push had Beaufort sitting down on the edge. His knees dropped apart as he sat down, and Stephen stepped between them.

"I like this view." Beaufort laughed softly. He pressed his lips to Stephen's groin, mouthed at the aching hardness of his prick through the layers of fabric. Stephen thrust reflexively into the pressure and the faint heat of his mouth. Beaufort pulled against the linen binding his arms and slipped his hands between Stephen's legs to toy with him.

"Not yet." Stephen stooped and slid his hands beneath Beaufort's shoulders and knees, like a groom carrying his bride. Beaufort yelped in surprise when Stephen tipped him backward, struggled in Stephen's arms. "Careful or I'll drop you!"

"You wouldn't dare."

Stephen set Beaufort down in the center of the bed.

He landed laughing, missing the pillows and the shirt still binding his hands at his chest. "Now you're just being ridiculous." Beaufort snorted. "What am I, a damsel about to be ravished?"

Stephen grinned. "If that's a game that pleases you," he offered without much interest of his own. The scornful look back from Beaufort gave him all the answer he needed. "On the contrary, tonight I am entirely devoted to your pleasure." He knelt on the bed, the mattress denting underneath him as he sank into its luxurious softness.

Beaufort sprawled on the white sheets, acres of bare skin crying out to be tasted. Stephen straddled Beaufort's hips, resisting the urge to grind down against him and sate the throbbing ache in his cock that was begging for pressure, friction and release. *Patience.*

He smoothed his hands along Beaufort's arms, lean lines of solid muscle that tensed beneath his fingers, and pressed Beaufort's charcoal-stained hands up above his head. He went willingly, his hips rocking up against the air as Stephen leaned over him. The small, taut nub of his nipple slipped easily between Stephen's lips, and he rolled it over his tongue

Beaufort gasped and arched his back, tangling his hands in the fabric. "In that case, that's an excellent start," he said, his breath catching as he spoke. "Keep doing that."

Stephen swiped at his nipple, bit down lightly and laved his tongue over the spot to soothe the sting.

Beaufort groaned, his fingers curling. His chest heaved as he drew in a deep breath, his muscles defined by the faint golden hair scattered there, leaving faint swirls on his skin. Thicker hair ran down from his navel to vanish beneath the waistband of his trousers, the fall front tented obscenely at the groin.

Stephen could almost make out the shape of Beaufort's cock, the curve of the ring pierced through the head. Stephen nuzzled the rigid line, ran his nose along the solid length of it. The wool of Beaufort's trousers was soft against his skin, the thick smell of his lust heady, musky and dark.

He dropped his feet to the floor and stood. Beaufort propped himself up on his elbows, a cry of protest on his lips that died away as Stephen grabbed his own shirt by the back of the neck and hauled it off over his head.

Beaufort settled against the pillows, and watched with half-lidded eyes and a gaze so intense that Stephen all but forgot what he was doing.

Turning his back, he took longer to undo his trousers, threw in a sway of his hips for Beaufort's benefit. He was rewarded with a low chuckle that had more need in it than mirth.

Stephen turned back to face him, his prick jutting, hard and red-tipped, from the thatch of dark curls between his thighs. The look of desperation on Beaufort's face only made the moment better. Stephen gripped his cock and stroked it, only once, all he could allow himself. The contact burst over him in a wave of pleasure so intense it was almost pain, and Beaufort made a noise that sounded halfway between a whimper and a whine.

"Come here," he begged, the rasp in his voice making it husky. "I need to touch you."

"Not yet," Stephen decided aloud, forcing himself to drop his hand away. The cool air hit the hot skin of his cock and it almost hurt to let go, but it would be worth it. It would. In the meantime—

"You're wearing too many clothes," he said with a grin, and Beaufort lifted his hips obediently. He took his time on this as well, gliding his fingers over the brass buttons of Beaufort's fly. His cock jerked under Stephen's touch, his hips riding up to chase it, and Stephen grabbed him solidly, gave him a squeeze through his trousers.

"Yes," Beaufort hissed, and Stephen could wait no longer.

He opened the buttons with an easy flick of his thumb and drew the pants down Beaufort's thighs.

His cock popped free to slap against his stomach, red-purple at the head, the gold ring that ran through it heavy and bright and wet with precome. It left a gleaming trail between the head of his cock and the flat of his stomach, a thin line of fluid that Stephen lapped at.

The salty-sour taste spread over his tongue, the pure and distilled essence of Beaufort's lust for him. He breathed over the fat head, ran the tip of his tongue down along the slit, gathering more of Beaufort's precome as he went, then tugged gently on the ring with his lips.

Beaufort gasped and keened deep in his throat, his cock jerking again. "What are you going to do?"

"What God gave us mouths for," Stephen replied cheekily, blasphemy in his heart and in his prick, alike. "And hands big enough to span your girth."

He wrapped his fingers around Beaufort's cock, let him thrust up into his fist. The sight of it was enough to set fire to his spine, the dark crown of Beaufort's cock sliding up between his fingers, the gold ring between his thumb and forefinger, only to vanish, then reappear again.

Beaufort's breathing grew ragged, his eyes dark as he watched. Stephen bent his head and licked the crown as it appeared again, opened his mouth and let Beaufort thrust inside. It was easy enough to control his depth like this, with Stephen's fist wrapped securely around the root of Beaufort's prick. Beaufort thrust again, his hands tangling and clenching in folds of his shirt, sliding deep between Stephen's lips.

His cock was heavy on Stephen's tongue, a thick and solid weight that pinned him down, grounded him, made him forget everything but the slick slide through his hand and between his lips. The ring caught on his bottom lip with every push, holding there long enough for Stephen's tongue to play at the underside.

He pressed his tongue against the place where the ring vanished into Beaufort's cock, licked it and sucked at it, the contrast between skin and gold the most amazing textures.

Up and off, then squeezing his lips at the end. He breathed along the damp skin until goose bumps appeared on Beaufort's thighs, then sucked him in again.

Stephen could easily spend an hour like this, lost in the rhythms of sucking and kissing, tracing circles on hot, wet skin with the tip of his tongue. He ran the flat of his tongue down the base, around Beaufort's balls and up the strip of skin between, felt them begin to draw up into Beaufort's body. Beaufort's breathing came in short, fast puffs, his head tipped back and his body tight.

Stephen stopped and sat up, pressed his thumb to the base of Beaufort's prick in an old trick he had learned once when he was rather more…impetuous in his lovemaking than he was now.

Beaufort groaned, long and low, and his body shuddered, but he did not come. "Bastard," he cursed when he had enough breath back. He glared at Stephen venomously, a posture made somewhat less threatening by the solid and almost-purple erection rising to sit hard against his stomach.

"Did you say something?" Stephen teased, and he lunged forward to seize Beaufort's mouth, suck at his bottom lip, already red from being bitten. Beaufort kissed him back just as fervently, running his tongue along Stephen's teeth and— God, he would be tasting himself on Stephen's lips.

The notion coiled flames in Stephen's gut and he rutted up against Beaufort's stomach, leaving a damp streak of his own.

Beaufort nudged him up and kissed his way down Stephen's throat, detouring to suck and lick at Stephen's nipples. He bent his head and worked them, laving and biting each in turn, nibbling until they were hard and erect. They ached as Stephen's prick ached, throbbing in time to the beat of his heart.

Stephen pulled back, raised Beaufort's hands back over his head again and licked a wide, wet stripe up the underside of Beaufort's arm. He tasted of salt and soap, the thin layer of sweat from their exertion prickling on Stephen's tongue.

"Please," Beaufort groaned, and he seemed shocked at the rasp and rawness of his own voice, lust-hazed and thick. "I need more, please."

He raised his leg between Stephen's and rocked his hips up to chase the pressure, but Stephen pressed his hand flat against Beaufort's stomach and held him gently in place.

"I want—" Stephen began, then Beaufort's thigh brushed against his prick and the shock stopped him dead. He *needed*, more than ever, and he took the invitation, rolling down against Beaufort, his hands gripping Beaufort's wrists, still pressed up above his head.

"Tell me," Beaufort urged, lifting his hips, arching his back, thrusting up to meet Stephen halfway.

Their cocks slid against each other, hot and slick from precome and sweat, the back-and-forth motion almost enough. Almost, but not quite.

"I want to fuck you," Stephen gasped. He sat up again, gripped his prick at the base and squeezed *hard* until the urgency flagged and he could think a little more clearly. "I want to make you feel as good as you make me. I want to take your cock in my mouth," he promised.

Beaufort's eyebrows went up and his tongue flickered out to wet his lips.

The pink flicker and the gleam on his lower lip drew Stephen in, and he couldn't look away. "I'm going to suck you until you're sated," he continued, gripping himself tighter and trying not to look down at his cock or at Beaufort's, mouthwateringly fat and straining for him. "Then fuck my prick into you and learn the way your body feels from the inside."

"Yes," Beaufort said instantly, almost before Stephen had finished speaking. "All of that, yes, now, please." He laughed, and there was an edge of nervousness to it which vanished when Stephen let himself fall forward.

He caught himself on his arms, balancing above Beaufort, hands on either side of his head.

Beaufort's arms still rested easily above his head, the linen wound around each finger as he held on to his bindings in a loose grip.

Stephen seized the middle of the shirt, between Beaufort's wrists, and held it down against the pillow. He kissed down the length of Beaufort's arm, licked the muscles of his forearm, the vein that ran down from his elbow to his armpit, nuzzled into the clean-smelling tuft of hair where his arm joined his body.

Down then and farther still, only letting go of the shirt when his arm could no longer reach. He licked and suckled at Beaufort's skin, his nipples in turn, delved the tip of his tongue into Beaufort's navel and laughed when the man squirmed beneath him.

"Ticklish?" he asked, amused, and Beaufort groaned.

"Only when being mercilessly teased by a minion of the devil himself," Beaufort grumped from where he lay. Anything else he was about to say died in a groan and a gasp when Stephen took his cock back into his mouth.

Beaufort's prick was velvet and marble, harder than Stephen had ever felt him, angled so high and so firm that he barely seemed human.

Stephen ran the flat of his tongue down along that solid shaft, the foreskin where it lay below the crown. He toyed with the ring and tugged it, licked through it, teased the places where it broke Beaufort's skin with the barest tip of his tongue.

Beaufort groaned and cried out, writhed and pleaded, and still he kept his hands in place. Stephen flattened his own hands out over Beaufort's hips to hold him steady and took him in entirely. Beaufort arched, pushing his hips up against Stephen's hands in vain attempt to thrust in.

He sucked, opening his mouth and throat and dropping his tongue to take Beaufort as deep as he could, the scent and taste of him filling Stephen's mouth and nose with sweet musk.

There, down, *there*— He sucked as he came up again, his cheeks hollowing out and tongue curling around the ridge, then into the slit, then back down again to play with the jewelry.

Everything ached, his hands, his mouth where his lips stretched around Beaufort's gorgeous girth, his balls, the coils of desperate fire in the back of his spine, building with no release in sight, and his cock, leaking against his stomach and throbbing more with every minute that he refused to spend himself on Beaufort's belly.

Beaufort writhed under him, made little whimpering pleas and abortive thrusts up, his whole back bowed and toes curled tightly into the sheets. "More, more, more," he chanted, and Stephen flicked the tip of his tongue lightly over the crown of Beaufort's cock. It was meant as a tease, until he saw the tears in the corners of Beaufort's eyes, the panicky rush of his breath and the way he scrabbled for purchase to get deeper inside.

"You utter *bastard*," Beaufort gasped out, and Stephen took him deep.

He grabbed Beaufort's buttocks, lifted them up as he sucked him down, buried his nose in the thatch of red-gold hair, opened his throat and swallowed around Beaufort's prick, the head pressing against the back of his throat. He would choke on it and die fulfilled.

He slid off, back down, off again.

He tugged at the ring one last time in passing, twice, again—

Beaufort came with a desperate and muffled shout, dropping his arms and biting hard into the linen stretched between his hands so that he would not wake the next rooms. He came, his entire body shaking with it. His emissions spurted, hot and white, over his own stomach, his chest, between Stephen's lips, his eyes squeezed so tightly shut that wrinkles creased his cheeks and tears spotted his temples.

Stephen had tasted a mango once, a fruit from a distant shore. This was like that first unguarded rapture, burst full across his tongue, ambrosia, thick and heady. Pure and distilled essence of *man* flooded Stephen's senses, bitter and salt in his mouth.

He swallowed, laved Beaufort's stomach with his tongue to clean him, capture his taste and the smell of it, take him in so completely that he could never, ever forget it.

"Holy God," Beaufort muttered, his eyes wide as he watched, his head propped up on his hands. He stared at Stephen, his tongue darting out to wet his own lips, his pupils still blown dark and wide and his skin gleaming faintly with sweat. "Do you have any idea what you look like?" He shook his head in answer to his own question. "No, you couldn't possibly. I will paint you like this one day," he promised, breathless. "As the image of Lust, or some figure from myth. Bacchus. Patroclus. Cupid."

Stephen bit his nipple, and he squirmed.

His own cock was screaming for attention. He pressed the heel of his hand against his prick, rolled against the pressure. Good, but not good enough, Not nearly.

Beaufort untangled his hands and flung his shirt over the side of the bed. He ran his fingers through Stephen's hair, the dark curls sweat damp and tangled, and drew him up close to kiss him.

The oil sat on the night table where Stephen had dropped it, and he grabbed for it as Beaufort released him. He stole another kiss from those plush, kiss-reddened lips, then settled back on his heels between Beaufort's legs.

The view here was magnificent, Beaufort's cock, still half-hard and spent, against his muscled thigh. The flat plane of his stomach extended way above that, a few pearling drops of come gleaming on his skin. His chest flushed red down to his nipples, the color only barely beginning to recede. His lips were open, his eyes bright and his hair a tousled mess sticking up in all directions. He was beautiful, utterly, spectacularly beautiful.

Something inside Stephen expanded sideways and upside down, before tangling into a knot so tight he could never unpick it.

"I need to—" he began, and Beaufort nodded, breathless.

"I want you to," he replied, though whether they meant the same thing Stephen would never be sure.

He tipped the bottle over his hand, smeared the clear, sweet-smelling oil over his fingers. He leaned in and kissed Beaufort again, slow and deep, and slid his hands between Beaufort's legs. He circled the sensitive skin at the entrance to his hole, pressing in gently as Beaufort shuddered, spread his legs wider.

This wasn't entirely new to him, being on this end of the proceedings. Evander had let him, once, and sometimes liked to watch Stephen take one of their guests while he stroked himself and gave direction. But this—pressing his fingers, first one, then a second, deep inside Beaufort's body, sliding slowly past the tight ring at the entrance, a little more slack now from satiation and relaxation than it might have been before, watching the way Beaufort bit his lip, teeth making white dents against the red—this was utterly new and delightful.

He opened his fingers and Beaufort groaned, pressed his feet down against the bed to lift his hips. A pillow had fallen to the floor and Stephen slid it beneath them, lifted him up so that Stephen could kiss his inner thighs, the insides of his knees, lick and suck at his balls. Stephen drew his fingers out, then pressed them back in and curled them forward. Here, somewhere, was a spot that gave more pleasure than he had ever dreamed possible as a young man, and Beaufort rocked up into his fingers as he found it.

"All right?" Stephen asked, though finding breath was difficult. He trembled with the effort, his body shaking with the ache of going slowly, preparing him carefully, when all he wanted was to push in, to break him open, to take and take and take until they were both reduced to nothing but quivering wrecks upon the bed.

"Good." Beaufort rocked his hips up again to take his fingers deeper. He was tight, so tight, slick and hot inside, and relaxed even as Stephen tried to add a third. "It's good," he repeated and, "I'm ready." He made to turn over, his hands braced against the bed, but Stephen stopped him.

"Don't," he begged, his hands on Beaufort's thighs. "Don't become a body for me, stay yourself. I need to see you."

"It's easier this way—"

Stephen shook his head, trembling with the effort of finding the words. He settled for "I want to see your eyes", as though that made sense, but Beaufort seemed to understand. He settled again, let his knees fall apart so that Stephen could place himself between them.

It would work better if... Stephen slid his arms beneath Beaufort's knees, lifted them up and onto his shoulders. He seemed to catch Stephen's meaning and raised his hips in easy invitation.

There was no way he could wait any longer, his hands already trembling. Stephen dropped a hand from Beaufort's hips to take his own cock and guide it to the cleft of Beaufort's buttocks. He slid easily along the channel, skin on skin, so desperately good, and Beaufort rocked up to clench around him. And yet it was not enough, not nearly enough.

He pressed against the tight circle of muscle at Beaufort's entrance. He had to go slowly, draw out the gorgeous thick slide as Beaufort's body opened for him.

Heat, so hot, so slick with oil and tight around him, and to think he had been letting all of this go by in search of the pleasures that came from *being* fucked. He would—he would never be able to choose from here on in. This was beyond perfection, cleaving Beaufort in two, watching the white dents of his teeth dig into his bottom lip as he breathed in, feeling his pulse and the way his body shuddered when Stephen bottomed out.

Beaufort was perfect inside, opening for him with only a little pressure. Stephen drew back, slid partway out, and they groaned together. Even slicked with oil and opened with three fingers, Beaufort's body was snug around him, every movement and roll of hips zinging along his bones and muscles, pushing his hips forward, making his skin sing with need and want and pleasure.

Nothing would ever be as incredible as this, the way Beaufort pulled him in, clutching at Stephen's forearms and his ankles pressing down on his shoulders to spur him on. Their bodies slid, slick with sweat, Stephen's fingers gripping Beaufort's thighs and hips as though this all might vanish in an instant. The room was silent but for the harsh rasping of their breathing and the wet slap of skin on skin, bodies undulating and Stephen's guttural groans of pleasure.

He turned his head to muffle the sound, pressed his lips against the inside of Beaufort's knee.

He pushed inside, slid out again along that tight, sweet glide, Beaufort's skin burning with fire against his own. Lightning flickered along his limbs, sparking in his fingertips and toes.

Stephen fell forward again, let Beaufort's knees down, and Beaufort clasped his legs tightly around Stephen's waist. He got tighter yet, merciful God in heaven, and each drag back and almost out of his body sent a million little flames licking up the inside of Stephen's thighs and his groin.

He thrust faster, harder, pushed himself inside like he could bury himself under Beaufort's skin and become a part of him.

Beaufort pulled him deeper inside with every thrust, his feet crossed behind Stephen's buttocks, urging him deeper, his hands buried in Stephen's hair and his tongue dancing, tasting Stephen's lips, his mouth, fucking into it as

Stephen's cock fucked into Beaufort's arse, a tangle of limbs and privates and precome from Beaufort's prick slicking their stomachs with wet. Joshua's cock was a rigid line between their bodies, the ring rubbing solidly against Stephen's skin as they moved.

Too soon, too soon and this would be over if he wasn't careful, the steam rising inside him like a kettle on the fire, an imminent explosion that would mean pulling out, losing the connection that meant everything.

Stephen slowed his hips, his head buried in the join of Beaufort's shoulder and neck. Beaufort tried to thrust up against him, to urge him on, but he did not, could not.

He rolled instead, intimate and slow, rising and falling as the waves against the shore. He could push himself up again after a moment, pulling back and out so slowly that it was all but painful, the drag of tight muscle against his skin so brutally good. He trailed the tip of his nose along Beaufort's and won a smile, blinding and joyous.

He followed that with long and yearning kisses, the hot puffs of breath. He scraped his teeth against Beaufort's throat and won a gasp, a stuttered thrust, the muscles in Beaufort's long, lean thighs contracting all together to wrap around Stephen's hips more securely.

That was it, he could hold out no longer, the coils of pressure and heat burning him from the inside out, his balls drawn up tight and heavy against his body.

He braced himself and pushed in deep, thrusting faster and faster now as Beaufort gasped and urged him desperately on.

There, there, *there*—snakes of fire ripping through his skin.

He convulsed, shuddered, pumped deep into Beaufort's body and claimed him, the blinding light behind his eyes so bright that, for a brief moment after it faded, he imagined himself blind.

He trembled through the aftershocks, rolling gently in and out of Beaufort to steal those last few sparks of pleasure before everything became too much. Hands played over his back, stroking and caressing, and Beaufort whispered nonsense syllables into his ear. He started to roll away, let Beaufort find some comfort, but Beaufort stayed his hips and held him in place.

"A moment longer," Beaufort begged, and dropped a hand between them.

Stephen nodded, resting his head on Beaufort's chest so he could watch, their hearts thundering along together too loud, too fast.

Beaufort took hold of his cock and stripped it, stroking himself with furious intensity, Stephen still buried, slowly softening inside of him. He pulled at the ring, harder than Stephen had dared, a tug that seemed to send all his limbs trembling.

He followed Stephen over the brink a moment later, spilling white and hot over his fingers, stomach and hand.

Stephen held himself up over Beaufort a moment longer, then slid out of him and collapsed to the crumpled sheets, utterly spent. There was a washbasin across the room; he had noted it when he came in. That would do in a moment. But not yet. He sprawled, arms wide. Beaufort curled in, nestling his head on Stephen's chest and breathing him in.

"Thank you," Beaufort murmured minutes later, then pressed his lips chastely against Stephen's shoulder.

"For this?" Stephen asked, confused. Confused and a trifle sticky. The washbasin was sounding like a better idea every passing moment.

"For this, and for coming tonight," Beaufort elaborated. "Alone. I know things are...complicated between you and Cade. In a very selfish way, I hope this means they have become less so."

And that was an excellent point at which to extricate himself from Beaufort's arms, as warm as they were, and cross the room in search of washcloths and clean water.

Beaufort sat up when Stephen draped the cold, wet cloth across his stomach, and then only to snap it at him with a wrinkled face.

"I think..." Stephen began, hesitating—he could draw his clothes on and leave, or be selfish and take his ease a little longer, "...I think things will always be complicated," he finished lamely.

Beaufort reached out, snagging his hand and drawing him back into bed, making his decision for him. Strong arms settled around Stephen's shoulders and back, and he rested his head on the pillow beside Beaufort's. Red-golden hair tickled his nose, and he nuzzled in to press his lips against Beaufort's ear before he said more. "We have built our lives around each other for so long, I know no other way to live."

Beaufort's fingers moved to Stephen's hair again, rubbed gently against his scalp as he brushed them through

Stephen's tangled waves. They fell around his shoulders, the ribbon long discarded somewhere between the door and the bed, the soft press and release of Beaufort's tender ministrations draining any remaining tension out through the top of his head.

"There are other ways," Beaufort said quietly. "Other places which do not hold the kinds of danger that England does for men like us."

That phrase again, reflections of Cade's endless arguments as to why the rules of society should not apply to them (more properly, to *him*). This time, though, it was not used as a weapon.

Stephen shifted in the bed, unsettled. "You would leave England," he said, instead of anything else that was on his mind. "You who did not like to leave his studio for a house party? How are you so fearless all of a sudden?"

Beaufort stayed silent for a moment, his lips pressed against Stephen's forehead and his fingers stroking through his hair. "At first, only because of Sophie's urging. Now, it is my own inclination as well. The Swan," he said finally, grief around the edges of his voice. "Watching needless death after death, the hatred only growing as time passes. Things were freer a decade ago than they are now, and yet we are all supposed to be enlightened men.

"Sophie has a cousin in Belgium, you see, who works for a French aristo-in-exile, who may have need of a painter. I wrote to him. Perhaps it is time to pay a visit in person, if he will see me."

And that—no—none of that was the sort of thing Stephen expected to hear from the man who had once professed that his idea of adventure was a good novel in front of a calm fire.

"French?" he replied, seizing on the first thing that came to mind to express his shock. He sat up, resting on his hip and elbow, staring down at Beaufort beneath him. "You would turn traitor? *You?*"

"No such thing," Beaufort argued, and he too sat up, the sheets pooling in his lap. "But have you not read France's new laws?" He gestured in the air. "Buggery is no longer a crime. They have no stockade and pillory in wait for men who dare to love. They execute aristocrats, certainly, but the empire has no regulations at all regarding sodomy."

That seemed unreal, too good to be true, even if it did involve the French.

Beaufort may have misunderstood his frown, for he ran his hand down the length of Stephen's arm, his eyes old and sad. "I have seen too many dear friends beaten or hanged. I am tired of it all."

"And you will go when?" Stephen formed the question, his mind trying to race and finding itself sluggish. Seeing him at the Horlock estate would have been difficult; spending time with Beaufort once he sailed across the Channel, utterly impossible.

"I have no immediate plans," Beaufort said, and Stephen relaxed. "I should wait for the vicomte's answer before making travel arrangements. But think of it, Stephen—" Beaufort blurted out, using his Christian name for the first time. The familiarity was unexpected, but Stephen's name sounded good in Joshua's mouth. Considering they were naked in bed together and but ten

minutes ago Stephen's cock had been up Beaufort's—
Joshua's—arse, it probably shouldn't have been such a
surprise.

Joshua stopped talking abruptly, all but holding his
breath until Stephen smiled.

"Go on," he said, and Joshua slowly smiled back.

"Think of it," he repeated. "The vicomte is in Belgium
right now, but it would be easy enough to slip from there
across the border, move down into France once we found
somewhere safe, far from the fighting. Then we could live
free and easy, our only worries finding clients and
audiences, not arrest and ruin simply for loving." He
grabbed Stephen's hand as he spoke, rubbing his thumb
across the breadth of Stephen's palm.

It was an intoxicating idea, however impractical.
"We?" he asked, just to be sure.

"We," Joshua said, half-breathless. "If you like. Come
with me."

Could he do it? Abandon Evander, pack his violin and
his music, his books and his clothes, latch a trunk closed on
all of his worldly goods and simply…go? He had done it
once before, sliding away in the night before he could be
packed off to the army like so much unwanted baggage.

And now, another offer to run.

Evander would be furious. As would the earl. But in
Belgium and France, who could touch them? (The
revolutionary army, he supposed, and they would never be
allowed back into England if it came out that they had
defected, no matter what their reasons. "Evading arrest"
would never be a good answer.)

And on the other hand, here was Joshua Beaufort, bolder and stronger in spirit than Stephen could ever be, holding his hand and promising a chance at something new and better.

"I—" Stephen began, and then he stopped. "Let me think about it?" He did not need to be watching too closely in order to see Joshua's face close in, his fearlessness fade. "It is a decision I cannot undertake lightly," he tried to explain, scrambling for the right words.

Joshua only nodded, and kissed him, his hand pressed against the side of Stephen's face.

"It is," Joshua agreed simply, and Stephen had done the wrong thing again, said the wrong thing.

They tangled together, their lips locked and chests tight against one another.

"You should go," Joshua said as they parted, with a glance at the clock sitting on the mantel. "The hour is late, and you cannot be found here in the morning."

"'Tis the nightingale, and not the owl," Stephen joked, but he slid out of bed and drew on his pants, buttoning them up without looking. "I will go, you get some rest, and we will talk about this again tomorrow."

"Tomorrow."

And Joshua said no more.

The earl's library contained an atlas, a massive, hand-colored tome filled with maps and diagrams, legends of obscure symbols, portraits of strange and exotic peoples decorating the corners of the pages. That was where

Evander found Stephen the next day, the book open to a map of Northern France before the war and the Belgian border.

"Planning a trip?" Evander's voice cut through the quiet, speaking over the trill of midmorning birdsong outside the partially open window.

Stephen jolted upright, his heart thumping in his chest.

"I beg your pardon." Evander held up his hands in a conciliatory gesture. "I didn't mean to break your concentration," he added, moving into the library and closing the door behind him.

The click of that particular door was a sound Stephen would be happy never to hear again. "Only passing the time." Stephen shook his head, flipping the pages over to hide his research. "I'll leave and let you to your work."

"I came here to find you," Evander said, and caught Stephen by the arm as he stood to make for the door.

Stephen looked at him for the first time that day and tried his best not to frown.

Evander's cravat hung about his neck, tied loosely in the kind of simple knot he would usually chide Stephen for. His cheeks were pale, circles under his eyes from lack of sleep. He looked altogether unlike the polished and perfected young man who could squire about an earl's daughter. He was just the vicar's wayward son, alone and unhappy, and once more he turned to Stephen... But for what? Solace? Affection? Unlikely.

"You made your feelings very plain the other day." He could not bring himself to shake Evander's hand off of his arm, however. Not as bedraggled and pathetic as he seemed now. Perhaps they could part ways as friends, instead of letting the unresolved anger simmer forever. Who better to be a comfort than someone who knew you so well? "I have been doing my best to stay out of your path. I thought that was what you wanted."

"I was unkind, I know." Evander shook his head and took a step closer. He was still beautiful, damn him, even pale and upset. But his eyes had been cold and cruel, and Stephen could not allow himself to forget. Evander was all warmth now, though, which made that particular resolution that much harder. "I am sorry, you must believe me. I said things I didn't mean, lashed out at you for no fault of yours. I have not been myself these last few weeks, for reasons you well know."

And he did, for they had sat together in the barn and listened as Joshua read out the lists of the arrested and of the dead, each name falling like a drumbeat in a funeral dirge. He had seen the fear in Evander's eyes, felt the chill settle deep into his own bones.

He had repaired things with Joshua with a humble apology—perhaps now he could find the strength of character to grant Evander the same.

"I know," Stephen said, and Evander smiled, mollified. "We have both been upset and spoken harshly."

There, that was easy enough. He could be an adult as well and apologize for his own faults.

"I do not want to leave here still upset with one another," he added for good measure. Because the thought of it—going back to their shared lodgings, trying to pack up his things, all with Evander erupting at him at random, like a furious blond volcano—was too much.

"Nor do I." Evander was all smiles again, his eyes alight, a sunrise that now left Stephen cold. (He had smiled at Charlotte that way, brightened when she'd come into a room.) "I promise you, I will do everything in my power to make it up to you."

Stephen's gut clenched. "That won't be necessary," he forced out, a heavy tangle sitting in the pit of his stomach. "I think it might be best..." he broached the subject tentatively, watching Evander's face, "...if we begin to sever our partnership. I can start looking for other work— perhaps an orchestra or the opera. Phillips is always hounding me to play with his ensemble." His voice felt close to breaking under the strain, and Evander gave no sign of a reaction. Maybe he wanted Stephen gone as much as Stephen wished to be away?

"We have become too close over the years, and perhaps some more distance will do us, and our friendship, some good. You, I am sure, will have no trouble finding another violinist to play for you. As you keep telling me," he added impetuously, regretting the daggers in his words as soon as he let them fly, "there are a great many who could fill my shoes easily enough."

Evander's face went dark for a moment, his brow coming down like a thundercloud. "Are you going to throw that back at me forever? Words spoken in anger, you know I didn't mean them."

"You meant them enough at the time."

"And you have never said things that you later had cause to regret?" Evander said, something hot and mean sparking in him.

He closed his eyes, and when he opened them again, the rage was gone. He caressed the inside of Stephen's elbow with his thumb, a crawling, clammy thing. Had Evander's hands always been so cold?

"Come, sit with me," he asked, rather than ordered, drawing Stephen toward the settee.

It was barely large enough for the two of them, and they ended up sitting one at each end, legs touching. It was a sensation so familiar and so instinctive that Stephen almost put his hand on Evander's knee before he remembered that they were not in front of their fireplace at home, and that he was still angry. (Though it was growing harder and harder to hang on to that spark of fury, with Evander sitting there, his head bowed, taking both of Stephen's hands in his.)

There were a dozen things he could say now—accusations, demands to know how many others there had been.

He could beg, plead to be returned to Evander's good graces.

Or he could walk away and leave Evander to his dramatics in peace.

In the end he did none of those, and Evander was the first to speak. His hands warmed as he clasped Stephen's, and now he brought them to his mouth to press a gentle kiss along the red-scabbed broken skin on Stephen's fingertips. "I get hasty with my words, and I've hurt you. I am so sorry."

The words fell like diamonds from his lips, crystal clear and so precious. Was that not what Stephen had been waiting to hear?

Somehow the victory rang hollow. "You don't need to—" he began, but Evander laid a finger over his lips.

"I do, I think," he said, soft and tender, and his eyes were blue as the summer sky. "I *have* hurt you, and I didn't realize how badly until now." He couldn't be anything *but* sincere, searching Stephen's face for something, his smile so tentative and gentle. "I swear to you, it will not happen again. I am nothing without you, and from now on, a changed man."

Stephen should back away, say that his mind was made up, and yet… Evander had promised things before and not delivered, but he had also made many of their shared dreams come true.

"When you say you will change, what do you mean? Will you give up your pursuit of Lady Charlotte?" *Let us get right to the heart of this.*

Something flickered in Evander's eyes, but he nodded without more than a moment's hesitation. "Instantly," he vowed. He stroked his thumbs across the backs of Stephen's hands in a rhythmic caress. "I only wanted to do right by you, don't you see? My plan was to make sure we would both be taken care of. But I should have told you beforehand. I simply wasn't sure it would work," he admitted sheepishly, ducking his head so that his hair tumbled boyishly over his brow. "And I would have been doubly embarrassed if you had seen my failure. I hate to fail you. You have always been my—"

"Don't say 'muse'," Stephen interrupted him, his voice sharper than it should have been.

Evander looked stung, then seemed to shake it off. "My particular friend, then," he said instead. "My confidant, the one who knows all the secrets of my heart. It kills me that you thought I would ever willingly betray you." He sighed, shaking his head. "I thought—"

But he stopped there. Whatever Evander thought, it would not come out now. "Never mind," he declared instead. "It is all over with now."

So Evander had decided, and so it was fact—one bad habit of his that didn't seem nearly so dire as the rest. But where did that leave them?

Joshua's offer tempted him, not because he had always had the urge to move to Belgium or France—God forbid—but because he had been wounded to the core. And now Evander was saying all the things Stephen needed to hear, his eloquence wrapping Stephen in indecision.

"This is not only about trust," he said after a moment. The right words could never come when he needed them most. "Though, if you promise not to lie to me again, I will be satisfied." Evander nodded and spread his hands, looking vaguely scornful at the smallness of his request. "But we must talk about our work as well."

That got more of a reaction, Evander's body stiffening. Something about the way the light hit him brought back a rush of memories.

Sitting on the fence alongside the pasture, Evander hanging over it with his pants muddy and stockings torn. Sprawled on the sheets in their first lodgings, a rat-infested room barely large enough to unroll a straw mattress. The warm summer night with the stars dotting the sky overhead, no voices yet calling their names, no signs they had been missed and the road stretching on forever in front of their feet. He had taken Evander's hand then, begun to run, laughing with the sheer giddy joy of freedom.

"What do you mean?" Evander said.

Once he would have known every thought in Stephen's head. Once, Stephen would have spilled his heart without worry or fear. What had happened to those hopeful boys?

"I mean that I live in your shadow, and until recently I have been content to do so," Stephen began. Joshua had berated him, and had been more right than Stephen had wanted to think about. Now that Evander was being reasonable, his artifice stripped away, it might be his only chance to make him understand. "But I too have skills and should like the chance to develop them."

Evander sat silent, and Stephen pressed on. "There is a sonata I have been practicing, the Kreutzer. It is quite long, but perhaps the third movement only, when we play next. The piano line is not difficult—"

"But of course!" Evander straightened. He crooked an eyebrow at Stephen, lit up with an idea. "Coventry has requested a concert, you know, before we go. You choose the program, we shall play your sonata," he offered grandiosely. "That gives us today and tomorrow to rehearse." He clasped Stephen's hand again and brought it to his chest, all earnest and bright. "Then you will see how devoted I am to you and your success."

He wanted to stay angry, should stand firm in his resolve to leave. But how could he be so cruel now, when

Evander gazed at him with hope and adoration, Stephen's hand pressed over Evander's beating heart? He had complained about their inequality, now Evander was repairing that. He had been hurt by Evander's foolish attentions to Charlotte, now he swore that dalliance was over. What more right did Stephen have to complain?

Had he not done worse, by running to Joshua's side when Evander was righteously angry?

Stephen's mind swirled, thoughts coming at him in disjointed fragments. Joshua's arms, his kisses, his laughter and his quiet conversation, the peace that suffused Stephen's soul when they were in the same room.

Then, Evander's wildness, his charm, the way the company revolved around him, pulled into his wake and trapped there, the fire in his touch, and the past they shared.

"Say you will stay with me," Evander said quietly and firmly. "And you will not abandon me to go play with the *simpletons* at the opera house. They would not know syncopation from *alla breve* if you inscribed it on their eyelids, and are universally drunkards, to boot. Your talents would be utterly wasted."

Evander looked so upset at the prospect, his brow furrowed in consternation, that Stephen couldn't help laughing. He shook his head to signal his no, and Evander relaxed.

"That I can swear with easy conscience," Stephen promised. "All I want is for us to be equal partners in this venture of ours. Remember how things used to be?"

"Very well indeed." He turned Stephen's hand over and traced his fingertips, examined the cuts and bruises on his fingertips with a dispassionate eye. "We are bound together, you and I," he said after a moment, all trace of humor gone. "We have been all our lives. Promise me you will not fight with me again. I couldn't bear it."

"I cannot promise that," Stephen replied lightly, and he took his hand back. "You know how we are. But I can promise that I will try to fight only about ridiculous things. Such as which of us ate the last of the jam, and whose turn it is to go to the butcher's."

"Always thinking with your stomach," Evander teased him. He stood, pressed a kiss to Stephen's forehead. Stephen flinched without thinking, and Evander pulled away. He looked Stephen over and frowned. "You'll end up too fat for your good suits if you're not careful."

Stephen stretched, leaning back on the settee, having it in his mind to look as casual and unaffected as possible. "That's your fault for convincing me to come to a house party with a very well-stocked larder," he jibed back, and Evander chuckled. The laugh didn't reach his eyes.

"Point well taken," he said, and straightened his waistcoat. He took off his cravat and began to retie it, his fingers moving confidently over and around the fine linen. "I will see you at dinner tonight?" he asked pointedly.

Stephen nodded. "You will." And then the thought of *that*—of facing Charlotte and Joshua at the same table, all four of them knowing some of the undercurrents, but not all of them, and the rest of the guests oblivious—

Joshua. Only, inside his head, he must still be "Beaufort" when spoken of aloud, in case of discovery.

Joshua would not be pleased. He disliked Evander, more so now than before.

The thought of Evander touching Joshua, kissing him, fucking him the way Stephen had just fucked him—it all turned his stomach into knots in unpleasant ways and left a painful lump in his chest.

"I know you have been concerned for our safety," Stephen said carefully. One wrong word could send a thousand things spinning out of control again in an instant. "Perhaps it would be better for us to continue to stay in our own rooms for the next few nights. Once we are home again and no longer in danger of discovery—"

"You are wise, as ever," Evander agreed easily, too easily for Stephen's ego. But no matter. Bruises to that healed easily, and he wouldn't be put in a position to mediate between the two men. He could work with Evander, spend precious time with Joshua, and neither would have to deal with the other.

For at least a little while longer, he would not have to choose.

Chapter Sixteen

"I don't think that it looks like me." Lady Amelia pursed her lips and created some unattractive wrinkles around her mouth as she did so. Joshua barely resisted the urge to draw them in to his pencil sketch. "Do you think that looks like me?"

The girl hovered over his shoulder as he added a last few lines on the canvas to round out the fullness of her skirts. The sun was setting, their light going, and the sitting that had begun just after nuncheon was finally, interminably (after four *"but I don't think that's quite* right, *Mother"* trials and an agreement on a pose dragged out of them like a dentist with an aching tooth) complete.

"I think it looks very well, darling," Lady Chalcroft pronounced with an eagle eye staring down at them both. "Now for colors—of course, you will use blues and greens primarily in the background? Amelia looks her best in darker shades."

Amelia gave him a flat smile from within her cream-and-lavender muslin gown.

"I think," Joshua said, biting his tongue, *that you two are pains in my—* "that we should reconvene at a later time. Tomorrow, perhaps? And we can discuss it further. Or, should you care not to miss the earl's picnic, I can carry on based on my own judgment and you can give the yay or nay upon your return." *Please choose that option.*

"The picnic will be dull." Amelia sighed, gathering her shawl about her shoulders and wandering away from Joshua to circle the drawing room and survey the paintings on the walls. "You know as well as I do, Mother. There is not much point now."

"The Downe boys are going, and that will do just as nicely," Lady Chalcroft answered with a face as pinched and sour as if she'd bitten into a lemon.

Joshua tuned them out as he tidied up his materials— no sense leaving the mess out for the servants to trip over or have to dust around. Too many projects and too much time spent thinking about other things when he should have been working, and the small space had suffered for it.

The door was still closed when he looked at it again. Stephen had not come to find him. He wasn't likely to again. The reality settled hard around Joshua's heart, a heavy millstone of disappointment around his gut. Still, the day was not over. Asking a man to uproot his entire life was not the kind of request that should be answered quickly, no matter how good it would have been to hear the words "yes, yes, I will run away with you" fall from his lips.

"Thank you, Mr. Beaufort," Lady Chalcroft said, drawing his attention away from sorting the handful of preliminary sketches. "We shall see you on the morrow and resume. Will you have something for us to look at by then?"

And there went any hope of joining the others for anything approaching a leisurely dinner, or finding time afterward to speak with Stephen again.

"Yes, I think so," Joshua said calmly, reordering his calendar in the back of his mind. Paying clients first, always, then personal projects, then personal life.

It was not as though Stephen could go too far. He would find him tomorrow, or the day after, and have a conversation then.

The meeting the next day turned into a longer consultation, and then a session to prepare his pigments and lay down his base colors. Joshua did not leave the studio until early afternoon, his neck in a crick and his hands spotted and smudged with paint.

He heard the music as he passed by the closed doors to the conservatory, a complicated piano-and-violin piece that stopped, started, stopped again. The wood of the door was cool beneath his fingertips, the brass handle cooler still. Should he go in? He had nothing at all to say to Cade, and nothing that could be said with Cade nearby.

They had obviously worked out some of their differences, which, he supposed, gave him the only answer he needed.

He let go of the door handle and kept on walking.

As tempting as it was to stay in his room and avoid the concert entirely, his absence would be far too conspicuous. Joshua dragged his feet on his way down to the drawing room, though. He was in no particular hurry to take his seat and listen to ten minutes of Horlock droning on about grouse or guns, before having his suspicions of a reconciliation confirmed. Imagining Sophie's critique if she caught him hiding from his problems was the thing that finally had shifted him out of his chair before the hour grew too late.

He obviously had not been in hiding long enough. For there was Stephen, turning the corner in the hallway just ahead of him. He carried his violin case and his hair was tied back. He had dressed for the occasion, his suit of charcoal-gray wool cut to cleave to his back and shoulders, a dark-green waistcoat bringing out the thousand shades of brown of his eyes.

"Ashbrook!" Joshua called out without thinking.

Forget the dozens of sketches already in his book—this was how he wanted to paint Stephen. He would hang this portrait in a drawing room with curtains the same deep-red velvet as the bow holding back his hair. He held himself differently, back straight and his head high. His color was up, a faint flush across the tops of his cheekbones, his eyes so alive that he all but crackled with anticipation. There he was—the seraph Joshua had seen at Vauxhall a lifetime ago.

At Vauxhall, and then a hint of it the previous night when Stephen had looked up at him, Joshua's emissions still wet on his lips, his hair tangled and his eyes blown wide with desire. Joshua had never wished so hard to be sixteen again, capable of becoming aroused to full strength over and over in a single night. He would have taken his pleasure in Stephen's arse, in his mouth, stroked himself to orgasm and splattered pearling drops of come across Stephen's chest, his face, his hair.

He lost his words, his mouth dry.

Is this how you seem every time you play for an audience? Or is this somehow for me?

"Beaufort," Stephen greeted him, glancing each way down the hallway as he said it, as though saying chaste hellos would somehow reveal them. "You are coming, are you not? I would be exceedingly pleased if you would, and then give me your critique after. It is not as grand as the concert halls in town, nor do we have a proper chamber group, but nevertheless!" He all but burbled, the words spilling out thick and fast. He bounced lightly on his toes, an excited boy trapped in a man's body. Joshua could not help but smile, his excitement contagious.

But you have still had no answer.

No news may be good news.

"What have you done with the real Ashbrook?" Joshua teased him, letting his worries and resentment float away on the wind. What good would it do? "I let a morose and pondering soul out of my room two nights ago, and here before me is a man so buoyant he is at risk of floating away."

Stephen smiled, and God himself would have wept for the beauty in it. "It is always like this," he confessed sheepishly, "right before a concert. I feel bubbly inside, twisted and tight. Then when I play, I can fall into the music, and it falls out of me, and I disappear entirely. It is the greatest feeling in the world, Beaufort, and I cannot begin to explain it."

"I think, perhaps, I can imagine," Joshua said softly. He wasn't thinking of his painting. "You and Cade, then— you've decided to play with him after all?"

Stephen nodded, some of that ebullience vanishing. He glanced down the hall at the closed parlor door. "We are still here as players at the earl's invitation," he said simply. "When he asks us to play at the party, we need to do so, regardless of what else may have transpired." He didn't seem nearly as angry or upset about it as perhaps Joshua might have expected. "We can act like adults, I think. It will be fine."

Joshua barked out a short, sharp laugh. "You can. Possibly. Can he?"

"We have come to terms with some things," Stephen said, obviously hedging around some less comfortable truth. "You worry too much." He tugged his waistcoat into place and posed, hand over his stomach and one at the small of his back. "Tell me honestly." The subject change came out of the blue. "Does this fit me properly? My coat is not too snug?"

It was akin to driving in a buggy with his brother, the frame sliding to a sudden stop before sending the horses galloping off in another direction entirely. "No," Joshua said, trying to keep up. "It fits as it should, and you look very well in it. Is this some ploy to distract me?"

"No," Stephen argued, but he dropped his arms and looked thoughtful. "No... Never mind. Things are changing," he said and smiled, his eyes alight. "You will see. All will be well for us."

"By 'us', do you mean you and Cade, or you and I?"

Stephen frowned, his brow furrowing. "You're angry with me for speaking to him?"

"What?" Joshua asked. "No, of course not. You're free to speak to whomever you please." Was that not obvious? "I'm worried that you're setting yourself up for another fall. Or have you forgotten how he deceived you?" he finished, concern thick in his mouth.

Stephen curled his fingers in, rubbing his thumb across the scabbed-over cuts on his fingertips. "He's sworn to me that he's done with her," he said quietly, and Joshua's heart sank. "He's promised to make the changes I asked for. He is a good man at heart."

"When it suits his own devices! Listen to yourself, Ashbrook. He has you so turned inside out that you would sooner accuse your own mother of treachery than admit he has done you wrong."

"You don't know him...you didn't hear him yesterday."

"I don't need to hear him to know what kind of nonsense he's capable of making you believe." Could he not see that he was being manipulated, that he was being played as skillfully as he played the violin in the case in his hand? Joshua could not fathom Cade's endgame, but this he was sure of—the man was no innocent naïf.

"Ashbrook?" The parlor door opened and Cade stood framed in the space, his back tall and tailored black suit sitting just so. He looked from one to the other and arched a perfect golden eyebrow. "Are you coming?"

"Yes, of course," Stephen answered. He met Joshua's eyes for a moment, some nebulous and unasked question there. He turned away, violin case in hand, and he headed past Cade and into the parlor.

Cade watched Stephen as a hawk watched his prey, then turned the force of that speculative stare on Joshua. They locked gazes for a minute, maybe less, Cade's steel-blue eyes cold as the grave. Then he followed Stephen into the room beyond.

A chill ran down Joshua's spine, a reaction to the malevolence that had flashed there before Cade had stuffed it down again. Was he imagining things, or was there something vicious lurking below the surface?

The house assembled. Joshua found a seat on the far side of the audience, which left him staring at the back of Stephen's shoulders and at Cade's face above the pianoforte.

He knew the first two pieces that they played—naturally, both Cade's work. But this was the first time Joshua had been this close to see Stephen perform, his eyes closed, his fingers dancing along the frets, his body leaning in to the bow so that it all became a part of him.

Applause rang out when they finished, genuine and pure. Stephen bowed, gestured to Cade, who rose and bowed as well. Charlotte leaned in, her face flushed and eyes bright, her applause louder than any of the others.

"Please…" Cade gestured and the audience fell silent, "…allow us to hold you here for one more piece. It is not one of my own composition," he said as though in apology, pressing his hand to his breast when Charlotte made a soft sound of disappointment, "but one of Ashbrook's favorites, and I am promised that you will like it just as well."

Stephen chuckled and shook his head, but the whole introduction sounded somewhat hollow and false. Had this been Stephen's price for forgiveness, playing something not of Cade's making? Was his sense of self-preservation really so cheaply bought?

The piece began well. The light and exuberant joy in the music was as unlike Cade's moody melancholy as it was possible to get on the same instruments, tripping through the rhythms and the melody like sun bursting through clouds in the spring.

Until it changed, and Stephen faltered, not missing a note but bowing furiously to keep up with Cade's new tempo. And then again, Cade slowing, not by much, but enough to throw off the harmonies.

Stephen's head came up, his shoulders tight, and Joshua could not see his expression. From the corner of his eye, though, he did catch the smug flicker of a smile that flashed across Cade's face when he varied his tempo once more and Stephen could not follow.

Bastard!

The applause at the end was scattered and thin, nothing like the thunder of approval Cade's compositions had received.

Joshua could not go up to them immediately, not until the room cleared, not with what he had seen and heard still thundering angrily through his mind.

Coventry got to them first. Stephen's shoulders slumped as he listened to the hissed diatribe directed entirely at him, Cade looking ever more like the cat who had found his way into the larder, self-satisfied and ready to purr at his own cleverness.

"…when I pay for musicians, I expect decent music! Enough with this foolishness, Ashbrook," Coventry said as

Joshua drifted closer, trying to look innocuous. "You will play as Cade dictates. If you must pick other pieces, for God's sake, practice them first!"

Stephen saw him coming and waved him off. Joshua stopped, because he could say something, intervene! Stephen shook his head, and Cade glared, and that was enough. Joshua turned away and against every ounce of his own better judgment, left them to their fate.

"Why would he do such a thing?" Stephen paced restlessly, the crackling frustration and bottled-up anger emanating from him in almost-visible waves. The wine sloshed in the crystal glass, splashing out over his hand as he gestured in the air. "I believe what you say you saw, but I cannot fathom it. Why would he sabotage his own concert and then lay the blame for it at my feet?"

"To control you." No need for diplomacy or secrets here—they were utterly alone in the parlor and all others had long since gone to bed. "To make you unsteady and uncertain, as he has most definitely achieved. You stood your ground with him yesterday, and this is his revenge."

And, once again, Stephen flatly refused to *listen*. "Maybe I misunderstood," he ventured, scraping his hand back through his hair. Joshua's scornful look in response was enough to stop him from carrying on down that path of excuses again. "I could have chosen something that did not require so much rehearsal."

"There is no excusing bad behavior," Joshua said. "Cade intended to hurt you, and he has. The only question that remains is, what do you intend to do about it?"

"It's not that simple," Stephen said once again, and Joshua utterly despaired of him. "Though it was the news from the Swan that shook him and began all of this nonsense with Lady Charlotte."

"He has been capricious before." Joshua felt compelled to correct him, though he may as well not have spoken.

"What if we all went abroad," Stephen suggested halfheartedly. "Your invitation to travel with you—"

"No," Joshua said instantly, gripping the stem of the glass so tightly that he half feared it might snap in his hand. "My invitation was for you and you alone, not for you to bring the man who belittles, torments and publicly humiliates you. And even if you are so attached to him that you are willing to accept that treatment, know that I most certainly am *not*."

Stephen nodded, laid his empty hand on the mantelpiece and stared into the fire, his head low.

Joshua sat on the couch and watched him, cataloguing the lines of his body, the way his shoulders sagged, the defeat in the lines on his face. Joshua closed his eyes and tried to bring back the vision of his dream cottage: Stephen curled beneath a blanket before the fire, chopping wood in the back lot in nothing but his shirtsleeves and buckskins, lovemaking and tasting wine off of his lips in their own small bed beneath a thatched roof.

Stephen, watching restlessly out of the window in rainy days. Getting a letter from Cade and ripping it open with joy in his eyes. Walking out of the door with everything he owned in a bag on his shoulder, leaving Joshua alone again, with nothing but faint memories of a time he was almost loved.

"And if I said I would come?" Stephen finally said, bringing his glass to his mouth once more.

"No," Beaufort said slowly, and his first dreamscape shattered and vanished before the second version faded. "No, I think not. How do I know that you will not turn tail and run from me as well? How do I know that, the next time he calls for you, you will not drop everything and fly to his side?"

He picked up speed and force as he spoke, the pent-up flood of words spilling from him, as water over a crumbling dam. "Now that I've seen you disregard your own pain moments after a wound, how can I trust you to remember it once months or years have passed?"

"I will not!" Stephen said angrily. "Once I make a commitment, it is made. What you think of as passion for Evander is only this—loyalty to the man I thought I loved. A reminder that I *did* love, even though he's broken my faith, and I his."

"Why do you feel guilty, when he is the one who betrayed you?"

Stephen balled his fist but did not strike out, laying the side of his hand against the marble of the mantelpiece. "Because he was right, in a way. We never made any promises. I was the one at fault for overreacting."

Joshua rolled his legs out from under him and stood, pacing the couple of steps across the room. "You know as well as I do that that's a foul lie. And I'll tell you another thing…" he pointed at Stephen's chest, not allowing himself to get distracted by the pink pout of his bottom lip or the way Stephen's stubble was growing in along his jaw, "…I'll tell you why you feel guilty, and it's not because of *anything* you and I did.

"It's because when he threw you to the wolves—not once now, but twice?—you felt a tiny flicker of relief both times. That, *finally*, it would all be over. That you wouldn't have to be the one to make the choice to leave."

Stephen backed up, putting space between him and Joshua's accusatory finger. "You don't know what you're talking about."

"On the contrary!" Joshua shook his head. "I see it all very clearly."

It all spread itself out for him in easy-to-dissect pieces, the bricks and mortar of a man's life laid bare. He spoke quietly as the enormity of it impressed itself upon him. Stephen's brown eyes bore the pain of a thousand ancient and fresh-made scars, crying out for understanding, patience, love—all the things Joshua desperately wanted to lay at his feet, but could not.

"You pretend at being an adult, but you're terrified of standing on your own. You won't leave him until he destroys you or abandons you of his own volition, just so that you will be the blameless one.

"I'll not be your fallback, Mr. Ashbrook." Joshua drained his glass and set it on the side table for a servant to clear later. "Stand on your own two feet."

And if he was being a coward as well, so be it. He was used to surviving on his own. One brief affair changed nothing. Not if he did not allow it to.

"Are you done?" Stephen challenged him, his raw and bleeding heart so evident in the sound of his voice.

"I believe I am," Joshua said, and without another word, he left the room.

Chapter Seventeen

Leaving Belmont House without saying farewell to Joshua was easily one of the most difficult things Stephen had ever done.

Trying to convince Armand to take a message had been no help at all. She had slammed the trunk lid down, narrowly missing his fingers, and pointed toward the sitting room door.

"Out."

"You helped us at the stables," he pleaded, not too proud to make this his stand. "Why will you not do so again?"

"I helped *him*," she corrected him sharply. "You were a side effect and nothing more. Get yourself gone, Mr. Ashbrook. And if you want what's best for Mr. Beaufort, you'll stay away from him as well."

He had no illusions, following that exchange, that Joshua had received any message.

So be it, then. In his uncertainty, he had burned a bridge that had once promised him salvation. Fighting back tears on the journey home had been more difficult than ever, a desperate ache consuming his organs one by one and leaving him a hollow shell of a man. The last, long look of disgust in Joshua's eyes floated in the black every time he tried to rest.

"I'll not be your fallback."

And he had tried to use him that way, hadn't he? Taken something as perfectly precious as Joshua's affection for him (he dare not be so arrogant as to think of it as love—the word had never once been spoken) and turning it into a safe place to fall. Joshua deserved so much better than that.

"You won't leave him until he destroys you."

That wasn't true, though! It hadn't been an exaggeration to call things complicated. How did one untangle half a lifetime and begin again? He should have said yes when Joshua first made his offer. He should have told Evander to go hang, come home alone, packed his belongings and left. Then he would have Joshua in his arms even now, and he would deserve to call himself a man.

Then maybe it wouldn't hurt every time he breathed.

Evander said little, passing the time writing letters when the road was smooth and reading a book when it was rough. Hours bled into each other, and the countryside sped by them, all clothed in shades of gray.

Light and color returned when the carriage rumbled through the streets of London, the familiar scents and sounds of the city rising up around him as he half dozed on the uncomfortable seat.

Evander slept, his arms folded across his chest, seemingly untouched by their return to the world of the living. His chest rose and fell evenly, his face unmarked by the traumas of the past six weeks.

There were fewer familiar faces as they progressed through St. James, but Stephen looked for them anyway. Tattered and mud-splattered newssheets proclaiming the local disgrace burned into his eyes at every lamppost, the "Vere Street Coterie" to be tried and condemned all together.

The Swan was gone, the building empty, and men crossed the street to avoid being seen walking near it. Another few weeks and then the papers would be full once more with names and dates, columns thick with damning testimony. Riots would fill the streets again.

A cold chill settled down Stephen's spine, one that not even the sultry summer heat could touch.

Stumbling up the stairs to the sounds of Annie's welcoming catcalls did help a little. The familiar old walls and the rise of the wooden steps under his feet grounded him in something real and solid, better than the disconnected self-loathing in which he was floating.

Evander moved through their rooms like a whirlwind, unfastening the shutters and throwing them wide, letting in air and light.

Stephen flinched away from him as he brushed past, even the faint contact setting off something dark and uncomfortable in the pit of his stomach. Easier to drag his belongings into his bedroom, plead exhaustion and sickness from the carriage ride, and close the door.

He flung himself on his bed, the mattress hard and low, compared to the luxury at Belmont House. But the linens smelled faintly like Annie's homemade soap, the dents were in the shape of his own bones, and he could put the pillow over his head and block out the rest of the world long enough for his turning gut to settle and his aching head to begin to clear.

It had seemed a simple plan at the time. Pacify Evander, take his concessions for the peace offering they had seemed to be and not rock their already shaky boat any further. Wait until everything was calm again and only then broach the subject of leaving. Or once they returned home, simply pack and take his leave. He was an adult, and as long as he left money for his share of the rent, there was nothing that could hold him here by law.

Only it hadn't worked the way he had intended. He had said the wrong things, waited when he should have given answers immediately, prioritized Evander's moods over Joshua's and generally made an enormous mess of things that should have been simple.

Unfit to call myself a man.

And what had been the end result? Back in the place he had left six weeks ago, a changed man and, yet, not changed enough. What choices did he have?

Only one. To keep on living, stay clear of the law and be sure he did not make the same mistake again. If he ever had another chance to be happy, to seize it and never let go.

Please let Joshua be well. Let him, at least, find peace.

Days passed in a blur, the first few after their return spent unpacking, putting out the word they had returned. More raids had followed the evening of terror on Vere Street, and even the boldest among London's mollies had gone to ground. Rumors swirled, as they always did—

another tavern, another place they could once again safely call home. It was too soon to go prowling the streets in search. It was too soon for a great many things.

Evander seemed less affected by the changes than he had in the country, contradictory creature that he was. He moved through his days in a haze of preoccupation, sitting at his writing desk and his pianoforte, with equal concentration.

The cuts on Stephen's fingers healed, the thin, dark scabs becoming faint pink lines, all traces of Joshua's gentle ministrations long gone from his body. He could not bring himself to wear the green waistcoat again.

Evander took it upon himself to retrieve the post from the table in Annie's back hallway, though the first week saw little coming from anywhere. Stephen had hoped…he had hoped in vain, obviously, since not once did Evander return with a letter for him.

He could always take the initiative, write to Joshua and beg his forgiveness, pledge—what? What did he have to offer now that would be enough to make up for his offenses?

The clatter of the door drew Stephen out of his reverie. He set the violin under his chin and adjusted his hold on the bow. The notes on the sheets in front of him swam in his vision, spinning around each other until they became incomprehensible, and all he could draw out of the instrument was a low, dire-sounding cry of distress.

"You are sounding better and better all the time," Evander teased him, his eyes showing more life than they had in a while.

He brandished an unfolded letter, as though the neat, cramped lines of handwriting could tell Stephen anything from that distance. The rich smell of stew and bread wafted through from the sitting room. Evander had brought dinner up from downstairs again.

"If you keep at it, you may be back to your first year's lessons in no time."

Scraping his bow across the strings to make them scream was more satisfying than it should have been, Evander wincing and making a face at him for his troubles. Stephen ran his scale one last time, just to enforce his point, and set Rosamund in her case.

"Your support spurs me onward to new heights," he replied churlishly. "I have lost my music in all this business and cannot find it again."

It lay in the pit of grief within his gut, chewed to pieces by the ravenous hunger of the black void.

"This will lift your spirits, then." Evander dismissed his complaints with an airy wave. "I have repaired relations with Coventry. It required some doing, of course, after your little display, but he is a magnanimous man, and we shall not lose our living after all."

"*My* display?" Stephen echoed in disbelief, but Evander only nodded as though he had agreed.

"All will be forgiven, in time," he said in what was obviously meant to be a kindly voice that rang with condescension. "All you'll need to do is apologize and we shall both be reinstated to his affections. We shall not need to set the hat out in the tavern again after all."

Of course, it would always come down to Stephen apologizing, abasing himself, begging for a chance to repair the things that he had not been responsible for breaking. The dagger twisted deeper into his spine, and defeat pressed down on his shoulders, a thick fog coating the world in gray.

"Apparently not," he said, for lack of anything else that would not begin another battle that he was fated to lose.

"Come and eat," Evander said, apparently oblivious to Stephen's turmoil. He folded the letter and tucked it into his pocket alongside another one of similar size. "Your food will get cold."

Stephen rested his head back against the window frame and looked out. The world moved by outside as though the hand of the Creator had slowed them all to half time, figures drifting through the streets, slow as a draining vat of molasses.

"I'll be there in a moment," he agreed, and hated himself even for that.

Evander went out that night and left Stephen behind. Noise floated up the stairs from the tavern below, raucous voices rising and falling, their words indistinct, but the joy and camaraderie in them clear. He could go down, fit himself among them again, remember the man he used to be. Or he could sit here and stare daggers at his music stand, and accomplish absolutely nothing of any worth.

Sighing and kicking his feet back, Stephen rose and took up his violin again. If there was nothing else left to him, at least he could play without care for being overheard.

Perhaps that might unblock the piece of his soul that he had lost.

Rosamund. He drew her out and inspected her lines with a practiced eye. He had been thinking of her as a tool again, not the lady she was, and she deserved better. Oil, then, to keep her pegs turning smoothly, a new set of strings fresh from their paper packet to make her sing with a clear, bright voice. His old bow, frayed and tattered and long overdue for repair, he left in the case and drew rosin down along the clean, taut hair on the newer of the two.

When Rosamund gleamed again, her wood polished and strings tuned, he set her under his chin. His bow came to her strings like a caress, gentle and tremulous, and she squawked in protest, no virgin to be touched with uncertain hands.

Scales to begin, as he had every time since that first month of lessons, the movements coming back to his fingers as the breath came back to her song. Once he had run them all through, his fingers warm and the tips only aching a tiny bit, he changed, his eyes closed, not following any music except for that which bubbled up inside.

It began as the piece he had played in the conservatory the night he had stumbled upon Evander and Charlotte, a dirge that howled pain in a minor key, gathering up the darkness in a whirlwind and setting it spinning through his mind.

Joshua had found him then, cared for him and kissed him, taken him to bed and shown him what it meant to give his heart away, as well as his body. He hadn't understood, then, what a gift it was. The longing flowed from him, pure and sweet, strains of a melody that still sang in his heart.

Blue-gray eyes, sleepy and sated. He had pressed his mouth to Joshua's eyelids, so soft against his lips. His hands, stained with pigment and charcoal, limning out a sketch as deftly as a sailor played out line to a filling sail. His laugh, the curve of his neck, the fierce intellect behind his dry wit. The peace that surrounded him, restful and calm, a rock of strength around which all other points circled. His compassion in attempting to care for an idiot man who barely knew his own mind half the time.

Stephen played until his fingers cramped and calluses stung. No Joshua to bind his wounds this time, he had to take care of himself.

Opening his eyes, he set Rosamund down in her case, flexing his hands to ease the tightness in his bones. The strains of the solo curled around his thoughts, the melodic line clearer than ever.

He could write it down, he realized slowly, write it down and not lose it, maybe build something of his own on top of the melody, something he could play that was untainted by his roiling and conflicted emotions.

There would be paper in Evander's desk—he had purchased a ream of it only the other day. He would never miss a handful of sheets, and Stephen was the one who had paid for the ink!

The mess on the desk spilled over onto the chair, nothing meticulous or organized about it. Old pages tumbled over in a loose stack beside his inkwell, scraps of notes fighting with a handful of farthings for surface space, a playbill from two years ago and an ink-stained handkerchief. A half-eaten apple rested inside his pewter mug, the beer long gone but for a sticky film around the edge.

The drawer was no better and he should not have expected it to be. Underneath a handful of old laundry lists, he found not the new paper he had been expecting, but a handful of letters—unfamiliar, the address written in a round and girlish hand.

Mr. Evander Cade, the top one read.

Who? Not his mother—she had died some years ago. No sister that he still spoke to, and cousins would have no way of knowing where he was.

Stephen should not open the letter on the top of the pile. Curiosity never did anything but harm, and Evander had every right to his privacy.

He opened it anyway.

My dearest love, the letter began, and Stephen's stomach clenched.

You cannot imagine how thrilled I was to receive your letter yesterday.

He did not need to look at the date at the top to know what it would be—the day before, which meant Evander had written this week, in secret, and more besides.

My body yearns for your touch again and my mouth for your kisses, pleasures such as I had never known before and

303

now die to know again. How much longer before we can meet, my darling heart? We arrive in town tomorrow. Tell me the plan and I will be yours.

Stephen deflated, air spilling out of him and his body slumping back into the chair, the darkness inside mercifully making him utterly numb.

So that explained it. The reason for Evander's cheer, his lack of interest in Stephen's bed. (To which, truthfully, Stephen had not objected. There was only one touch he wanted now and it was not Evander's.)

He had said he was done with her, but he would be off to meet her…

Stephen looked out the window, the darkness of night settling in. Now. He would be with her now, unless Stephen missed his guess. He had given up his own dreams for a house built on a foundation of lies, and the letters from Evander's secret mistress were his proof.

Stephen pushed his chair back with such force that it toppled over with a crash, and swept the papers off the desk with his arm, the mug and apple core clattering and spinning across the uneven wooden floor.

"God *damn* you," he hissed, and could not be sure whether he meant Evander or himself.

He was alone in the flat when he went to bed, Evander humming somewhere in the sitting room when he awoke.

The sun streamed in through the shutters he had forgotten to close, piercing through the fog surrounding his brain. The empty bottle on the floor and taste of stale wine in his mouth explained why his head thrummed with pain and how he had ended up draped half across his own bed, still in his shirt and stockings from the day before.

Dulled the pain of our own stupidity in the arms of Bacchus, did we? How novel.

Sitting up was difficult, his head swimming, but he managed. Washing cleared some of the fog away, enough to make him feel mostly alive. Breakfast would do the rest. He dragged on trousers and fastened them as he left his room, memories slowly filtering back around the gray.

Evander went to Charlotte last night, and I left Joshua behind.

And there he was, the man himself, spreading jam thick on toast and so relaxed in his bearing that one would think he had the sure and certain prospects of a king. He sat back in his chair when Stephen entered the room, his eyes crawling over Stephen's body in a way that used to make him feel desired, and now only left a film of dirt behind that he would never be able to scrub away.

"Good morning to you," Evander said, amused.

"And to you," Stephen replied, purely by reflex. Breakfast first, to fortify himself, and then—

Evander rose from his chair, oily as a snake, and insinuated himself between Stephen and the bread. His hands fell to Stephen's hips, his shirt bagging over the waistband of his trousers, and he leaned in as though to deliver a kiss.

Stephen twisted away sharply, forcing Evander off-balance and the kiss to land on air.

"What has gotten into you?" Evander asked peevishly, grabbing for Stephen's hip again.

"Nothing, and I prefer to keep it that way," Stephen snapped. He pushed Evander's hand away, the flash of fury on Evander's face spurring on his anger, rather than fear, as it once would have. "I know full well where your mouth has been."

Evander cocked his head, his eyes narrowing. "You've lost your mind," he said flatly, inspecting Stephen as though he were some kind of specimen on a tray.

"Oh no, I have not," Stephen retorted. "I have found it." The black pit inside him flushing bright and red. Fire clawed around the edges of his vision, his chest tight. "Does Charlotte carry your bastard yet? Have you planted your seed in noble soil?"

He lashed out, his hands landing on Evander's chest. He pushed, his rage blinding, and Evander stumbled back a step, his mouth hanging open. "Does that girl have any idea what kind of depraved monster she's given herself to?"

That got him talking again, Evander's voice a low hiss of fury. His hands clenched and his lip curled in a snarl. "You are just as depraved as I, if you want to discuss our sins, *Mr.* Ashbrook."

"Do not mistake me," Stephen snarled because he was *finished* with all of this. Finished taking orders, bowing and scraping, spending his life walking on knife edges because every misspoken word could start a conflagration. He lived with a cannon on a hair trigger in the bed beside him. How dare he imagine that Stephen would simply roll over and accept the correction? Except…except that he always had done so before, and the shame of that realization cut him open stem to stern.

"This is not because you prefer arse to cunt, but because you will sacrifice everyone around you to advance yourself. You care for nothing, and for nobody." Evander fell back another step and Stephen followed, driving him backwards with the force of will alone until Evander's back was against the sitting room wall. "You don't have the facility."

"And *you* do not have the balls," Evander spat. He grabbed Stephen and turned them both, his strength and surprise attack both catching Stephen off guard.

His back slammed against the wall, Evander's hand at his throat. Stephen scrabbled at Evander's arm, air cut off and his head throbbing with pain.

"You are *nothing*, a puling schoolboy, a sad *parody* of a man."

Stephen kicked his foot forward but only hit Evander's leg. Evander loosened his grip and Stephen dragged in a breath, his lips parted. Evander used the moment to force his mouth over Stephen's, his breath cloying with the taste of jam.

His hand tightened at Stephen's throat and black spots swam before his eyes. Evander forced his tongue between Stephen's lips, sluglike and thick.

Stephen pushed at him, brought his knee up between Evander's legs with as much force as he could muster, bit down with all his strength. In an instant he was free to breathe.

Evander staggered and caught against the edge of his writing desk. His mouth was open, his lips stained red, his hands dropping to the tender spot on his thigh where Stephen's blow had landed. An inch to the left and perhaps all Evander's dynastic dreams would have been shattered—worse luck!

Stephen's mouth filled with sour iron and he spit on the floor, his saliva streaked red with Evander's blood.

"You utter *bastard*," Evander cursed. He lunged forward, the letter opener from his desk gleaming sharp in his hand, now aimed for Stephen's throat, and his words chosen to slice open Stephen's heart. "I should have thrown you over for Beaufort long before now. At least he knows how to use his prick!"

"You don't get to say his name—not now, not ever!" Stephen did not make the conscious decision to let his fist fly, but in an eyeblink, it had, his knuckles striking Evander's cheek and nose with such force that he felt the bone splinter beneath the skin.

Evander fell, dropping the wickedly pointed blade. It clattered on the floor, spinning away to land beneath the desk.

Stephen lunged and pinned him down, Evander's stomach flat under the pressure of his knee. He pulled his fist back again, the world bathed in red, red of fire and blood, his pulse hammering like a drum in his ears.

Evander froze beneath him. He didn't fight back, only flinging his hands up to protect his face. The flush of anger drained from his skin, silent hopelessness and acceptance sitting in the grim lines of his face and the bleakness in his eyes. Stephen paused, the red mark on Evander's face already bright and swelling.

He couldn't do it. Stephen pushed himself back, the nausea thick in his throat. He stumbled away, his hand against the wall to brace himself.

"Stephen—" Evander said softly, sitting up. Blood ran freely from his nose, splattering his shirt with gore.

"Don't."

Stephen staggered to his feet, reeling, his knuckles throbbing and his throat worse. He would bruise; he and Evander would both be purple and blue by morning, their shirts stained blood red.

They had run together down the dark and starlit road, laughing, hand in hand. Evander had kissed him, shy and trembling, and they had sworn to be each other's.

How had it come to this?

"Don't," he repeated needlessly and gripped the doorframe until he could catch his breath once more.

His bag, then, and his clean clothes—he shoved the one into the other, grabbed the first waistcoat from the pile and slung it around his shoulders. Green, unworn since— A coat overtop of it to hide his shirtsleeves, his boots on his feet and hat on his head. His music, books, everything he could not replace easily. Rosamund in her case—she fit perfectly in his hand before he even realized he'd taken her, as though she had been anticipating flight.

Back on his feet, Evander tried to stop him as he headed for the door, but a hand up gave him pause as it had never done before.

Stephen's feet clattered on the stairs, the bag on his back no weight at all.

Evander threw the door wide before it could close, his hands on the frame, his face and shirt spattered bloody and his eyes burning with thwarted rage. "Where will you go?" he shouted down at Stephen's retreating back. "What will you do with yourself, now that you are alone?"

"Play for myself!" Stephen called back, his mood lifting higher, the black clouds parting with every step that took him farther away.

"You are *nothing* without me!" Evander cried out in desperation.

Stephen turned at the bottom of the stairs and spread his arms wide.

Evander loomed out at him from the top step, a gore-splattered gargoyle, spitting in his rage and unable to touch him.

"I am *music*," Stephen shouted, his triumph echoing up the stairwell.

The sunlight burst across his face, golden and warm, as he jumped down the outside stairs. He lifted his face into it, let the midmorning light burn across his eyelids and cheeks, soothe the burning, throbbing pain that circled his neck. He breathed in, his body shaking and tears welling up in his eyes. He blinked them away—men did not cry! Especially not at their moments of triumph!

Something crashed above him, sound echoing down the busy street. Stephen paused, his hands up behind him to tie back his hair, and the shutters of their flat flew open.

Evander appeared, only briefly, his face wiped mostly clean and his fist raised. "You forgot this!" he spat, and something winged at Stephen's face, a dark shape in the corner of his eye.

He stepped neatly aside, ducked his head, and the old leather-bound book clattered to the ground impotently.

He recognized it a moment after it landed, his ancient copy of Chapman's *Iliad*, annotated and stained by years of schoolboy pencils and sticky fingers. He picked it from the cobblestones, saluted with the book held high above his head. "Thank you for your kindness, Mr. Cade, as ever!"

People were staring, old ladies stopped in their shopping, Bunsen with his broom on his stoop, but Stephen broke into a run and waved as he passed them by. He was free, with the world open before him, wings on his feet and absolutely no idea where he was going.

He ran out of wind a few minutes later and sagged back against the stone wall of a tavern, laughing and breathless. The bag could sit on the ground for a few minutes while he sorted himself out, made himself look like less of a criminal on the run.

Shirt tucked into trousers, all buttons done, his waistcoat properly buttoned, his coat back on both shoulders… He slid his hand into his waistcoat pocket to check for his watch, and his fingers closed around fabric instead.

What is this, now?

It didn't come back to him until he drew it out and looked at it—the linen square with carefully monogrammed initials on the corner, *JBM. Joshua Beaufort.* The white linen still bore a few faint traces of rust-colored stains in the middle that Stephen had not been able to soak out, unwilling to entrust the handkerchief to the laundress. Unstarched or pressed, it fell softly across his hand. He curled his fingers into it and brought it to his face, but no trace of Joshua's scent lingered. Not after all this time.

Still. Perhaps it was an omen, or a sign. He drew it out between two fingers to smooth the wrinkles, folded it so the faint brown stains would not show and tucked it into his waistcoat pocket. A talisman, for luck.

John Meredeth had a guest bedroom that was not always filled with his wife's relations, and Stephen had long promised him those lessons for little Susannah. It might not be somewhere to keep him for more than a day or two, but it was a place to start.

He pulled his bag back up over his shoulder and set off in a new direction. He brushed his fingertips against the corner of the handkerchief and breathed out into the warm late-summer air.

More than one person had believed in him. Perhaps it was time to try to believe in himself.

Chapter Eighteen

August passed for Joshua as August always did, sultry and slow. Even the birds and beasts on the Horlock estate remained the same, cows with their jaws working for hours, placidly staring and seeing nothing, horses with their fine necks and long manes that deigned to allow him the occasional ride. The brook flowed as though every crick in the bed took more effort than it was worth to navigate, eddies and shallows capturing little minnows who were themselves too bored to attempt escape.

September kept the heat, lingering far longer into the fall than usual, as though Nature herself still clung to those last, lingering threads of summer.

This time, even taking his paints out to try and capture the perfection of the sunset failed him. The colors ran flat, the lines untrue, and in every cloud that smeared in gray across his canvas, he saw a thing he could not have again.

Letters came every day, and some for him, but never the one he watched for.

No! He did *not* watch for a letter. That was a ridiculous thought.

He could write to Stephen if he wished to. He simply...didn't wish to. No good would come of it.

If Stephen was ready to be with him, then *he* would write. He had cared for Joshua once; his devotions and the promises he had murmured against Joshua's skin had made that clear. But he was not free of Cade, and that was where Joshua had drawn his line. Stephen would have to come to him.

Until then, he would pick up the pieces of his life from where he had left them, his books on their shelf in neat array, his canvases stretched upon their frames, waiting to be splashed bright with color. He had been content here, among his paintings. He would find that again.

Except now, standing on the hillside and staring at the reds and oranges that streaked the darkening sky, even that was mocking him.

He closed his eyes and saw Stephen, as beautiful as crystal and just as easily broken. How could a soul with so many scars produce the music of the spheres, make it sing for him, and the universe pause to take notice? How could a man so badly wronged still trust? How did he keep enough passion burning within him to willingly give his heart to Joshua's keeping?

Joshua could not heal him. So he'd run away instead.

Memories pounded in his brain, voices and breathy moans and sweet, solemn oaths—all blending together until he could no longer remember who had said what and when. He tugged at his hair, his fingers buried in it, to have something to focus on other than his spinning thoughts—anything else! The pulls stung, sharp and ready, and his eyes filled hot with the faint pinprick of tears he had never shed.

Joshua fell to his knees, the heels of his hands pressed tightly against his eyes, stars bursting in the blackness of his vision.

I cannot save him. I cannot save myself. I am drowning.

No one was around, not for a mile at least. Safe in that knowledge, he let out a howl of frustration, struck at the easel with his fists and his feet. It toppled over into the grass, the canvas flying off to land elsewhere, wet paint smeared across his hands. It was barely satisfying, not nearly enough.

The world was dark, but not yet dark enough for stars. He let out a single, shuddering sob that seemed to echo in the twilight gloom. And he sat. He sat until the day's warmth had entirely fled the ground beneath him, until the heavens overhead were dotted with a million tiny flames, until his pulse had slowed in his ears and he could keep his breathing calm.

Two months was nothing in the grand scheme of things, and time healed all.

Or so he had once been promised.

The rain began as he trudged back to the house, lights flickering from only a handful of windows to guide his steps.

"Mr. *Beaufort*!" Mrs. Colby's shriek of dismay cut through him worse than the cold and wet as he slunk through the kitchen door, his paint box tucked under his arm. The walk back to the house hadn't been so bad, but the sudden rain, on top of the dark and the chill and the pounding in his temples from his emotional outburst—all that together was enough to make him feel, and apparently look, like something one of the dogs had found on the side of the road.

"What on God's green earth happened to you? And what were you doing out so late at night? You'll catch your death of cold, you will."

"I was caught in the storm, Mrs. Colby," Joshua protested, "nothing more."

But he had the bad luck to sneeze at precisely that moment, and the cook, all iron-gray curls and shoulders like a burly forester's, had his paints away from him, a blanket around his shoulders and one of the scullery girls spooning soup into a mug for him before he had the chance to look for his handkerchief.

"Honestly," he mumbled from deep within the wool blanket as she pressed him down into a chair in front of the banked fire, "I'll be fine."

"If you catch your death, Mr. Beaufort, I'd like to know who, precisely, is going to paint me my picture?" Mrs. Colby drew herself up to her full height, all of five feet, if that, dug her knuckles into her powerfully Teutonic hips and beamed down at him with a look of triumph. "It's not as though I have girls sitting about doing nothing and waiting to bring you medicines, either."

He had no choice but to concede to the superior force, waving his hand in a pale imitation of a white flag. The soup did smell good, the rich savory broth making his mouth water. He'd forgotten dinner, and the last thing he'd had to eat that day was a heel of bread and a cold sausage during his hike out.

"You're quite right," he conceded contritely, his fingers tingling as they dried and his toes warmed from the coals. "My apologies to you and your staff."

Drips of rainwater ran down his hair and splashed on the end of his nose. He shook his head violently, making water spray across the room in all directions, and the scullery girl broke into a cascade of giggles. He should draw her, as well as Colby, Joshua decided impulsively. And give them the pictures as presents when he…when he left.

Of course. When he departed for the Continent. Because what had seemed like such a bold plan at one point now seemed distant and trite. The vicomte had not responded, not yet, and he had only just begun to weave fantasies of himself and Stephen, setting out together to forge a brand-new life. And then it had all gone to pieces.

A foolish notion, and he would do well to forget about it.

He sipped at the soup, the peppery heat of it sliding down to puddle in his empty stomach and warm him through. The embers in the fireplace winked at him, glowing red eyes in the dim light of a single candle, and he solemnly blinked back.

"Finish that up—it'll do ye some good. You're too skinny as it is." Mrs. Colby patted him on the shoulder as she passed, her broad hand comforting. "And get yourself to bed. I'm off myself now, unless you'll be needing anything else."

"No thank you, mum." He found it within himself to tease her, just a little, and she beamed back.

"Cheeky," she reproved him. Then, "Sleep well then, Mr. Beaufort." She set her apron on the hook and bustled herself off, leaving the candle stub so he could see his own way to bed.

More than anything, at the moment, he needed sleep. Sleep and the numbness that would come with it, blanketing himself away from the world. Water trickling down his forehead blurred and prickled in his eyes, and he closed them against the insipid, flickering light.

The morning dawned with Joshua apparently little the worse for wear, only the linens hung over the grate to dry, a reminder of his lapse into morbid sensibility. His toes ached with the trace of a bruise, probably from when he had kicked the easel, but otherwise he remained unscathed. He stretched, his shoulders and neck clicking and cracking, the muscles in his arms and sides pulling luxuriantly against each other.

A new day was dawning, another chance to get his head on straight and rededicate himself to finding satisfaction in his life as it was. He was not an ungrateful man; he needed to remember that. His existence was a pleasant one overall, far beyond what many could claim.

Washed, dressed and looking like something approaching human once more, Joshua turned down the hall toward his studio. There were hours yet between the sunrise and the time when breakfast would be set upon the table, and he had work to do. The portrait of Lady Amelia, for one. He would be glad to get that canvas away from him and out of his life.

He saw Belmont House and Stephen whenever he looked at it, the drawing room in the background, the trees outside the window behind her. It was no wonder he was still fixated on his ridiculous summer dalliance, when he was surrounded by daily reminders!

The studio sat empty, curtains drawn back and windows opened to let in the air, the sound of birdsong outside lifting his spirits further. Yes—that would be his task today. But, first, to limber up his fingers and finish waking his eye…

He laid his hand upon the sketchbook sitting on his writing desk, the leather binding a soft and warm old friend. It fell open when he picked it up, not to a blank page, but to one so familiar that he could redraw it in his sleep.

Stephen Ashbrook arched across the paper, nude and yearning, his prick hidden in shadows and his teeth leaving impressions of passion in his dented lower lip.

Joshua slammed the book closed, a tremor in his hands.

He could burn the damn thing. Or at least those pages. He had the knife in his hand before he could develop the conscious inclination to seize it, to take the sheaf of pages in the other. One slice, rip the pages from the binding with the edge of the blade, and he could throw them away. One more step toward excising Stephen from his life.

Trembling, he pressed the tip of the blade against the page, denting it. And he could go no further. Light played over the lead and charcoal lines on the page, highlighted the angles of Stephen's face, touched his eyes, until it looked as though some of the sketch studies were pleading with him, yearning and alive.

Kiss me, Beaufort. Come to my bed tonight.

Joshua threw the knife aside. It clattered against the wall and fell to the ground, harmless. He slammed the book shut and pushed it back on his desk. *Enough.*

Enough yearning, enough pining, enough self-torture over someone he would never see again.

Clean paper, then. He drew it across the surface of the table, swiping his arm to push all else aside. Nothing here but untapped potential, the beginning of something fresh and new.

A figure study, if he was so obsessed with bodies today. A couple dancing, flowing out from under his fingers. Smudge the charcoal to shade the side of her dress, feathers cascading behind her head, and then the man. Tall and lean, his hand raised to turn her beneath his arm, long, lean fingers, deft and capable, a clean jaw and full bottom lip that he could catch in his teeth to elicit a gasp—

His cock ached, heat pooling in his gut at the memories, the sensation of that mouth trailing down his body.

"Damnation!" Joshua exploded as Stephen and Sophie stared at each other, smirking, on his page. Even the curve of the dancer's smile resembled *his*, the familiar sardonic edge and the shy evidence of a dimple lurking in the hollow of his cheek.

That too he pushed aside, buried under a pile of random pages that signified nothing.

His head followed, thumping against the smooth wood. The desk lay cool against his forehead, sturdy and unmoving. He ran his fingers through his hair, longer now than he usually preferred it, and prone to sticking up in all directions.

That was an excellent idea. He would ride to town, see a barber, order some materials for new pigments and revitalize his inspiration. A few days in London would do more to restore his spirits and his perspective than he could find in another month staring at the same four walls.

And once there, came the treacherous internal whisper, *who knows whom you might encounter?*

He shut that down without a word. He was going solely for himself and because he required a change of scenery. Nothing else and nothing more. And if he *did* happen to see either Ashbrook or Cade, his only logical course of action would be to turn around and walk away.

Isolation in the country had seemed like a terrible thing until Joshua found himself in London once more. The summer heat beat down on the cobblestones in greater force than on the grassy hills of Berkshire, compounding the sweat already prickling at the back of his neck and knees. Late afternoon crowds on the streets went about their business with little regard for the man standing and looking about.

The list of things Lady Horlock had asked him to acquire crinkled in his pocket, and his own requirements would necessitate a few very particular, personal stops. But not immediately. For the moment, at least, lodgings secured and his belongings stowed, he had the time to be his own man.

His ears ringing with the raucous calls of the shop owners closing for the evening, Joshua held his head high and scanned the storefronts for a likely place. His feet turned him toward Vere Street, at first, to the old haunts that he had once known so well. But memory caught up with memory before he went far. Nothing but death lay that way now.

Even if he were to go prowling among the pretty, young men clustering at Moorfields or St. James', none of them would recognize him, and they would all be strangers. Could he bring himself to do that now, be nothing more than a body in the night after having tasted something more?

Nothing stirred in him when he thought it over, no hint of interest from mind or prick. Dinner it would be, then, and back to his rented bed alone. A copy of the *Times* to keep him company, and he was set for entertainment as well.

Joshua stopped and stared at himself in the plate glass of the shop front, his reflected head superimposed on a bottle of perfume. He was undoubtedly as dull and boring a person as Sophie liked to tease, but there was something to be said for knowing what he liked.

He wrinkled his nose at the floating head in the reflection and caught the eye of a woman behind him just as he stuck out his tongue in impulsive response. The old dowager tut-tutted at him and he whipped his head forward, his cheeks flushing hot. There was a public house next door and he ducked inside before she could say anything to compound his embarrassment.

See? That's what being impulsive gets you.

It was early yet for dining and the pub was not nearly as full as it would be later on. Joshua claimed a table off to one side, the sturdy oak furniture worn down with years of use, but cleaned and polished until it gleamed.

A slab of bread and cheese, hot pigeon pie and a pint of good beer later, he felt almost—though not entirely—human once more.

There was little interesting in the paper. Parliament would argue about the same things in the same order from now until kingdom come and nothing there would change. That the king was unwell again was unpleasant, but he had an heir and so there would be few disruptions should he pass away.

Life continued as it must, despite the travails of a handful of men who had been trapped together at a house party. There was comfort to be found in that.

Bursts of laughter from another table broke into his reading. Two men sat over a cribbage board, cards in their hands. He couldn't catch all their conversation, but their rapid gesticulations back and forth and the way one of them was deliberately shaking out his sleeves as he laughed suggested enough for him to understand. The one accused of cheating had dark hair, worn long, that curled around his collar, and the golden afternoon light coming in from the windows cast shadows over his face that looked too familiar.

That could have been them, had the world been different, sharing a bird and a bottle at a pub. Joshua had a decent hand for cards, but Stephen would be too distracting to let him keep his mind on the game. His smile alone would be enough to throw Joshua off, to let him slide cards under the deck and play perfect hands, to bluff and not be called on it, to win cheerfully, and Joshua would let him, just to see that smile turned upon him again...

(He would exact his revenge later, binding Stephen's wrists with his own cravat, *"to stop you from cheating this time"*. Stephen would be pliant underneath him, gasping and writhing as Joshua sucked his half-hard member into his mouth, licked down between the cleft of his buttocks to tease the sensitive skin there, bite at the firm flesh of his thigh.)

Dark Hair turned out his pockets—empty—to prove his innocence, his opponent pointing out other options and laughing at the spectacle all the while.

There was no reason for his breath to come in short, painful bursts or for his gut to knot around the hard lump of his dinner. Read the news, think about war and parliament, about import taxes and the colonies. Anything but sitting across a table from Stephen, their boots barely touching beneath it, his finger catching the edge of Joshua's newspaper and dragging it down to force him to make eye contact.

"What will induce you out from behind there?" he might ask. *"Shall I play something for you? Or, better yet, you read to me while I rehair my bow. The chore goes faster that way."*

He was torturing himself, and to what purpose? Stephen Ashbrook was gone from his life, and Joshua was the one who had sent him away. Whether it had been the right thing or not seemed moot. The look he had worn at the end, a wounded animal trying to gnaw off its own limb, had been answer enough. Looked at to be a savior in a lifetime filled with hurt, Joshua had only caused him more pain.

They were better off apart.

If God or the stars or whatever mad forces ruled the universe wanted them to meet again, there would be some sign of it, instead of two long months of silence.

"Government this morning received dispatches from Lord Wellington, at Alverca…"

"Here you go, sir." A rustle disturbed his paper, but the voice behind it was boyish and high.

Joshua lowered the pages and frowned at the schoolboy and his stack of handbills, before noticing the one he had already laid on the table.

"What's this, then?" he asked, more out of surprised politeness than any real interest.

The landlady noticed and was gathering up her skirts to approach on a rescue mission.

"Concert, sir, at the Hanover. It's not a subscription event, tickets at the door, sir. Supposed to be right good, if you like that sort of thing, sir."

"Out of here, you rapscallion!" The landlady descended on the poor boy like a harpy from the trees of myth, making sweeping motions with no broom in her hand, as though to shoo him out the door. "Don't you be bothering customers with your papers."

"As you like, missus—I'm paid my shilling either way!" The boy ducked out of the way and dropped a handful of his printed bills onto the table with the cribbage players, before scooting under her waving arm and making for the door.

The landlady sighed her long-suffering sigh, shaking her head as she tidied up. The card players paid her no mind, but she frowned in apology in Joshua's direction. "In here every blasted week, he is, leaving papers everywhere, cluttering up the tables. Why they can't take space out in the paper like anyone else, that's what I want to know. Soon there'll be nothing but bills posted everywhere and paper instead of stones lining the streets!"

"It's no bother," Joshua said with faint sympathy. The handbill lay on the table, half-hidden beneath his paper, and with a gentle press of a finger he stopped her from clearing it away. Idle curiosity, nothing more.

Once she was gone, he turned it over, the cream paper inscribed with swirling lines of ink that were more elegant than the printed bills he had seen posted on empty walls and in alleyways between his lodgings and here.

Three Quartetts, for Two Violins, Tenor & Violoncello, Compofed by Guiseppe Haydn, and Performd at Mr. Salomon's Concert, the Festino Rooms, Hanover Square. With solo Performances by Mr. Robert Phillips, Violin, and Mr. Stephen Ashbrook, Violin.

The stab through the walls of his chest was coincidence only. The clenching ache there was indigestion brought on by eating too quickly, and at an odd time of day.

The boy was in here with his handbills every week, she had said.

This was not a sign.

And yet. Cade's name appeared nowhere on the bill. Could it be that Stephen had listened, taken Joshua's words to heart? Could it be that he was free of the man, finally, after all these years?

Elation, then, swift and rising, a hot-air balloon inside, filling him with something he had been denying himself for so very, very long.

Hope.

But if he is free, why did he not write?

The answer was as obvious as it was swift and brutal.

Because he neither needs nor wants you anymore.

He crumpled the handbill in his fist, the crunch of the paper gratifying in visceral ways. It only made sense. Joshua was the one who had walked away, and he had said harsh and unforgivable things, fought with him not once but twice. Stephen must despise him, and rightfully so. Whether he had been correct or not, it didn't matter. He had not been kind.

Damn him, anyway.

Joshua had been fooled once—he would not be so eager to fling himself headlong into danger again. He had sunk himself in false hope over Mr. Ashbrook already and been burned for it.

No more.

He rose, leaving money on his table to pay for his meal and some more besides. The handbill he tossed into the fire, the soft pop and crackle it made as it lit drowned out by his footsteps as he walked away.

Chapter Nineteen

"They sold *how* many tickets?"

"It'll be a wonder if they can all fit in the rooms to listen."

"Well, that's hardly our problem, is it?"

"It is if they have to move chairs up closer to the music stands. Do you remember how they crowded us last time?"

Stephen slumped back on his bed and banged his head against the wall, his writing slope sliding off his legs. Wren and Pembrey's footsteps rattled past the door, their voices loud in the shared lodgings, and Stephen stuck his thumbs in his ears. It didn't help.

A glance in the chipped looking glass hanging on the wall showed him the image of a petulant child, and he rolled his eyes at himself. He had to laugh, despite the small garret room—scarcely large enough to be called a room rather than, say, a large wardrobe—and the very unfashionable area where he now parked his boots. Despite the endless chatter from his newer roommates and the October wind that was currently invading in the form of a draft around his knees, Stephen had to admit that he looked happier than he had done in a long while.

More relaxed as well. Less like he was going to vibrate out of his own skin, given the right incentive. Or have himself a palpitation if someone shouted his name too loudly.

If only he could get this letter drafted, if only he could make words come the way music came to him. Then, perhaps, he could fix the wrongs he had done. It was a worse gamble than some of the horses at Newmarket, with far less chance of success, but he could not let things lie as they were.

He had imagined, when he left, that it would be Evander's face haunting his nights. For the first week or so, ensconced in Meredeth's spare room, it had been. But those dreams had been filled with flames and blood, with shouting and fists, and all the words still left unsaid. He woke in a hot sweat every time, his palms clammy and shirt damp. No one in the house ever admitted to hearing him shout in the night, but he woke with a raw throat and had to wonder.

The night terrors faded, slowly, as he set himself to finding steadier work, as Evander kept himself away. More doors had opened to him than he had imagined possible. A few closed, oh yes, and doubtless remained open to Evander, but the penalty Stephen had imagined—the world knowing his dark and private business—never came. Evander too concerned for his own skin, most likely, or too embarrassed.

Whatever the reason, he had escaped, and with Robert Phillips's invitation to take up the empty room in *his* shared lodgings in return for a small portion of the already paltry rent, well. That was shelter and company provided for. They were four young men, musicians all, and between them made enough to cover a pleasant, if not extravagant, existence. He had a place to stow his coat and music books, food to fill his belly and companions to while away the lengthening evening hours in practice and conversation.

The general agreement not to bring mistresses or whores back to the lodgings helped immensely. Whether they thought him temperate in spirit or too consumed by work to join them when they went carousing, he paid it little mind. He had no interest in skirt chasing now.

Not when this all still lay unresolved, the paper in front of him blank but for a name.

Mr. Beaufort,

He scratched it out.

Joshua, he began again, then scratched that out as well.

Stephen set his pen down and linked his hands behind his head. Assuming he could decide upon a salutation, what then would he write? Had he even improved himself enough yet to be worthy of reaching out?

Was the fact that he was even asking that question to begin with a sign that he still yearned for Joshua's approval?

"Stand on your own two feet."

He had done it.

Joshua had told him to grow up, to become his own man, to learn what he wanted for himself. To stop trying to please others. But he was a musician, a performer by trade—his *life* was devoted to pleasing others. So there was a limit to how far he could follow that command.

Surely there was a balance to be struck, somewhere between chasing his own desires and abandoning everything in favor of another's wishes.

He was closer to finding it, but maybe Joshua would not think so.

"Oy, Ashbrook!" Wren stuck his head in the door, his wavy hair in a permanent state of disarray. It was that nondescript sort of color that hovered between brown and blond, not helped by the faintly insipid brown of his eyes or the cheap suits he wore. But his smile lit up a room, women flocked to him (though whether to feed him or pet him, it seemed they could never decide) and the violoncello sang in his hands. "Are you ill?"

"Only of seeing your face." Stephen took up his quill and waved it at Wren as demonstration of his task. "Finishing some correspondence." *I barely know where to begin.*

"I hate letters," Wren answered, with what he imagined was sympathy over a mutually loathed task, and barreled on without a second glance, "Phillips is talking about going over to Bath for a few weeks, doing some concerts there for new faces. It would break up the slow pace before the winter really starts. What say you?"

Bath. Unbidden, the thought rang through him. *Bracknell is between here and Bath.* He skimmed his fingers over the paper, barely aware that he was doing it. *I could do this in person instead.* "It's worth a thought," he replied as casually as he could with his heart suddenly racing faster than before. "Is Pembrey interested?"

"Pembrey wants Scotland," Wren said with thick and utter distaste, and the tall, dark-skinned man passing behind him in the hallway slapped him casually on the back of his head in reply.

"Scotland in the winter? He's gone utterly mad," Stephen called out, loud enough for Pembrey to hear them before he got too far.

"It comes of living with you daffocks," came the call back before Pembrey's door opened and then shut again.

"You'd miss us if we were gone!" Wren turned his head, his hands still resting easily on Stephen's doorframe, to holler back down the corridor at his oldest and closest friend among them all.

"Come on, you shit sacks." Pembrey reappeared in his field of view, casting a look over Stephen, cross-legged on the bed. "We'll be late for rehearsal, and I have no wish to have my ancestry threatened in brutalized Italian."

Wren let go of the doorframe and fell into conversation with Pembrey, everything about the pair of them relaxed and easy. "Oh, but having it insulted in German would be fine?"

"Don't play the fool with me; you know what I meant." Pembrey took the teasing with the good grace of familiarity, before dragging his attention away. "Coming, Ashbrook?"

Stephen nodded, and that mollified them both. "In a moment," he promised.

Bath. Joshua.

It was something he hadn't considered, not sure of his welcome if he turned up on the doorstep unannounced. He would have an excuse, this way. *Just passing through, happened to be in the neighborhood...*

But then, Joshua had also shouted at him for making excuses, for looking for a reason to leave Evander that was not solely about his own selfishness.

Whatever he chose, somehow, it would be wrong.

He crumpled the paper and threw it petulantly into the corner, where a small pile of similar paper balls now rested. He would go plead his case to Joshua as a changed man, not a half-formed boy with his voice still breaking.

Give it more time, just a little more time. Then he would be even better situated to make his case.

And maybe convince Joshua to come home.

Chapter Twenty

Giving his notice didn't go nearly as poorly as Joshua had been dreading.

Lady Horlock took it worse, of the two of them, which he should have expected, all things considered. "But to leave so soon," she said. Her expression showed "taken aback", but gears turned behind her eyes as though she were already four steps ahead in figuring out how to rearrange her calendar. "I wish you had said something earlier." The mask slipped, then, and she clasped his hand with a sort of apologetic look. "Dear cousin, has our house not been satisfactory?"

"Nonsense," Horlock grumped from his chair before the fire, brandy snifter still in his hand. "You speak as though he's gone forever. A year abroad to study on the Continent hardly counts as abandonment, my dear. Pull yourself together."

"I am contracted for a year," Joshua cautioned him, two fingers brushing against the pocket where his letter rested. The time frame was the truth. He had not been entirely honest about how the vicomte had come to know of him or why he had accepted, but the less they knew, the better. "What happens after that, I cannot say. But the opportunity to expand my skills is something I cannot pass up."

"Of course you cannot," Horlock agreed, nodding sagely.

"I have been very comfortable here, cousin," Joshua promised Lady Horlock, squeezing her hands gently. "But I cannot live off your generosity forever."

Especially not after this summer's interlude.

It had not been spoken of since, Sophie taking more care not to be caught in his presence, but tensions hung over them now that could not be entirely ignored or forgotten.

"Also very true." Horlock put in his verbal shilling, and Lady Horlock glared darkly at him over her pince-nez. "I thought something like this might be coming, you know," Horlock continued on blithely, his thick mustache bristling as he spoke. "You've been off your feed since this summer."

Joshua froze, Lady Horlock's hand very still in his. He remembered how to breathe, barely, waiting for Horlock's next pronouncement.

"Aha!" Horlock crowed, and Joshua let go the lady's hand. "I've hit on something indeed. An unreturned *tendre* for one of the young ladies at Coventry's house, hmm? I knew it!" He chortled. "That Chalcroft girl is quite the beauty."

Oh, thank the Lord. He had the sum of it, but not the parts.

Lady Horlock sucked lemons, her lips tightly pursed.

"Time away will resolve that, no doubt, no doubt," Horlock continued.

"Indeed." Lady Horlock looked him in the eye, radiating disapproval.

"It was nothing," he said, and that was a lie. Though it had *come* to nothing, hadn't it? "I am all but mended now." Except that every figure he sketched had deep, dark eyes and hair that curled about his shoulders. "Enough so, that I cannot turn down opportunity when it comes. I promise I will write."

"Well and often," Lady Horlock instructed him, her words friendlier than her eyes. "Stay out of danger, and none of your 'all is well, nothing is exciting' two-line letters, either. I had quite enough of those from *him* while we were courting."

"German girls are lovely," Horlock added, a twinkle in his eye. "Or so I've heard."

"I will write, I promise." Joshua itched between his shoulder blades and restlessness pooled in his feet. He had to end this, to go before he started to second-guess everything and nothing, all at the same time. "Though not about the girls," he dared to joke, and to his vast surprise, Horlock chuckled and Lady Horlock gave him a small, tight smile which vanished as soon as it had begun. "But if you will both excuse me, I must go and further my arrangements."

A hint of melancholy settled over him as he closed the door behind himself and walked away, but it was utterly eclipsed by his certainty that he was making the correct decision. Let him get away from this damned island, this winter, the letters that never came and the face he would never see again.

Come two weeks from now, he would be putting the entire Channel between himself and Stephen Ashbrook, and be all the better for it.

A candle was burning on his windowsill when he returned to his room, one he had not left there himself. Odd, that. Perhaps the maid? It was unwise just to leave it, though perhaps she had been interrupted? No matter. There was no singeing of the curtain edge, and no harm done.

Joshua untied his cravat, the flicker of the flame holding his eye. He unwound the strip of linen and tugged it free from his collar. The jacket buttons next, popping easily with the pressure of his thumbs. He stopped dead at the discreet coughing sound from the far corner, whirled on his heel, his hands still at his waist.

"Sophie!"

She sat in the chair in the corner, her feet curled up under her and hidden in her skirts, her arms folded in front of her. It was too dark in the room, the shadows too heavy to see her face, but the hunch of her shoulders suggested unhappiness. Because of him or for him? Or for some other reason entirely?

"When do you leave?" Her voice had no ragged edges, so at least she had not been crying.

He left off with his buttons and crossed the room to join her. Dropping to the floor on his knees put him slightly below the level of her shoulders, but she folded in and hugged him fiercely. His arms went about her, and the two of them clung together. Her hair smelled faintly of perfume, and the bit of lace on her cap tickled his nose.

"In a fortnight." He let go and sat back on his heels, clasping her hands in his. "We still have time, sweetheart. I'm not dead to you yet."

Sophie—*Sarah*—smiled tightly and brushed her thumb along the curve of his cheekbone. "I shall miss you, Mr. Beaufort."

"Wish me well, dearest," he begged impulsively.

"I do, I only wish…" She trailed off, her desires unspoken.

"Name it," he said instantly. She was the closest thing he had to a sister, the one who knew him better than anyone. She had instigated this trip and would never seek to hold him back from it, but none of that negated the simple fact that he was leaving her behind.

Her answer surprised him more than anything else that night. "That you were leaving for the right reasons," she said simply, and squeezed his hands.

"I thought you were the one telling me to go," he chided her gently, and she smiled.

"I was, but to add some excitement and risk to your life, you boring old man. Not to go nurse a broken heart."

"I *am* leaving for the right reasons," he promised, and knew she didn't believe him. "I shall be glad to put this island behind me. There is only one thing I shall miss." He curled his fingers more tightly about hers when he said that and flashed her a grin as cheeky as he could make it in the flickering half-light.

She scoffed at him, but squeezed back. "Liar."

"Perhaps. I shall write you often."

Sophie unwound herself from the chair, rising to her feet and poking him once in the gut as she passed him by. She picked up her candle, and lit one from it to leave behind.

"Be well, Mr. Beaufort," she said softly. "Travel safely."

"And you must stay well too," he answered her. "It shall be *à la prochaine*, sweetheart, and never *adieu*. Not between us."

He kissed her on the cheek. She flung her arms around his neck and embraced him again, and he held on to her for as long as she allowed it.

Sophie left, closing the door gently behind her, and he was truly alone.

Chapter Twenty-One

The door of the concert hall clanged firmly shut behind them, leaving the players standing in the chill of the November night. Their final performance, one last round of applause, and now there was nothing left of this series but to keep an eye on the papers for write-ups after the fact. Nothing left to look forward to but Phillips's Bath proposal, somewhat further along in the planning than when Wren had first spoken of it a month ago.

"Ashbrook!" Wren slung his arm about Stephen's shoulders and tugged him toward the other two waiting by a streetlamp. "You're doing an excellent imitation of an icicle. Come along with us—we're taking Pembrey out to dinner."

"I'm not in the mood," Stephen objected weakly, the coin in his pocket from the performance not giving him the usual opportunity to plead poverty. It was not that he disliked going to *dinner*, particularly, but what would inevitably come after made it more awkward than he cared to handle.

"It's his birthday, Ashbrook! You owe it to him to celebrate."

Stephen made a face at Wren as they drew abreast of Phillips and Pembrey, the former as pale in the lamplight as the latter was dark. "You're a cruel taskmaster." Stephen made light of his complaint, giving in to the inevitable.

"We'll need you to chip in your coin." Phillips fell in step with them, his square shoulders hunched under the heft of his cloak and his collar turned up against the cold. "We're buying him a proper girl."

Pembrey laughed at that, a rich and hearty sound, and elbowed Wren with affection. "I can find my own woman. You should spend that coin on Ashbrook—he could benefit more than the rest of us from a plump miss to dandle on his knee." Pembrey pushed open the door to the King's Oak, the warmth and light of the tavern spilling out onto the street.

"Among other things!" Wren joked back, following Pembrey inside.

The rush of noise and smoke overwhelmed Stephen for a moment, taking his breath more than the cold had done. Serving girls moved through the crowd, trays on their shoulders, the landlord busy filling glasses at the bar.

"Leave off him." Phillips's voice cut through the joking before Stephen had a chance to defend himself. "He's said before he's not interested."

Pembrey put up his hands in mock surrender, but Phillips and Wren shared a look that Stephen did not dare consider too closely. The subject dropped, at least for the moment. It was simpler by far to let the heat of the wine pool in his belly and argue good-naturedly about what, precisely, *rascaglione* meant when Moretti had bellowed it at Pembrey and whether it had anything to do with his parents' status as freedmen.

In a perfect world, he would have Joshua beside him now, laughing at their jests, mocking their impassioned proclamations and making wry asides for Stephen's ears alone. His hand might brush against Stephen's on the table, the barest contact of skin on skin as a reminder and a pledge.

How many months had gone by since he had last seen Joshua, that last, brutal conversation where his heart had been ripped out of his chest and displayed before him?

Three and a half, that was the total now, with no word sent or received. He would be lucky if Joshua even remembered his name.

For Stephen, time had alternately crawled along, minute to minute, and sped by when he was not paying attention. In every waking moment, he yearned for something indefinable, an itch like a phantom limb. He could push the sensation aside on occasion, ignore it when he played, at rehearsals when surrounded by his comrades, when the everyday business of life threatened to overwhelm and bury him. At night, though, the world and his bed cold and empty, the void waited.

How much of it, Stephen argued with himself, ignoring Phillips as he stole the last sausage link from Stephen's plate, was because he missed someone in particular, and how much because he simply was not used to existing alone?

Joshua would want to know the answer, and he was running out of time to untangle the Gordian knot of his own emotions. A fortnight, that was all, before they left for Bath and Stephen could divert himself to Berkshire and the Horlock estate in Bracknell.

It would not be enough time.

And if he had to spend one more night in his bed alone—the sheets colder than winter, the ghostly fingers of memory tracing teasing circles on his skin—he would go utterly and completely mad.

"Why do you not indulge, Ashbrook?" The question was too timely, coming hard on the heels of his memories of Joshua's hands, his mouth, his prick. Wren leaned on his elbow on the table and grinned at the heat Stephen could feel rising in the tips of his ears and across the tops of his cheeks. He could not be referring to *that*. None of them knew Stephen's private inclinations, of that he was sure.

"A vow of celibacy?" Pembrey guessed, gesturing with the wineglass in his hand. The wine splashed over the edge, dotting his cuff with spots of red. He cursed and dabbed at them with a napkin before giving up.

"He thinks himself above it," Wren replied, grinning. "Master of your urges, channeling it all into your art? I should try such a thing."

"It still would not improve your playing," Stephen shot back, placing himself on the offensive.

Pembrey hooted in appreciation.

But no matter how he maintained his privacy, they would stay curious if he gave them nothing at all. Curious friends poked their noses where they did not belong, and that way led ruination for everyone.

Wren pretended to sulk, and Phillips shook his head at all of them. "Enough, both of you. Leave him be."

"No." Stephen frowned into the dregs of his wine, his head spinning from the spirits, the late hour and the heat. "They are fair questions, I suppose—we share rooms, do we not, and style ourselves friends. I..." he drew out the moment of suspense until Wren was leaning forward, almost toppling over into his stew, and Pembrey was laughing at him for it, "...have a sweetheart."

"Balderdash," snorted Pembrey.

Phillips looked sour, as though he had bitten into something foul. "Will you two not hold your tongues, for once in your lives?"

"No, no, this is brilliant," Wren exulted. "Is this new? Getting yourself bedded will soothe those jagged nerves of yours, my anxious friend." He gave Stephen a mockery of a toast, then turned to Pembrey, sitting on his other side. "Do you think his mistress is a blonde, or dark? Don't you think he'd look well with a blonde?"

Phillips shifted in his seat and Pembrey jumped, rubbed his leg with a dark glare at his friend, then shrugged. "It's not redheads, I can guarantee you that, or he'd have taken Johanna up on that offer she made him last month." He looked off into the distance, a nostalgic smile playing across his lips. "I have never *seen* a girl with a bosom more spectacular."

"He turned her *down*?" Wren gasped, and Stephen sank his head into his hands.

"Aye, that he did."

"There's something funny in your head, Ashbrook," Wren saw fit to inform him, and the irony was so bitter and so real that Stephen felt his own mouth twist into a parody of Phillips's glower.

Since they seemed unlikely to exhaust themselves any time soon, he had best answer as well he could and attempt to fight his way out of the hole he had dug.

"There is not, I promise." *Such lies.* "Since this summer I have been..." *How to even begin to phrase this well?* "...out of her favor," he compromised with a half-truth. "I am trying to be a better man and make amends."

They exploded, as much as any two loud men could explode, with "oohs" and "ahhs" and various tidbits of sage advice, including a sermon about his foolishness and earnest declarations that his sweetheart had likely taken up with someone else already, so why worry? Phillips brooded thoughtfully over his ale and said little.

Stephen parried as best he could, drank more than he should and left the rest in God's uncaring hands. The bitter taste in his mouth that came from lying to the men whom he called friends—well, it was his own and most familiar kind of gall and wormwood, and something he should be well accustomed to by now.

They left in a hubbub, Wren and Pembrey already planning their next stop and Stephen calculating the time until he could make a polite escape. He had his coat buttoned and was most of the way to the door when Phillips stopped him, his hand flat against the wall and his thick arm barring Stephen's path. He was a head taller than Stephen and had muscle mass that stopped Stephen from even contemplating ducking under his arm or around his other side.

"What can I do for you?" Stephen asked, his chin up. They reeked of brandy and wine between them, the air almost fetid.

Phillips looked at him seriously, looked *through* him, as though trying to divine something that Stephen kept shut behind his eyes.

If he meant to accuse or threaten, turn Stephen out of doors for being a sinner and a pervert, back to Meredeth's he would go. He was not helpless, nor hopeless—not yet!

Phillips drew a breath.

"Cade is not worth your heartbreak" was all he said.

Stephen's mouth worked but he could not speak, his mouth dry and his throat closed with a lump that appeared out of nowhere. Phillips was no stranger to Evander, none of them were. But Evander had isolated himself since the summer, spent his days doing God knows what, and Stephen had apparently inherited their mutual friends without huff or complaint. He had thought most of them oblivious. Wren might suspect, perhaps, given his usual train of thought, but he had never said anything. How long had Phillips known? Did he mean to turn Stephen over to the law?

No. If he did, he would have done so by now and not confronted him here, in this public place.

Trust. He had to trust his own instincts. Evander would call him a fool for it.

Leap of faith.

"It is not Cade I love," Stephen managed to croak, not knowing what he was going to say until the words were out and said and done. It hit him like a thunderbolt and burned through his blood. He hadn't ever dared to admit it, even to himself, hiding behind words like "desire", "loneliness" and "need".

I love him. I love Joshua. I may once have thought I loved Evander, but it was never, never once like this.

"Good," Phillips said. He dropped his arm. "Then you need to stop allowing him to shape you."

With that most cryptic comment, he turned to catch up with the others, clapping Pembrey on the shoulder and leaning in to speak as he drew close.

"Ashbrook?" Pembrey called, but Stephen shook his head and flipped a coin to Wren.

"I'm not entirely well; I'll see you at home. Enjoy your birthday, Pembrey."

"I shall!"

And with that they headed off, heads bent together in cheerful conversation.

Stephen watched them go, hands in his pockets, and then he turned towards home. His feet dragged at the idea. He had no particular desire to go back to his little room and his tiny fire, and sit and think about all the things lost to him. Nor had he been at all interested in accompanying the boys on their whoring. Where did that leave him? Not part of their world, and no longer a part of his own. He had not been to any of the molly houses since the spring, since the raids on the Swan and the trials.

He had not been with anyone in over three months, the longest span he could remember since he and Evander had shared the sweet, stolen kiss that began it all. More than three months since he had lain with Joshua, traded breaths in their kisses, given himself over utterly to their mutual pleasures.

Would he ever know it again?

If Joshua wished to see him, he was not difficult to find. He had moved, true, and if any letters had come for him after he left, then it was most likely that Evander had destroyed them rather than pass them on. And yet.

Sometimes, like now, the wind whipping cold around his legs, the streets he kept to mostly empty but for a few others about their own secret business, it all felt futile. He had nothing new to offer.

"It would calm your jagged nerves."

The words rang in his head. Wren might have a point. There was peace to be found in someone else's arms, even if just for an hour or a night. He wasn't far from a tavern he'd once frequented, another place of vaguely ill repute, but for a rather different sort of clientele than those his friends attended.

A few minutes' walk put him directly outside, the sign for the Apollo's Arms rattling on its hooks in the stiff breeze. Muffled sounds of music and laughter came to him from inside, light spilling out from the cracks around the window shutters to cast beams of yellow on the road. Someone played the piano, another sang. Everything in there would be pleasant and warm, the revitalizing and enthralling company of pretty men, eager for new partners and new experiences.

And then what? Stephen paused, half in shadow.

The door opened and a pair stumbled out, arms flying away from each other as they made it, mostly upright, into the public street. They wandered off together, silhouettes in the darkness. Before they turned the corner, one reached out and grabbed the other's hand to squeeze it. Only for a moment. Just a single squeeze. But it ripped through Stephen like a saw blade, grating his flesh from his ribs.

Joshua, smiling up at him from their bed, inviting him to kiss and touch and taste anywhere he pleased, any way he liked.

Meredeth and his wife staring at each other as though the world around them ceased to exist when they caught one another's eyes.

Joshua's head bent over his sketchbook at the riverside, the sun gleaming off his copper-golden hair and kissing his face. His fingers pressing between Stephen's as Stephen sucked him down, twining their hands together as they gave and took pleasure from each other in equal measure.

He could not do it. There would be no way to take some other man to bed and not imagine him, not remember *him*, not cheapen everything that they had tried to steal. There was so much more that it could have been, and they had come so close to having it.

If he had been brave enough to say yes.

"Damn it!" Stephen shouted in frustration, and wheeled to kick the wall before catching himself. Broken toes would not make his situation any easier to manage.

...and who said anything about having to manage it?

The idea crept over him, slow and steady, a dawn inexorable in its approach and just as implacable as the rising sun. If he wanted it badly enough, then why wait?

Why should he wait for someone else's timelines to bring himself within striking distance of his desires?

Let him be a man for once, and not a coward.

Wings on his feet, Stephen ran for home. He took the stairs two at a time, no one else inside when he turned the key in the lock and let himself in.

The flat was dark, but he knew where to find pen and paper, lamp and ink. A note, then, for the others, to say where he had gone and when he expected to be back. There was a midmorning coach headed for Berkshire—it would have him there by late afternoon. If he could only talk to Joshua, face-to-face, man to man, he could prove that he had indeed changed, express himself in all the words he could not find to put on paper.

He had failed them both once with his doubts and hesitation. He would not fail again.

To Bracknell, and let not even the hounds of hell stand in his way.

Chapter Twenty-Two

The morning dawned cold and heavy, gray skies lowered overhead.

No letter came. He didn't really think it would.

Neither of those things helped Joshua's mood. The prospect of sailing the Channel the next day was daunting enough; to do it under thunderheads was worse luck. Even if he *had* made the idiotic decision to flee the country in the depths of November, the least the universe could do was provide him a clear day to set out on.

Mrs. Colby scolded him for being an impetuous boy and handed him a packed supper, Horlock arranged for his driver to take Joshua as far as the Bath Road to meet his coach, and the morning both sped on and crawled in equal measure.

Finally, the hour nigh, Joshua stepped up into the carriage, his trunk settled behind. The horses pulled away and the house began to recede into the distance.

Some small part of him had hoped to hear from Stephen before he left. It had been a ludicrous dream, one to be harbored in the dead of night and never spoken aloud, not even to Sophie, who kept her counsel close. But, surely, if they had been meant to be, there would have been some last-moment bolt of lightning to set them on the right path once more.

He could have written, Joshua reminded himself severely, the trees slipping by on either side. He hadn't. He could have gone to that concert. He hadn't. He had no right to expect any different from Stephen.

Even still, that childish and unworthy refrain sounded over and again in his mind. *If he loved me, he would have come.*

So let it be, and let it die.

Far easier said than done.

Chapter Twenty-Three

The rain began as Stephen walked along the side of the road, heading deeper into the woods at Bracknell. Horlock's estate was supposed to be close to the road—at least the coach driver had not laughed too loudly when told that he would walk the rest of the way.

He had not gotten wet at the change at the turnpike, and counted himself lucky for it. Now, though, he was a sodden mass from his hat to his boots, his shirt sticking to his back and cold rivulets drizzling down the back of his neck to work their way down the length of his spine.

What a wretched figure he would cut, showing up at the earl's front door. *Hah.* Some suitor or gallant hero.

If he'd had a horse, that might have worked better.

Mud squished up around the toes of his boots, staining the leather and adding to the chill in his bones.

Not much farther now.

Then he would see Joshua again. And even if he was thrown out on his arse into the storm once more, at least he would have *tried*.

Not much farther now.

The mantra kept him going, one foot in front of the other, a steady, careful plod along the fence until the drive turned away from it and opened up toward the Horlock house. He turned with it, his heart leaping up into his throat. Light shone from the windows, a glorious and welcoming thing, promising heat and warmth and...

He was an idiot. He could not walk up to the main door, knock and request entry. They would ask why he was there, what had possessed him to walk. He had not been invited, after all, and it was entirely possible that Joshua would refuse him entry, and then *he* could be forced to explain.

The kitchen door. If they could not call Joshua down, then at the very least Armand, if she would forgive. The cook would be able to send a message to her, and then through her to Joshua, and get him down there without attracting undue attention from the master and mistress of the house.

No dogs had started barking at his approach, which was good. Between that, the slow descent of the sun, thanks to the lateness of the year, and the clouds doing their best to drown him, he could make it up the hill and to the house unnoticed.

He slipped, stumbled and almost fell on the stone outside, catching himself just in time. Around the house, then, and to the side-door servants' entrance. This was more where he belonged anyway, a hired player, no name nor family to boost him, surviving on nothing but his addled wits and his cold, *cold* hands.

A maid opened the door when he knocked, took one look at him and ushered him into the hall. Heat from the kitchen struck him hard in the face, a blissful tingling pain that suffused his body from the outside in, soaking into every exposed surface. He flexed his hands, the stiffness in them aching under the change in temperature, before they began to loosen.

"Can we help you, young man?" A broad-shouldered barrel of a woman in apron and cap plumped her fists on her hips and stared him down. "What on God's green earth brings you out-of-doors on an afternoon such as this?"

"I-b…" he began, stuttered and stopped to find his kerchief, sneeze into it and compose himself. "My name is Stephen Ashbrook, madam. I am a-an *acquaintance* of Mr. Beaufort and I've come to speak with him. Please, is he about the house?"

Her expression softened as she looked him over, which meant he must be an utter fright. Her next words, though, did more damage than weather ever could. "I'm afraid you've missed him, Mr. Ashbrook. He's gone."

What?

Not dead, never dead, or she would not say it so easily.

"When do you expect his return?" He was assuming trouble where there was none to be had. Joshua could have gone to town for the day, or to visit family, or—

"Next year, possibly, or perhaps never. He's gone to Belgium, you see. To paint for a viscount."

"Gone to Belgium," Stephen repeated dumbly, the words thick in his mouth. He slid down the wall, landing on the old, wooden deacon's bench by the door. He had imagined a handful of different scenarios on the long walk over—Joshua welcoming him, Joshua furious with him, Joshua refusing to speak to him entirely. But never this. And

355

it was foolish, because he *knew*…he had been invited on this very trip, and he had hesitated.

How could he have imagined that Joshua would put his own life on hold, when Stephen had kept moving? He was an impulsive fool!

He stared at his clasped hands in front of him, tried to organize his maddened and swirling thoughts into some more logical plan of action. Above all, of one thing he was certain—he had come too far to give up at the first setback. That acknowledged, he looked up at the cook and tried to ignore the rainwater dripping onto his nose.

"Do you know where he is staying?" he asked, subdued. "Or a way to get a message to him?"

"Polly," the cook called, apparently ignoring his request, "go fetch Armand, will you? That's a girl. In the meantime, young man," she addressed him again as the scullery maid scurried off, fists on her substantial hips, "you'd better give me your coat and take off those boots so we can get you a little dryer than you are. I'll not have anyone catching the ague on my watch."

He should have argued the point, but, frankly, he was too exhausted to begin.

By the time his boots and coat had been taken to sit nearer the fire and a blanket placed around his shoulders, Sophie Armand had appeared in the hallway. He stayed on the bench, pulling the blanket closer around himself.

She stared at him as though seeing a ghost, her face pale but cheeks flushed, everything about her carriage taut as a string being plucked. "He's gone, you know."

"I know," Stephen replied, his grief bleeding around the edges of his calm front. "When? How long ago?"

She hesitated, as though weighing what to tell him, how much or how true to be. Her fingers twisted in her apron, bunching and unbunching in the fine white fabric until they left creases behind.

"Please," Stephen asked. She was his only link, his only chance to make everything right again. "You have to help me. Tell me where, when, how long ago. How can I find him again?"

They were alone in the hallway but still she looked over her shoulder, into the open door to the kitchen. The clanging of pots and calling of orders meant that dinner plans were well underway. A good thing, since it left them less likely to be overheard or disturbed.

"Why should I?" Armand said finally. "He's been miserable since the summer, because of you."

That gave him pause. "He has?" Stephen asked, wondering, and the look she gave him was filled with such contempt that he slammed his mouth closed again.

"He waited for you to write," she said, venomous in her anger.

Stephen closed his eyes, sank into the deep pool of despair and remorse inside. "I didn't think he would read it," he confessed.

She snorted. "Then you don't really know him, do you?"

"No," he admitted, after a long pause. "Perhaps I don't. But I want to."

"You're too late."

"No!" Stephen said forcefully, then paused to see if the noises from the kitchen had stopped. They continued and so did he, his blood rising, finally, as his body thawed. "Not so. Not until one or both of us are dead, and I will not believe it even then." If he could suffuse enough emotion into it, cut open his chest and let her see the beating of his heart, would she capitulate? "I could not make him promises this summer, but I can now, and I promise you I will not give up trying to find him."

Armand frowned, a crease deepening between her brows. "And if he does not wish to hear from you?"

"I will obey his wishes. But only once I hear it from him." He was hardly anything to be impressed by, wet and bedraggled, huddled as he was in an old blanket that, for a moment, he thought smelled faintly like Joshua. He drew himself up on the bench, set his shoulders and tried to show some vague force of character.

She stared, her arms folded, and he held her gaze as steadily as he could manage. "Please," he said simply. "We belong to each other."

"No." Her jaw set, she was as implacable as the mountain, a barricade that no cavalry could break.

He had but one option left, a ploy that surely she would see through and mock him for. But what was dignity in the face of losing the one thing he wanted most—and had so stupidly thrown away?

"That is your final word?"

"It is."

"Then, madam..." He swallowed hard against the lump in his throat, one altogether too real. He fumbled in his pocket, his fingers still too stiff and cold to work properly, until he could draw it out. He unfolded the square of linen, his constant companion, so she could see the monogram on the corner. "...would you be so kind as to return this to him in your next letter? I have been keeping it, you see..." and then his voice did break, the sheer stupidity of the whole mess crashing down over him, "...until I could give it back in person."

Armand took the handkerchief, smoothed it out over her hand, traced the embroidery with a finger. The frown line cut deep between her brows. "You have this?"

He nodded.

"You kept this?"

"As a talisman." And why should he not tell her now? She knew everything else. "There has not been a single day these past four months where he has not been at the forefront of my mind."

A drop of water rolled down his forehead and splashed off the end of his nose. He blinked, trying to maintain some form of dignity that did not include scrubbing his hair and face with the back of his hand.

A smile tugged very briefly at the corners of her lips before it was gone once more. The curse she muttered under her breath was most certainly *not* something she had learned at any French boarding school. Was that a good sign? Maybe, perhaps...

"He left four hours ago."

Only that? Only that? Then there is still hope. Oh, there is hope!

"He left for London this afternoon and meant to take the Bath Road," she continued, but he could barely hear her over the exultations in the back of his mind and the rapid thrumming of his heart. "Given the weather, he might have stopped instead of changing in Slough. If so, he prefers the lodgings at the Holly and Ivy." Every word was clipped as she spoke it, as though every letter was painful, but she gave him what he needed, nevertheless.

Stephen rose, grasped her hands impulsively and squeezed them tight, then tucked the handkerchief back into his pocket. "You are a blessing and an angel," he declared, and heard a giggle from the doorway. The scullery maid vanished again and there would be rumors spreading soon, no doubt, but what mattered that to him now? He had a chance.

And so did Armand. He had closed the distance between them and she narrowed it further, leaning in to murmur in his ear, "Be good to him, or I *will* find you." Her accent had changed—the sleek and sophisticated daughter of France gone, and in her place, a Bankside girl, thick canting drawl and all. "I will expose you only insofar as it hurts you and keeps him safe, and then I will destroy you."

That threat was legitimately terrifying, and Stephen nodded seriously as she pulled back and removed her hands from his grip. "I will," he pledged, and meant it. "I will be good to him. I swear it."

And thank God, if there was such a thing, for she seemed to believe him. "Then wait here and dry some more," she commanded. "I'll go see about finding you a drive to Slough. I've no interest in explaining to my employers how the corpse of Coventry's pet violinist ended up cold on their lawn."

"You're too kind," he murmured, but he was too warm through and through to put any venom in it. Joshua was still in England. All was not yet lost.

Assuming he could get his boots back in time.

Chapter Twenty-Four

Rain drove down in sheets outside, and Joshua scowled at the shutters. The weather had him stranded, the coaches to London staying put for fear of flooding, and he was here until the morning. Thank goodness he had booked passage on a ship that would not leave until the following evening or he would miss his chance altogether.

At least the coaching inn was not terrible, as far as these things went. The Holly was certainly the best choice of the options available in the area, and he'd secured a small but private room. The furnishings were no great luxury, but the sheets were clean, and if he went downstairs, he could find some stew and a crust of decent bread to fortify himself against the damp.

Voices rising from below stopped him dead at the top of the stairs. One was the landlord, the other familiar. Too familiar, *dreadfully* familiar, and the nausea rose high in his throat. *No. Not him, not now, it cannot be.*

One look, to prove I am mistaken, and then onward for supper.

He crept forward on the landing, every inch the ridiculous boy, and peered over the railing.

"Will you take a message, then? I need to speak with him urgently."

It was Stephen indeed, resembling nothing so much as a cat that someone had tried to drown in the Thames. His hair stuck to the side of his neck, his coat hung on him, a wrinkled mess, and water stains ran up both his boots where mud had no doubt been half dried on and then scraped away.

Joshua's heart stopped within his chest, a lump the size of an apple grew in his throat, and he struggled for breath. *Here. He is here, he is here.*

In almost four months, Stephen had not changed. Even as much a mess as he was, battered by the storm, his beauty still shone, still eclipsed everyone else in the room, in the country, possibly even in the world. He was luminous, and Joshua…

Joshua adored him still.

What do I do now?

"And who shall I tell him is here?" the landlord asked, mirroring Stephen's posture and endlessly amused by the figure of despair before him.

"Tell him…" Stephen paused, and his head hung low.

A new ache set up residence in Joshua's heart at the sight. *I did this. I did this to him.*

"Tell him Miss Armand sent me," Stephen said, his head jerking up as though he'd had a flash of inspiration.

Joshua grinned, and, oh, how must that conversation have gone? He could barely picture it, but could not imagine that Sophie had treated him with any degree of kindness.

He should be kind now, should reveal himself in the shadows on the stairs and give Stephen a reprieve from his troubles. But then they would have to talk, and who knew what he had come to say?

No, Joshua would take this moment for himself, selfishly, absorbing everything he had tried to forget about Stephen's voice, his lips, his eyes, the way his hands gestured in the air as he spoke.

"Ohhhh, there's a 'Miss Armand', is there? You her brother come to drag him to church?"

"Nothing so dire, I promise. But he will want to hear me out."

Stephen leaned over the desk, and perhaps he was about to do something desperate?

Joshua stepped down a few treads, emerging into the light. He cleared his throat, and both Stephen and the landlord paused in their negotiations to look up. Stephen's face went pale, paler than before, white as the grave.

He had lost weight where he did not have much before to lose, his cheekbones sharper and his jaw more perfectly defined. Was he eating? Did he have a home? Did he still live with Cade?

"I'm here," Joshua said, once he found his voice again. He could not move, could not force his feet to the step below or draw any closer. What should he say? How? What questions could he ask?

Stephen made the move for him, bounding up the stairs two at a time until they stood face-to-face on the small landing. Joshua had been entirely mistaken—Stephen had not lost weight. His shoulders were still firm and strong, his arms and slender waist the same as they had always been. His face was the thing that had changed, all the last, lingering remnants of puppy fat or boyish softness carved away, until only the man remained. Now he burned with fierce determination and a new kind of fire, all of it directed at Joshua.

He pulled in a soft breath, and that seemed to break the dam penning in his thoughts. After months of yearning, on the eve of his escape Stephen stood there, so close that Joshua had but to reach out with a single finger and touch him to bring it all back.

"Why are you here?" he asked instead, in the vain hope of regaining some distance. "We have said everything that needed to be said."

"No, we have not," Stephen insisted, keeping his voice low. "You do not know what has happened these past few months, what I have done and learned."

"Yes, I do," Joshua interrupted. "I have seen your playbills. Nothing for you has changed, and for me, everything has."

Stephen shook his head and spread his hands wide. "I left," he said simply. "I have been playing for myself, taken lodgings elsewhere. I have not seen Evander since the summer. The week after we returned from Belmont, I *left*." There was so much more there, things he seemed to be holding back, but the words he had spoken aloud were enough to send Joshua's heart racing.

Enough. Did you not say yourself that you have been hurt too many times? Cut this off now, before you are wounded so deeply that you cannot recover.

"Are you telling me the truth?" he asked, instead of sending Stephen away.

"Yes," Stephen replied simply. He looked down into the room below them, the landlord hurriedly casting his gaze elsewhere. "Is there somewhere more private than the stairs?" A puddle was slowly forming below him, from the steady drip of rainwater coming off the hem of his coat, and yet he waited for Joshua's invitation.

"I…that is…yes," Joshua admitted in defeat. "Come with me, and you can borrow some of my clothes while yours dry."

Oh, that's precious. Finding an excuse to get him naked in your room already. His inner voice sounded much like Sophie at that moment, and he could not hide the small smile.

Stephen said nothing until they were in the room and alone together, the door closed and latched firmly behind them. He took off his hat and held it in his hands, the damp felt squelching between his fingers as he turned the brim nervously.

"I am my own man," Stephen began, and he lifted his chin to look at Joshua directly. There was no falsehood in his dark-brown eyes, no dissembling, just honest passion, laid so open and bare for Joshua that it felt as though they were already naked, already entwined, already forgiven.

"And I am neither broken nor lost, as he predicted," Stephen continued, seemingly unaware of Joshua's churning thoughts. "I am enough of a man, perhaps, to be a partner to you in truth."

"After everything that has passed?" Joshua blurted out, the world shifting unsteadily beneath his feet. This, this was everything he had imagined, and so much like it that he could not be sure he was not dreaming now. He would wake to an empty bed once more, his heart sore from promises broken in the harsh light of morning. "I meant what I said at Belmont."

I was cruel and cold.

Stephen nodded slowly. "And you were right. I have built a life for myself again these past four months. I have survived, and, more than that, I have thrived. I have friends and a home, albeit smaller than my previous one, but it is mine and my bed is my own, no longer subject to Cade's whims and moods."

He reached out, his hand hovering near to Joshua's, but he dropped it again when Joshua could not, did not, yet reach out to meet him partway.

"What I have learned, most importantly, is that I can survive without you as well. And be as content as any man within the world has a right to expect."

That, no—those were words he had not anticipated, and Joshua's brow furrowed tightly as he tried to parse them out. The burgeoning excitement in his chest emptied and became a void, one more disappointment to add to the tally that made up the years of his life so far.

"This is what you rode through a storm to tell me? That you do not need me in your life? Better that you had not come at all, if that is your only message!" He could not help the anger in his voice, sharp and hot, but Stephen only bit at his bottom lip and shook his head.

"You don't understand. I *can* survive without you, but I do not wish to. *Ever* again. I want you beside me, with me, always." He reached out again and this time did grab Joshua's hands, stroking his thumbs over the palms as though divining Joshua's future.

"Look at us," he pleaded, as if Joshua had any other choice in the matter!

Stephen's hair stuck to his forehead, ragged and tousled curls plastered here and there in haphazard swirls, and he blinked water out of his eyes.

"Six weeks changed everything in my life. Not just because of you, but because of the potential you awoke in me. Think of how well we could grow together in twenty years, or forty!"

No, there were too many doubts, too many things left insubstantial. "What of Evander? You grew together—do you now say that you have left him utterly behind?"

"I have nothing more to say to him. I left and he did not pursue."

And once again there was more there, much more, that he was not saying, but the core of it rang true. That, or he had learned how to lie to Joshua with his tongue as well as his eyes. If Joshua settled on that explanation, though, with everything in his heart screaming out against it, how could he believe in anything again?

What to do? How to be in any way sure that the decision he made now was the right one? He needed, he wanted, he feared, he *hurt*, and it all tangled up together in ways he thought he had long put behind him.

And in front of him, Stephen, his arms open.

Stephen pressed on when he said nothing, holding his hands tightly. "At the very least, please—if you will take nothing else that I offer, take my gratitude. I could not have done this without you." He blinked fiercely, his eyes shining in the candlelight.

"I did nothing," Joshua demurred. Stephen's hands were cool against his, but solid. He wanted to close his hands, tangle their fingers together, hold on so tightly to this gift he had been given back. "Nothing but walk away."

"You showed me I didn't have to accept my fate. Beaufort—*Joshua.*"

He spoke Joshua's name with such tenderness and longing that he was sunk, utterly and entirely sunk, before he could escape. Joshua's hands tightened on Stephen's, and Stephen brought them to his lips. He kissed Joshua's knuckles fervently, and Joshua's stomach tangled into a solid-iron knot.

"Listen to me now. Don't accept loneliness and exile as yours."

"What?" His mind was jumping too quickly for Joshua, stuck as he still was on the apology, on the firm pressure of Stephen's lips against his hands, on the way his soul had settled back into his skin the moment Stephen had stepped into the room behind him.

I am meant for you—this is all just a formality.

"Be with me?" Stephen asked, neither begging nor pleading, his back straight and his eyes alight. "Take lodgings with me in London or allow me to come with you to the Continent, I no longer care. But do not run away because of what transpired between us. There is nothing, now, to drive you from England, if you will forgive me my trespasses. I have forgiven you everything. I miss you, and your particular affection."

"I leave for Belgium tomorrow—I will not be persuaded otherwise," Joshua cautioned, his head spinning.

Joshua owed him something…what? Some kind of excuse? He was not *running away* because of Stephen, that was ridiculous. Ridiculous and embarrassing and *wrong*.

"I have been on this path before, burned by love," he tried to explain, searching for words. "Blisters on the soul take far too long to heal. I do not want to live it again."

Stephen did not move. He stared at Joshua as though there had been some brilliant revelation there, and Joshua tried to think back over his words. What had he done?

"You said 'love'," Stephen said with such tremulous and disbelieving awe in his voice that it broke Joshua to pieces. "You love me?"

Yes.

He still had his pride, damn it all to hell and back! "I said no such thing."

"You did and you do," Stephen insisted, joy overtaking the wonder and surprise. "Look me in the eye and tell me that you do not."

He looked. Stephen's exhilaration shone from him, golden and silver beams of light, his hair starting to dry at the curled ends, wisps bending up around his temples, and so soft. He knew what it would be like to twine his finger in one of those curls, bury his hands in Stephen's hair and claim his lips again, just kiss him and kiss him until there was no breath left in the world but the one they passed between them, lung to lung.

"Say something," Stephen pleaded in the face of Joshua's dumbness, that joy beginning to slip. And still, still he was tongue-tied, his throat tight and fear overriding all his sense and form.

"I'll go down on bended knee if I must, only smile at me and tell me that you love me. I saw it in your eyes in Belmont but I would hear it in your own words."

And he did it, right there in the inn room, falling to his knees in a parody of a proposal.

He was utterly ridiculous, kneeling on the floor, damp clothes and all, a faint whiff of steam rising from his side where the fire warmed him. He was no portrait now, but a floppy-eared, half-drowned spaniel, wide, plaintive eyes and all.

Joshua had to laugh, a short huff of breath that broke the spell. "I cannot dissemble." He admitted defeat.

He stepped backward, claimed space between them and sank down into the chair behind him, rubbed the bridge of his nose as though the pressure and contact would give him the clarity of mind that he lacked. Stephen rose to his feet and took a tentative step toward him as Joshua found his words and began again.

"I have desired you for years. I have loved you since I saw the sun in your hair and heard you laugh by the banks of the river. And, for the life of me, I think I have been spoiled for all others."

There—it was out, his heart was in a million shards that littered the inside of his rib cage, and Stephen could do with his new power whatsoever he willed.

Stephen braced his arms on either side of Joshua in the chair and leaned in to claim what had always been his.

The kiss was soft and gentle, and in that dry press of lips, a tentative reclamation of something Joshua thought was forever gone. He allowed it for a moment, tilted his head to lean in to it for longer than that, and then finally broke, burying his hands in Stephen's hair and holding him there. He tasted the seam of his lips and Stephen opened to him, the tip of his tongue a teasing and tender thing.

And this—this was everything he had thought never to have again, the weight of Stephen pressing down against his shoulders, the slide of his hair under Joshua's fingers, the huff of his breath as he laughed softly against Joshua's questing and needy mouth. He was *there* and he was real, yielding happily under the gentle pressure of Joshua's kiss, and he was *everything*.

When they parted, finally, Joshua's lips buzzing and sore, Stephen's eyes were wide and joyous.

"I asked you once before," Joshua said, his heart an entire percussion section within his ribs. "I'll ask it again. Come with me?"

"I will," Stephen answered with no hesitation at all. "And gladly."

That deserved another kiss, and this time Stephen's teeth grazed Joshua's lower lip. He sucked at it, bit it, kissed away the sting and left him breathless, everything about his mouth hot, slick and needy. Then he was gone, and Joshua's eyes snapped open.

He didn't go far, kissing down Joshua's throat, past his loose cravat and down his shirt, stopping only to nuzzle at the bulge beginning in Joshua's trousers. Stephen's breath was warm, even through the layers of wool, the barest grazing contact enough to send Joshua dizzy with months' worth of constrained desire.

He slid his hands through Stephen's hair, held the loose curls back from his face so he could watch as Stephen mouthed at him gently. He laid his cheek against Joshua's thigh, his eyes closed and with a look of such exhausted contentment that Joshua almost cried.

Stephen popped the buttons on Joshua's fall front and ran his nose along the stiffening line of Joshua's prick, only a layer of linen now between them. He tingled, everywhere, craved the feel of skin on skin, of more than just where this was heading.

"Stop," Joshua asked, gripping Stephen's head, his thumbs along the line of his beautiful jaw, and tugged gently to draw him away.

"What's wrong?" Stephen asked immediately, dangerously close to a pout.

"Not like this." Joshua shook his head, dropping his feet to the floor and rising to stand. "Not after so long."

It didn't take much to pull Stephen toward the bed after that. Clothing hit the floor in equal piles—waistcoats, trousers, shirts—until they were both gloriously nude, that long, lean expanse of Stephen's skin now Joshua's to taste and touch once more.

"Like this, then?" Stephen asked, as Joshua suckled at his nipple, the high pink nub hard even before his mouth had brushed across it.

Stephen rolled his hips up, his cock a thick and solid pressure between their stomachs. It slid along Joshua's erection, the heads catching each other, knocking his pierced ring. A shock burst through him, settled deep in his lower back where heat and pressure coiled around each other. He shuddered and Stephen laughed, his rippling mirth a sound that Joshua could never tire of.

"Like that, I see now," Stephen murmured, and did it again.

Joshua slid up Stephen's body, grinding down into his hips as he did so. The ache burned in his shoulders from propping himself up, sweat stinging in the bend of his knees. He kissed Stephen's mouth, sucked his lower lip between his teeth. Stephen opened for him, deepened the kiss into something hot and filthy.

Their cocks slid against each other, now slick, now rough, the scattering of dark hair on Stephen's stomach adding another layer of sensation to the needful drag of skin against skin.

Joshua kissed down Stephen's jaw, and Stephen lifted his chin, baring his throat in delicious surrender. Joshua tasted the salt there, his tongue darting out to flick at the lobe of his ear, leave wet trails down the straining tendon along the side of his neck, delve into the hollow of his collarbone where the sweat was gathering. It was too easy to nuzzle into the join of Stephen's shoulder and throat, to press his face into the familiar curve and breathe him in for a moment. He smelled like travel, dust and horses, and damp wool—so good, so *real*, so far beyond the realms of his fantasies and memories.

Stephen arched his hips up against Joshua, trapping their cocks between their bellies. "Please," he gasped out, and Joshua kissed the words from his mouth.

Stephen licked a wet stripe up his hand and slid it down between them, past Joshua's arms where he propped himself up, down to where their cocks dragged together. He wrapped his hand around them both.

Joshua dropped his head to brace against Stephen's chest—the hard pressure of Stephen's prick and the tight, wet heat of his hand was too much, too soon!

He needed to move, had to thrust, to ride up into the circle of Stephen's fingers and slide through the slick that was forming there.

He felt rather than saw the progress of Stephen's other hand, wrapping around his buttock, the pads of two fingers pressing against the tight muscle between. Those questing fingers traced circles on the tender skin, but with no oil on hand there was no further entry possible.

"Not yet," Joshua begged shamelessly. The pressure began to build.

Stephen's fingers toyed over the sensitive skin behind, while his fist gripped Joshua's prick against his own. His thumb flicked at the ring, flicked and tugged, adding to the overwhelming wave crashing down around Joshua.

It had been so long, too many months apart, and now to lose all control like this, to be taken apart so easily—

"Stop, or I am lost!"

"Do it," Stephen begged, arching up beneath him and thrusting faster into the circle of his own hand. "Fuck me just like this, finish on me. Mark me as yours. I need to see you do it."

Their cockheads emerged and vanished back into Stephen's hand. Joshua could look down between their bodies and see them, red and purple, gleaming wet now, their foreskins riding along the slickness of their shafts. The sight struck him like a thunderbolt—he could not stop now if the world itself collapsed to pieces around them both.

"Please," Stephen begged again, and Joshua caught his gaze and held it.

Stephen's eyes were black, tears gathering in the corners, his hairline dotted with gleaming beads of sweat. He panted, his lips parted, and he stared up into Joshua's eyes as though he saw revelations playing out inside them.

"I love you," Stephen gasped, wonder filling those eyes again. "I love you."

His hand tightened, Joshua's toes curled and his fingers dug into the sheets on either side of Stephen's head. Lightning bolts rushed through his body, coiling, boiling and exploding out along his cock. He came, fiercely, more powerfully than anything he had managed on his own. A thousand pearls of white splattered across Stephen's stomach, gleaming in his dark hair.

"Mine," Joshua announced triumphantly, exultantly, still hovering in that realm between desire and disbelief. He shuddered and clenched, Stephen's fingers pressed firmly against the entrance to his arse, his other hand closed tight around Joshua's cock. "You're mine and I am yours," he said again, Stephen's body rising underneath his. "I love you."

Stephen cried out, kissed Joshua to muffle the sound that wrenched out of him. He came, hot and wet between their bodies, his emissions splattering across Joshua's chest and abdomen.

Ripples of ecstasy ran through Joshua's body as the aftershocks took him, Stephen's hand slowly stroking back and forth along their pricks to work the last of their pleasure from them. It was too much, finally, his body recoiling from the contact, and Joshua let his arms buckle. He rolled to the side as he collapsed, exhausted.

The sheets crumpled beneath him, warm from their skin and wet from Stephen's damp hair, the mattress firm and just yielding enough to let him sink. He closed his eyes, his entire body tingling.

And so he missed the moment when Stephen rolled over to flatten on top of him. The breath would have been knocked out of him if he'd managed to catch it yet, his lover's dead weight pressing him down into the mattress.

Joshua opened his eyes into a mass of dark-brown curls, and he reached up to push them out of the way.

Stephen captured his hands and brought them back down to their sides, lacing their fingers together securely. He hummed to himself as he lay there, his head on Joshua's chest and their legs tangled, semen drying between them to fuse them together even more permanently.

That would become a disastrous mess at some point soon, but Joshua could not bring himself to care. Not just yet.

For now, he would lie here, Stephen's solid warmth secure above him, their chests rising and falling in unison, their hands locked together in a wordless and unnamed pledge.

He almost fell asleep that way. Or maybe he had, and it only seemed like he'd just been dozing. Either way, the sky outside the shutters had gone fully dark, the candle the only light.

Stephen still lay on his chest, occasionally pressing a tender kiss against Joshua's naked skin. He needed to wash—things were itching where they should not be itching—and he desperately wanted to crawl beneath the counterpane and sleep. Which was not going to happen while he was still sticky.

"Stephen?" he murmured, flexing his fingers.

Stephen snored once, going limp and pretending to be asleep.

"I know you're awake," Joshua added, a smile playing over his mouth. "Get off me."

"No, I shan't," came the mumbled retort, vibrating against his collarbone. "And you can't make me."

That sounded like a challenge if ever he had heard one. Joshua extricated one of his hands from Stephen's clutches, ignoring the small whimper that followed. He ran his fingers down Stephen's neck, which got him squirming but not moving. Down his spine, then, as far as Joshua could reach from that angle—no luck. Under his arms, then, into the tuft of dark hair that trapped and held his scent.

Stephen yelped and rolled away, jamming his hands into his armpits to protect himself from the threat of tickling. "Ugh!" he declared, half sitting on the bed, the sheet tangled around his legs. "Cruel man!"

"One of us needs to be the practical one," Joshua said easily, and he leaned over to kiss Stephen, tender and soft against his lips. Stephen pressed into him, all but falling over when Joshua rose to soak a cloth in the washbasin and attend to his ablutions.

He returned to the bed a few minutes later, clean, cold and with a fresh pair of smalls dragged over his bare skin.

Stephen's turn for ministrations, then. He took longer than he probably needed to, for the sheer novelty of being able to do this again. To draw the cloth across Stephen's chest and watch his nipples tighten, to run it through the tangle of coarse, dark hair below his stomach and watch the curls bounce back into place, to roll the cloth over Stephen's soft prick, stroking the silken skin and letting it tap lightly against the firm muscle of his thigh.

Stephen shivered, his arms up over his head and his knees fallen to either side, granting Joshua all the access he could ever desire.

And because Joshua could never leave well enough alone, he had to break the silence to ask, "You meant what you said?"

Stephen opened one eye and looked at him, his brow coming down low. "Which part?"

Joshua frowned at him. "All of it."

"That I love you? Yes." Stephen sat up, his eyes open and tracking Joshua's movements carefully. He drew back the counterpane and slipped beneath it, holding the covers up for Joshua to join him in the warmth. "That Evander is no longer in my life, most emphatically yes."

Joshua followed his lead, more for the chance to end the shivers than anything else. Stephen wrapped his legs around Joshua's almost immediately, facing him as he laid his head on the pillow.

"That I followed your advice and have built a reasonable life for myself, yes. That said life would be infinitely improved by your permanent presence in it, a million times yes, yes and yes again." He punctuated each of those affirmations with a gentle tap of his fingers on Joshua's chest, directly over his heart.

Said heart swelled until it pushed the tears up to his eyes, and Joshua blinked them away hurriedly. Words were easy.

But he rode through a storm to find you, chased you down until he had the chance to plead his case. What further proof of his devotion do you need?

"And you will sail with me tomorrow?" Joshua asked because he needed to know, now, with their lusts sated and their bodies quiet. "Leave this new life of yours and willingly begin over again, somewhere entirely new?"

Stephen nodded, his smile all the sunshine needed in the room. "My trade is portable. Where I can take my instrument and music, I can find employment of some kind. I would rather be with you in a peasant's cottage than alone in a vast mansion," he pledged, a teasing light in his warm, dark eyes.

"It may yet come to that," Joshua answered dryly. "There are no guarantees in our types of lives."

"Nonsense," Stephen replied blithely. "And either way…" he wrapped his arms around Joshua and curled in close, "…we have each other to keep warm."

"Are you sure you're a musician? With lines like that, one would swear you're a writer of ladies' romances."

Stephen laughed, despite Joshua's fond sarcasm. "With smudge on his fingers and paint on his nose," he recited in a singsong rhythm.

Joshua rubbed at his nose automatically, but no color came off on his hand.

"And you shall have music wherever we go."

"I don't think that's how it goes."

"Really? Hm." Stephen hummed against Joshua's Adam's apple, nuzzling up beneath his chin.

Joshua slipped his arms around Stephen's shoulders, traced the bumps of his spine, the gorgeous curved arcs of his shoulder blades, memorized the triad of moles that spotted the back of his right arm.

The candle end guttered out and died, leaving the room to settle into darkness. Joshua tipped his chin and found Stephen's mouth with his own, their lips moving sleepily against each other's. His prick stirred faintly, but gave up before making its presence too well known to ignore. Stephen traded kisses back with him, soft and tender, their mutual lust momentarily abated.

Curled into each other, hearts and hands pressed together and the blankets drawn snugly over them both, Joshua drifted into a content and dreamless sleep.

Birdsong woke him the next morning, announcing the beginning to a bright, new day. Joshua floated into consciousness more slowly than usual, everything around him conspiring to keep him snuggled deep in the bed.

The blankets drawn up to his ears were warm, in contrast to the sharp chill of the morning air. He was without his nightshirt, but the body pressed up closely against his back, knees fitted tightly against the back of Joshua's knees and arm draped over his hip, went a long way toward explaining that.

He's still here.

The press of something long and half-hard against Joshua's arse suggested that Stephen was subject to the same sort of usual morning affliction as he, a sweet possibility that suggested so many future pleasures. This morning, though, he was not quite tempted enough to spoil the perfect beauty of this single moment.

Joshua lay there for a while, time passing as the sky lightened outside the shuttered window. How long could he hold on to this before something ruined it, brought him crashing down to the prosaic reality of the world?

Stephen woke between breaths, one moment his body soft and pliable, curved against Joshua's back as a second skin, the next suffused with faint tension, like someone filling a wineskin and stretching the surface taut. Joshua held his breath and did not move.

Lips brushed softly against the nape of Joshua's neck, and he let out the breath he was holding. Stephen's mouth lingered on his skin, and his hand flattened out over the plane of Joshua's stomach. He expected something to follow that, a drift southward, to take up where they had left off the night before. It didn't come.

Stephen simply lay there, his nose buried in Joshua's hair, his cock semihard against the curve of Joshua's arse, and the pressure of his hand warm and solid.

Getting out of bed could wait.

Later, when Joshua woke again and they were pulling on clothes for the day, Stephen looked up from where he sat on the edge of the bed, trying to fit himself into a pair of Joshua's spare trousers. "When do we sail?" he asked, the first real logistical question he had put forth about the whole venture.

"At four this afternoon." Joshua glanced at his watch and frowned. Three hours to get themselves to London, then four more to settle accounts and get themselves to the ship. It would be tight, but possible.

Stephen managed to get the trousers buttoned, the muscles of his legs enough to haunt every one of Joshua's most fervent dreams. "Time enough for me to gather my clothes, then, and settle with my lodgings," he said blithely, either not aware of, or entirely ignoring, Joshua's distracted scrutiny. "Will you come with me, or shall we meet again at the ship once we've completed our business?"

"At the ship, I think." Joshua knelt to finish repacking, but could not hide the worried frown that crossed his face. "I'll be there," he said. "Will you?"

Stephen nodded. He took Joshua's face in his hands, and their kiss was the sort that could lead to a couple of men missing their coach and having to rebook passage entirely.

"See that you are, this time," Stephen murmured against his lips. They rested their foreheads together, and his warmth was everything Joshua had needed. "I've done enough riding cross-country to find you. I don't intend to lose you again."

"Never," Joshua promised, and kissed him again.

The coach would not wait, but they would be on it, and then onward to the tides and the Channel, the sea that promised to give him back his life, and the wide world that called to them beyond.

Together.

Epilogue

Mud squished up around Stephen's boots again, the spring thaw turning the usually firm path up to the little cottage into a black and sucking mess. It would be better by tomorrow, one more day of sunshine to warm and dry the earth, but that didn't help him much tonight. The air was warmer, at the very least. No more need for scarves and muffs to protect him from the elements.

Light flickered in the windows ahead. Joshua had a fire set, then, and the sitting room would be cozy, a welcome respite from the chill still lingering in the early April air.

His ears still rang from the noise at the pub in the village, his head muzzy from drink, but there, there was the firelight bringing him home.

The wind blew him up the last of the path, and he slammed the door tightly closed behind him before throwing the latch to block out the night. Boots off in the hall, mud and all, or Joshua would gleefully murder him, and he padded through to the sitting room in his stocking feet.

The cottage was not what anyone could call large. The sitting room doubled as the dining room, parlor, dayroom and whatever other downstairs space one cared to name. A kitchen off to one side was adequate enough for them to sort out basic meals. Sausages, cheese and good bread bought in the village made up the bulk of the rest. They had two bedrooms but only used one for sleeping—the other a painting studio so much smaller than the one Joshua had at Bracknell that Stephen sometimes felt physical pain looking at the cramped space. But he professed to be happy, and so Stephen had to take him at his word.

There was the man himself, stretched full-length upon an old and battered chesterfield that had come with the cottage. He was in his shirtsleeves, a blanket cast over his legs and the golden glow of the fire playing over him. He sat up when Stephen entered, set his book aside on the end table and gifted him with a warm and beckoning smile.

"My weary traveler returns," he said, and Stephen vaulted the arm of the chesterfield to sprawl across his warm body. "My *cold* and weary traveler," Joshua corrected, tugging the blanket out from between them and draping it over them both. "How go matters in town?"

"Well enough, for a border town in an encroaching war zone." Stephen shrugged. They were so far from the fighting that in reality there was nothing to concern themselves with. "A couple of letters. Those brushes you ordered came in." He pressed up on his elbows and kissed Joshua soundly, his lips warm and pliable, soft and yielding.

"You taste like brandy" was all Joshua said when they broke away, and Stephen covered his mouth in a burst of shame.

"My apologies." He started to sit up. "I can go clean my teeth—"

"I didn't say I minded." Joshua reached out to pull him back down and kissed him again, as though to prove a point.

Stephen sank in, Joshua's legs spreading to fit him softly between. "Gustav's wife is pregnant again," he explained after a moment more in the drowsy heat. "He says she means to make him sleep in the attic from now on."

Joshua snorted. "You should give him some pointers on how to avoid that. And a gift of a bottle of oil."

"Hah! I doubt that would go over well." He nuzzled in, Joshua's arm about his shoulders, the two of them trading soft and slow kisses that warmed him through to his very center.

"Any news from London?" Joshua asked, and Stephen shifted to draw one of his letters from his coat pocket. Joshua's hips hitched up against him when he moved, a slow and comfortable roll together that held sweet promises for later.

"A letter from home. Pembrey." Stephen had left his address, made at least one of them promise to write, since Wren most certainly would not.

"My sweetheart has forgiven me," he had told Pembrey to his face, watched those full lips break into a broad white smile. *"And we leave for the Continent today. Wish me well."* And he had. After insulting about four generations of Stephen's family and calling him a ninnyhammer for leaving them in need of a new soloist for Bath.

"And Phillips sent a note inside."

Joshua raised an eyebrow, tangling his fingers in the shorter hair at the nape of Stephen's neck. He had put up a fuss originally when Stephen had decided to have it cut, but seemed to enjoy the new, more fashionable length. *"As long as I can still get a grip on you,"* he had said, and laughed.

"And what do they say?"

"Lady Charlotte is married," Stephen reported, and felt no sting in the words whatsoever.

"Oh, is she now?" Joshua said, a ripple of sardonic amusement behind his words. "But not to Cade?"

"No." And a small, satisfied smile flickered over Stephen's lips. "I imagine there would be very little that Evander could do now to earn Coventry's favor once again. Not after being caught in Charlotte's London bedroom the way he was. No, she's been married by special license to the elder Mr. Downe, who will be Viscount Downe eventually. It's better than being the wife of a disenfranchised minstrel, and he's not such a bad sort. Handsome enough to suit most girls, at any rate, and he has pleasant manners."

He nuzzled Joshua's chest, and was rewarded by a soft and pleased rumble. "And the new Countess of Coventry— Miss Talbot that was—was safely delivered of a baby boy in February. A full two months premature, but hale and hearty as can be. Fancy that. A true miracle."

"Gracious. A husband and a baby brother all within the span of a few months. Such a grand summer the new Mrs. Downe must have had. What a pity we missed all of the excitement." Joshua's voice was as dry as hardtack, but his eyes sparkled with barely concealed amusement.

Stephen said nothing, running his fingers over the edges of the folded papers, soaking in the warmth and the gentle caresses from Joshua's hands.

"Do you have regrets?" Joshua ventured softly, his hands stilling.

Stephen shook his head. "No," he said, and meant it. "Evander's misfortunes are all of his own making, and I have what I have always wanted."

"Your dream is a tiny cottage within spitting distance of a war zone?"

"Not for me an aristocrat's house with all the problems that accompany such things." Stephen sat up partway, drew Joshua into his arms and rested his chin upon that dear and familiar shoulder. Joshua leaned into him, fitting perfectly into the curves and angles of Stephen's body.

The letter from Baron Terlinden burned hot inside his pocket, the promise of patronage and stipend memorized from tracing his fingers across the dark letters. Money for ink, new strings, time to compose a waltz to be played at the baron's only daughter's debut ball.

He would tell Joshua all, share the good news and trace the shapes of letters across his lips with fingers, wine and tongue, celebrate their success in the appropriate ways. But for now—

"I have you."

And that itself was enough.

Author's Note

**If you enjoyed this book, please leave a brief
review at your online bookseller of choice. Thank you!**

-

History has been my passion for as long as I can
remember. I devoured stories of knights and damsels, kings
and queens, battles and victories across time periods and
continents. As I grew, I started reading more about the lives
of the regular folks, the you-and-me people whose lives
tended to fade into the background in the grand sweeping
epics. *Rite of Summer* grew out of that reading, with my
earnest, somewhat emotionally constipated artists living
and loving in the middle of turbulent times.

A quick note on Joshua's dressing ring. While the
popularity of that piercing in England has been attributed to
Prince Albert in the mid-nineteenth century, that is most
probably an apocryphal story. Men in India, however, where
Joshua's late lover Charlie was briefly stationed, have been
performing apadravyas (vertical glans piercings), and men
in the Philippines and Borneo have used ampallangs
(horizontal glans piercings) since long before European
contact. If you can forgive me the stretch and the potential
anachronism, I'm sure we can all agree that it's just plain
fun to indulge in the fantasy!

I first began to write this story after stumbling across
historian Rictor Norton's essays and books on gay and

lesbian history in Georgian England. His descriptions of illicit queer life under the noses of the London magistrates fired my imagination, and the sources he dug up brought everything to life. His work is the rich, dark garden where the seeds of this tale were planted, and in that, I owe him everything.

The Vere Street raid that so terrifies Joshua, Stephen and Evander took place in reality on July 8, 1810, when the White Swan, a secret gay bar, or "molly house", in Marylebone was raided by the Bow Street police. Twenty-seven men were arrested for sodomy—nineteen released for lack of evidence, eight tried, six placed in the public pillories to be assaulted by the mob. Two regulars at the club, John Hepburn and Thomas White, were executed by hanging. And yet, despite the terror and risk of death that surrounded them, gay and bisexual men and women continued to search for romance, find true love and create secret ways to spend their lives together.

That message of hope in a seemingly hopeless time is magical to me, and a reminder that love can always, for every one of us, conquer all.

About the Author

Tess has been a fan of historical fiction since learning the Greek and Roman myths at her mother's knee. Now let loose on a computer, she's spinning her own tales of romance and passion in a slightly more modern setting. Years of obsession with the early modern era have provided the basis for her current novels, most especially with the performing arts communities of Georgian London. She has a Masters degree in History, which has proven very useful for things that would utterly dismay her professors.

Tess lives in the Canadian Maritimes with her partner of fifteen years and two cats who should have been named Writer's Block and Get Off the Keyboard, Dammit.

Learn more about Tess and her projects at her website, http://tessbowery.com, or on social media at @tessbowery on Twitter, and http://tessbowery.tumblr.com.

Also by Tess Bowery
She Whom I Love

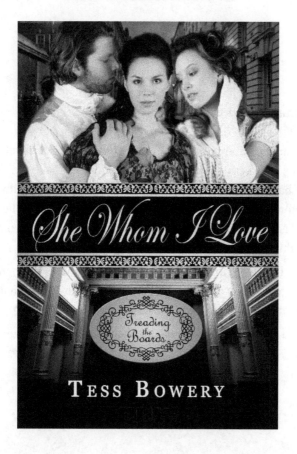

Treading the Boards Book #2

ISBN: 978-1-7753003-1-1 (print)
ISBN: 978-1-7753003-2-8 (digital)

Love would be simpler if it came with a script.

Marguerite Ceniza dies on the London stage each night, but her own life has barely begun. The ingénue is on the prowl for a lover, but while she burns with desire for Sophie, a confession could ruin their decade-long friendship. In the meantime there are always men vying to be her patron, and square-jawed, broad-shouldered James Glover can't help but catch her eye.

Sophie Armand has been a lady's maid for too long, and she's sick of keeping secrets. Her hidden scripts and the story of her birth are only the beginning. Her nights are haunted by desperate thoughts of the beguiling Marguerite, and of James, the handsome tradesman who whispers promises of forever into her ear.

James has the kind of problem a lot of men would kill for—two women, both beautiful, both sensual, and both willing. Sophie wants marriage, while Marguerite's only in it for fun, and choosing between them isn't easy.

What's the worst that could happen if he secretly courts them both?

That Potent Alchemy

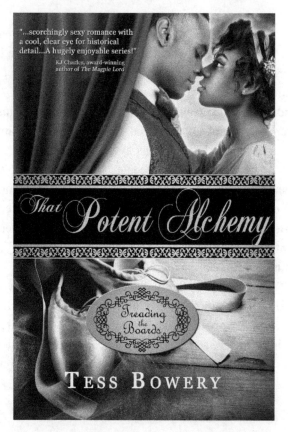

Treading the Boards Book #3

ISBN: 978-09866184-7-5 (digital)
ISBN: 978-1-7753003-3-5 (print)

Love can be the hardest leap of faith.

Child prodigy Grace Owens left dancing behind years ago. Gossip said she cracked under pressure, but the truth was harder to explain. Four years later she's made a fresh start in London, where she doesn't have to play the perfect femme. The other actors don't ask questions about her fondness for breeches, or why she's never married, or whether this is truly what she imagined her life would be.

Isaac Caird is a stage machinist and special-effects man, a showman invisible, the hand behind the wheel that makes the world. He's seen a lot of actresses come and go on the Surrey's stage, but no-one has ever caught his eye quite like Grace. He wants her on his stage, in his workshop... and in his bed.

Grace wouldn't give a smooth-talker like Isaac the time of day under normal circumstances, except nothing about the summer of 1811 is *normal*. The Prince Regent has taken the throne, the aristocrats are restless, and the Surrey playhouse's very future could depend on the two of them pulling off the greatest spectacle London has ever seen.

But can Isaac and Grace survive the curse of the Scottish play... and each other?

CPSIA information can be obtained
at www.ICGtesting.com
Printed in the USA
LVHW081400180121
676797LV00032B/651